was born in St. Louis, Missouri. Leaving Bryn Mawr College, in a hurry to get started, she arrived in Paris less than a year later, after two jobs, on the *New Republic* and the *Hearst Times Union*. She had decided to pay her way around the world as a reporter and write about it in fiction. Returning to the U.S. in 1934, she was hired by Harry Hopkins to report on the way the Federal Emergency Relief program really worked. The result, in 1936, was a widely acclaimed book of four linked novellas about Americans in the Depression, called *The Trouble I've Seen*. In Spain, in 1937, she sent to *Collier's* in New York an unsolicited article on daily life in besieged Madrid, and so began her career as a war correspondent which lasted for nine years and covered five wars: Spain, Finland, China, the Second World War and Java. In intervals between assignments, she wrote two novels and a book of short stories. After 1946, journalism became occasional and free-lance, a means to see for herself whatever absorbed her interest and concern, ranging from the Eichmann Trial to Nicaragua. She wrote short stories for American magazines and nine more books.

Martha Gellhorn has written five novels: *A Stricken Field* (1940; also published by Virago), *Liana* (1944), *The Wine of Astonishment* (1948), *His Own Man* (1961) and *The Lowest Trees Have Tops* (1969); two collections of short stories: *The Heart of Another* (1941), *Honeyed Peace* (1953); four books of novellas, *The Trouble I've Seen* (1936), *Two by Two* (1958), *Pretty Tales for Tired People* (1965), and *The Weather in Africa* (1978). Her non-fiction is *Travels With Myself and Another* (1978) and *The Face of War,* originally published in 1959, reprinted to include Vietnam as a paperback in 1967, and republished with additional wars by Virago in 1986.

Martha Gellhorn now lives in Wales.

Liana

MARTHA GELLHORN

With a New Afterword by the Author

PENGUIN BOOKS–VIRAGO PRESS

For Edna Gellhorn

PENGUIN BOOKS
Viking Penguin Inc., 40 West 23rd Street,
New York, New York 10010, U.S.A.
Penguin Books Ltd, 27 Wrights Lane, London W8 5TZ
(Publishing & Editorial) and Harmondsworth,
Middlesex, England (Distribution & Warehouse)
Penguin Books Australia Ltd, Ringwood,
Victoria, Australia
Penguin Books Canada Limited, 2801 John Street,
Markham, Ontario, Canada L3R 1B4
Penguin Books (N.Z.) Ltd, 182–190 Wairau Road,
Auckland 10, New Zealand

First published in Great Britain by
Home & Van Thal Ltd. 1944
First published in the United States of America by
Charles Scribner's Sons 1944
This edition first published in Great Britain by Virago Press Limited, 1987
Published in Penguin Books 1987

(CIP data available)

Offset from an edition published by Popular Library 1958

Printed in the United States of America by
R. R. Donnelley & Sons Company, Harrisonburg, Virginia
Set in Times Roman

CHAPTER ONE

In the afternoon at five o'clock he took his wife for a
drive. He turned left at the gate of his house and drove
up the narrow, bad road into the hills. At this hour there
was a green underwater light in the forest. Along the
road on both sides the flamboyante and the palms, the
bamboo, ceiba and eucalyptus grew like a wall cemented
together by vines. The trees thinned out near the crest
of the first hill and they could look back at the blue of
the water over the reefs, at the curves of sand between
black rocks on the coast, and on the pink and white and
lemon-yellow town.

He turned the car here. There was a small open valley to their left, with a great square of sugar cane growing in it. The leaves of the cane moved stiffly in the
afternoon wind. Beyond the sugar cane clean cows
grazed in a meadow. The road led through more tight-
growing forest to a higher hill and another cultivated
valley. In this valley was the farm of his sister-in-law,
called Le Paradis. He always stopped the car on the first
hill. The woman who had married his brother was the
woman he had wanted to marry himself. His brother was
dead now. He went to Le Paradis alone three nights each
week. Every afternoon he stopped his car at this unmarked frontier and he and his wife looked without
pleasure at the Caribbean and the faded little French
town. Then they drove home.

"Julie," he said to his wife in an easy voice, not a
voice for a quarrel, "as you have nothing to do, I find it
absurd that you do not arrange better meals. You get
plenty of money for housekeeping."

Her name was not Julie; Julie was the name he chose
for her. She despised it knowing that he wanted a wife
who would fit that name, neat faced with a small pink
mouth and a terrible tidiness in her and around her. Her
mother had named her Liana.

5

"I do my best," Liana said, sitting far away from him against the new gray upholstery.

She did what was required, as he knew, without enthusiasm like a servant who does not yet want to be dismissed but does not really want to stay.

"You did not care for dinner last night?" Liana had learned this voice. It was an even high way of speaking with every word accented like the last word, which she believed to be the voice of a white French lady. She wore her face to match her expressionless voice. In the beginning she thought that by behaving like a white lady she would be one and her husband would think she was one, and they would be happy. He was not deceived but he found this post decent; it separated his wife from the servants. Liana's acquired voice and acquired dead face and expensive clothes gave him a feeling of dignity in his home. But he would not rely on these things enough to take her among white people nor would he risk inviting them to his house. They had all seen Liana on this island where she grew up and grew always more beautiful, with her long eyes and dissatisfied, dark-red, promising mouth. They had seen her in a cotton dress and bare feet, careless and laughing and lovely, and never one of them.

When Marc Royer took the sixteen-year-old Liana (who had no last name that anyone knew) into his house and into his bed, the men of the island thought he was lucky, but then he was always lucky. Liana was another thing to envy him. He had more money than anyone and he was always making money. It was amazing and disgusting to them that anyone should be so successful on this small island where no one was hungry and no one else could get rich. He had built a house and furnished it with tasteless and elaborate furniture imported from America; he had the biggest radio, the biggest electric ice-box and his own power plant to run it, the newest car; he had champagne to drink and he bought and enjoyed scotch whiskey, his servants wore uniforms and shoes, and he ordered books from Paris and from New York. Everything he had and everything he did was different from everybody else. Yet he had been born here as they had. He was just Marc Royer, the son of a fairly rich man but not too rich; he was Marc Royer who had

6

always been short and stocky and strong, blondish because of some distant Breton blood, not goodlooking, no longer young, no better than any one else.

There were handsomer men and stronger and braver men living here, but each man secretly wondered whether anyone was as clever as Marc Royer. He did not seem very clever. He had a loud, vulgar voice and he was friendly and open; yet he always had ideas and the ideas made money. People said he owned property in Nassau and Florida, that he had accounts in New York banks, that he had a factory of some kind in Paris. He was a man with a great life stretching out beyond this place, and no one understood it. If he could afford the most beautiful mulatta on the island it was only the way things happened for Marc Royer but it was still enviable. Men who could offer a woman much more, as a man, would have to take what was left.

The ladies of Saint Boniface, drawn and pale and soft from the heat, with worried and discontented faces, accepted the news that Marc Royer had a colored mistress as they had always accepted this news. A man could not have any other kind of mistress; the few white women were only obtainable through marriage. The heat and their gossip and their ambitions had made them ugly but they kept up their value by being respectable. Until Marc Royer married, it was natural that he would sleep with a mulatta. It was not a subject that was discussed between white men and women. But when after four years of living with her he married the girl Liana the women were as furious as if each one of them had been mortally insulted, and the men were as furious as if their wives had been humiliated in public. The envy of the island turned into hate. Marc Royer's marriage did not make Liana respectable, it simply mocked the respectability of the white women.

During the first year of Marc Royer's marriage the three thousand inhabitants of Saint Boniface, the whites and the blacks, had plenty to talk about. There was the fall of France; and the boatload of English sailors who drifted here from their ship which had been torpedoed in the Anegada Passage; and the new school teacher, young and directly from the army and from occupied Paris, who had come to replace the schoolmaster who

7

finally died of old age after thirty years in the islands. The new school teacher stayed, though the sailors did not, and therefore was better material for talk. There was the marriage of the Mayor's daughter to a presentable young man from Guadeloupe, a fine old Guadeloupe family everyone said, even though he had the rather odd name of Pinelli.

No one really understood about the fall of France, nor did they see clearly why the Mayor had to take another oath of allegiance after the Maréchal became Président de la Republique or whatever it was. The Boches were in France and that was terrible enough. As for all this Vichy business it was more politics. They had watched the politics of France without comprehension or interest ever since they could remember. Nobody in France bothered the island of Saint Boniface; it was strategically worthless and produced no raw materials of any kind. The Ministry of Colonies sent a school teacher when the acting school teacher died or was transferred, and every three years or so the two gendarmes were changed. The Mayor handled what business there was with the French government through the authorities at Martinique. There had never been any trouble about it. Everyone on the island was against the Boches, absolutely. No óne on the island had been in the last war nor in this war, except the new schoolmaster who never spoke of it.

The boatload of sailors made much better talk than the politics of France, but when the Becquat family got a letter saying that their first cousin, the son of Uncle Guillaume, was in a German prison camp, the island talked suddenly with real interest and fury about the war. The war was over for the French; why didn't the Boches let the boy go home? It was like the Boches, who were and always had been barbarian monsters. Young Pinelli on the other hand said that what had ruined France was the Jews. Who knows? people said. There had never been any Jews on Saint Boniface. Of course young Pinelli had visited Europe and lived on a big, important island. That talk about the Jews ruining France would have died at once since no one understood it or had any ideas about it, if it had not been for the new schoolmaster who became white with anger when he heard it and raised his voice for the first time

8

and said Pinelli was a dangerous fool. This was recklessly indiscreet as Pinelli had married the Mayor's
daughter and everyone talked about that in excited whis-
pers for two weeks.

They listened to the radio and were horrified to hear
that German submarines hunted and killed in their own
Caribbean. But the sea around them was safe; no shipping lanes led through their waters. Still, it made you
sick at heart to think of it. Pinelli said that scores of
shipwrecked sailors had landed on Haiti and Puerto Rico
and Trinidad, starving sun-blinded men. They knew
the sea and knew what it would be to drift in an open
boat on this hard blue water, for days, for weeks. They
felt strongly sympathetic to the sailors. The Boches had
always sunk ships, which was wicked and cowardly and
just like them.

The luxuries and comforts and some of the necessities
the island used to import no longer arrived as they once
had; but there was plenty to eat; the soil in the little
bright green valleys was rich and there was enough rain.
It was infuriating when the ice factory broke; the Americans would not send new parts to repair it. Some said
that was because there were no ships, look how many
were sunk in the Caribbean; some said it was due to the
foreign exchange restrictions and the way a dollar was
worth forty francs now; some said it was because of
politics and Vichy, they had heard it on the radio.

It was a terrific year for talk. But through it all the
talk would come back to Marc Royer and Liana. That
subject never failed; it belonged to the island entirely.
Everyone asked everyone else, during that whole year,
why Marc Royer had married her.

Liana did not know why Marc had married her but
she knew how. It began when she left him. It was a
March day with a strong east wind blowing; they had
not quarrelled, she was not ill or unusually sad. In the
afternoon while Marc was in town, Liana rode up the
hill path to the shack Marc Royer had bought for her
mother. It took two hours to ride there and though Marc
gave old Lucie a cow and chickens and four pigs, he
did not give her a horse. He did not want Lucie to come
and visit with her friend, his cook. He could not have

9

his mistress's family eating furtive meals in the kitchen and borrowing slyly at the back door. Liana made a package of the clothes Marc had paid for and put them on a shelf and told her mother she was home to stay. This seemed to Lucie an ungrateful stupidity; no negro girl on the island was as well placed as Liana.

"He beat you?" Lucie said. That would be a reason, though women had been beaten before and stayed where they were.

"No."

"He made you work too hard?"

"I did no work."

"He quarrelled with you; he screamed at you?"

"No."

"What happens with you, my daughter?"

"It is like prison. I will stay here and help you on the farm. Later I will find a boy I like and marry him and go to live with him. I am not going back to Monsieur Royer."

Lucie did not answer and they sat in the dark small room, Lucie sewing and Liana waiting, waiting for an order or an argument. Later Liana said, "He despises me except at night."

Lucie shrugged her shoulders, just a little, so that Liana barely saw her. She was thinking that such things did not matter; the girl had always been vain and proud but this was exaggerated. No one should spend time seeking reasons to be unhappy.

Liana said, "A boy. A boy like me."

"Who is it?" Lucie asked sharply. "That young Roland? That worthless boy of Joséphine's?"

"No one. How could there be? When would I see anyone? But someday I will know one. A black," Liana said, her voice bitter and clear, using the word the white people used.

Lucie thought, Marc will take away the farm now. And there are four other children, all eating and eating, and I am getting too old to do washing and they are still too young to earn for us. None of them are light colored as Liana; none of them had a white father to give them loosely curling hair and a small pretty nose. Only Liana has a chance like a white girl. Liana was no worker anyhow; she would sit about all day playing with her hair,

10

looking at her face, smiling, making plans and telling herself stories and finding excuses to go in town.

Lucie said·to her daughter, "Go and milk the cow. When you are through you can feed the pigs."

Liana went slowly and sullenly; she understood how she would be punished for running away.

That night at Le Paradis, Marc told his sister-in-law Marie. They were sitting on the veranda looking at a hill that climbed straight up before the house. In the day time it was a high smooth wave of green, at night it looked like a great broken black tower. He said, "Liana went home today."

The woman beside him laughed. "Poor Marc," she said, laughing, "poor Marc."

"Why do you laugh?"

"Without reason."

"Tell me."

"I do not know, my dear. I simply laughed."

She laughed, Marc thought, because it was another triumph for her. He sat hunching his shoulders with rage against himself and against this woman. His light eyebrows went down over his eyes and the blue eyes were squinted and hard with anger. If Marie had seen his face she would have laughed again.

She might well laugh without reason, Marc thought, she is fool enough for that. She is so stupid that she can never know why she does anything. She had laughed at him with malice, but even her malice was pointless. She was too lazy and too stupid to plan malice, to work for it or invent it. She would only take whatever happened and delight in it, maliciously, because for the moment that suited her. Why am I here, he groaned, why do I come? His mind ached with the helplessness and folly of a man who could be used for fifteen years by such a woman. She tells me I may come three nights a week, Marc thought, she has no reason for it. She might as well say five nights or two nights or never or always. And I come, as she orders. I do not discuss it since she cannot understand reason. She says three nights because the number pleases her. She will never change; she will never make it four. She laughs because another woman is making a fool of me. She laughs because Liana does not want me either.

11

They often sat, half the night, in the cool dark of the veranda without talking. Marc imagined that Marie sat there, comfortable, smiling to herself, with her mind as smooth and flat as a sheet. He sat and talked to himself, thinking over and over the long incomprehensible story of himself and this woman. He had tried to think his way out of it and now he knew his mind could not help him. He had thought himself out of loving her but he could not stay away from her. All he had done was destroy the old happiness, his happiness, since Marie had never loved him nor loved anyone as far as he knew.

Marc went over it again now in the dark, watching the spray of stars over the hill. Was Marie ever beautiful, he asked himself. He thought not, but he could not remember. She had been tall and well-made and she held herself as if no one could touch her because no one would be good enough. That was the first thing. He had thought it was pride, and years later he thought it was something as unnameable and mindless as the way she decided on three nights a week instead of four. No, he told himself viciously, she was ugly: the dark skin, the smudged black eyes and dull hair, that short flat-looking nose. Marie either did not care how she looked or else she thought it was the best possible way for a woman to look. What does she want, Marc thought, what has she ever wanted?

When Marc was in Europe his older brother married her. Marc had gone to Europe, hoping to forget Marie. He knew she would not make a good wife and he did not want to spend his life tormenting himself in an effort to understand her. When he came home Marc knew he would have to marry her and she was married. People said that his brother had pursued Marie and bullied her and bribed her family: and she married Jean Royer as indifferently as she would put two lumps of sugar in her coffee in case someone made a scene and insisted (after she had refused to put two lumps of sugar in her coffee for years). Marie certainly did not love his brother and his brother was trapped as Marc was, beating against her silences and her unreason. At last his brother too thought there was nothing behind the silences except more silence and nothing behind the unreason except blind stupidity, and he had hated her, and

12

been fiercely jealous of her. Marc believed that his brother purposely rode the unmanageable horse which killed him.

Marie would not marry Marc but after a time she slept with him because he was there, he begged for it, and because she apparently enjoyed sleeping with a man when she felt like it. Her body fits my body, Marc thought. And then he thought: why not, what is so wonderful about that? Now, not touching her, he could deny whatever power Marie had, saying to himself that many women had had it for him. He was not difficult, he was healthy and coarse and easy; any woman or almost any woman would have been as good. Liana, he thought, and felt suddenly choked and dry-mouthed and hot, Liana is far better.

Then Marc stopped thinking about Liana because this recital inside himself had to go on as it always did through all the facts to the end .that decided nothing. So Marie consented to sleep with him, sometimes with pleasure, sometimes with detachment, exactly as she liked, but in no case did it make any difference afterwards. She treated Marc as if he were no more to her than anyone else. He would have found some flattering explanation for this if Marie did it on purpose, but she never acted; she was incapable of imagination.

Marc gave her presents and he gave her money; he bought her more land and she had the finest cattle on the island. Marie took whatever he gave and thanked him as if he were loaning her a book. For a time Marc had thought she was greedy and shammed indifference for fear he would use the gifts to control her, forcing her by withheld bribes to be loving or attentive or gentle or even interested. Marie was greedy as she was everything else; she liked what she got but she would not work for it. Once Marc stopped giving her money or any other thing for six months, and she was as serene and indifferent as always. There was no way that he knew to fix her mind on him. She was not unfaithful but he had his own answer to that. He turned and looked at her profile and said it to himself with a hurting pleasure: who else would want her? She is forty-six now, two years older than I am. She is not fat but she is heavy and her skin is dried and lined and darkened by sun, and her

13

hair is ugly and shapeless on her head. Who would want her? But he knew that if he died or went away, Marie would find someone else as soon as she needed him and would take that one too and give nothing in return.

This was the end of his thinking. He wanted to beat his fists on the arms of the chair. He wanted to scream at her: what is it, what have you done to me, why must I live this way? It would have been useless to ask her any of these questions. She would have said, "Marc, do not be tiresome," and gone inside and turned on the radio. Or she would have stared at him a moment, and her dark eyes would gleam with pleasure—though why, what pleasure?—and she would go on rocking and smiling to herself.

If he could accept Marie as she was, and accept his own humiliation and helplessness, then it would be bearable. Or if he could say to himself coldly: you only want her because you cannot get her, because you will never have her, it is nothing but vanity; then too he might be free. But he could do either and he did not believe in it: if it were as easy as that, surely he would long ago have forgotten her. So he made money because he knew how to do that and because the money gave him comfort. It was not the money Marc liked, it was the knowledge that he could make it. And he needed to be envied, knowing how everyone on the island would pity him or laugh at him if they saw what his life really was. The white people thought Marc slept with his strange sister-in-law because he had once loved her and it was a sentimental habit. They were a little sorry for Marie. She was a woman growing old, not an attractive woman, and she had no children and now no family, and if Marc was kind enough to be attentive to her, it harmed no one. When Marc took Liana, they decided he was tiring of Marie and for a time they hoped Marie would be publicly tragic or make some sort of scene, but as she did nothing they imagined she accepted the inevitable fate of a woman which was to grow old and be discarded.

In the beginning, Marc had told Marie about Liana gently and with shame. He said he was lonely the other nights and if she would let him come more often he would send Liana away at once. Marie said she did not see how Liana concerned her. Then later Marc taunted

14

her with Liana; he spoke indecently and in detail of Liana and some nights he would lie on his back in the big bed at Le Paradis and compare Marie and Liana aloud, in a hating mocking voice. Marie told him to be quiet, she wanted to sleep. Finally, because he bored her, Marie explained that in case his taste ran to mulatto girls it was his own affair but no reason to make himself ridiculous, bragging and boasting. Marc felt at once that he was a vulgar and disgusting man, which was what Marie intended. It never occurred to Marie that she could be insulted by anything Marc did. After all, she said, you are really no relation of mine. That night Marc dressed in the dark and drove his car crazily down the hills to his home and frightened Liana awake at four in the morning and made love to her until daylight.

Now Marie was laughing at him because Liana had left. He had tried to make Marie jealous or angry or ashamed and in the end he had not hurt her at all and Liana apparently did not need him either. Suddenly Marc decided to get Liana back and keep her. He would not let Marie think that any woman could treat him as she did. He would not let Marie believe that he was entirely, and in all of him, a man to be used and despised by women.

CHAPTER TWO

Lucie and Liana heard the pebbles rattling in the path and then the soft clop of the horse's hoofs sinking into the dirt at the edge of the field. Liana wanted to hide but she knew she would be dragged out like a bad child; it would only be worse when they found her. The two women stood in the pink painted doorway and waited. They were both very straight and slender, and both now wore the same face. It was the deaf-mute face that negroes have learned to wear, the maddening, unanswering, not understanding face which is their protection against whatever damage the whites can do. At least the whites can take no satisfaction from the misery they make, since the black face admits nothing.

15

Lucie thought Marc Royer bad come to send her and
the five children from the farm. She did not blame him;
the farm was payment for Liana and Liana had run
away. She lay awake the night before, trying to plan
another life. But there was nothing to plan with: there
were only two things Lucie knew, the daylong bending
over a washtub, or the daylong work of a farm. The first
was harder work and the money earned bought very
little food. Lucie thought against this idea, trying to invent out of nothing some other way to feed her family.
When she slept she had resigned herself to it. She
thought: one never knows . . . who knows . . . one
will see . . . something good may happen . . . there
is so much movement in the town . . . something will
happen. She talked to herself automatically with this
sighing optimism: these were the old cheerful lies she
had been forced to use all her life.

Liana saw Marc and her flesh tightened and felt cold.
The jailer was riding toward her; his linen jacket flapped
against his sides, his wide straw hat shadowed half his
face, there was red clay on his riding boots, he had not
shaved. If Marc could force her to go back it would be
the dead life of the other years. (All day Liana waited
in the silent house. She was not allowed to talk with the
servants; she was not allowed to see her friends. At the
end of the day Marc came home and read in a chair by
the radio and drank whiskey. At dinner, he ate steadily
and heavily; if he talked to her it was only to ask questions about the house or the garden. Marc read again
after dinner; then he told Liana to come to bed. In bed
she served him and he spoke to her but it was not loving or gentle or gay. In the morning Marc gave the day's
orders and went into town.) I will not go back, Liana
thought, let the other children work; I can be a servant;
Lucie can take in washing. Let them starve then, she
thought, I will not go back.

Marc was determinedly pleasant. Even when they
could not see him he started to smile his hearty town-
smile, the one he had for the judge and the priest and
the Mayor.

"Bonjour Lucie."

"Bonjour Monsieur."

16

He looped the bridle around a branch and walked toward them.

"Your house looks very pretty."

"Yes Monsieur."

"I see the corn is doing well."

"Yes Monsieur."

"How is the cow?"

"Very good, Monsieur."

"Plenty of milk?"

"Yes Monsieur."

"Aren't you going to say hello, Liana?"

"Bonjour."

"Well," Marc said, as if he were rubbing his hands together. "Shall we sit down and have a little talk?"

He wanted to beat them both. He wanted to slap their faces so that they would show something, pain or anger or fear or anything. The time that women take, he thought furiously, even black women, my God; there is no end to it.

Marc would have preferred to stay outside where the wind twitched at the yard dust and the leaves of the lime tree and the mango and the flamboyante flickered in the sun. The sky was paint-smooth and solidly blue and now, in the dry season but before the burning summer, the air smelled sharp and new. The mango tree was covered with yellow pyramid flowers. The air around it held a special sweetness.

The land makes up for the people living on it, Marc thought. Even Lucie's shack, which would be dark brown and rotting inside, looked delightful. Red and purple bougainvillea and heavy orange trumpet flowers, all violent clashing colors, hung and climbed on the sun-faded pink wooden walls. Green lizards, with black blinking eyes and red throats, ran like light among the flowers. The ride through the close-growing slender forest had pleased Marc. He thought he would keep his temper better if he stayed outdoors. But as he was being docile on purpose he went inside when Lucie held open the door. Obviously Lucie felt that conversation in the dooryard was not serious.

Lucie offered Marc the only sound chair; she sat on a box and Liana sat on the floor against the frame wall of

17

the house. Anything Liana did was wonderful to see. She leaned against the wall with her long bare earth-colored legs crossed before her and Marc saw, unwillingly, that her instep was faultless and exciting.

"I would like Liana to come home." He said it very nicely.

The women looked at him with the same faces, as if they did not understand the language. Marc waited.

Then he said, "I will make it happier for you."

Liana looked at the opposite wall, through it, and at nothing. Lucie moved her eyes, without moving her head, to watch Liana.

"You like this farm, Lucie?" Marc said.

"Yes Monsieur." He was going to take it away anyhow; she would not cry for it and be refused.

"I will give it to you, in your name. The notary will make the papers, as it is done for white people's land. The farm and everything that is here now."

Lucie watched Liana.

"I will settle three thousand francs a year on you, for as long as you live. Lucie. You hear me?"

There was a restless sound or movement from Liana, but when Marc turned to see, her face still had the deaf-mute look.

Suddenly Marc knew what to do. He had not planned it but he knew now that he wanted the girl. He wanted her at that moment so fiercely that he was ready to order Lucie from the house and lift Liana to the grayish, shapeless bed in the corner. But it was more than that, it was better still. It was for Marie too. There would never be a triumph for Marie again. Even she would notice this. He thought of Marie's anger and Liana's body and he leaned toward the old negro woman and stretched out his hands to her because she was the one who would give him what he now knew he must have.

"I want to marry Liana," Marc said.

Liana pulled herself back against the wall by her hands and her legs lay flat and stiff on the floor. Her eyes were frightened staring negro eyes. Lucie looked at Marc with suspicion. She had been cheated before by the whites. She did not care for this marriage idea but she did not like to be fooled when a bargain was being discussed.

18

"You will bring the priest?" Lucie asked.

"Yes."

"And all that you said before about the farm and the money?"

"I mean it as before."

"But with the priest?"

"Yes."

Liana watched them both. Since her mother was not afraid, and did not seem to think this was some wicked and fearful trick that Marc had invented to hurt them, she listened with amazement and slowly with pleasure. *Madame,* Liana said to herself, *Madame, Madame,* turning the word over in her mind as if it felt like satin.

"I will speak to the girl alone, Monsieur."

"I wish the answer now."

"I must speak to her alone."

Marc Royer walked through the doorway across the beaten earth of the yard to the shade of a great flamboyante. It relieved him to breathe; the dirty human smell of Lucie's shack was disgusting and he had been taking in that polluted air with caution. Now the wind blew his shirt back from his neck and cooled his face. This month the wind blew strongly from the east and the trees made a night and day murmur of shallow waves. The island seemed larger: you felt that the wind had blown across hundreds of miles of fertile sun-cleaned land. Marc leaned against the trunk of the flamboyante and looked over the fields to the distant hills where Marie lived, and smiled to himself. Lucie and Liana would not refuse: there had never been an offer like his.

The women stood together with their backs turned toward the door and Lucie spoke softly but quickly.

"He could not despise his wife. What you said before. The wife sits at the head of the table. The wife is the one who orders in the home."

Liana looked at the iron cook pot on the smoke-blackened hearth. She was thinking: dances and card parties and all the lights burning in the house at night. Picnics, she thought, and birthday presents and going to church on Sunday wearing fine clothes and a hat and gloves.

"He is not bad. You said so. It was only that one thing. He would not despise his wife."

"You would be happy?"

19

"I am getting old," Lucie said.

"He is not young. He is not beautiful."

"No one is young long who is poor. You would not be beautiful for long if you were poor. When he dies you will have everything he has; it is that way for wives."

"Ah," Liana said, turning away from her mother. The money meant nothing to her and this talk of the future, what might happen some time that she could not even imagine, meant nothing to her. She could think only of now. All the lights burning in the big house and she would stand at the head of the steps on the terrace, wearing a dress made of lace, shaking hands with the other wives who came to play cards in the evening. Liana walked across the room to the one good chair and sat down with perfect and formal elegance, holding her back straight and her legs neatly crossed at the ankle. She leaned forward to talk to an unseen lady and balanced an invisible teacup in her hand. Then Liana smiled like a child, delighted, loving her masquerade, and said to her mother, "Madame Royer."

Lucie called Marc.

Marc had to tell the Mayor his plans. The Mayor was speechless, which was the only acceptable way he could behave. Marc said coldly that he wished the marriage to be secret until he announced it himself and he would thank the Mayor to post the banns—pendant huit jours dont deux dimanches, as the law required—unobtrusively somewhere inside his office.

Marc made it clear to the Mayor that he would hold the Mayor responsible for any gossip which might precede the ceremony. The Mayor, though horrified by Marc's intentions, was not foolish enough to argue. Marc knew that the Mayor would not forget his dependence on Marc's schooners and the money he had borrowed from Marc last year at a friendly 3 per cent interest.

Marc said that he intended to marry Liana at her mother's house in the country (the Mayor did not even smile with his eyes). The Mayor pointed out that civil marriages were performed in the mairie, with the register and all the rubber stamps at hand. Marc said that the Adjoint-au-Maire could ride upcountry with him, carrying the register and the necessary stamps. Well, the Mayor said uncertainly. Why not, Marc asked sharply. I suppose it can be done, the Mayor said. But naturally, Marc said. The Mayor thought it was the worst thing he had ever heard and that if Marc was having a child by the girl for God's sake why didn't he simply let the girl have it, and give her some money: practically every white family on the island had cocoa-colored half brothers and sisters. Marc must be insane. It was too awful to think about. Possibly Marc would change his mind before the eight days was up. Posting the banns engaged no one; especially if they were posted in this canny and secretive manner.

Marc waited impatiently. He knew it was impossible to hurry the law. He made his arrangements with the priest after he received the civil certificate, and the Mayor did not instruct his aide until early in the morning of the day Marc had set: he was not going to risk his aide's possible indiscretion and Marc's anger.

Lucie decided Marc was forgetting his bargain: it was ten days now since he had come to see them. This did not surprise her. There was always a difference between what the whites said and what the whites did. Anyhow they had been untroubled for ten days and you could only live in the time you had, and it was a lucky thing when each day passed and there was no misfortune.

Liana hated the farm work and thought bitterly that she was in prison wherever she was, in Marc's house or in Lucie's upcountry shack. She never saw anyone, there was no excitement, nothing to talk about and no place to go. Half the time Liana told herself that of course Marc was not going to marry her; he had only spoken of it to trick them in some way which they could not understand. Half the time she told herself that he was coming soon, and she dreamed of herself as a wife, a new free Liana who would live in a world full of movement and pleasure, laughter and clothes and friends.

Then one morning they heard the horses and stood at the door to watch four men ride silently out of the forest across the open field. By their faces, the men had not spoken for a long time. Marc was scowling and the priest, the notary and the Mayor's aide looked worried and resentful.

Liana's two little sisters sat happily in the dirt of the

21

front yard and ran the dust through their hands and looked at the feet of the big people and laughed with amazement and joy in all this excitement. Her brother stayed near the cow shed covering his shyness in work. The sister who was sixteen, not sixteen as Liana had been, but thin and awkward and with thick lips and corkscrew hair and a wide comic smile, stood in a corner and held her hands behind her and teerered on her bare feet and stared. Marc ordered them all out.

"Tell the children to go away and not come back until we have left."

The little ones cried as their sister dragged them across the yard past the flamboyante tree into the farthest field.

The priest could not refuse to perform the ceremony. There was no law against it. Liana and Marc were both Catholics. He could not even delay by saying that he had to obtain permission from the Bishop of Martinique before dispensing with the religious banns. He had the necessary authority himself; Marc knew that. Of course his little church would benefit from this hurried transaction. New candelabra, an altar cloth, repairs to the south wall, he thought. In God's eyes, the priest kept telling himself, but he was full of nervousness and doubt. The notary, who served as witness with Lucie, could not refuse either. He would be well paid, too. The notary thought Marc Royer was mad but it was not his business to say so. He would be glad when this insane performance was finished and they could get out into the air again. My God, how these negro shacks smelled. It was certainly not etiquette, the notary reflected grimly, for the witness to cover his nose with his handkerchief.

"We will have an extra clause in the contract," Marc said to the notary. Then he turned squarely to Lucie. "We must agree on something else. Neither you nor any of your family nor any of Liana's friends will ever come to my house. Ever. Liana may come to visit you here for a few days every four months. This will be written into the contract which gives you the farm and the money. Do you agree?"

Marc had not recovered from the shock of seeing the children. He felt cold with fear when he saw the sixteen-year-old girl with her hair sticking up in sooty points over her head.

"Yes." Lucie said, not giving Liana time to speak.

The civil ceremony was brief and mumbled; they signed their names in the register as if their hands were cold. It had the air of a customs inspection or some formality about cashing a check. The Mayor's assistant looked at no one; he pounded down the violet-inked rubber stamps where necessary and closed the large black register and went outside. He was taking the safe attitude that he was scarcely here, and was only completing an impersonal procedure which really had nothing to do with marriage. The responsibility and the emotion were the priest's business.

Liana did not answer during the marriage service until the priest reminded her. She seemed to understand nothing. When Marc put the wide new gold band on her hand, she held her hand away from her and looked at it as if it were diseased. Then she shook her hand and the ring fell off, as it was too large. She did not pick up the ring but stood staring at the shine of the gold on the hard-packed dirt floor. Marc picked it up impatiently and put it on her hand and closed her fingers roughly, so that she would not drop the ring again. There was a line of sweat over his lips and on his temples.

Whatever way Liana had dreamed of her wedding, whatever way Marc had thought of it himself long ago when he thought of Marie, it was not like that. They rode from the house in single file with the priest leading and then the notary and the assistant Mayor, then Liana and Marc. Liana looked back at the house once, and saw her mother standing in the doorway. Her mother did not wave. They had not said good-bye. The pale, tight and almost sick fearfulness of Liana's face loosened and she bowed her head and cried. Marc pretended not to see this and spurred his horse and rode ahead of her.

Marc called the servants together and stood with Liana beside him, with her hand on his arm and the wedding ring bright on her hand.

"Mademoiselle Liana is now Madame Royer. You will obey her as you obey me. She is the mistress of the house."

He had Liana moved from the small room at the back into the elaborate and always unused guest room

23

across the hall from him. He drove in town and made brief frozen calls on the judge, the doctor, the hotel keeper and the man who owned the garage. He announced his marriage and his eyes warned them to say nothing. They gave him what congratulations they could manage, being too startled and horrified to think of anything else to do. Marc knew they would inform the town and the news would spread instantly over the island.

Marc told the maid to take Liana's measurements and he cabled his agent in Florida to buy fifteen dresses and fifteen pairs of shoes and hats and bags and whatever women needed. Let your wife do this, Marc cabled. He said these things were a present for his bride; he did not say more. The package was to be sent by airmail to Saint Thomas and one of his own schooners would call there to collect it. He told Liana to pin up her hair and found a magazine with the picture of a sophisticated and dazzling movie actress to serve as model. He corrected Liana's table manners and her speech and her voice.

Liana accepted Marc's orders with humility and gratitude. She knew she would have to practice being a white wife before she became one. She thought Marc did all these things to help her and because he cared for her and wanted her to be as fine a lady as anyone. Liana tried very hard and wore without complaint a pair of shoes Marc bought in town which blistered her heels and cramped her straight slender toes. She waited with excitement for Marc to come home at night, to show him how much more she had learned.

Then the American clothes arrived and Liana was enchanted and dressed and undressed all day long in her room, arranging herself to be many different women and all, she believed, elegant and wifely and what Marc wished. The wife of the agent in Florida did not have faultless taste, but these were definitely white clothes and better than those of the Saint Boniface ladies. Surprisingly, this masquerade was becoming. Liana wore her hair in a high smooth wave and she had natural style and made the dresses smarter than they were in her manner of wearing them. All this time, Liana was shy and gay and thankful and as soft and loving as a man could wish. Marc did not notice.

On his wedding night Marc had gone to Marie, want-

24

ing to be the first to tell her. Marc waited until he felt
Marie at ease beside him on the veranda, comfortable,
mindless and certain of everything. Then he told her
and the seconds of silence between his telling and her
answer were the beginning of peace. Marc felt tired and
empty and perhaps it was not the revenge which made
him glad but the knowledge that at least they were
equals.

Then Marie laughed. The few seconds of peace were
only the time it took her to understand what Marc had
said. She laughed as if the laughter of all the years was
collected to make this mockery. She laughed as if she
knew him to be, without question and for all time, a
helpless man and a weak one and a fool.

CHAPTER THREE

Liana's table manners were certainly better than Marc's,
as she was graceful and full of care and he was neither.
She had learned this finicking voice to go with the cautious and tidy French she now spoke. She wore her elegance like varnish all over her. The servants did not
smile when she gave them orders. They did not even
smile secretly with their eyes. Liana was haughty out of
fear, but after months of use her haughtiness looked
genuine. And still Marc did not take her to town and
no white people ever came to their house. There were
no parties, the lights never burned at night. Before the
servants Marc was formally respectful.

When they were alone he was always polite but he
did not see her or hear her. He never spoke to Liana
badly, he simply did not trouble to speak.

The silk of her fashionable city clothes began to
weigh on her; everything felt tight and everything felt
heavy. Her shoes crippled her; she thought she would
never walk or run freely again. The pins that held up
her hair hurt her. Liana did not talk unless she had to,
because that strained voice and those controlled sentences tired and finally sickened her as if she were listening to a pretentious stranger.

25

In that first spring of her marriage Liana had been busy with her new wifehood; by the end of summer she believed herself ready for the wonderful life that wives were supposed to have. Now the third summer was beginning and nothing had changed; the house was a jail and on Mondays she began to wait in despair for the week to end. But after this week there would only be another, as bare and as lonely.

There was something else which Liana had not questioned before their marriage and had only begun to notice when she saw that her learning and trying were for nothing and that Marc never intended her to be as other wives. Three nights a week Marc left her without explanation. Liana knew where he went. Before Marc had closed her into his house, Liana had seen Marie in the town and she had heard the talk. She could not understand why a man would want that ugly shapeless old woman. Marie's skin was the color of mustard; her clothes looked gray no matter what they really were, and hung down at the sides like sagging curtains; her hair was dirty or if it was not dirty it was dead like the stuffing of a mattress. Liana could not be jealous of such a woman. She could not be jealous anyhow since she did not love Marc; and as the months went by and Liana saw how Marc had cheated her, she hated him. But Liana was jealous for her wifehood. No white wife would have been treated this way. Marc had made her into a white wife and all the island must know that she was still a mulatta mistress.

Liana would wait in her room, those three nights, until she heard Marc come home. Sometimes he came at dawn and sometimes he came back before midnight. She locked her door when she heard his car turning in at the gate, and put out her light and lay in bed hating him and waiting. Some nights Marc beat on her door; one night he had tried to break it down. That night Liana called to him saying she would wake the servants if he went on. All the servants would see him hurling himself against his wife's locked door. Liana knew that he only wanted her those nights because the other woman had refused him or angered him; and she was his wife, she was not to be dirtied in this way. But slowly Liana came to loathe him on all the other nights, thinking that Marc took her because he could not have Marie; she was something he had bought for use when he could not have what he loved.

Liana never spoke of Marie because she did not dare but she let Marc see her hate and she let him know the door would always be locked on the nights he went to Le Paradis. Marc did not care whether Liana hated him or not and he accepted the locked door rather than make a scene and be laughed at in the town when his servants told the other white people's servants. And every night, after the heavy steady eating, Marc read by the radio. Liana embroidered in the other great chair under the other lamp, until her hands fumbled and her body felt torn and crazy with anger.

But she was surprised herself when she flung down the embroidery hoop and broke the thin wooden band with her heel and picked it up and clawed at the cloth and, failing to tear it, suddenly ripped the pins out of her hair and let her hair fall wildly about her shoulders and hurled her shoes across the room and wrenched her neat close dress away from her throat. She was surprised because it had happened without her thinking of it. She turned to Marc and said to him in her own voice, furious and breathless, "Why should I? What for? What good does it do? Why? You sitting there always. Sitting and reading." Her voice failed her. She was too angry to talk and she stopped for fear she would cry and show Marc truly how helpless she was.

Liana looked very lovely and very young, like a little girl in a fierce but harmless temper and Marc watched her and was amused by this sudden spirit. It changed the flat boredom of every evening into something new which might end anyway.

"Why don't you read, too?" he said reasonably.

Liana turned sullen then. She could see what he planned. He would be sensible and cold the way white people were, and she would gain nothing.

"Can you read?" Marc asked. He did not know. He had never thought about it.

"Naturally." She had gone to school for four years. How dare he ask if she could read, in that way? Liana wanted to take his book and throw it at him; no, she wanted to cut his face with her fingernails and make him bleed and cry with pain.

"Have you ever read a book, Julie?"

He would always win. Nothing moved him; nothing would ever change. He would look at her like that and ask a question and she would be wrong, as she always was.

"No," Liana said and turned away and walked slowly across the room.

"Don't go," Marc said. "Come here and sit down. I want to talk to you."

"I do not want to talk."

"Julie, come here. I have something to say to you."

Liana stood before him but she would not sit down. She knew she would have to obey sooner or later. She did not listen to what he said, standing before him with her mind closed and ashamed and bitter, but as his voice sounded gentle he began to listen out of surprise.

"I think you would be happier if you read. It is a pleasure women know very little about." Liana looked at Marc suspiciously then. If he was only going to laugh at her in the hidden way he had, she would go to her room whether he permitted it or not.

"I am going to have a teacher for you," Marc went on. "He is a very agreeable young man who came here last year to teach in the school. He does not work in the afternoons. I will have him come out several days each week and you can read together. It will be company for you and it will give you something to do and if you learned to read, you would be happier."

"May I go to my room now?"

"You do not want the teacher?"

"What is the use?" Liana locked her door that night though it was not Marc's night to go to Le Paradis. She wanted to cry and she had to do that alone, with her mouth against the pillow so that Marc would not hear. Marc must not know that she cried; he must not be able to laugh at her crying. She had never rebelled before and the rebellion had failed. Marc would bring a teacher. That was all. There was no hope now and every week would be like the last week until she died.

Marc mixed himself another whiskey and soda and

tried to read again but he kept thinking of how Liana looked and most of all how young she looked. He had never really thought of her; he gave her clothes and money and treated her properly and her body excited and sated him. How young, he said to himself, and suddenly he was sorry for Liana as he would have been for a sick child. The idea of hiring the teacher was not a bad idea, now that he considered it. Pierre Vauclain was an intelligent and attractive boy and he came from Europe; he did not have the prejudices of the island. He must be poor too, and his work here was surely not enough to keep him busy all day. For fifteen hundred francs a month, Marc thought, which is certainly more than his salary, he would be enchanted to come here and teach Julie.

Marc knew very little about Pierre Vauclain since Pierre had come to Saint Boniface after Marc's marriage. Marc would not admit to himself that he had been afraid to ask for friendship from the new school teacher, for fear of being refused. The envy of the island had been a satisfaction to Marc but their new hate, the hate because of Liana, suffocated him. He liked to be with men. He liked to shoot the blue pigeons in the hills and he liked to fish in the deep water beyond the reefs. He liked to play cards in the only café and he liked to get drunk and tell stories. Before his marriage, Marc would have invited the young schoolmaster to go hunting or fishing; he would have bought him drinks and loaned him books and talked. There was almost no one here to talk with. The island men had no need of ideas and nowhere to get them; but the young schoolmaster would be able to talk about the war and Europe and Marc was hungry for talk and cruel for want of the easy laughing company of men.

Pierre Vauclain would have heard all about Marc. Perhaps, from discretion, he would follow the island men in their hate. Perhaps, and this was worse, he would pity Marc as a European might. But that would be if Marc went to him asking for friendship; he could with dignity and without risk propose a business deal to the teacher who must need money as everyone did. If the man refused there would be no insult in it; a business offer may be accepted or rejected without offense.

29

Marc thought: later, he and I might become friends and in the evenings he could come out here and we would have a few drinks and talk about things. Marc only knew then how lonely he was because he knew how passionately he wanted it to be like that, to hear a man's voice, to have an intelligent cultivated man sitting in Liana's chair discussing things which concerned neither of them, and opening the trap of the room and the house and the island because their minds could go anywhere.

Pierre Vauclain had been on the island for more than a year and the people no longer talked about him because he did nothing they could talk about. Everyone was a little disappointed and the men were even a little contemptuous and the women a little condescending. To be virtuous to this point was almost like not being a man. He rented two rooms from the baker's family and his rooms had a staircase leading directly up to them from the outside, so in a way he was free. Even if he had not been practically in his own house, he could arrange things. It had been done before. In the beginning the white people hoped he would court one of the four marriageable girls and there would be the pleasure and interest of following his success or failure. The girls were quite pretty and three of them had adequate dowries but Pierre Vauclain was as agreeable to them as he was to their mothers and no more. The men thought he probably did not want to get married which proved that he was no fool and knew his way around, but then they expected him to find a dark-skinned girl to keep him company at night. They believed rightly that if Pierre Vauclain took any girl on the island they would hear of it. They heard nothing and Pierre could have announced everything he did from the church steps and shocked no one.

During the first months the white people tried to make talk out of his sunbathing (though no one had ever seen the teacher naked on a beach which would have been better than nothing). He spent his free time along the shore but always wearing swimming trunks perfectly decently. He made collections of everything, of shells and coral and seaweed and the bones of fishes.

He also lay asleep or seemingly asleep, his body shining with coconut oil, and his face turned gratefully up to the sun. He also read a great deal, lying on his stomach, with a cheap wide straw hat shading his eyes. For the rest, he played dominoes at the café and drank a little beer and a little coffee and never was drunk and spent almost no money. He had his breakfast in his rooms and ate his lunch at his desk at school and at night he ate at the hotel unless he was invited out for dinner. All the white people except Marc had invited Pierre and the families of the four girls had invited him several times. He did not go to anyone's house unless he was asked. He was pleasant and never talked much and never said anything exciting when he did talk. Gradually the white people decided Monsieur Vauclain was a good teacher and an inoffensive young man and they felt cheated because he was surely not more than thirty and blonde and slender and with a nice face (but a soft face, the men began to say, a girl's face when you really looked at it), and he could have provided them with far more amusement if he had only troubled.

The negroes liked Pierre because he was always courteous to them. He called the old women Madame and he paid Joséphine for his laundry promptly and without argument and he stopped to talk and joke with the negroes who fished off the pier and with the shop assistants and the market men and the ones who lived by odd jobs and had a great deal of time on their hands. He taught the negro children and the white children together. There were only fourteen white children in the town and they sat on the front benches, by old custom, and the negro children filled the rest of the school room. The white people were surprised that the children seemed to like school now and went without complaint promptly at seven-thirty in the morning. But Monsieur Vauclain could not be teaching them anything bad or modern because the children never said anything unusual at home. On the whole, they might congratulate themselves on having a serious and reliable teacher; it was a pity that he added nothing to the life of the island.

The school house stood next to the old unused church, on the road behind the water front. The school house

31

was painted yellow and was a long rectangular box with a sharp roof. Wisteria grew over the small front porch. The children had worn out the grass around it and only tough weeds stuck up through the sandy soil. There were three fine old Spanish laurel trees to give shade. Marc sat in his car and watched the children spill out of the door, laughing and shouting, and chase each other across the school yard down the road to their homes. He heard the windows closing inside and Pierre Vauclain came out and turned to lock the door behind him. He leaned against the white pillar of the porch and smiled as if he owned the place and as if it were very beautiful and he was happy to have it. Marc felt his heart beating as he watched the man; he knew what that look meant but no one else would know. Marc felt it himself; it was why he had always lived here when he had money to live anywhere. The man has eyes, Marc thought with joy and recognition, he can see.

"Hallo," Marc called. Pierre Vauclain looked toward the car and did not seem surprised or ashamed that someone had seen him dreaming like a woman.

"You remember me," Marc said. "We have spoken together a few times at the café."

"Of course. You are Monsieur Royer."

"Yes. May I drive you home?"

"I was not going home. I was going to the Roches Noires beach up the coast."

"Let us talk here then."

Pierre Vauclain waited; Marc liked the way he did not speak when there was no need of speaking. But suddenly Marc found it harder to say than he had thought; harder at any rate to say in the casual half-true way he had planned.

"I want to make you a business proposition. It is worth fifteen hundred francs a month if you care to accept. It will only take three afternoons or so each week. It is good pay." Marc talked faster toward the end and almost angrily.

"It is very good pay but what is the work?"

"I want you to teach my wife Julie," Marc said and stopped, red with embarrassment as he heard the words. How absurd they sounded. Who ever hired a man to

32

teach his wife, unless it would be tennis or riding or the things women learned in Europe?

"Yes," Pierre Vauclain said without surprise.

"She has had very little education. There is nothing much for a woman to do here. She is bored, you see. I thought it would divert her and occupy her mind."

"Yes. What would you want me to teach her?"

Marc could not say: I want you to teach her to read a book. "Some history," Marc said vaguely, "some literature. She has had very little education. You know how it is for women in these islands."

"It is too much to pay."

"No. That is what I wish to pay."

"I will be very glad to, Monsieur. I have a great deal of time too. And of course the money would be welcome. But I do not want you to pay more than I deserve."

"No, no," Marc said, "the money is quite right as it is. Will you start tomorrow?"

"Yes," Pierre Vauclain said, but he was thinking and Marc feared that he might now make a condition so as to give himself time to change his mind. "I think I can find some books that would be suitable. The studies in the school are very simple, you realize, but I think I could start with what I have and perhaps we could order more books. If you think that would do? For a start, I mean?"

"Oh, yes." Marc began to dread how this young man would look at him after he had talked to Liana and seen what the teaching really must be. Pierre Vauclain would know then that Marc had half lied, from shame. It was too late now; he would have to act his way out of it. All three of them would have to act. No, Marc thought, I will not start any more of that; it is better to give it all up now than to get caught again in the falseness and the weariness of pretending.

"My wife has never read a book," Marc said. "I will call for you tomorrow afternoon."

CHAPTER FOUR

Pierre Vauclain sat in the dark with his eyes closed, by the open window. There were no lights burning in the town and hours ago he had heard the last negro voice talking under his window, then farther along the road, then out of hearing where the road became a path and the negro shacks began. In three hours it would be dawn and the white men would leave their close mosquito-netted beds and dress and go down to the pier. Every morning they studied the sea and the sky and took the new day's air as if it were a medicine their bodies needed. The white women, wearing kimonos and curlers, would lean on the balconies of their houses and turn their faces to the breeze that came out of the white-green sky over the flat ocean.

Now the sky lay like heavy black cloth above the island and the air was damp and whining with mosquitoes. These had been terrible hours for Pierre before, if he could not sleep. It was in the empty night that he felt France to be farthest away and lost. He was not thinking about France. He was thinking about himself and Marc Royer.

Greedy, Pierre decided, you wanted the money and you did not consider whether you could do the work. I do not know enough about people; I have not had enough experience as a teacher. It was impossible for him to imagine a life without reading and he had spent this whole night trying to imagine such a life and trying to find a book which could be a first book. You had no right to make fumbling experiments with a woman's mind. This was not a light thing like teaching a child who had missed some time at school from sickness, or like giving extra lessons to a stupid child who could not keep up with the class.

Royer did not understand of course because he had always read. He did not realize that each book rests on all the other books that have come before it. You grow to fit books or they grow with you or something like

34

that; they are not thrown recklessly into your mind. This
is only stage fright, Pierre told himself; after you have
met her it will seem as reasonable as any other teaching.
Now the money talks, he thought. And you hate to make
a fool of yourself; there is that too. You do not want to
face Royer and admit you were greedy and that you are
no great teacher at all. He would think you were crazy
if you told him that as a teacher you only hoped never
to damage the children.

His head ached and he knew he would not sleep and
he was ashamed of himself. I will talk to her, Pierre decided, and then I will tell Royer as best I can and he
will have to think whatever he likes. It is the only fair
thing to do.

Marc Royer and Pierre did not speak in the car. Marc
did not see the anxious lines in Pierre's forehead nor
the way his lips seemed almost to be forming and prac-
ticing words, and Pierre did not see the sweat on the
backs of Marc's hands and around his mouth, and the
stiffness of his shoulders. Marc was preparing himself,
with pain, for another humiliation. Liana had wept all
morning for reasons Marc could not discover, weeping
in her room like a child who has both a tantrum and a
broken heart. It had made Marc furious and finally wild
with nerves. He ordered her to come down to lunch and
she came, unwashed, wearing a kimono which had never
before looked slatternly and soiled. She refused to eat
or to explain her tears. Marc told her to make herself
presentable and to bathe her eyes and finally he threatened to beat her if she made a scene when the school
teacher came. Liana answered him by silence, sitting
slouched and sullen in her chair.

Pierre Vauclain sighed with pleasure when they turned
in at the gate. The drive wound up the hill to the house;
it was bordered by hibiscus bushes and lined with mango
trees. Their leaves looked sharp and slick and dark,
fresh after a morning rain, and the hibiscus were velvety
and brilliant against the gray coarse trunks of the trees.
They could see the house to the left, placed at the crest
of the lawn. The lawn sloped down to the road. Beyond
the road the land fell away so that only the palm thatched
roofs of the negro huts could be seen standing in the
thick greenness of sugar cane. Royal palms towered out

35

of the canefields. Beyond the roofs and the palms was the shining line of the ocean.

When they entered the house, Pierre hid himself behind a polite face. Only his eyes looked shocked. The front door opened into a square room that ran through the width of the house. The walls were panelled in a varnished dark brown wood, to the height of a man's head. Above the panelling the walls were mud-brown stucco. From the center of the ceiling hung a chandelier of amber-colored glass, the glass all smooth tubes blown into many elaborate curls and twists. Small orange-colored conical electric bulbs flowered out of it. A wide oak staircase led up from the back of the room. An enormous tapestry hung over the stair railing at the second-floor level. The tapestry was covered with fat goddesses and overdressed sixteenth century gentlemen and it looked like a rug which has been hung out to air. There was a certain amount of badly placed furniture around the walls, mahogany rockers with cane seats, stiff chairs with high carved backs and flat plush cushions, tables with dragons' legs and tables that could only be there to be knocked over. There was a large ebony black radio in one corner and two standing lamps with fringed shades. The room did not look like a hotel foyer because everything had cost too much and everything was too clean and new. It was one of the ugliest rooms Pierre Vauclain had ever seen and he started to dislike and distrust Marc Royer because of its ugliness.

Marc had stopped noticing Pierre when they came into the house. He was waiting for Liana. Marc was sure she would be wearing a kimono and would stand at the head of the stairs and glare at them like an animal. Then he would have to find some way to get Pierre out of the house and would have to invent a falsely cheerful excuse for her behavior. Marc had called to her, when they came in the door, and there was no answer.

"Julie," he said the second time, "please come downstairs."

He heard her door open and for a moment he shut his eyes, wanting to postpone this scene. Then Marc looked quickly and saw that Liana had on a plain white dress and was very pretty in it and then he looked at Pierre Vauclain.

Liana rested one hand on the tapestry and stared at Pierre. She had expected a cold secretly contemptuous man who would come here to please Marc and earn Marc's money. She was prepared to cheat the teacher of his scorn, by not showing that she felt it. There was no scorn in his face. His eyes were warm and gentle. Liana smiled at him suddenly the way children make friends with strangers. Pierre smiled at her.

Marc had not known, until he saw Pierre's face, that he had feared something else. He feared something as intimate and insulting as a wink or some sort of murmured leering congratulation. He had unconsciously been ready to resent this and accept it, since he could do nothing else. But the man was looking at Liana as if he were grateful.

Liana came down the steps slowly and gave Pierre her hand. She was shy and she did not speak. She wore her hair pinned up, but not in the elaborate pompadour wave she had copied from the movie magazine. It was drawn away from her ears and folded on the back of her head as simply as if she had just pinned it up to be cool. She wore a white silk dress with an open collar and short sleeves. Her legs were bare and she had on rope-soled espadrilles so that she walked as she was meant to walk and not with the studied walk of the high-heeled shoes. Pierre took her hand and did not speak either. They stood there smiling at each other, apparently happy and not troubled by their shyness. Marc did not understand this and he needed time to straighten out his mind.

"You may as well begin your first lesson immediately," he said. "I am going back to the office. I will call for you later, Monsieur Vauclain."

Pierre nodded. Then he remembered where he was and became businesslike. "I did not bring any books today. I thought Madame and I could plan our studies together. If we finish quickly I will walk to town."

"Good. Good-bye, Julie."

She led Pierre across the room and out to the veranda. There were white wicker chairs and they could look at the sea. Of course, Pierre thought, she must hate that room. I know I can teach her; I am sure I can do it without harming her. Royer did not say how young she is. There was that boy I tutored who had not had any

schooling until he was fourteen, the one with weak lungs.
The boy was happy; I managed to do it slowly and fit-
ting it into what he already knew. And nothing much
can have happened to her, she won't be complicated,
Pierre thought, forgetting all the gossip he had heard and
ignoring what he could see: that she was a beautiful mulatta girl married to a rich white man twice her age and
living on a small Caribbean island where the people had
too much idle time to be forgiving.

Pierre did not speak, as he was thinking about her
and what kind of lessons would be best. Liana sat beside him and, without really noticing it, he felt her ease
and unnervousness and grace.

"Julie," he said absently. "You don't mind if I call
you Julie?"

"Yes."

Now this was different. He had offended her already.
Why? he wondered. This was no way to start.

"I beg your pardon, Madame," Pierre said.

"My name is not Julie."

"I beg your pardon, Madame Royer. I am so accustomed to teaching children that I forgot for a moment.
I assure you."

"I don't want you to call me Madame Royer. Julie is
what my husband calls me. It is not my name. My name
is Liana."

She waited to see whether he would find that strange;
whether he would smile because it was not a proper
French name. But she could not stop herself from telling
him even if he spoiled everything now. She was not
going to be Julie and she was not going to be Madame
Royer.

"I'm so glad," Pierre Vauclain said. "Liana is a beautiful name. You permit me to call you that?"

"Please, Monsieur." Liana drew her feet up under her
and settled back to wait for what would happen next.
This was like opening presents. You did not know what
would be hidden inside the wrappings.

"Liana," Pierre said. What a fool Marc Royer was,
really. Imagine changing a beautiful name like Liana
for a little dumpy name like Julie. "What shall we do?
What do you think would be amusing for our lessons?"

38

She laughed aloud with delight. He was a kind, funny man and not at all like a teacher. "Anything."

"I think you should teach me, to begin with, and then I will teach you. You can show me the island and tell me about it and then I will tell you about books and we can read together. What do you think?"

"You mean take walks in the country?"

"Yes, and on Saturdays we can take picnics and go swimming."

"Oh."

Or isn't that right, he thought. "Do you want to?"

"Oh, yes."

Pierre turned in surprise, hearing her voice, and saw that there were tears in her eyes. My God, he thought, doesn't she have anyone to play with; is she that lonely?

"We are going to amuse ourselves very much," he said. Liana looked away from him. She could not believe this because it had happened so fast. He had only been here fifteen minutes and already he was her friend, as if that were normal and everyone behaved this way.

"I don't know anything to teach you," she said.

"You know the trees?"

"Don't you?"

"We don't have these trees in France."

"I can tell you their names," she said proudly.

"You see. And you know the flowers?"

"Oh, yes, of course I do."

"And everything that lives on the island?"

"There are deer up in the hills," Liana said, as if she had put them there. "I know all the kinds of fish they catch. I know where the beaches are, the good ones where the sharks don't come. I know the fruits you can eat and the ones that will make you sick."

"You see?"

"Will you tell me about Paris?"

He had not wanted to talk of Paris, not for years anyhow. He had not wanted to talk of it until he had forgotten the pain. Pierre said, "Yes, I will tell you."

"What is it like?"

"The Germans are in Paris now."

Liana did not know any Germans. The way he said it sounded as if someone in his family had died. This was the war probably and she knew nothing about the war. He looked sad and far away from her. It did not make him happy to talk of Paris.

"I'll tell you the names of the trees now," Liana said quickly. "That's a banyan tree. And that shiny one is a soursop. If you want to walk around I can show you the others."

That night Pierre put the magnolia flower Liana had given him in a water glass on his table. The whole room smelled of it and when he looked up it was all he could see, the creamy petals growing from the black stem, and the tight velvet heart of the flower. He was happy and excited and a little doubtful. Should a man be paid for what was surely not work? Marc Royer was presenting him with fifteen hundred francs a month and the first person he had felt at home with since leaving France. He smiled thinking of how earnestly Liana had warned him against the poisoned burning leaves of the manicheel plant, and how she had identified the leaves of the avocado and the tamarind as if she were giving him street directions in a foreign city.

"What are you reading, Julie?" Marc said.
"A book."

The night before, Liana had been laboriously pinning butterflies into a sort of wooden tray, surrounded by glue, paper strips, scissors, colored inks and pins. She did not answer when spoken to, being absorbed in the problem of getting the butterflies pinned straight and without damage to their wings. After this came the slow printing of names under the insects.

Liana was busy all the time now. She no longer wore her hair in the stylish way and she did not wear the elegant dresses, with pleats and tucks and rhinestone ornaments, that had been part of her airmailed trousseau. She looked very young, as if she really were going to school Marc thought. And there was something absurdly like a little boy about her and it was not unattractive. It was exciting in fact, because it was new and it did not belong to him and he did not understand it.

Liana read bunched up into a comfortable ball; and on occasion, thrilled by what she read, she kneeled straight up on the chair and seemed to be following the lines in the page with breathless surprise and emotion. Sometimes her lips moved and she turned the pages violently, entering into the action of the story. Marc had watched her weep as she read, without noticing that she was weeping or that he was in the room. And once she threw a book away from her saying, "What a monster!" and then picked it up and went on reading. She was evidently indignant against some character in it. Marc watched all this, enchanted and bewildered. But when he questioned her, when he tried to join in the tears or the anger or the butterfly pinning, Liana closed herself against him. She hid her books so that Marc could not find them and locked her butterflies and her shells and her pressed flowers into a bureau drawer and carried the key with her.

"Do you like it?" Marc asked.

Liana looked at him with suspicion. She liked all the books. Of course she liked it. Why shouldn't she? Was he now going to twist it so that it was foolish of her to like the book, or wrong, or not something a white lady would do?

"Yes," she said and turned a little in her chair, away from him.

But she could talk to Pierre. She could tell Pierre how sorry she was for Heloise and how she thought Abelard was a pig or he would not have let Heloise suffer so terribly. But then she had not finished the book and perhaps Abelard was better at the end. Only what did the houses look like? Liana wondered. What sort of clothes did Heloise wear?

"Will they talk about Paris on the radio tonight?" Liana said.

"I don't know." Marc realized that he had to say "I don't know" a great many times. This was probably the way people felt with their children but they could invent authoritative lies or tell the children not to ask stupid questions. "Do you want to listen?"

"Yes please."

"Are you interested in Paris now?"

"Oh yes," Liana said, in a smiling superior way. She needs a spanking, Marc thought, and then was amused to find himself so irritated. I'll have to tell Vauclain to cane her, she's at the nasty age like fourteen-year-olds.

41

"What do you know about Paris?"

"They shoot people in Paris." Liana said it with horror. She was looking at Marc quite differently now, forgetting that he was the man who had to be kept out and kept away lest he ruin this lovely new life. "Pierre told me."

She used to call him Monsieur Pierre, as if he were a coiffeur or she a servant, Marc thought, but apparently Vauclain also found that an embarrassing form of address. Marc tried to remember the tone of her voice as she said the name.

"The Germans shoot them," Liana went on, "if the people do anything against the Germans. But you see, they don't shoot the one who did it. I mean if I killed a German they couldn't catch me but they would shoot my mother or my sister or any one. They kill many people if only one German is shot. Anybody can die for no reason, Marc."

"Yes. But you don't know any of them."

"It isn't that," she said furiously. "It's wicked. It's cruel. It's just as bad if I don't know them."

Marc thought: in three weeks Vauclain has taught her to have a conscience. Surely Julie had never thought of anyone except herself and perhaps him and her mother. She had never thought of anything outside this island. Marc did not know what to expect from her next. But he liked it. Marc decided he would join in some of the lessons or at least insist on Vauclain's coming to the house at night. He wanted to know more of this lively little world they were building. After all, he thought, Vauclain would never have given her lessons if I hadn't arranged it; if I didn't pay for it.

"Come to bed, Julie."

"I have a headache." She started to droop and passed her hand across her forehead and sighed, acting without talent the part of a sick woman.

"Nonsense." This was a new tiresome trick she had, feigning illness at night. She had never done it before, though she had often come to him sullen and hostile. But Marc knew that he could override these delays and that once she was with him, beside him, she made love as well as always. He did not know that afterwards, while he slept, Liana stayed awake hating herself because she

42

could not make her body as cold as her mind. He did not know that she felt herself to be weak and shameful and that she hated him for forcing her into a pleasure she did not want.

"Nonsense," Marc said again. "Come upstairs."

Marie said, "Really?" "How amusing." "Think of it." "Not really." She yawned twice, carefully covering her mouth with her hand. The third time she yawned openly. Marc talked more these nights than he ever had before. He talked so eagerly that he did not notice the dryness of Marie's answers. He talked through her yawns; he covered and obliterated her with talk.

Marc was telling her, laughing with surprise and pleasure as he spoke, of the newness of Liana.

"Vauclain gave her an old copy of *L'Illustration*. I don't know how he happened to keep it," Marc said. "It was one of the war numbers. He told her about the refugees on the roads leading to Paris. He told her about the bombers. She wanted to know if I had ever seen a bomber. What did a bomb sound like? The poor people, she kept saying. She was actually wringing her hands, terribly agitated about it. Don't you think it's fantastic, Marie? She has never seen anything, you understand, she imagines it all and uses a few pictures in *L'Illustration* to help her. I am not sure it is wise of Vauclain; she is so distressed by these things. I don't want her to become nervous and hysterical after all."

"My God it's hot," Marie said. "We need rain."

"Now she wants to listen to the radio every night." Marc went on, untroubled, "She asked me if there were no maps in the house. 'Where is France?' she said, 'I mean where is it exactly, not just across the ocean.' So in the evenings I explain geography to her. It is very good for me too. And I have to be sure I am right; she is upset and disgusted if I make mistakes." Marc leaned back in his chair and laughed to think how he had studied the Atlas in his office in order to impress Liana with his accuracy.

"It's like having a child," he said. "Like having a son you are teaching things to. She doesn't seem at all interested in girlish things, but I suppose she knows all those. Sewing and cooking or whatever girls do. And she's so funny with her toys, her little collections. She shows off a good deal, telling me the names of things."

Marie held her dress out from her neck and fanned air down between her breasts. *"On étouffe,"* she said irritably. "I've never known a hotter July." Everyone on the island said this every year.

"Vauclain does not like to come to the house in the evenings. I wonder why?" Marc was talking to himself now.

Marie heard this. "Probably he does not want to become intimate with you. After all, he is paid by the town. He has his situation to consider. It is quite different simply to give lessons to a mulatta; but I mean to say, dining with the husband and wife is something more."

Marie waited. She smiled to herself. Now Marc would come back to himself. He would be again the large helpless animal she knew, foolishly and comically beating against the bars of his cage.

"Oh, I think not," Marc said calmly. "He isn't at all that sort of person."

She shrugged her shoulders. If Marc wanted to be so smug and stupid, let him be. Marie rose, yawning, and walked to the screen door of the terrace.

"Well," Marc said, "good night."

Marie stopped by the screen door and her face in the dark was hard with anger. This was the second time Marc had come, bored her all evening talking about his negress and her lessons until she felt sick with irritation, and then told her good night comfortably and gone home. He had not tried to kiss her; he had not so much as stretched out his hand to her. Before, sitting there on the terrace, waiting for the late coolness of the night while slowly between them and without words they built up the old hurting hurrying desire, she could almost tell when Marc's need for her became unbearable. She could almost feel his hands before he reached toward her, making some gesture that meant he was ready. Now Marc only wanted her to listen. He did not seem any more man-like than the priest. He was as friendly and placid as a brother.

"Don't bother to come any more this week," she said.

Marc stopped at the head of the steps and looked at

her and then he laughed. "You're jealous, Marie," he said. But he did not say it slyly or with triumph; she would have recognized that. She would have thought it was part of a scheme he had invented to give himself power. She would have been amused and fought against him, matching malice with deeper wiser malice. Marc said "You're jealous" as if it did not matter to him one way or the other.

She opened the screen door and went in and latched it behind her. He could only see her as a shadow in the dark room.

"It is you who should be jealous, my poor Marc," Marie said softly.

Marc did not speak again but went to his car and started down the hill towards town. He drove slowly at first, denying what Marie had said. Marie is trying to make trouble as she always has, he thought. She spoke simply from wickedness, to torment me and take away my pleasure. Vauclain would not consider anything of that nature. He does not think of Julie as a woman; he thinks of her as a child, his pupil. I would notice in Julie if there were any change. I am not going to allow Marie to poison this for me. It is only that, it is only Marie's wickedness.

But when Marc was nearer his house he found himself clenching his teeth; Marie's voice buzzed in his head, saying the same thing over and over. Have I been made a fool of again, he thought; are they laughing at me, laughing at the way I enjoy her questions and humor her and allow them to be alone as much as they like. Marc put his foot all the way down on the accelerator and the car leaped ahead and raced over the bad dust road and turned dangerously at the gate. He stopped with grating brakes and ran from the car and fumbled with his key at the front door and ran up the steps to Liana's room. He hammered on her door and after a few moments he heard her voice, husky with sleep but angry.

"What do you want?" Liana said. "I will not open the door. You know that."

"Where have you been all evening?"

"Here. Where else would I be? I will call the servants if you do not go away."

45

No, Marc thought, I am crazy. It is Marie who made me crazy. She was lying as she always does. There is nothing to fear.

CHAPTER FIVE

Marc told the cook to make extra paté sandwiches as a treat and to pack a bottle of good red wine. He put cigars in his pocket for Pierre. He wondered what else he could add to the picnic so that it would be a richer, tastier meal because he had decided to join them.

"I think I'll go with you and Vauclain today," he said to Liana at breakfast. "I have nothing special to do at the office."

She kept her face down. "Are you going every Saturday then?"

"Not every Saturday," he said cheerfully.

"But often?"

"From time to time."

She ought to be pleased that he wanted to come. After all, hadn't she once complained and often made him feel that he neglected her? And who pays for all this, Marc thought, she forgets that there wouldn't be any Vauclain and no picnics at all if it weren't for my money.

"He doesn't do this for his health," Marc said.

"What are you talking about?"

"After all," he said, and suddenly changed his mind and tried to make it into a pleasant joke, "I'm entitled to a little amusement, as I am the financier of these excursions."

"Oh," Liana said. She went to her room without finishing breakfast.

Pierre came to the veranda door at ten o'clock. He looked sunburned and young and happy, wearing faded khaki shorts and an old open tennis shirt, with a cheap child's knapsack on his back. He brought from town little presents for their lunch: candy from the store, a bottle of cider and some not too soft square sponge cakes. He brought also *Twenty Thousand Leagues Under the Sea* which they were reading aloud and two home-made

46

diving masks. He carried a spear he had made out of a broom handle because he was teaching Liana to spear fish off the reefs. It was their newest game and the most exciting one they had found. Liana now made collections of coral and underwater plants, and drew inexpert pictures of the bright little fish which swam in hordes through the coral cities of the reef.

When Marc announced that he was coming along, Pierre said, "Naturally," agreeing to terms he could not reject but did not care for and then he said with unwelcoming politeness, "Where would you like to go, Monsieur Royer?"

"Wherever you had planned to go," Marc said impatiently.

"We were going to walk up to the point beyond Rives Mortes and fish from that reef."

"Is it a pleasant place?" It was at least six miles away and the day was hot. There was no comfortable beach there; but only black smooth rocks and a deep channel close to shore and then the curve of reef before the open sea.

"Whatever you wish," Pierre said.

"No, of course we'll go there."

Liana always carried sandwiches and whole tomatoes and hard-boiled eggs and a water bottle and her bathing suit in another knapsack like Pierre's. Walking was easier that way. But Marc had told the cook to pack the picnic in a basket and when the butler brought out the basket, Liana and Pierre looked at it as if they had never heard of anyone carrying a basket, as if it were both impractical and vulgar to have a basket. Marc picked it up angrily and said, "Well, why are we waiting?"

Marc walked last in line on the path behind the coast. The ground was sandy and his feet slipped and sank in it. They tried to avoid the long silver thorns of the acacia bushes that grew like weeds in this bad soil; they were cautious with the leaves of the manicheel; they had to push through the tough branches of sea grape. The trees here were scarce and small, not nourished by the poor earth and stunted by the wind, and there was little shade. Liana and Pierre did not talk. Marc was sweating and uncomfortable. Liana looked cool and untired; Marc was not tired himself but he was hot and the handle of the

47

picnic basket cut into his hand and the basket swung against his legs and was a nuisance on the narrow sand track. Pierre walked easily and without noise. Marc had to walk with his head down, watching for roots and stones and land-crab holes in the path.

Marc thought that they had probably picked the farthest and least attractive point to go to, and taken the most trying path at the hottest hours of the day, simply to make him realize he was not wanted. He planned sentences in his mind but he did not speak. Everything he thought of saying sounded either whining or angrier than his dignity would permit.

They came out on the barren coast and stood in the sea breeze high on the rocks and looked down at the deep clean blue of the Caribbean. No one swam here. The white inhabitants of Saint Boniface did not often use the sea for pleasure and when they did, in the summer, they stayed together on the beach near town for the sake of the talk and the company. No one had ever heard of picnics; people ate reasonably at home, a good solid hot meal with a nap in a shaded room afterwards for the digestion. You went swimming, if at all, at four or so in the afternoon. The women took parasols or umbrellas or wide straw hats so as not to dry their skin in the sun.

Liana and Pierre, looking out now at the brilliant blue of the water over the reef, the narrow white line of coral that showed above the sea, and the smooth fall of the boulders down to the deep water, had the same happy look on their faces.

"Shall we swim first?" Pierre said. He was more friendly now; he loved this place and could forgive Marc for intruding and trying to spoil a Saturday.

Liana climbed down the rocks below them out of sight to change her clothes. The two men undressed outlined against the sky. Marc was standing behind the younger man; he did not mean to look at him but he could not stop himself and he saw Pierre's body, silhouetted in the glare of the sun, and he thought with envy that he had once looked so finely cut and swift himself. Ten years ago, Marc thought, ten years ago I was like that too. But he knew he was lying; his body had never been different.

"Are you ready?" Pierre called without turning around.

Marc had forgotten that he was staring. He had forgotten that he was in the ridiculous position of a man trying to take his trousers off over his shoes.

"I'll be down in a moment," Marc said. He noticed that Pierre did not ask Liana whether she was ready. I wonder if they bother to separate when I am not here, Marc thought, or if he just climbs down and finds her half naked on the rocks below him. Then he was appalled at what this meant if it were true; it meant so much more than getting into bathing suits without privacy. Marc hurried and clambered down the rocks after them. Liana was wearing a white suit and was standing with lovely magic grace, her head bent, pulling her cap on over the forward swept mane of her hair.

Marc lay on his back with his eyes closed. The sunlight made a reddish glare under his lids and he could feel a tickling drop of sweat run down his right side and another under his left knee. The black rock was not comfortable to lie on and he knew that unless he dressed or went inland and found a shade tree he would be covered with tiny flat water blisters and his face would hurt badly and peel. He had never lived for long out of this sun but he took no beauty from it. Pierre's skin was the color of dark honey and his hair was bleached and streaked so that it was blond as sand. Liana and Pierre were still diving from the reef. He could hear them.

I must stop this, Marc thought, I am getting sick in my mind. First I am jealous and then I am delighted to see them because they look so suitable together, so healthy and ornamental and the way every one should look. Then I am furious that I came on their wretched picnic and then I am enchanted to see how beautiful it is under the water by the reef. He had never dreamed that you could make a diving mask out of useless inner tubing and some window glass and wire, and then swim about exploring inside the ocean. I have no imagination, Marc said to himself, I am a man without any talent for making life pleasant. That was an idiot way to think, like a neurotic woman who wandered off into self-accusation, regret and anger. I always knew what I was doing, Marc thought, and then he doubted it.

I like the boy, he told himself, I like him very much. He is the most interesting man who has ever come here. It is undignified and stupid to be jealous. I have seen them, haven't I, they are fine friends, they are as contented as children. There is nothing more to it. I am happy to be with them; this is not a Saturday like all the others. But I am not happy, Marc thought, I feel old and ridiculous and awkward and ugly and in the way.

Marc sat up and shaded his eyes and saw Liana's white cap bobbing above the water, and then saw it rise, curve in a circle, and next he saw a little splash where her feet had slapped the water as she dived down. She swam under water as if she belonged there; Pierre too was graceful and strong. Then he saw that Pierre was swimming toward shore and calling to Liana and she laughed at him, with the water flashing on her brown face, and swam after him.

Pierre was carrying two lobsters and some yellow grunts in a small string sack. He held the sack away from him with his left hand and swam an awkward sidestroke. They left the day's catch in the shade where the rocks had been cooled by high tide.

The day is very long, Marc thought, what is the matter with me?

They made their picnic low down on the rocks near the water. The boulders behind them curved up and gave shade. The rocks were uneven and Liana found a small hole in the surface where she put the eggs; she leaned the bottle of cider, the water bottle and Marc's wine against the rock which was serving her as a back rest. She placed the sandwiches in mounds and used Pierre's candy as a centerpiece. She takes more pains about this picnic than she ever did about our table, Marc thought. And though Liana did not speak, she seemed gay and serene. This was nothing like the hard watchful silence she kept at home. Evidently Pierre was not much of a talker either. What do they do, Marc wondered, sit and eat like an old married couple? But he knew it was not like that: there was no boredom or resignation in them. The next thing Marc thought impatiently, they will begin smiling to themselves or looking at each other and laughing without having said a word. Yet you could not criticize them. Liana was not flirting, Pierre's eyes were loving but it was a friendly kind of love.

"What do you plan to do when you leave here?" Marc said.

Pierre was surprised. "I'm not leaving," he said.

"I don't mean that. But you aren't planning to stay here all your life. You're a young man. What will you do after the war, then?"

"I will go back to France I suppose and get a job with all the others to build up what has been bombed. Or else I will work on a farm to grow food for all the people who have none. I will do whatever there is to do in a disaster, like everyone else."

"Why did you leave?"

Liana made a little waving movement with her hand, as if she wanted to brush Marc aside and stop this talk. She knew this was the talk that hurt Pierre. Why did Marc come, she thought bitterly, he is only going to make people unhappy.

"I left," Pierre said slowly, "because I wanted to live. And I knew that if I stayed I would not live because it was getting too bad. It was so bad that when I would see one on the street I would walk away in a hurry because I so wanted to kill him. And then you see, I reasoned; because I have been taught to do that. We learn it in the lycée. We believe very much in reason. We think very highly of the controlling, orderly brain. We are probably quite wrong."

Marc laughed. "What did you reason?"

"I reasoned that though I would kill one German, I would be shot. I reasoned that this was a bad bargain: I was more valuable alive than one nameless dead German. If I had ever entered into politics or belonged to a party I would have worked with other men and perhaps it would have been different. I mean to say: my ability to kill one German, as a civilian, might have been part of a pattern and a sensible thing to do. The way things are in Paris now you cannot present yourself to the Communists or the Union people or a de Gaulliste group and say: here I am, let me be one of you, and presently allow me to kill a German. They do not take chances any more, even if you could find them to talk to. You might

51

be a police spy or a French-Nazi or simply insane; in any case you bring to other men the chance of quicker death. One is very alone in a country which the Germans occupy."

"I can imagine it."

"No," Pierre said. "You would have to see it."

Liana watched Pierre's face anxiously. He sounded as if he were talking for himself. She could tell that Marc did not mean to be cruel with his questions. Marc and Pierre seemed to understand each other though they were not friends and had scarcely spoken together before. Pierre had always treated Marc with the politeness due an older man and his employer. Marc had always been jovial but unreal with Pierre, as if excusing himself for giving Pierre money. Now this was gone and there was nothing false between them. Even their voices had changed. It is France, Liana thought with envy, it is knowing about France where I have never been and will never go. She was jealous of Marc for taking Pierre where she could not follow.

"I was in France at the beginning of the last war," Marc said.

"I do not think it was the same. I do not think it is only the dying that makes war horrible."

"No. And I was very young. My father brought me home. I did not belong in Europe, you know, and it did not matter much to me."

"It is not a thing one can think about," Pierre said.

"Nor stop thinking about."

"I am happy now," Pierre said, "I don't think about it. I do not look even a day ahead."

Then he was ashamed to have talked so much and he asked Liana for something to drink. Marc uncorked the wine and Pierre took a glass from politeness but when Marc turned to reach for the fruit, Pierre poured the wine down a crevice in the rock. The red wine was too hot and heavy, at noon in the sun. Pierre made talk about the food, complimenting Marc on the paté sandwiches and praising the tomatoes which came from Marc's garden. He talked unnecessarily and uneasily and suddenly he stopped talking altogether.

Liana saw the day ruined as if it had rained. Only it was worse than rain; the rain would have passed, they would not mind getting wet, and when the sun came out again there would be the sweet green smell of the land as they walked home. But now the day was hopelessly ruined; they were all strangers. Pierre would not read to her. They would not swim again. He would not help her remember the colors of the angel fish so she could paint them in her notebook. He would not tell her stories about the theatre in Paris. It was all lost and Marc had done it though she did not understand how. Will Pierre ever come again on Saturday, Liana thought in panic, will he ever come? Marc was the one: Marc only made people unhappy.

The old hated trouble woke in Pierre's mind. The memories he thought he had burned out with sun, the places he had tried to forget by loving new places, the people he had mourned until he could no longer endure mourning and had finally buried, all came back. And with them, bright and feared and painful, came the memory of streets he had walked on in the spring for happiness and streets he had walked on in the winter hurrying to get somewhere, the houses he had lived in, the tuning-up voices of women in the foyer at the Sunday Pasdeloup concerts, the Mayday parades when you watched in the Place de la Bastille and felt excited and full of good will and brief hope, the color of the sky from the Pont Alexandre Trois looking up the river at sunset, the smell of the flower stalls around the Madeleine, the first morning when the horse chestnuts bloomed on the Champs Élysées, the sound of the brasserie on the Boulevard Saint Michel that you could hear before you went in the door, the sound that made you laugh and feel at home even before you got to the table where your friends waited with beer-soaked cardboard discs and a damp disorder of one-franc-fifty glasses before them.

He had never intended to tell Marc Royer anything. In his shyness, and because of the long habit of not talking about himself or what concerned him, Pierre imagined that he had given all his secrets away. Marc Royer had robbed him or cheated him of his privacy, though he recognized it was unfair to blame Marc because he had talked himself back into the past. I need not have spoken, Pierre thought, but why did he have to question me? It is none of his business.

53

"It is very hot. Shall we go home?" Pierre said suddenly.

Young Pinelli had never gone back to Guadeloupe. There were many good reasons. He would have to transport his bride home in a sailing schooner which often took three weeks to make the trip, and was not only uncomfortable but possibly dangerous. Though the German submarines did not in principle menace French shipping, you could never be sure they would not make a mistake. Of course, as people pointed out, they did not often waste shells on schooners but it had happened to some English boats. Pinelli's little bride was terrified at the thought of all the hazardous water between her home and her husband's island and besides she was young, accustomed to living with her mother, and finding it pleasant to be a married woman in her own town.

Pinelli was a shrewd young man. His father-in-law the mayor could afford to give him a good position, the Mayor's house was very fine, and Pinelli was more of a figure on Saint Boniface than he had ever been in Guadeloupe. He supervised the Mayor's salt ponds, which was not difficult work, and he became one of the biggest and most authoritative talkers on the island. The only person who was not impressed or did not pretend to be impressed by Lucien Pinelli was the school teacher Vauclain. Pinelli had not forgotten that Vauclain called him a dangerous fool, publicly, some time ago. And he resented almost daily, in the café, the unobtrusive way in which Vauclain ignored him or, if called upon by some islander to check Pinelli's statements, smiled a sort of indifferent denial.

Pinelli had been thinking and whispering about Vauclain and Liana for weeks. It surprised Pinelli that the island was not more interested in these two; but the island had decided Vauclain was a model man and the island simply was not able to change its mind after Vauclain's months of proved virtue. Though Pinelli did not understand this the white people had no special feeling about Liana, as you would not become distressed over the actions of an animal or a child. The island's resentment was against Marc. Negroes did not misbehave, according to doctrine, unless they were encouraged. More-

54

over Liana never tempted them to disapproval by giving herself airs and appearing too smartly dressed. She had vanished; and if anything the whites were a little sorry for her because she had been forced out of her class and must, they thought, be miserable up there in the big house all by herself and not knowing how to act.

Pinelli was drunk, since it was Saturday, and as usual when drunk he was loud and full of vanity. The café was in the downstairs room of a dingy house at the far end of the main street. It was a low, hot room with unpainted board walls and an army of insects beating against the light bulbs, and it smelled of rum, beer, sweat, the pissoir whose door would not shut, and strong black tobacco. Pinelli's voice was the only clear voice in the place; the voices of the other men, drinking or playing dominoes in the yellow light, rumbled together but Pinelli's voice could not be escaped. He was telling lies about an alleged airplane trip he once made from Paris to Marseilles and Pierre Vauclain, entering the café, could not help hearing the story. Pierre had come this evening with the intention of getting drunk; he felt empty and sad and angry without knowing whom to be angry against. Now, hearing Pinelli, he forgot all this and listened with wonder. At the end of the story he shook his head and laughed to himself. This Pinelli was a clown, after all, the most romantic liar you could hope to meet. When the poor idiot was only telling lies to appear heroic, he was quite entertaining; it was when he started on politics that one wanted to mash him like a mosquito.

Pinelli, standing at the bar and looking toward the door, saw Pierre, saw the smile and the head shake, understood them for what they meant, and being drunk, they seemed to him the final insult after countless studied insults. He walked across the room.

"What are you laughing at, Professor?"

"A joke."

"What joke?"

"It is my affair, cher Monsieur Pinelli."

"Why don't you tell us your little joke, Professor? Why don't you let us in on the fun? I can guess what makes you smile with such contentment for yourself. You are thinking what an agreeable afternoon you had, making love to the beautiful black wife of our honored millionaire."

The café was perfectly silent; a flying beetle knocked against the light bulb. A man put his beer glass down softly on the table and it sounded as if he were trying to break it.

Pierre stared at Pinelli. He felt paralyzed and cold with surprise; he could not believe what he had heard. Pinelli's face looked terribly big in front of him, blurred as though he himself were drunk. There was the great pink-cheeked face with black greasy hair curling up over it, and the face swam and wavered and leered at him. Nothing happened. Then Pinelli laughed.

Pierre hit him as hard as he knew how and as well as he could, given the fact that the face floated so it was difficult to be sure where it was. Pinelli staggered back, talking to keep his prestige intact.

"A glorious cavalier," Pinelli said. It sounded to Pierre as if he were singing. "A glorious cavalier defending his black mistress."

Pierre sprang at the man: he felt quite blind now and only directed himself toward the voice. He could scarcely see the outlines of the room and no other faces. His body worked without conscious plan, and was cold all over, and he was angry enough to kill. His hands slipped off Pinelli, he did not know whether he had clutched at the shoulders or the sweaty neck; but they slipped. And then suddenly Pinelli was near and easy to see; Pinelli had hit him though it felt as if he had cut him, perhaps Pinelli's knuckles had cut his cheek under the eye. He saw Pinelli close up, his mouth open and his eyes bright with a dirty hating anger in them, and Pierre swung again. This time he connected well and Pinelli sat down, and looked up from the floor with a stupid expression and blood running from the corner of his mouth. Pinelli was confused by drink and by the taste of blood in his mouth and amazed that this light-boned quiet peaceful man could have hit him hard enough to knock him down.

"More?" Pierre said.

Pinelli got up without much conviction. He was not talking. He knew he would have to go through with this show now; but later he would see to it that Vauclain paid. He could hear the sentences going around in his

56

head: "Imagine, the pretty little school teacher tried to beat me up because I spoke of his mulatta mistress; pretty little school teacher, mulatta mistress, an affair of the heart actually, too absurd, imagine it. . . ."

Some men had started from the corners of the room to stop the fight but another group made a solid ring around Pinelli and Pierre Vauclain, and guarded their right to go on. Their only interest was in seeing a good fight. Someone called out from the bar, as if it were a match for fun, "Hit him Pinelli. Come on Pinelli. Give it to him." This partisanship produced an opposition group who started to shout, "Come on Vauclain. In the body. In the *buffet*. Give it to him in the old ice-box."

"This is like the good old times," someone said at the bar.

Pierre did not hear or see; he felt the dark straight bodies of the men around him, keeping space cleared near the door. The surprise and rage were wearing off. Pierre could not now believe that Pinelli had said these things and he had hit him. It seemed unreal and disgusting and he wanted not to believe any of it, but simply to go away and deny it by acting as if it were not true.

Pinelli moved closer and Pierre smelled rum, tobacco, lavender brilliantine, and a strong acrid underarm sweat smell and he hit with all his force and heard himself saying, in a voice he had never heard before, "Learn not to talk about ladies."

Pierre had put all his weight behind his right arm and now when Pinelli's head snapped back and Pinelli dropped like a flour sack, he fell over on Pinelli, unable to save his balance. He felt his right knee in Pinelli's groin and he held himself up with his left hand on Pinelli's chest. Pierre was trying to keep his face from pressing against that sweaty, red and white, eye-closed face beneath him. Everything felt soft, the layer of fat over Pinelli's breast bone and the soft inner fat of the groin. Pinelli's head did not move. It seemed to Pierre that he hung above that repulsive face, loathing it and slipping down toward it so that at last he would feel that skin against his skin. Someone pulled Pierre up by his elbows. He could not get his footing properly.

"Learn not to talk about ladies," Pierre said in a strange, hoarse voice. "Learn not to talk about ladies."

57

The face was receding. He must stop saying that same thing over and over. His mouth and throat were dry and his legs trembled but they held him. Learn not to talk about ladies, Pierre thought fiercely and stupidly, and watched while someone threw water on Pinelli and someone who was drunk threw beer on him.

Pierre pushed open the torn screen door and walked out into the street. Negroes were hanging around the door staring quietly. They made a lane for him to go through. When he had gone, two boys ran softly down toward the negro section to tell the story. The men in the café found the evening flat, after Pinelli had been helped home. They talked for a while about the fight, saying with amazement that this Vauclain was quite a hitter, who ever would have thought it, he looked so thin and easy-going.

Then the garage owner said, "Pinelli had no right to speak of Vauclain's private affairs."

There was general agreement.

The butcher said, "It is all the same droll to fight for a thing like that."

Everyone agreed.

The hotel keeper said, laughing, "I'd never have thought of Liana as a lady."

No one had anything to say. This was a new angle on the business.

"Evidently," the huissier said, "Vauclain wouldn't have hit Pinelli unless it was true."

"Then why make such a noise about it?" the butcher put in. "It is not as if she were white."

They broke up into groups to talk over the finer features of the evening. In the end they agreed on two things: Vauclain was the lover of Liana (that Marc, they told each other smiling, first he married a black and then she puts horns on him) and beyond that, Vauclain exaggerated. It was pretentious to call Liana a lady just because he slept with her, and to make a public scandal about her honor as if she were white.

CHAPTER SIX

When Pierre heard the bells ring for early Mass, he decided to get up. He had been lying awake, staring at a brown stain on the mosquito net and trying not to lie too heavily on the rumpled sheets. Since daylight he had studied the stain and disliked the feel of the sheets and tormented himself with the memory of last night. He followed in his mind the itinerary of scandal as it would travel from house to house across the island. He imagined Liana's eyes and what Marc would say. He twisted on the torn-up bed trying not to picture the faces of all the people he knew, looking at him in a way he could exactly foresee. I might as well go to Mass, Pierre thought. The Mass would be like all the others he had ever heard; it would be reliable in this maddening confusion of strangers and lies.

On Sundays the town slept, or at least stayed indoors, because this was the day of rest. The men did not meet at the pier and the women did not show themselves as if they could not be seen, pallid and sleep-marked, on their balconies. At eleven, they would all be stiffly dressed and in their places in church. The early Mass on Sunday was attended by negroes.

Pierre saw Liana at once though he had never met her in church before and he had never seen her dressed like this. She wore a black dress with long sleeves and on her head a plain black chiffon scarf. The ladies of the town wore small unsuitable city hats: only the colored women wore head cloths. Pierre guessed that Liana must always come to the early Mass because she could not come later; she could not sit with the whites nor with the blacks. Though everyone is equal before God, local custom had divided the church so that the whites worshiped on the left side of the altar and the blacks on the right. Liana sat far back near the door in the left section of the church, which was empty at this hour. You are not supposed to hate your neighbors on Sunday, Pierre thought. Liana had never looked more alone; Pierre had

59

not thought of her as thin before. Her being so young had seemed to him lovely and lucky, now it made him sick with pity.

Liana looked up when she felt him beside her; and was surprised, and glad, and smiled at him. Pierre kneeled and folded his hands on the bench in front of him. He did not seem to notice that he was in church but went on studying her as if he were looking at a picture alone. Liana had never seen this intended gentleness in Pierre's eyes. She smiled at him again. His face was white and tired.

Pierre closed his eyes then and bowed his head. Our Father who art in heaven, Pierre began and did not finish. Hail Mary full of grace. He had no interest in these prayers now. Seigneur, he prayed, make them be kinder to her. Then Pierre stopped praying; he did not believe that God occupied himself with the small problems of mankind. What am I going to do, he thought, how am I going to take care of her?

The votive candles on the altar made the white side walls look pink. The rest of the narrow church had a cool green light as if the green early morning air and the trees outside had washed their color over it. The altar was white and gold, dressed with a starched embroidered cloth. It made Pierre homesick. He had seen many altars like this, always the richest possession of the village, and because the village and the faithful were poor the richness of the altar was touching and the way they made their altar so innocently gay was touching too. There were tuberoses and gardenias on the altar between silver candelabra. No church he knew in France smelled of these flowers.

Pierre listened to the priest droning the old fine words. He noticed that two of his boys from the fourth class were serving. They looked sleepy but proud, and much cleaner than they looked at school. He was amused by their self-confidence and the evident pleasure they took in being so important. The boys he had taught in France were paler than these, wiser, quicker.

There was no safety in thinking of French churches or French school boys. There was no safety left and he had built it slowly and carefully for himself, wanting nothing else. Nothing else, Pierre thought. I only wanted to be quiet. I believed a man could at least save that. Liana touched his sleeve. They were the last people in church. Pierre heard one of the altar boys whistling Tantum Ergo very softly in the sacristy.

The church was not far from the school on a narrow road lined with pepper trees. Pierre and Liana did not have to cross the main street nor pass the pier. The negroes saw that Monsieur Pierre had met Liana at church and walked home with her, but they would not gossip about this with the whites. It was fortunate that none of the whites saw Liana and Pierre. It would have outraged them all: no one was supposed to carry love affairs into church except the young girls of good family who could walk to and from Mass with their fiancé or those young men whom they hoped to have as fiancés.

"I did not know you went to early Mass, Pierre."

"I couldn't sleep. I don't usually go at all."

"You look tired. You aren't sick are you?"

"No." He ought to tell Liana about last night. Someone would tell her.

"It is nice to see you on Sunday."

"Liana," he said. He thought he must tell her that it would be better not to see her at all. He could not say that. Pierre knew that her only pleasure was their lessons which had become daily lessons, and their Saturday picnics. And my only pleasure too, he told himself.

"What do you do on Sundays?" Pierre asked.

"I wait."

"What for?"

"I wait for Monday," she said and laughed.

Pierre stopped her in the road and held her elbows so that she faced him but he did not pull her close. He saw behind her the fawn-colored trunk of a flamboyante with its roots growing out like stretched tendons. It was cool in the shade and silent. Somé black Jew-birds made a rumpus in an acacia tree and flew off bumping across the sky. Then it was silent again.

"Liana, are you very unhappy?"

"Not now."

"Tell me."

"Now we have so many things to do. And the books.

And everything you teach me. Are you going away, Pierre?"

"I don't want to hurt you."

"You are going," Liana said. She did not move and she made no sound; she only lowered her head.

Liana felt the island suddenly as if she could see it all: green, pointed with hills and dented with valleys, oval, growing in a blue sea with reefs as its roots. It felt too small to live on. It felt so alone that beyond it there was no more land. There was only this tiny island and she could never leave it.

It is more than that, Pierre thought, there are many people I would not hurt. I do not hurt people anyhow, I am not a man who ever hurt people. I would take care of any child who was entrusted to me. It is more.

"Why did you marry Marc?" So now I will hurt her with that. What concern is it of mine? Pierre hated the words as he said them. But that was there too and he had never admitted it and never spoken of it. I don't mean why did you marry him, Pierre thought, the marriage part is only a legal mistake. I mean why do you go to bed with him, why did you ever go to bed with him, why, why? It is that, he thought. I do not know how he treats her body. He took his hands from Liana's arms. He was frightened at the pain and the anger inside him. She could refuse, he thought. Or is she docile and obedient? Or worse than that, is she flattered? My God, Pierre thought, because the picture of them was as revolting as if he had been in their room. That heavy common insensitive man used her and she accepted it, her body all pliant and warm. If she were white, it would be better; the way it is, it makes her like an animal. Does Royer dismiss her afterwards, Pierre thought, and groaned aloud as he imagined it.

Liana stood back against the tree in the deeper shade.

"Why?" Pierre said.

"I wanted to be a wife. It was good for my mother."

"But now? Now?"

She knew what he meant. Liana turned her face away and slowly started to walk up the road. She had suffered through this alone, night after night, and now Pierre despised her as she despised herself. It must be even more terrible than she had thought, because Pierre was always right. He would not be cruel to her without reason. Pierre watched her passing from shadow to sunlight, under the trees. In the sun the black of her dress looked a little rusty; in the shadow the cloth looked heavy. He could see her shoulder blades through the dress. He watched her until the road turned and she was gone. Then he walked back to town.

There was something wrong. When Marc came down to breakfast, Liana looked at him as if she were going to be sick and pushed back her chair, overturned her coffee cup, dropped her napkin on the floor and ran to her room without speaking. Marc followed and called to her, outside her locked door, but she did not answer. He was not going to stand for this; first he had been treated like a leper at their picnic, and ignored all evening, and now Liana fled from him apparently because the mere sight of him was horrible. As if I were carrion with the buzzards and the ants on it, he thought. When Marc came downstairs again he could hear the servants gossiping in the kitchen. He flung open the pantry door and shouted to them, asking what they meant by making this noise and what had happened for them to talk so idiotically much. They separated and each one began to do something unnecessary (the butler polished a glass as though he were trying to wear it away) and did not answer. But they looked at Marc with a sly wondering look in their eyes. They were not afraid; they were laughing about something.

Marc drove in town after breakfast because the butler had let the cigarette supply run out. Marc told the butler that if he ever did anything as careless as that again he would make him crawl to the tobacco shop on hands and knees. No one on St. Boniface had a chauffeur; the rare cars could not be entrusted to blacks. The quickest way to get cigarettes was to drive in town for them himself. The main street was full of church-goers on their way to late Mass. They were all talking in a most irreligious and excitable way. People who normally did no more than bow were now practically hanging on each other's necks. What can have happened, Marc thought contemptuously, to excite the gentry? He passed a group composed of the hotel keeper, the Mayor, one of the

63

gendarmes, a sugar cane planter and their wives (where do they buy those hideous hats, Marc thought, looking at the women) and the group stopped talking as Marc came up to them, waited for him to enter the tobacconist's, then put their heads together and began to talk again but in a whisper he could not hear. They had all said good morning to Marc formally, but there was something in their eyes too. They looked like the servants if that were possible.

Marc came home in a temper and shouted for Liana. The maid said Madame Royer had gone out. Where? Madame did not say; Madame went for a walk probably. The maid knew this was not true. Liana had taken her horse and ridden up the hill path; she was going home to Lucie. Marc would come for her as soon as he learned where she had gone. But at least tonight she would be away from him. At least tonight, when all she could think of was Pierre's face and Pierre's disgust, she would not have to lie in Marc's bed.

At five o'clock, by threatening to dismiss them all without pay and without references (which was the same thing as sending them out marked as thieves) Marc learned from his servants that Liana had gone to her mother's house. It was too late to follow her. He could not get home again before dark and he could not sleep in Lucie's one room shack which smelled of negro bodies and negro food and the old rag smell that came from negro beds. He would ride up early in the morning, Marc told himself, and he would beat Liana. White wives were beaten from time to time and it proved healthy; negro women always had to be beaten sooner or later. They had no sense of responsibility; they behaved like spoiled half-witted children unless you forced them to behave better.

At six o'clock Marc had drunk more than half a bottle of scotch whiskey, broken an ash tray against the wall, pulled down a hanging book shelf in fury because he could not find the book he wanted, and his anger was growing drunkenly and recklessly. There was no one to talk to and no place to go. He looked at the large elaborate living-room with hate. The café in town would be pleasant; you could get drunk with other men and forget why you got drunk and talk about anything and

64

forget there were women, or secretive servants, or a big room like a cage that you could not escape from. He might go to Marie's of course; Sunday was one of her nights. The thought of Marie started the anger again; another woman, worse than Liana because she was older and she was white.

He would not go to Le Paradis at all. Never again, Marc told himself, drunk and certain. Women were all disgusting, full of trouble and insults and stupidity and greed and all of them were cold, really; they had nothing in their hearts. If they wanted you it was only for lust or for money. "Women never have any ideas," he said out loud. "Women can't talk about anything." Women just made scenes. That's all they could do; stir up trouble until men went crazy and then made scenes.

The café was a pleasant place; it always had been. What prevented him from going there?

"There is no law that says I cannot go to a café if I feel like it," he said.

"Is there?" Marc shouted in the empty living-room. He mixed himself another heavy drink. Don't know why I don't go to the café every evening, he thought, it is a pleasant place. Have a game of dominoes with that old crook Baudier; have a few drinks with Merey and Luc and Captain Saldriguet; see what's going on; find out if old Berthold is doing any hunting these days. No reason not to go to the café if a man wants to, Marc thought, don't imagine anyone would say anything to me, what right has anyone to make observations to me. Might find out what all that noise was about in town this morning. Probably some other thing the women started. Perfectly ridiculous for a man to drink alone at home if he doesn't want to. And I will beat her tomorrow, Marc thought, with a riding crop so she will remember. And after I beat her I will lock her in her room and she can stay there until she behaves. She can do without her precious lessons until she learns manners and stops making senseless scenes.

"When does Monsieur wish to eat dinner?" the butler' said.

"No dinner," Marc shouted. Then he laughed and threw his glass with the dregs of whiskey in it. The butler shut the door behind him and ran to tell the servants, who were waiting in the garage, that Monsieur was drunk and crazy and did not want to eat. The servants decided to go to their homes for the night. Monsieur would probably be calm in the morning. He must have heard the story in town and that was making him crazy, but it was neither safe nor sensible to stay around here tonight.

"Mary pity Liana when she comes back," the maid said. She was very frightened.

"Liana got her trouble when she married Monsieur," the butler said.

"That Lucie's a fool," the cook remarked. "She's my second cousin. She was a fool from her childhood. I'm going home where it's good for me."

The maid and the cook walked off under the trees, taking a short cut to the town road. The butler went softly up the veranda steps and peeped into the living-room window and saw Marc, with a glass in his hand, staring wickedly at Liana's chair. He turned and ran down the drive. Monsieur would have to shut the house himself tonight; he was not going to wait around any longer. When the white people got mad drunk they did anything; and afterwards they could always fix it up with the Mayor.

Gaston Drieu owned the café and was a smooth-talking man who had made money running rum to St. Thomas during Prohibition and lost the money playing cards in Trinidad and you always had to count your change when he gave it to you. Marc and Gaston had gone to school together in the yellow clapboard school-house and had disliked each other all their lives. When Drieu saw Marc stagger through the screen door, he moved out from behind the bar, wiping his hands on his apron, and walked quickly past the domino players and stopped Marc with his hand on Marc's shoulder. Marc was drunk as anyone could see, a red-faced hot-eyed mean-looking drunk. Not many men were permitted by their wives to go to the café on Sunday nights. There were only two tables of domino players and three men at the bar. They watched Drieu and Marc in pleased and interested silence.

"If you're looking for Pinelli, he's not here," Drieu

said. "He's not coming either. And I'm not going to have any fights in here tonight nor tomorrow nor next week. If you want to fight you go and do it somewhere else, Marc. Besides you're drunk and you better go home while you can. You're too old to start fighting with young men."

"Take your hand away."

Gaston Drieu dug his fingers into Marc's shoulder.

"Are you crazy?" Marc said. "Take your hand away, you bastard. What are you talking about, fights and Pinelli? I have come to drink."

"You have had enough."

"Listen, little man, since when do you give orders to the customers? You are trying to begin something, aren't you? You talk like a crazy man and try to push me out of your dirty café. We will see about that."

"You only come to make trouble. You can't make it here."

"Gaston," one of the domino players said. "Hey, Gaston. It is possible he has not heard."

"Bah."

"Heard what?" Marc shouted. "*Salauds! Emmerdeurs!* What are you talking about?"

The domino player opened his mouth and laughed like a horse whinnying. Two other domino players slapped each other on the back and laughed as if they had won the National Lottery and were already drunk with joy. One of the men at the bar beat on the wood with his beer glass and said, "That is something. That is the funniest thing I have seen for years." Gaston had dropped his hand and was staring at Marc. Then he laughed too and walked back to the bar. This could not be happening to him, Marc thought. This was insane. He went across the room to the domino player who had laughed first and grabbed the man's collar and shook him.

"You, Paul," he shook the man into silence, "tell me."

Paul coughed as the pressure on his windpipe grew. He pulled at Marc's hands. He was getting angry too.

"Let go of me, you fool. Stop acting like a poor little innocent. We are laughing at you. Pinelli told everyone

67

here last night. Pierre Vauclain hit him. Why weren't you here to defend your wife's honor instead of leaving it to the schoolmaster?"

"Vauclain was very noble," one of the men at the bar said. "He did your work for you. Of course he was personally interested."

The laughter started again.

The whiskey made Marc uncertain on his feet and he swayed; he had the lost, whirling, smeared feeling of a man going under ether. It was impossible. Still, he had understood them. Pinelli said Liana and Pierre were lovers and Pierre had hit him; and everyone on Saint Boniface knew about it except Marc Royer. Liana must have run away because she was afraid. Marc heard the laughter as if it were cyclone wind, blowing down this house and the town, roaring over the island. He turned and tried to pull the door open but it was swung on hinges that opened outwards, and he stood battling the door foolishly and heard the laughter driving him on. When he got out in the street he thought he would vomit, because suddenly the whiskey and the shame would not mix inside him. He hurried down a side street and leaned against an unlit lamppost (when the electric bulbs burned out they could no longer be replaced), and tried to breathe quietly and wait for this attack to pass. Then he walked back to his car, walking in the shadows for fear someone would see him and laugh at him.

Marc did not turn on the lights in his house because if he were hidden even from himself he might really be hidden; he would not exist. The island had envied him and then hated him, and now it laughed at him. He would have to stop the laughter. If he were to live here, if he were to live at all, he would have to stop the laughter.

The Mayor and his wife and Geneviève his daughter and Lucien Pinelli sat at the dining-room table after the plates had been cleared away and the servants sent home. The curtains were pulled and only the hanging lamp in its glass mosaic shade lighted the room. This was the first time during the day that anyone had been able to sit down and talk reasonably. When the Mayor heard the story, on his way to church, he had refrained

68

from comment and during Mass his wife watched him nervously, knowing all the signs. He walked home without speaking and so fast that his wife had to take running steps to keep up with him. Geneviève was in the bedroom, trying futilely to make Lucien's face look better. She had no practice in such first aid and had done everything she could think of, and finally she had put liquid powder around one eye and foundation cream and more powder on his puffed and reddened chin. She was in tears.

The Mayor stood in the doorway and watched this scene and then said, "You should have gone to Guadeloupe the day of your wedding. You are a newcomer here and you behave like a fool. I do not know why I allowed Geneviève to marry you."

Madame Berthold listened in the hall behind her husband and Geneviève buried her face in a pillow and sobbed. Pinelli sat up in bed and tried to look indignant.

"I will arrange passage for you both this week," the Mayor went on. "Marc Royer owns the schooners. It is possible he will not accept. He can take you on his boat and have you drowned, as far as I am concerned."

"Papa," Geneviève said, "do not talk like that. How can you be so cruel?"

"We will discuss it later; whenever Monsieur Pinelli feels able to get out of bed," the Mayor said.

Madame Berthold came upstairs after her husband was settled in the salon, pretending to read. She advised Lucien not to appear for a while. Give Papa time to calm himself, she said, stay out of his sight.

"I didn't know he was such a friend of Royer's," Pinelli said, almost crying with nerves. "Royer never comes here."

"He has always kept good relations with Marc," Madame Berthold said. "Papa owes Marc money and he cannot ship his salt except on Marc's schooners. Oh, why did you have to make a public scandal, Lucien? Have you no good sense?"

"He did it for me," Geneviève said, wiping her eyes. "Because Vauclain has been here to dinner and Lucien thought it was an insult to me to have a man who was . . ."

"Stop it," Madame Berthold said crossly. "Do not be

69

such a little idiot. Your precious husband was probably drunk."

"No," Pinelli lied indignantly.

"Tell Papa," Madame Berthold advised. "And stop whining, Geneviève, and get dressed. This is the stupidest thing I have ever seen."

The Mayor was cold and sensible. There was no way to unmake that dangerous scene in the café and it was useless to waste time blaming Pinelli. One could of course dislike the boy heartily but that did not improve matters. He waited until he heard the servants leaving by the back door. Then he poured himself a glass of brandy and offered none to his son-in-law.

"Marc will probably challenge you," the Mayor said. Geneviève gasped and held her napkin against her mouth. The Mayor looked at his wife irritably, as a man does who says: she is your daughter.

Madame Berthold said, "If you cannot behave quietly, leave the room Geneviève." Lucien had forgotten his bride; he was listening to the Mayor. Geneviève, after all, was not the one who would have to duel.

"We must prevent that," the Mayor went on. "Marc is a fine pistol shot. I cannot have him arrested and thus prevent it, though duels are illegal; and two gendarmes cannot patrol the entire island day and night in order to intervene at the proper moment."

"Why can't you arrest him?" Geneviève said.

"Don't be too great a fool," the Mayor said icily. "Even in France, the law does not interfere until afterwards. A man has the right to demand satisfaction."

Pinelli wanted to say: "What shall I do?" but he did not dare.

"There is only one solution," the Mayor said. "You will have to apologize. I imagine he will ask for a public apology. It is possible that he will not accept an apology, but I shall urge him to do so. I will point out that if he kills you, it becomes a matter of law." The Mayor was taking a certain pleasure in this. Let the great talker suffer, he thought, he has caused me enough trouble. God knows I have been distressed all day.

Madame Berthold said, "If Lucien apologizes publicly, will it be all right?"

"He will apologize and then he and Geneviève will

go to Guadeloupe. It is only reasonable that Marc would not wish to pass him every day in town. I must explain to you, my dear Lucien, that we do not make public scenes about private affairs on this island. Possibly in Guadeloupe this sort of thing goes on every day. Here we have worked out a system whereby the women can gossip as much as they like amongst themselves, and the men can gossip too, but we do not get drunk in cafés and make accusations."

Pinelli blushed. He was too wise to launch into a moral justification of himself. The Mayor was capable of reminding him, before his wife and Madame Berthold, of the little colored girl Isabelle with whom he had slept during his three months' virtuous courtship of Geneviève.

"Furthermore," the Mayor said, "There is almost no one on this island who does not depend on Marc Royer in some way. You seem to have forgotten that in your enthusiasm."

"I regret it very much," Pinelli said, looking at the table. Geneviève touched his hand tenderly. Madame Berthold looked at them with gentle eyes; they were really a charming and devoted couple. When Lucien was older, he would become more discreet. The Mayor remained unmoved.

"We will call on Marc at his house, the first thing in the morning," the Mayor said. "I believe you will have to invite him and Liana here for dinner, Jeanne."

"No," Madame Berthold said, shocked. "What would the servants think? Everyone in town would laugh at us."

"I regret it very much also," the Mayor said coldly, "but Monsieur Pinelli has unfortunately left us no choice. Marc is not such a fine Christian that he will forget insults and treat us with kindness. We can either make up to him for all this stupidity, or we can eat salt since we will have very little else to eat. And now I am tired of this and I suggest that Geneviève and Monsieur Pinelli go to their room. I will be ready to call on Marc at eight o'clock tomorrow morning."

"I know you did it for me, my beloved," Geneviève said softly when they were in their room. "Let me put some more cold water on your poor eye."

71

"I'm content to go back to Guadeloupe anyhow. I was getting sick of this boring little hole."

"Poor Lucien," Geneviève said.

"It is Vauclain's fault. I would like to arrange things with him before I go."

"Oh, Lucien," Geneviève said, "I beg you not to see him. Papa would never forgive you."

"It's all ridiculous anyhow. A huge noise for nothing. Ridiculous. Very provincial. The civilized thing would be simply to overlook it."

Geneviève sat on the bed and admired her husband as he stood in his pale blue rayon silk underpants, frowning at the littleness of little people. She did not notice the beginning of the stomach he was going to have, nor did she notice the red veins in his cheeks which could still pass as youthful high color.

CHAPTER SEVEN

They could give me time for breakfast, Marc thought. He had an iron-hard, hollow, burning hangover. The butler showed excitement like a man who has just seen a serious street accident: the fool was hissing at him. Wake up, Monsieur, wake up. Monsieur le Maire and Monsieur Pinelli are waiting in the salon. The butler loved all this. Marc opened his eyes a little and the light hurt them. What do they want, he said. I did not ask; should I ask them, Monsieur? Take that look off your goddamned face, Marc thought. He imagined the servants pressed silently against the pantry door, listening. Tell Monsieur le Maire that I will be down, Marc said. When he stood up, it jarred the back of his head. They might have given me time for coffee, he thought. He rubbed cold water over his face and combed his hair and put on the shirt he had thrown on a chair last night and the trousers which lay stretched on the floor like the skin of an animal.

The Mayor and Pinelli stood like two extra pieces of furniture in the middle of the salon. You can almost taste this place, the Mayor thought disgustedly, it is a mixture of cough medicine and mustard. He had not spoken to Pinelli in the car coming out, nor here in Marc's house. Silently the two men considered and rejected the idea of sitting down. No chair was so placed that you naturally went to it. They would have to make a definite decision and choose where they were going to sit. It was not a room that you could possibly use unless you were invited to use it and even then you would sit up straight and feel spacious silence behind you and around you. The Mayor doubted that anyone had ever rested a drink carelessly on the polished tables or taken off his coat and lighted a cigar and felt comfortable here.

Outside the lawn flowed downhill like water and the grass looked new. Later in the day the grass would have a yellowish burned color and the trees would be dark green with hard leaves. But now in this early light everything was lime green and soft as spring and the air which later smelled only hot now smelled of flowers. From the living-room, the terrace seemed to belong to another house; it was part of the morning. Nothing of the morning entered and shone in the house.

Marc was painfully aware that he had not shaved and that his bedroom slippers made a shuffling old man sound on the stairs. The Mayor was dressed as for the annual Armistice Day banquet. Lucien Pinelli looked frightened and thinner; he could not meet Marc's eyes and he kept one hand in his coat pocket where March saw it opening and shutting as if this small movement was comfort for his nerves. Marc did not greet them nor offer them chairs. They stood like three strangers who have been held up by traffic on a street corner.

"My dear Marc," the Mayor said, "I cannot tell you how I regret the necessity for this visit; I would wish only to see you on the terms of our great friendship and in the cordial spirit which we have always shared. I have come with this boy" (the Mayor had decided that boy was the best word; it made Lucien seem so young as to be irresponsible) "in order to beg your pardon most humbly. This boy, as you have heard, made certain untrue and harmful statements in the café on Saturday night. I can only say he was drunk, which does not excuse him but which explains his shocking behavior. It appears that he was motivated by a desire to anger

73

young Vauclain, whom he dislikes personally, and did not consider the effect of his words."

The more I say the worse it gets, the Mayor thought. Pinelli said nothing. Marc looked at the Mayor in silence. His eyes were almost hidden by his heavy blond brows. He was facing the front windows and even the thin light that filtered through the beige net curtains hurt his eyes. He could feel drum beats of pain behind his temples. Black coffee, Marc thought. He felt himself trembling but he knew it was all inside; it is the whiskey, he thought. I have to be careful. I must not do anything suddenly. He wanted to kill Pinelli with his hands and end the whole filthy mess. Kill him and never hear about any of it again, he thought. Be careful, Marc told himself, if I do anything violent they will have that to laugh about too. He clasped his hands behind his back because they were shaking.

At least there was no sign of mockery in the Mayor. The Mayor was as anxious as he had ever been and as nervous. And it was good to see Pinelli so frightened and for once so silent.

"Any satisfaction which Lucien can give," the Mayor went on. "I want also to assure you that he will leave the island on the first sailing of one of your schooners if there is place and that is acceptable to you. Naturally I would not consider allowing him to remain here after the offense he has given."

The Mayor wished someone else would say something and that Marc would stop looking at him with those murderous eyes. He was tired of standing. How long will the bastard make me go on, the Mayor thought. Does he want me to kiss his feet? Is he ever going to answer?

Marc's face had not changed since they came. His face did not admit that they were in the room. He watched his voice now so that it would tell them nothing. He spoke only to the Mayor because he was not sure he could handle his voice if he talked to Pinelli. "One does not allow one's wife to be insulted by a worthless drunkard. If I kill him, I would come under police jurisdiction. I do not care to inconvenience myself."

Pinelli let his breath out little by little. He hoped Marc would not see his shoulders ease themselves. If I could only smoke, Pinelli thought; it is not going to be so terrible after all. These old men always try to make everything serious for their own importance.

Marc said, as if there were no need for further talk, "Monsieur Pinelli will call on every white family in the island, since everyone on the island has surely heard of this, and he will explain that he lied." This was the voice Marc used for giving orders to a servant who had displeased him.

Pinelli blushed. Tears of anger came to his eyes. He felt sick like the sickness in dreams when one discovers oneself naked in a crowd, as he imagined these house to house visits. Then his eyes gleamed a little; he would burlesque it. He would make a joke of it and everyone would know that he was forced to give his ludicrous speech because his father-in-law needed Marc's schooners.

Marc saw Pinelli's eyes and understood.

"In case Monsieur Pinelli should use this as an opportunity to insult us further, I will forget about inconveniencing myself. Unless Monsieur Pinelli prefers to send his seconds?"

Marc turned to Pinelli; the little blue eyes were so hating that Pinelli flinched. "I beg your pardon, sir," Pinelli said. He cleared his throat; he did not want to gasp or whisper. "I realize I did not behave like a gentleman."

Pinelli had never seen a face look so unpleasant and so dangerous.

"You will find no objection to saying you lied?"

"No, sir," Pinelli said miserably. The Mayor was as red as if he had a bad case of sunburn.

Marc turned away. It was a relief not to have the light in his eyes any longer. I must walk slowly and not touch the banister, he thought. The carved and varnished staircase seemed unusually big and long and far away. He said, with his back to them, "I shall expect this apology to be made to everyone by tomorrow evening. The *Pilote* sails Wednesday morning. There will be space for Monsieur Pinelli."

"And for my daughter?" Now he makes me beg, the Mayor thought. I could kill Lucien with pleasure myself.

"For your daughter also."

"Thank you for your very generous attitude, Marc. I want to disassociate myself entirely from Lucien and make you understand that I am only horrified and disgusted by his behavior . . ."

Marc was half way up the stairs. He pretended not to hear. I am doing this well, he thought, walk slowly, do not listen, do not notice them. He was sick of them both, the fifth-rate orator and the coward. They will find nothing to laugh about now. There is no way they can twist this interveiw to flatter themselves and humiliate me. Old Berthold would remember that he had not offered his hand at any time nor called the butler to show them to their car. He had carried it off as he had to, coldly and insultingly. There was nothing to regret so far. Marc walked around the open stairwell and up the hall to his room at the front of the house. But let them get out of here, he thought furiously, if they stay around any longer I may spoil it all. I can't go on acting all day. As Marc entered his room, he heard the terrace screen door being carefully closed.

The Mayor pushed the screen door and walked quickly on to the terrace. He let the door close against Pinelli who was following. There will be no more of this *mon cher fils* business, the Mayor thought, Geneviève can come home alone on visits from time to time. I should never have permitted the marriage; Lucien is not a man at all. The Mayor took a mouthful of air as if he were rinsing away a dirty taste. He shook his shoulders and the odor of mothballs came strongly from his cutaway. He would have to send these dress shoes to be stretched; the left one pinched his little toe and he could feel a burning pressure over the corn which he had been treating with a patent medicine guaranteed to lift corns out by the roots after two applications. Pinelli held the car door open and the Mayor grabbed the inside handle and slammed the door before Pinelli could perform this service.

The thought of sitting beside Pinelli all the way to town maddened him. He noticed that Marc's driveway was better kept than any of the roads on the island. He can afford all the crushed rock he wants, the Mayor thought angrily. And Marc had Chinese mangoes whose fruit was the color of peaches and bigger and juicier than

76

the ordinary almond-shaped kind that grew in the Mayor's garden. Marc has Chinese mangoes just to line his drive; he never loses a chance to show how rich he is.

Jeanne was the who who said Lucien was such a brilliant match, the Mayor thought, talking about his parents' position in Guadeloupe and how difficult it is to find a suitable husband here. I always knew he was worthless. Women never fail to admire braggarts. Marc was certainly as disagreeable as possible; there was no need to treat me as if I were responsible. Marc will never forget either. He will always be pleased to have humiliated me. He made a point of not asking me to sit down and of not shaking hands. At least I didn't have to invite him and his negress to dinner. In the town anyhow, we are not going to appear entirely ridiculous. It is shameful enough to have one's daughter married to a man who will be the joke of the island by tomorrow night.

The Mayor said, without looking at Pinelli, "I forbid you to speak of this when you return to Guadeloupe."

"No, sir," Pinelli said. He got out his handkerchief and wiped the back of his neck. He was trying to think how he would start. He could picture the hotel keeper, a fat dark man who wore striped shirts without collars, and his wife in her morning attire of flowered cotton kimono and leather curlers, and her daughter who had once been very nice to Pinelli, sitting in the lobby of the hotel with the sewing machine against one wall and the Frigidaire against the other, rocking and waiting for him to speak. "I have come to tell you that I was drunk on Saturday night and I lied about Madame Royer and Vauclain in order to make Vauclain angry. I know nothing about them at all; it was a pure invention which I most sincerely regret." Was that enough? And what if I refuse now? What if I say I have changed my mind and will not do it? But Pinelli knew he would not dare to refuse; he remembered Marc's eyes and the way Marc's face looked as hard as if there was solid bone under the skin. They are like animals here on their horrible little island, Pinelli thought, they have no sense of humor, no largeness of view. Detestable provincials; I am lucky to be leaving.

The harbor faced east and the main street of the town led from the harbor between two rows of houses, turned south after four blocks where the houses stopped, and continued as a wavering circular road around the island. This same road passed Marc's house north of the town, and finished its circle in the main street two blocks above the harbor. The Mayor honked his horn at this intersection, which was a local and unnecessary custom since there were only ten cars in use on the island and the chance of colliding with any of them was slight. *La ville,* Pinelli said to himself mockingly. At least there were pavements on both sides here and in the afternoon a wagon, driven by a very old black who laughed and talked to himself, sprayed water slowly and thinly down the center of the road to lay the dust. You did not actually choke like an Arab in a sandstorm, Pinelli thought, and the ruts were not as deep as river beds; but aside from that, they were certainly conceited to call this path *la Grande Rue.*

There were no stone houses, and the solid windowless first floors looked like barns, as if every one believed that in a town you still needed a place for cattle. No one lived at the street level; the balconies with their wooden fretwork railings served as open air parlors. Pinelli stared with contempt at the double line of pastel-colored houses. (Before the war, when occasionally a Swedish cruise ship put in here, the tourists exclaimed with delight; the town was so quaint, so tropical, so pink and blue and tiny. Just look at that enchanting old woodwork. Isn't it sweet the way they all live on stilts practically. It's so like southern France, the tourists always said erroneously, imagine finding the Côte d'Azur way down here in the Caribbean.)

The Grande Rue was not only the best residential section, it was also the shopping district. There were eight stores and various offices on the ground floors of the houses. Light and air came in through double wooden doors which were very high and wide enough for wagons to pass. During the day the doors were folded inside and the shops looked like· cool dark caverns, with their long counters and high shelves back in the shadow where sunlight would not spoil the merchandise. They are like shops for niggers, Pinelli thought, bolts of cloth, wine in jars, pots and pans hanging from the ceiling, shoes on the same shelf with canned soup. There is no

78

elegance here, no taste. And they are as proud of themselves as if they lived in Paris.

He saw Madame Boutellier and her daughter closing their parasols on the pavement in front of the hardware store. The white women behaved as if a single ray of sun would kill them. Probably they are going to buy face powder, Pinelli thought scornfully, knowing that face powder was on sale in the hardware store. They would buy a pinkish, heavy powder made by an unknown firm in France, with a picture of a Pierrot or the coy face of a blonde with a 1920 haircut on the cover of the box. In Guadeloupe the ladies bought Coty or even Chanel powder, at a coiffeur's which was a suitable place to buy. Of course there was no hairdresser here, as anyone could tell at once by looking at the women. And no lady in Pointe-à-Pitre would go out on the street with a hair net over her curlers, as Madame Boutellier and her daughter were doing. They probably haven't washed, Pinelli told himself with disgust; Geneviève and Madame Berthold never really dressed and fixed their faces until afternoon.

Of course they are all looking at us, Pinelli thought, and wondering where we have been. They will be whispering about that in ten minutes. They cannot help hearing us in this old iron pot. Monsieur le Maire and his 1936 Ford, he told himself, and the way they always talk about la voiture. On ira dans la voiture. Amenez la voiture. God, how have I endured this place all these months?

I am lucky to be leaving, Pinelli told himself again. He would certainly find a good position at home. The Mayor paid him 1200 francs a month and he had no expenses living in the Mayor's house. There was nothing to spend money on here; it was not like Guadeloupe where a man had to keep up appearances. We cannot live with my parents, he thought, there are the two girls still at home waiting to marry. Pinelli could not deceive himself about his father anyhow; the old man behaved as if his five children were an undeserved burden which God had inflicted on him, but it was a burden with a fixed time limit. After you are twenty, the old man always said, you can manage for yourselves. He had never even tried to find positions for his three sons. Of course it was not as if he had a business where the sons would normally be employed until they finally inherited. Monsieur Jules Pinelli was Receveur des Postes at Pointe-à-Pitre; it was a solid and dignified position and in the end he would receive a pension. He made it clear that the pension would care for him and his wife: he looked forward to living alone in his house, enjoying the entire fruit of his labors with no young Pinellis to feed and worry over.

I can always get back my job with the Singer Sewing Machines, Pinelli thought. He would not admit to himself how delighted he had been to leave this job and how little he ever wanted to be employed by that concern again. Americans were insane and shameless in their love for what they called efficiency: Pinelli had been forced to learn how to run a sewing machine as if he were a woman. The office manager boasted that he himself could sew a dress and Pinelli had passed an infuriating sort of test, before he was given work as second assistant at 800 francs a month, during which he had sewed a pinafore apron with ruffles, and completely dismounted and reassembled one of the machines. He did not know which he disliked most, the òbsequious geniality with prospective buyers in the Pointe-à-Pitre office, or travelling all over Guadeloupe in the office car collecting installment payments from harassed women who dreaded his monthly visits. It was the kind of work that you hid from your acquaintances, saying simply: I am connected with an American firm. And how those Americans worked people: he was really busy from eight to six for that wretched salary. No, I will have to branch out, Pinelli thought; but a married man was not free to get a fresh start in life as he should. A married man had responsibilities that held him down. On the other hand, old Berthold would not let his daughter suffer; he would surely make her some sort of allowance.

It all came back to Vauclain. None of this would ever have happened if Vauclain hadn't gone about sneering at people as if they were low colonials and he was the only gentleman because he was born in France. Marc Royer was merely grotesque and the way everyone cringed before him and his money was intolerable. There was nothing Pinelli could do about them now, but he would not forget. If it weren't for old Berthold he could settle this honorably. He was being shamed because of old Berthold's interests; he was forced to accept undeserved humiliation from two men with no chance of revenging himself. I will remember, Pinelli thought, and so settled the pattern of his life. There would always be someone to blame.

Marc watched at his window until the Mayor's car turned out of sight on the main road. Perhaps I have a touch of malaria, he thought hopefully. He would like to have malaria if that explained how he felt. The best thing would be to go back to bed for a while. Marc started to undress but the bunched-up sheets disgusted him. He kicked off his bedroom slippers and lay across the middle of the bed, staring at a crack that split the flat tan plaster ceiling like a black river marked on a map.

Except for the rumpled bed, the room looked as always like a display in a furniture store window. Marc had bought this set of modern furniture ten years ago when the style was still fairly rare. Not even a pair of brushes on the bureau or an inkwell on the desk showed that the room belonged to him and he lived in it. Ten years ago Marc told the sweating negroes who were moving these huge angular pieces into his house where to put everything: the desk goes between the windows, the bureau to the left of the door, the wardrobe to the right of the door, the dressing table (part of the set) to the right of the bathroom door, the bed against that wall, the two chairs on either side of the bed. Nothing had been changed.

After his first pride in having something no one else had, Marc was vaguely aware that the room was unpleasant. He did not believe that furniture which cost $2,000 could be ugly so he simply avoided the room, using it only to dress in and sleep in. Now the thought of lying here all day was unbearably depressing. I'm not sick, Marc told himself, I ought to take a stiff drink and a cold shower and go to my office. But this was not a day like any other; it had to be planned. Only what was there to plan?

The island would believe Pinelli's apologies because

he was generally known to be a liar and a fool. In two days the shape of the gossip would change and Pinelli would be the clown, not Marc. That part was going to be easier than Marc had expected. But what if it is true, Marc thought, what if Pinelli was telling the truth? His body felt limp and heavy like a drowned man's. What shall I do then? How can I know? He rolled over and beat the pillow with his fists, wanting to hammer this shame and anger out of his mind. I can do nothing, Marc thought, the only way to protect myself is to hide them. He noticed that he was driving his fingernails into the palms of his hands. He sat up and covered his face with his hands and rested with the good empty darkness pressing against his eyes.

Don't think about it, Marc told himself. Why did Vauclain hit Pinelli? There was no louder way to admit the whole thing. Or is he proud of having tricked me? Was he glad to show off before everyone? But Pierre was modest the way he was blond; it was not a thing he could change, it had been born in him. Then was Pierre ashamed to have it said he slept with a mulatta? He is a European; they are unpredictable. If that were his reason, it was as insulting as if he said, it's all right for Royer, but don't imagine it's good enough for me. My God, Marc thought, I have to stop this; I have to think clearly. I cannot lie here and do nothing.

Then Marc suddenly thought: there is more to it than all this business of people and what they will say. There is more to it than the faces of Drieu and Luc and Merey and Captain Saldriguet and how they look at me when they come in my office and what they say behind my back. There is something for me alone. Why wouldn't Marie have me long ago, when my brother died? If she had married me then she might have loved me, or at least we could have been together and trusted each other and been friends. A man needs someone. There is no one, Marc thought, I have no one. Liana does not belong to me any more than the servants do. But I have given her everything she wanted and lately I have taken an interest in her. I could not have treated her better if she were my daughter. No, Marc thought, that is a lie. He was ashamed to have used the word "daughter,"

82

remembering all the nights and the greediness of his desire.

He thought of Liana and Pierre standing on the rocks with the wind blowing her short dress against her legs and blowing Pierre's sand blond hair up from his head. Their eyes had the same look. Whether they are lovers or not, Marc thought, they have each other. I have never had anyone. Perhaps if I could explain it to Marie now, she would understand. If I could tell her it isn't only the body: I need her to be with me, I need to love her. But why should Marie change? Why would she become gentle with his trouble, and kind and loyal simply because he was sick with loneliness and cold with loneliness? It is different now. She will see that I am better; it has been my fault that she never trusted me.

I will go to Marie now in the daylight so that she will know I come with a clean mind, and I will ask her if we cannot still make a life. If she wants it, we can do it. I can arrange the practical details; they will not trouble us. We are the same age, Marc thought, as if that would protect him. We have lived here always, we have known everything that happened to both of us. We have known each other for thirty years, Marc told himself, feeling the time solid and comforting behind him.

Marc was surprised to see Marie rocking on her veranda at eleven in the morning. He imagined Marie was busy during the day, supervising her house and her farm. Her life was unknown to him too. Now Marc wondered if she ever did anything; if she read or sewed or tended her roses or talked with her overseer. Suddenly Marc was sorry for her; she looked old and very alone and he thought it must be a sad thing to wait day after day for nothing to happen.

The sunlight lay like paint across the lawn and up to the top of the steps. The veranda was in shadow. Marc could hear the farm hands talking in the barn, not the words but the singsong laughing negro talk. Inside the house a vacuum cleaner buzzed over the living-room rug. He saw the butler washing the windows of the dining-room, with his back toward the porch.

Marc bent his head to kiss her cheek. Marie turned

away from him with a shiver of disgust. His breath smelled sharp and evil; he had not shaved. There were loose bags of flesh under his eyes and he walked like a sick man. There is no excuse for him being so dirty and unattractive, Marie thought, he would do better to stay home until he is presentable. She picked up the crochet work that lay in her lap and began to work a fancy border on a doily. She held the needle close to her eyes. Marc was shocked to see how ugly she was and how careless of her ugliness. But it was for her that he felt this hurt recognition. It must be hard for women to grow old, Marc thought, they have to admit it so plainly; they cannot deceive even themselves.

"Have you heard the talk, Marie?"

"Yes."

"Do you believe it?"

"It could be true. Pinelli is a great liar of course. I suppose that if Vauclain wanted Liana he could have her. I doubt it though; he does not seem to me a man who is much interested in women. Those blond Frenchmen are usually anemic."

Marie spoke as if she were discussing mango rust. Marc was too tired to think about it.

"Julie went home."

"Liana," she said. "It is too silly to give her a white name."

Yes, Marc thought humbly, it is silly. Marie is right.

"Probably she was afraid you would beat her," Marie went on. She held up the doily for a moment and stared at a place where she seemed to have dropped a stitch. She made a little sound of irritation and pulled the thread loose with her teeth. Marc thought: this is wrong. Marie doesn't understand what has happened.

"I have never beat her," he said stupidly. Why were they talking about this?

"Much better to beat her. The best servant my father had was old Nanette. She came to us about the same age as Liana, he slept with her too I imagine, and he beat her quite regularly. She was a very devoted and capable servant, much the best, and lasted the longest."

Marc listened to her so fast that he did not really hear what she said, and he had forgotten her words before she stopped talking.

84

"I am very lonely, Marie," he said. This was all he knew certainly.

Oh, Marie said to herself, so that is why he came in the middle of the morning like this. He wants someone to cry on. It isn't my fault if Marc gets into these ridiculous difficulties and everyone laughs at him. Marie squinted her eyes to see whether she had pulled out enough thread. Yes, that would be the bad place. She hooked the needle carefully into the doily.

"We are the same age," Marc went on. He felt very tired. He could not plan how to say any of this. He would say it as it came into his mind.

"I'm two years older."

"But we are really the same; we have gone through all the same things. We knew each other's parents. Do you remember when you lived in the big yellow house at the corner?"

"Of course," she said impatiently, "why would I forget?"

"Do you remember the little cat I had when I was fifteen? My brother thought it foolish for a boy to have a cat. I called it Yvonne. It was a Persian. I don't know where it came from, now that I think of it. Do you remember?"

"No," Marie said.

"Aren't you lonely here sometimes, Marie? The house is so big and you are so far from the town."

"I am very well here. I am not in trouble. You're the one, my poor Marc."

"But Marie, we're the only two people here now. I mean, no one else knows us; we haven't any other friends. We're the only two."

"Nonsense. I know a great many people if I choose to see them."

"We have known each other thirty years."

"We've known everybody else here who's old enough for thirty years too. Really Marc. What's the matter with you? It's Monday morning. Haven't you any work to do?"

"I thought we could start again," he said. "And be friends. And look after each other and keep each other company."

Marie put her crocheting down and shaded her eyes

85

to look at him. The sun was higher on the veranda. There was no wind but the heat seemed to move in slow swells.

"Just because you married a mulatta," she said, "and nobody forced you to and she runs away and makes a scandal in the town, you come here like a sick dog looking for sympathy. I can't imagine why you think you have a right to, and I don't know what you are suggesting. If you mean you want to live in my house, you are being ridiculous. Now that Liana has cast you off, you think I will be delighted to take you in. My dear man, if I were you I'd go in town and behave as if nothing had happened. They'll forget it. And I'd beat Liana. And I'd stop crying about cats I had when I was fifteen and knowing people for thirty years."

Marc had stood up before she finished. "I regret that I have bored you," he said. "Forgive me."

Marie listened to his car going down the hill. She rocked faster and dropped another stitch and put her crocheting down angrily on Marc's chair. Imagine, she told herself, coming to cry on me simply because he's been made a fool of by that servant girl, and actually suggesting that I let him come here to stay. It's absurd, Marie thought, he goes too far. There's always something the matter with Marc and he behaves as if it were my duty to help him out. He has no one to blame except himself. Marie saw that the farm hands had left the barn door open, though she had told them only yesterday they were never to do this. The new calf had strayed into the high brush yesterday and two men wasted a whole afternoon finding it. Marie called to the butler and directed him to shut the door and said he was to send the farm hands to her when they came back from lunch. These blacks were absolutely irresponsible and careless of anything that did not belong to them, though they took good enough care of their own cattle. That Marc, she thought angrily, calling on me in the morning. He is surely old enough now to manage his own life without crawling to other people for comfort.

Marc stopped the car on the lower hill where he used to sit with Liana in the afternoons. The town was bright and little in the sun and no one moved in it. The sea was a hard blue and looked grained and solid as concrete. The sun beat down on the roof of his sedan and he felt sweat slowly oozing out all over his body and his back stuck to the upholstery and the sleeves of his shirt were streaked and clammy. He put his head down against the wheel and shut his eyes. He was too tired to go on and face the town and this day, this week and all the other weeks. Thirty years, Marc told himself, it does not mean anything to her. He had believed that today, when he came without pride or desire, the thirty years would mean safety to Marie too. I might have been trying to sell her a radio she does not need or a set of books. Perhaps if he rested here a while the hollow dead feeling inside him would pass. There is no sense in thinking you cannot go on; a man always goes on. There is nothing else to do.

The most curious thing was that it all seemed to happen behind glass or under water. His own voice sounded like the voice of a deaf man. Marc knew every tree and every rise in the ground; he knew how the cane grew and where the thatched roofs of the negro huts were. This was his veranda and this before him was the view that belonged to his house. It looked smaller or farther away, and Marc observed it with a vague impersonal attention as if it were a picture in a magazine. I must be ill, Marc thought, this is all very important to me. I should listen to what he is saying.

Pierre stood by one of the pillars of the veranda and faced Marc. Why is it that everyone knows how to behave, Marc wondered, and I am the only one who is stupid and uncertain? Pierre was so correct that Marc got the impression he had learned in school exactly how to handle such a situation; in dancing school, Marc thought with brief amusement, they teach the young gentlemen how to address outraged husbands.

In the late afternoon, Pierre knocked at the front door and asked the butler to call Marc. He did not come in the house nor offer his hand, and he remained standing so firmly that Marc was ashamed to ask him to sit down. Pierre made a little speech that was as cold as an engraved sentiment on a ready-made card of condolence. Marc found that he had a new habit which was to listen to a few words and stop listening before any sentence was finished. But he understood what Pierre was talking about. Pierre regretted the scene in the café, did not apologize for his own actions, and put himself at Marc's disposition. Marc was not sure what that meant. Je suis à votre disposition. It sounded absolutely right.

Marc thought: I must look terrible. I must stop looking this way or he will pity me. He thought Pierre had never been handsomer or more a man, standing there so straight and with such a cold unyielding face.

"I wish to ask you only one thing," Marc said. Where did this tired voice come from? Tired and pleading, Marc thought, and tried to rouse himself. "I ask you to tell me, on your honor, whether what Pinelli said is true?"

"It is not true."

Marc knew at once that Pierre did not lie. He would be too proud to lie. I believe he would have come and told me himself, if it were true. Like all really proud people, Pierre would not embarrass his conscience. Pierre would not think adultery was wrong, he would only think secret adultery was wrong.

"I believe you."

Pierre said nothing. He was not going to thank Marc for believing him. He was not going to thank anyone for anything. Thank you for dragging me into your mean little lives; thank you for giving me a chance to be star actor in your rotten melodramas; thank you for breaking in to where I live. Thank you for marrying a helpless little mulatta girl and never cherishing her, Monsieur Royer. Thank you for your sexual appetites and your lack of judgment; thank you for paying me to witness your lovely life.

Marc had been watching the contempt grow in Pierre's eyes. What have I done now, Marc thought wearily.

"It is best to keep on with the lessons," Marc said. "If the lessons stop, everyone will imagine I have forbidden them. They will then believe the story is true."

"Perhaps Madame Royer will not care to continue."

"She will do as I order."

It is not my affair, Pierre told himself fiercely. This is the life she got for herself and this is the life she will have to live.

88

"In future, however, I think it wise to have all the lessons here at the house. The Saturday excursions will cease."

"I resent the implications," Pierre said coldly.

"I am implying nothing." How could the man be so frozen and perfect? "I wish to avoid talk in the town. I am not concerned with anything else."

"On the other hand, Monsieur Royer, I am not concerned with the talk in the town. I will either go on as before, if Madame Royer wishes it, or I will not continue with the work. If we are constantly afraid of the possibility of gossip, the lessons will be pointless and painful."

Marc admired this tone. I should be in a rage and Vauclain should be cowering and apologetic, instead of which he looks wonderful and delivers ultimatums. I could deport him as easily as Pinelli if I decided to; but it is disgusting to threaten people. I wish he would like me, Marc thought, and was amazed to be thinking this now. I wish he would say something friendly and not too solemn. "We have a pretty little mess on our hands, Royer, what shall we do about it?" Oh, well, let it pass, Marc thought, Vauclain is probably right anyhow. Since everyone knows that they go off together on Saturdays they had better continue.

"I would like to ask Madame Royer how she feels about going on with the lessons," Pierre said stiffly.

"She is not here. She left after church on Sunday and went to her mother's house. I have sent the stable boy for her; she will be back tonight. Please come tomorrow afternoon."

"Very well. Until tomorrow, then. Au revoir, Monsieur."

Pierre stopped in the drive to pick an hibiscus flower; it would curl up into a tight veined and faded sausage and die, cut off from the bush. But now it was wide open and brilliant and the inside of the petals felt as soft as fur, as soft as a bird's throat. Pierre stroked the petals with his finger. Liana had not heard about the fight, he thought, she was not afraid of Marc. It was because of me. She seemed very young and alone and without help, and Pierre imagined her riding her horse up into the hills, with her eyes as hurt and pleading as he had seen them (and her hair, he thought, lifting from her shoulders when the horse cantered over the open fields, and she riding so lightly and naturally and never knowing the value of how she looks and moves). Then Liana does not want him, Pierre told himself, but she cannot live in his house and refuse.

He crushed the hibiscus flower in his hand and then, feeling it sticky in his palm, he shook it off and walked as if he were trying to leave someone behind.

It was unbearable to see this thing in his mind like those flickering movies they showed in cheap bordels on the side streets of the Marseilles port. Pierre imagined Marc's body in every detail, even his mouth, his eyes, the way he breathed. It was so horrible to him that he closed his eyes for a moment and stood still, hoping to lose this picture. Then unwillingly Pierre invented Liana naked, with the soft live brown of her skin toned down in the shaded light of the bedroom; her hair just falling to the curve between her throat and her shoulders, her breasts sharp and darktipped, walking toward the bed with her hands out, yes surely with her hands held out to protect herself. Her hands and her arms would bend as easily as willow branches.

Stop it, Pierre said aloud. Stop it. Stop it. It is none of my business. He no longer thought of Liana as young and alone and helpless. He thought of her with fury, hating her for this thing he imagined. I must get a woman, Pierre told himself, I am worse than men in jail with their filthy illusions about key holes and all the rest. Why can't a man be decent and quiet in his mind? Pierre had always walked this road with pleasure, noticing the green black tunnel where the Spanish laurel grew together above the red dust road, noticing the fern leaves of the flamboyante, waiting for the place in the road where he could smell a hidden magnolia tree and waiting for another place where he sometimes heard a negro woman singing in a shack behind a bamboo thicket. I see nothing any more, Pierre thought; my mind is like those postcards the rat-faced little men try to sell you by the fountains in the Tuileries. And there is no escape. The island is thirty miles long and we are all locked in. The world is no bigger now than any distance you can walk.

CHAPTER EIGHT

There was a black iron cauldron with rice in it. A dented aluminum pot, which Lucie had begged from Marc's cook, held the stew meat and greens. There were oily, dark, yellow plantains in the frying pan. A kerosene lamp stood on the bare wood table and the low fire on the hearth gave not light but a lighter shadow to that corner of the room. The shutters and the door were open but the heat was packed in the room. Mosquitoes hung in the air as over a pool of stagnant water; they were thickest above the rag beds. Liana brushed flies from the food and then stopped because there were too many of them and they always came back.

The children each had a plate. There were eight plates on the wall shelf and none of them matched and none was uncracked, and all of them had a smooth grease shine from having been washed in cold water and wiped with a soiled cloth. The children served themselves from the pots and the frying pan with their own spoons. The two little girls and the boy crouched on the floor to eat; there was a chair and two crate boxes for Lucie and Liana and her sister Antoinette. When they had all taken food, they ate hungrily. No one spoke. Their lips made a rubber smacking and sucking noise as they ate. Antoinette chewed with her mouth open. The meat slowly mushed together with the rice in her open mouth, then Antoinette swallowed and pushed in more food at the same time. The boy and the little girls held their plates close to their faces and did not raise their heads. Their spoons scraped on the emptying plates.

Lucie rested her head on one hand and ate as the others did, without seeming to notice the taste, eating for hunger; but she was tired and she did not eat as fast as the children. There would be no second helping. The pots and the frying pan were empty except for crumbs of rice and the gravy of the stew and the oily juice left from the plantains. After they had eaten they would wash the dishes and Lucie and Antoinette and the boy would go out, one at a time, to the shallow evil-smelling latrine behind the house. The little girls would raise their dresses and squat outside the front door. Then Lucie would blow out the kerosene lamp and shut the door and the board windows and they would find their way to bed without trouble in the dark. Antoinette and Lucie slept together and the little girls slept with their brother Alphonse. They did not undress. They would fall asleep at once and Lucie and the boy snored. It would get hotter and hotter in the room all night. The mosquitoes did not disturb any of them; their loud fading and nearing whine mixed with the slow, open-mouthed breathing of the negroes.

At dawn the room became a little cooler from the first morning air outside and Lucie would wake, open the door and the shutters and call the children. The morning air did not wash out the smell of the room. It kept the odor of their bodies and their beds, their food, the creeping smell that came in from the latrine which was too near the house, and the sharp rotten smell of the garbage dump. They fed the garbage to the pigs and sometimes burned over the heap, to discourage flies and buzzards; but the smell had seeped into the ground.

Liana had left the table and gone out to stand beneath the flamboyante tree at the far side of the yard. She turned her back to the house and tried to breathe off the choking sickness that the meal, and her family eating, and the smell of her family and their home had given her. When the dishes were put away Lucie came to the door and called into the dark, without any expression in her voice, "You too fine to eat with us now, Liana?"

Liana did not answer. She was ashamed to be sickened by her own people.

Liana knew she could not go near the latrine and she wandered across the nearest field, stumbling in the newly hoed dirt. What if I slept outdoors, she thought. But there was always the fear of snakes and tarantulas that would certainly bite you on the neck and kill you, and at night the woods were full of things that moved and that no one really understood. Indoors, the mosquitoes would settle on her clean flesh and she knew she would lie awake listening to Lucie and Alphonse and trying not to breathe that smell she had grown up with and now could not endure.

Would Lucie at least throw some stained and worn blankets together for her to sleep on alone? Liana could not ask for this. She could not hurt her brother and her sisters. When Liana arrived they ran to her like puppies, patting and pulling at her. They thought she was beautiful and rare. She had brought them no presents this time but they did not mind. They had nothing to say to her, after the first screams of delight on seeing her, but they stared at her and followed her wherever she moved, silent and adoring, and when she looked at any of them directly they laughed with pleasure and hung their heads until they could watch her again without being noticed.

Liana had heard Antoinette whispering to the two little girls outside the door, while she helped Lucie make supper.

"Did you see Liana's hands?" Antoinette said. Liana's nails were painted a dark rose color. "Did you see how her hair shines? She's a beautiful princess."

The two little girls said "Oh," and sat looking up at Antoinette.

"Princess," the oldest child said, slowly. It was a word she had never used but she knew what it meant; it meant someone lovely and strange, from a far away place, someone like Liana. The two little girls waited with joy and amazement for Antoinette to say more. There was a princess in their house.

I might as well go in, Liana thought, this is my home, this is where I belong. She met Alphonse at the door; he was twisting the loose cloth of his pants tight around his waist. He hurried now as if she were a strange lady and ran before her into the room. He dived into the gray shapeless bed on the floor with the little girls and they pulled the blanket up over their heads, in an ecstasy of shyness, and Liana could hear them giggling together in the suffocating comfortable darkness of their bed.

"You can sleep with Antoinette and me," Lucie said. She was closing the windows. Lucie's bed was made of four sawed-off logs, with a mattress woven of canvas strips. Lucie had fixed the bed herself because at night the dampness of the floor got into her bones and in the morning she was too stiff to work. Liana waited until Lucie and Antoinette lay down; then she lay beside them. Her skin prickled and she held herself tight, trying to make herself smaller and keep from touching them. If she moved, she would feel Antoinette's coarse woolly hair against her cheek. Her legs were already sweating alongside the relaxed sweating legs of her sister. Liana raised herself carefully so that she could lie on top of the blanket, though she knew that no matter how hot the night you had to keep covered or the sweat would dry on you and give you a chill. She turned on her side so that she had her back to Antoinette. She swept the whining mosquitoes from her face and then wearily and hopelessly she lay still. Lucie began to snore.

In the morning, Lucie sent the children with Antoinette and Alphonse to work in the vegetable patch beyond the cane field. "You keep your eye on them, Antoinette. Don't you bother your sister," Lucie said to the children. "I'll call you when I want you to come and eat."

She gave Liana a broom. Lucie shook the blankets and began to put them back on the beds. The handle of the broom was smooth and brown, polished by all their hands. Liana held it lightly, disliking the feel of it. It was senseless to clean anything as worn and dirty as this house.

"It's nice to have you visit us, Liana. We were expecting you some time ago." Lucie was not reproaching Liana. If Liana did not come, it meant that she was getting on well in the town.

Eight months ago, Liana had ridden up the hill path with a light small suitcase tied on behind her saddle. She brought with her two new dresses Marc had ordered from Miami. She thought her family would be dazzled to see her in the expensive clothes, with her hair waved in a high pompadour. But Liana had not unpacked the suitcase and she rode back to town the same afternoon. Putting on the dresses in Lucie's shack would soil them, and she felt disappointed and irritable with Lucie who did not appreciate the fine lady she had become.

There was always some excuse not to come for her visit, and after Pierre's lessons began Liana would not miss a day with him. When the summer vacation started in July, Pierre came earlier to Marc's house and stayed later, and Liana forgot about Lucie. She had not realized that it was now eight months since she had seen her mother.

Lucie finished the beds. Liana thought of Lucie day after day handling these things which were not fit to be handled. Suddenly she said, "Don't you get the money from Marc?"

"Don't you worry."

"Why don't you use it then?"

"What's the matter with you?" Lucie went on brushing ashes from the hearth into a wooden scoop. "Didn't you get enough to eat last night? There's plenty of food, isn't there?"

"But this house."

"This house is all right. Don't you worry about things you don't understand. I know what I'm doing. I'm saving that money in a good place where no one will find it. If Marc gives me the money for a few more years we won't have any more bother. I'm saving it for you too, Liana. I don't forget you got it for us, if that's what's troubling you."

"You'll get the money every month until you die."

"That's what it says on the paper," Lucie said. The white people made the papers and they could tear them up just as easily, and say you were lying, and you'd find yourself in court and what could you expect then? As long as Marc kept Liana, he would pay the money. But when he tired of Liana and took some other girl, he would stop paying. Lucie was glad Liana still looked beautiful and seemed to be pleasing Marc. If this lasted a few more years, they would all have enough. She had only to buy kerosene and matches and flour and rice and cooking oil and a few things like that; the children hardly needed clothes and with their own pigs and the vegetable garden they had enough to eat.

"Marc has to pay you," Liana said in exasperation. "I'm his wife."

"Oh, yes," Lucie said, "it's very good for you to be his wife." That business with the priest would probably make it last longer; it was a good thing. Still you should never be certain in this life. The safe way was to save.

"I'm not going to sweep any more."

"That's all right, daughter. When you come to visit

95

us you shouldn't have to work. You go out and rest yourself till lunch time."

In the daytime the woods were friendly. There was shade under a big pepper tree and no ant hills nearby and no fallen palm fronds where scorpions might be hiding. Liana lay down on her back and watched white cotton-flower clouds cross the sky until it seemed to her that the branches of the tree were moving with the clouds. She had thought she would talk to Lucie and Lucie would help her. Now, for the first time, Liana doubted Lucie; Lucie was not wise, as she had always believed, Lucie was not sure to be right. How could Lucie understand? Lucie would only worry about the money; she would see nothing except the risk of losing 3000 francs a year. But she doesn't use the money, Liana thought furiously, she is content to live like an animal. When she had said this to herself, Liana was shocked. Now I am despising my own mother, she thought.

Keep your fingernails clean: that was Marc's voice. Don't put your elbows on the table; no, use the other fork, hold it this way. That was Marc's voice again. The care of the hands is essential to feminine charm: that was the booklet in the manicure set from which Liana had learned how to paint on the pretty rose varnish. Dawn Soap preserves delicacy; the secret of beautiful hair is a rich-in-oil-shampoo; Nodo spares you those painful social moments; a great big puff, soft as a kiss, dusts the lovely gardenia scented bath powder over your body in a velvety cloud; just a sprinkle of these emerald green pine salts in your bath and you have the fragrance of the deep woods; Louis of the Plaza mixes your powder to suit your own fragile skin tones; the smooth, non-caking, non-smearing lipstick that all women have been looking for. Liana knew and believed the advertisements. She had secretly studied old magazines she found stored on the bottom shelf of the linen closet. Marc subscribed to every kind of publication; they were his only amusement and his only contact with the outside world. Liana waited until Marc had finished with the new ones and saved for herself all those which had pictures and advertisements. She treated these magazines as textbooks. Even if she had dared ask Marc, he could not tell her about these powders and scents and oils and soaps, with

96

their mysterious uses and fascinating effects, which gave the white ladies their power. Liana had determined to become as faultless and smooth and sweet as the advertisements urged.

I am, Liana told herself, I am, I am. But she was not now; under the rose varnish her nails would be grimy; her hair had not been combed; she could feel the coating on her unbrushed teeth.

The books she read now were written about white ladies too. White ladies must be very different; they must feel everything in a way that was their own. But since they were educated and admired and all the books agreed, that way was surely right. Love, Liana said to herself: love and making love were not the same. Anyone knew that. Making love had never seemed to her wrong. It was easy, everyone did it. Everyone ate too, and slept. It was not a thing you cried about or worried over. It was easy and quick and there was the great instant when it suddenly flamed in you and then it was over and forgotten. It was natural that Marc should want her. Marc did not love her and she did not love Marc. But in the books it was not like that; no white lady could endure to sleep with a man as Liana did; they would sicken or go mad. Pierre thought so too. Liana did not question the books or Pierre; she was not proud of what she did. Ever since she realized how wrong it was, Liana had tormented herself with shame. But she could not keep her body from responding as it always had. Her body knew nothing about books. Her body operated with appalling carelessness, as if there was no difference between now and when she first came to Marc's house and learned for the first time what a man was. So evidently her body was not like a white lady's.

But who paid for the white ladies? Who gave them the money to buy all the things that kept them lovely and clean? Who bought their soaps and their dresses and their perfumes and who paid the servants and who supplied the bathrooms and the table cloths and the silver forks that made them ladies? Or if they said to their husbands, no, I will not go to bed with you, I do not love you, did the husbands say I am sorry; and go on paying for everything? Perhaps that was what men did in Europe, but Marc would not do it. She could either

97

sleep with Marc or live like Lucie. There was no other choice.

It's easy for Pierre to look at me with hate in his eyes, Liana told herself, but how would he look at me if I lived in Lucie's house and was as dirty as Antoinette? Would he want to give me lessons then? I don't care if I am bad because I sleep with Marc. What does Pierre know about being a negro girl? What does Pierre care? He never had to live in a house like Lucie's.

This was worse than despising Lucie. Now she was turning against Pierre and making herself hard in her mind. They were the only two people who had ever taken care of her or wanted her to be happy, and she was blaming them both and denying them.

"Liana," she heard her mother calling from the house.

Liana stood up and cupped her hands around her mouth. "I don't want to eat," she shouted. She could not sit at the table and hear them over their food again. The forest was big and clean and she would stay here until she decided what to do. If Pierre knew what she had escaped from he would not force her back into it. I know I can make him understand, Liana told herself, he will not hate me if he understands. It was so simple if she could only explain it. To sleep in Lucie's bed was worse for her than to sleep in Marc's; it was as simple as that. The thing with Marc did not harm her; it had no importance. But Lucie's bed was the end of hope.

Alphonse tugged at her skirt. Liana stretched, with a long sleek pulling motion like a cat, not knowing what had waked her. The shade was deeper and cooler under the tree but the little puff clouds still crossed the sky. She must have slept through half the afternoon. Then she saw Alphonse's feet with the skin of them hard and wrinkled like buffalo hide. She rolled on her side and looked up at him. He said, sweetly and stupidly, "Bonjour."

"Bonjour," she said. He was a nice little boy, a kind and gentle one. Liana could not believe he was her brother; there was no longer anything in her that was at home with him.

"Jacques Petit is at the house. He says Monsieur wants you to come home this very afternoon."

Jacques Petit was Marc's stable boy.

If she disobeyed, Marc would come himself tomorrow. She could only delay her return and make trouble. But Liana knew really that she was glad, wonderfully and heart-lighteningly glad; because now she could leave and there would be no more tin spoons scraping on plates, no more mosquitoes hanging in the hot body-smelling air. She rose slowly as if she planned to take her time and make up her own mind, and followed Alphonse back to the house.

Lucie was sitting on a box before the front door and Jacques Petit squatted in the dust, talking. Even from a distance Liana could see Lucie making amazed gestures with her hands, bringing them together in a great silent clap and holding them suddenly over her ears. When they were closer, Liana heard Lucie saying, "Don't tell me! Holy Mary! What did Thérèse say?" Thérèse was Marc's cook and Lucie's special friend. But from the gestures and the tone of Lucie's voice, Liana knew that Lucie was excited and amused. The little children and Antoinette were still working away from the house; Lucie had called Alphonse to bring Liana. Jacques Petit's story was not suitable for the girls.

"You Liana," Lucie called, "hurry here and listen to Jacques Petit."

The stable boy said, "You better get your horse and come home with me, Liana, before Monsieur gets angry again. Thérèse says he is quiet now but she said to tell you she don't know for how long."

Jacques Petit called her Madame, at Marc's house, as did the other servants. At home he would not have dared repeat servants' gossip to her. Liana said to him coldly, "What were you telling my mother?" He was far too impressed by himself as news-bringer to notice the coldness of Liana's voice.

Jacques Petit told the story all over again. He had the fight in the café from his friend Coco who shined shoes during the daytime and hung about the streets at night. Coco had actually been standing at the door of the café and had seen Monsieur Vauclain leave and later seen Monsieur Pinelli being helped home. "Coco said," Jacques Petit repeated, " 'Name of God what a crack Monsieur Vauclain gave to Monsieur Pinelli.' " Jacques

Petit had almost forgotten what the fight was about; the fight itself was the event that filled him with enthusiasm. Liana questioned him sharply. Oh yes, he answered casually, Monsieur Pinelli said you and Monsieur Vauclain made love. Then he went on to the further delights and horrors: Marc's drunkenness, how he had almost torn down the house (this part was getting wilder and better every time the maid and the cook and the butler mentioned it), how Marc had received the Mayor and Monsieur Pinelli. Théodore the butler, who listened to that part, said Monsieur spoke big words to them and sent them away like beggars. Monsieur had been terrible and fierce. Monsieur Pinelli had already started to apologize. Thérèse knew this because her niece who worked for the Laurents, the garage owners, hurried out to Marc's before lunch, when the niece was supposed to be marketing, and recounted the scene at their house. After Monsieur Pinelli left, the niece told Thérèse, Monsieur and Madame Laurent laughed until they nearly burst.

Lucie listened to the story again as if she heard it for the first time. She followed each episode with motions of her hands and rocked back and forth on the box. "Listen to that," she kept saying. "Holy Mary! And then what happened, Jacques Petit?" It was the most thrilling story she had heard for years: there had been nothing like it since old Monsieur Leblanc (now dead) went after Monsieur Henri Gaston with a horse whip, right in the Grande Rue, because Monsieur Henri Gaston was hanging around Madame Leblanc who was much younger than her husband. Lucie did not consider that Liana was involved in this drama. This was a white people's scandal and wonderful and funny and she envied her friends in town who could watch every incident as it happened.

Alphonse stood open-mouthed and silent, twisting his toes in the dust. He did not really understand anything Jacques Petit was saying. He did not expect to understand; he knew that people in the town were cleverer than people in the country. The town people talked so fast too.

Liana stopped listening closely when Jacques Petit said, in passing: Monsieur Vauclain and you made love. she heard the rest of his story but it did not mean anything to her. She did not understand the use of the

Mayor's visit and Monsieur Pinelli's apologies. This was part of the unreasonable behavior of white people. It was another story altogether in which she had no share.

But Liana thought with horror of anyone saying: Monsieur Vauclain and you made love. People would be saying that on the street, as if it were a little thing to say. She had never imagined Pierre touching her; she had never dreamed or desired it. A woman would have to be fine and perfect like the ladies in the books to be worthy of Pierre.

"He wouldn't touch me," Liana said. Jacques Petit and Lucie stared at her. She stood with her hands clenched by her side. "It's a lie! They cannot lie about him!" She wanted to run through the town screaming it at all of them, "Stop talking about him! How dare you talk about him! He is better than anyone. He wouldn't touch me." Did they imagine Pierre would share her with Marc, Pierre who could have the finest new white lady in the world?

"What are you talking about?" Lucie asked reasonably. Jacques Petit thought that Liana looked crazy; she looked as if she would fall down straight and hard on he ground like a dead person with a little foam blowing out of her mouth, the way Tante Berthe did when the evil spirits settled on her.

"Pierre," Liana said, and suddenly dropped on her knees and put her head in Lucie's lap and wept. "Pierre wouldn't touch me," she mumbled. "Never. Never."

Lucie stroked Liana's hair. "Voyons, voyons," she said. "You've no reason to cry. Didn't you hear what Jacques Petit said? Marc made Monsieur Pinelli tell all the white people it was a lie. Monsieur Vauclain is a white gentleman. Everybody knows he wouldn't bother you. You stop crying now, little one, and wash your face and ride home. Don't you be afraid of Marc. This isn't your doing, Liana."

Liana did not move.

"Go for Liana's horse," Lucie said to Jacques Petit. "You, Alphonse, get to work. What are you standing there for, staring like a monkey?"

"Shall I call Antionette to say good-bye?"

"No," Lucie said. "Go away."

Presently Lucie coaxed Liana into quiet and brought

101

her a gourd full of water to wash her face and offered her a comb with many missing teeth which Liana refused. It was the comb that decided her. Pierre will never speak to me again anyhow, Liana thought, I cannot stay here. In two days, after the lovely months of the summer, trouble had blown up and whirled around her like a waterspout. She could not run away since there was only this one place to run to. Now she would go back and hide herself in a blank stubborn silence, behind a face that showed nothing. She could only protect herself that way against Marc's anger and Pierre's loathing. Liana stopped trying to understand her trouble; she knew that what she wanted above all else was her screened and orderly room, the tiled bath, the bed with white sheets. She did not remember to send a message of good-bye to the children.

"You be a good girl," Lucie called after her warningly.

Liana rode ahead of Jacques Petit. There had been no towel to dry her face and her hair was matted and wet around her forehead. She felt in her pocket for a handkerchief but finding none she furtively lifted her skirt to wipe her nose, and then hated that, and thought to herself that she hated Lucie and Lucie's dirt and Lucie's clutching for money, and she hated Marc who had fixed her life so that she would be a stranger everywhere, and she hated Pierre because he made her feel ashamed.

"Liana," Jacques Petit called.

He thought she had not heard.

"Liana," he called again.

Liana said, without turning, "Call me Madame when you speak to me."

He rode in silence then, with a sullen look on his mouth, thinking that Liana deserved it if Monsieur beat her. She needn't try to fool him with that Madame, she was just a black girl like all the others on the island.

Liana and Jacques Petit both feared the forest at night. Without speaking of it, they flicked the reins against their horses' necks and kept the horses trotting wherever the path flattened out into a level stretch. The horses were dark with sweat when they reached the coast road. Liana kicked her horse into a canter and felt safe only when they turned in at the lower gate. Then she held the horse

102

to a walk; she did not want Marc to hear her thundering home, as if she could not wait to be back.

She walked softly up the veranda steps, hoping that Marc would be at dinner in the dining-room and she could pass unseen. He was reading under the fringed lamp by the radio. He did not get up or speak to her.

"Bonsoir," Liana said.

Marc knew that voice; it poisoned him with anger. This was the maddening trick of the negroes, that secret flat sullen expression they took, and the dead voices, and the way they waited to be ordered.

"I want to talk to you," he said.

"I must take a bath first and get rid of these clothes."

Marc studied her now with interest and satisfaction. That was what he would have said, and meant, if he had been forced to spend a night at Lucie's shack. He watched the way Liana's nostrils flared and the way her shoulders seemed to shrink away from her dress, and he could imagine her disgust and how she felt debased and sickened by the contagion of that humid negro filth. Liana waited for Marc's permission to go upstairs, and his little blue eyes smiled at her mockingly. He would never have to argue or reason with Liana again, he would never have to give orders which she might choose to disobey. There had been no way to hold Marie and he had paid for his helplessness. But Liana at least could no longer make a fool of him. Liana would stay where he wanted her; Liana would behave as he desired. Liana needed him. She would not be allowed to forget her need. He knew how to control Liana from now on.

"I have only one thing to say to you." Marc spoke in a silky voice that frightened her. "If you ever run away again, you cannot come back. You can never come back."

CHAPTER NINE

In the afternoon the sky was a luminous milky white, with the sun hidden. The color deepened to gray and the trees and the grass looked yellow. The heat now was closed in between the flat but blinding grayness and the

103

yellow foliage. There was no breeze and the leaves burned and drooped and when Pierre put his feet down he pressed heat out of the ground. On unshaded stretches of the road the heat vibrated like a banging door, and Pierre was soaked with sweat. He put his hand to the top of his head, and felt his hair dry and really hot and he wondered whether he ought not to listen more to the natives and wear a hat in August, or rest indoors during the hot hours of the afternoon. Then a quick wind came up, blowing in gusts, and the yellowish leaves rattled in the trees and the dust stirred snake-like on the road. Pierre knew these signs and ran for the umbrella branches of a Spanish laurel and from this shelter he watched the rain pound down. This was the first rain in six days; the yellow would be gone from the leaves by morning.

The earth gave off a wet steamy heat that folded around him. His hair was now lank with sweat. Pierre imagined the rain itself would be luke-warm. The ground absorbed the first downpour slowly and the green smell came back into the air and Pierre felt a delicious release, as if the sky were higher and the trees not a close web shutting out the air. He watched the rain blowing in small waterfalls from the leaves, and watched the leaves sway in a new cool breeze. There was a final thin spouting of water and the rain was over. If he walked quickly, he could reach Marc's house before the next downpour. It would go on this way, in brief interrupted torrents, until five o'clock. Then the rain stopped for the day and the sun would set as usual in streaming red clouds.

A hundred yards farther on the road was dry and the dust twisted in the dead air. Pierre had cooled off but now his shirt stuck to him again and again he felt the heat dry in his nostrils. August was a terrible month and the end of the hurricane season in September would be no easier.

It's a wonder that anyone stays sane here, Pierre thought. He had started to hate this heat that tormented them all and gave them no rest.

Pierre ran up Marc's driveway and arrived at the steps with sweat in his eyes and his mouth dry and his heart thudding. He waited a moment to get his breath back. Then the rain came again, in a solid, gray, glass curtain before the pillars of the terrace. It was loud rain, making a grapeshot noise on the roof and a woodpecker tapping on the leaves. Pierre did not hear Liana open the screen door. He turned to enter the house, when the rain slackened, and saw her.

Liana wore one of the discarded trousseau dresses, a peach colored silk crêpe dress with a large rhinestone arrow piercing the folds of cloth at the neck. Her hair was lacquered with brilliantine and towering and wig-like in its order. If her skin were yellowish-white and caked with powder, Pierre thought, she would look exactly as Monsieur Royer's wife ought to look. It was shocking for Liana to look this way.

"Are you going somewhere?" Pierre asked.

"No."

There was a line of sweat above her mouth; the heavy silk was hot and her legs felt slippery with sweat inside the stockings and the high-heeled slippers burned her feet. She ignored her discomfort. She had dressed herself in armor, to be grand and imposing and sure.

"I should have worn a *smoking*," Pierre said unpleasantly.

Liana did not move. He had also never seen her face closed in this curious animal wariness.

"What's the matter with you, Liana?"

"Nothing."

But how could a girl change so in two days? She was a stranger and an unattractive stranger. I am becoming as hard and insensitive as Marc, Pierre told himself. I do not think of her at all, nor how she has been feeling with no one to talk to and no one to help her. I expect her to exist for my pleasure; just as Marc does in his way. We are a fine generous pair of men. How do I know he didn't beat her when she came home? How do I know he didn't order her to behave like this?

"Liana, you must not think of all the unpleasantness our little friend Pinelli stirred up. You aren't, are you?"

"Why?" She shrugged her shoulders. Where had she ever learned anything so concierge, so vulgar as that gesture? Stop criticizing her, Pierre thought, she is probably frightened. You forget that you were pretty confused yourself: you're the man who went storming down the road, crushing hibiscus flowers. You're the one who drove her away, asking questions you have no right to ask. I am acting like God these days, Pierre told himself disgustedly, trying to make people in my own image and pronouncing judgment on them. She trusted me entirely, and look what I have done to her.

Liana watched Pierre and waited. She would never be able to explain anything, though she had practiced what to say when she saw him. He spoke to her in a light unfriendly voice and he looked at her with distaste. In a moment he would say something more hurting and she would have to hold herself .straight and listen and not answer. But when he had gone she could hide in her room and hold her arms over the pain that was hard in her chest.

"You had nothing to do with it, my child," Pierre said gently. "I have talked to Marc. He does not blame you. Truly. And it is all over now and we must forget it."

Liana nodded her head.

"And forget what I said too. I hope you will forgive me for that, Liana. We can go on with our lessons as before, can't we?"

She sucked in her cheeks to keep her mouth from trembling and blinked back the tears. She looked like a child who is trying not to cry over a scraped knee or a cut finger. She looked innocent and funny and Pierre loved her for never using tears and being always so decent and secretive with her own sorrows. He laughed at her, and suddenly put his arms around her and said, "Darling, darling, you have nothing to cry about. No. Stop now, little one. Everything is all right."

Pierre raised her chin and looked at the smooth brown cheeks. She turned her head away from him, hiding her tears. He pulled her close and stroked her hair.

"My poor little child," Pierre said, "no one is going to hurt you any more."

Liana felt light and warm and cat-soft in his arms. Pierre loosed his arms slowly; he had felt a flooding happiness rise in him and this was the thing to fear and to avoid. She doesn't need that, Pierre thought. The only kindness is to leave her alone.

Liana smiled and wiped her cheeks shyly with the back of her hand.

"But go and change your dress. I don't know you like

this. You're too elegant for your old teacher," Pierre said.

"You'll wait? I can change quickly."

He had never called her "darling." Liana could not look at his face. It had sounded beautiful, lovely, and unlike any other word.

"Put on something really old," Pierre called to her. "And let's walk in the rain. Would you like to start a collection of orchids? I've been reading about them. We could walk up to the woods beyond the Palmiers. Perhaps there'll be water in that stream again."

"Just a minute," Liana sang, hurrying up the stairs. "Just a minute."

She pulled the silk dress off and threw it carelessly on the bed; she snatched the pins out of her hair and let it fall around her shoulders and did not stop to comb it. Darling, Liana said to herself. Hunting for orchids, walking in the rain, the new life was not lost. It was starting again as if nothing dreadful had happened to damage it. Darling, she repeated, and remembered how easily and belongingly Pierre's arms had held her.

CHAPTER TEN

All summer long the white women said, *"Quelle chaleur."* No matter what they were talking about, they began their sentences that way. *"C'est affreux,"* they said, *"quelle chaleur."* No one listened to anyone else, saying this. The women fanned themselves on their balconies, and wiped their necks with an ugly competent movement using their handkerchiefs like towels. The men went about with half-moons of sweat under their arms and dark wet patches on their shirts, and never stood on the street to talk; they sought the shade of doorways as if they looked for refuge in a bombardment. It seemed incredible that one day could be hotter than the next. The white people suffered and walked carefully and panted in the heavy, still air. They sweated through the nights too, lying naked under mosquito nets listening to the fast, hard-working little mosquitoes which never tired.

The heat was not unbearable since they had all borne it. But they began to fear the heat though they were used to it; they felt themselves endangered by the sun.

August was the worst month and they used up their endurance living through it. September should have been brisk and fine, but they could count on nothing. September might mean dead calms and a glaring white sky; September might be the extra strain that was not possible. Marc watched the heat and watched himself, gauging his resistance. He knew all the danger signals. There was a nerve under his left eye that started to jump in a maddening way. The sleepless nights filled him with panic instead of the dull exhausted irritation he was accustomed to. He waited for a curious inward shaking (his hands were steady) which he could not control. He knew that the next stage was shouting at people, making unwise decisions in his business which cost him money, and getting so drunk every night that he could sleep. Until the war Marc had always travelled north in September, but for two years he had been trapped by the complications of passports and visas and the uncertainties of Vichy politics.

It was no use to visit the other French islands, though that was possible, because they too would be cramped and suffocating: the people would have the same bright weary eyes and barely concealed nerves. The only restful or cool island was Saba, that the Dutch owned.

The French and the Dutch had broken off diplomatic relations but surely that would not matter to Hendrik Kerstens, the Governor of Saba. Marc had known him for years; Kerstens was not likely to forbid Marc to land because the Queen disapproved the politics of Vichy. Everyone knew everyone else in this group of islands, and they generally ignored the politics they had not made.

I will take the motor boat, Marc thought, and if the weather blows up they can run her into Statia harbor to lie over. The anchorage at Saba was eight fathoms of open sea with a fine rock wall of mountain to crash into if the sea got high and the anchor dragged. The motor boat was the crew's worry anyhow. This very minute, there would be a good fresh breeze blowing across Bottom. Marc reflected with amusement on the Dutch, who colonized a volcano peak in the middle of the Caribbean, carved steps up the face of the rock and built a neat little village in the crater and called it Bottom. For a practical stolid people, they went in for a great deal of unconscious fantasy. Kerstens himself was a rare character, tidily administering his mountain as if he were doing a routine job in Amsterdam. But Kerstens must be half dead from boredom now that no new people ever came to the island, and he would surely welcome a friend who brought gifts of whiskey and American cigarettes. Kerstens was a learned and eager conversationalist. It would be a pleasure to discuss astronomy and colonial administration with Kerstens, after this insect worry of women and gossip that had tormented Marc. On Saba, you actually needed a blanket at night; the little field stone houses looked like Europe (though what part of Europe Marc could not say); there was a doll-like virtue in the people and the place that now seemed to Marc different, refreshing and infinitely attractive.

Marc had been considering Saba in the afternoon at his office. At six, when the negro clerk started to shut the great wooden door, Marc told him that he would not be back tomorrow and that he was leaving for Saba the next day. I will be gone for a week or ten days; if there is anything important send me a cable in care of Governor Kerstens. In this month? the negro clerk said. What's wrong with the weather? Marc asked. On ne sait jamais, the clerk said. Nonsense, Marc answered.

Marc told Liana at dinner. He had decided not to take Liana. She gets seasick, he thought, it would be unpleasant for her. But he did not want Liana; he was tired of her too, she was part of the island and of the nagging constant irritation of the hot months. Besides, Madame Kerstens came from the Hague. Though the Dutch were tolerant of mixed marriages in the colonies, you could never tell how a continental Dutchwoman would feel. Marc wanted no problems. This was his vacation. He had become as excited over the trip as if he were really going far away to a new place and a new life.

"I arranged it with Gilbert Macon," Marc said. Macon was his white pilot. "He made a fuss about the weather but I told him he would be as safe in Statia harbor as here, if there's a hurricane. The only bad thing is not getting weather reports on the radio."

"The submarines," Liana said.

"There aren't any around here; why would they waste their time in these waters?"

"Do you think it is safe?" Liana was being polite and dutiful; she hid her pleasure. Pierre and I could take the horses and ride over to Basseterre beach at night, she thought, we could picnic when the moon comes up. She lowered her eyes so that Marc should not see the joy in them.

"Of course it's safe. Besides I don't believe there will be a hurricane this year. It doesn't smell like hurricane weather."

"How long will you be gone?"

"A week or more."

Liana said nothing. Marc imagined that she was hurt or angry at not being invited.

"I am not taking you Liana." She did not remember on what day Marc had started calling her Liana again. It was not her triumph since she had not asked him to do it. But it was a relief because now she need not stiffen with resentment every time she felt the accusation and the falseness in the white name that would never belong to her.

Oh no, Liana thought, do not take me.

"You get so seasick," Marc said awkwardly, "I thought it would be hard for you."

"Yes, I would be sick the whole time."

"I'll leave day after tomorrow. You'll be all right, won't you?"

"Oh yes."

Marc looked at her. Her answer was too eager.

"Will you have your coffee in the salon?" she said quickly.

I am not going to worry about it, Marc told himself. The hell with it. I am going to forget everything and get out of this damned oven and have a fine time with old Kerstens. I will take him a case of whiskey and six cartons of cigarettes. You had to have your own schooners to import such luxuries now. Kerstens loved to drink and despised the local rum. Marc began to feel happy as he imagined Kerstens loosening up, though Dutch to the

110

end, with the rare, desirable, now priceless whiskey inside him.

In bed Liana said, very softly, "I will miss you, chéri." She risked saying this because Marc had talked all evening of Saba and she knew he was determined to go. Liana had never used guile before. It was the first gentleness Marc could remember since the early days of their marriage.

"You're a good girl," he said and stroked her shoulder.

Liana was ashamed to see how easily she lied and how well it worked. Let the weather be good, Seigneur, so Marc will go. Oh, please let the weather be good.

"You must be very careful," Liana said, half ashamed and half curious to see the effect of this new lying talk. Marc wouldn't want me to think him a coward, she reasoned.

"There is nothing to worry about," Marc said. He rolled on his side away from her; he would not sleep in this black pasty heat but he did not want to talk. He wanted to think about his trip.

Marc had not been to Saba for three years. He remembered now the ruffled white curtains in the Government Guest House windows and the enormous white canopied bed. He remembered the ever-present pictures of the Queen and Princess Juliana and her daughters, all of them looking so good and sensible and healthy. He remembered the neatness of the cobbled roads and the endless steps that led up the side of the mountain to the town. The customs guard, who came down the mountain side when he heard the arriving boats blowing on a conch shell to call him, would be wearing a hot green uniform and sweating horribly, but the Dutch made no concessions to weather. The Guard would never take off his coat or wear something less stifling than leather puttees.

As Marc thought of Kerstens, Kerstens became more of a friend than he was, more charming and more understanding. Saba too became better than a quaint peaceful place that was blessed with a breeze. The need to be happy was always there, and a man could imagine that life would be good and full of friendship in another place.

111

CHAPTER ELEVEN

The beach was a great snow field. The air was silver and so was the sea. In the strong starlight, the trees behind the beach cast shadows on the sand and the black fringe of the tree tops swayed in the night wind. Liana and Pierre walked where the sand was wet and hard-packed, and the gleaming air flowed between them. They had nothing to say.

Their horses were tethered at the far end of the beach in a coconut grove. They had cooked supper over a small fire and laughed often and easily. Pierre said that people always sang at moonlight picnics. He stretched out beside the embers and sang *"Au Clair de la Lune."* The soft monotonous tune hung over them. When he told Liana to sing too, she was shy and would not.

Then they drowned the fire and scoured the pots and pans with sand. There was still daylight in the sky, a violet blue that had the burning sunset hidden behind it. This picnic was as familiar and gay as all the picnics in the sun. But now it was night and the night made them strangers. The darkness demanded something different of them; they did not know how to begin.

Liana had schemed to come here but she had not planned what would happen afterwards. She had not imagined they would walk all night aimlessly up and down the long beach. Their silence drove them apart. She felt she could not speak even if she had anything to say. She would have to cough and clear her throat and anything she might say would be ridiculous. "Comme la lune est jolie!" She could not say that.

Pierre was thinking: I was a fool to come. Soon I will have to make casual conversation and then suggest that we untie the horses and ride back to the house. This is a tricky place, he thought, it gives you romantic excited notions and you forget that there is also tomorrow. I wish I were in France: Oh God, let me go home sometime. The beach at La Favière was not as beautiful as this one, though years ago it had been empty and clean.

The Mediterranean was different from all other seas; or if not different it was his own. The last time he saw La Favière it was littered with papers from the workers' *vacances payées* and two White Russians had a lemonade stand at one end. It was an unremarkable poor man's beach in the south of France and he longed for it with such a passion of homesickness that it hurt him in his throat to think of it. This place was too far away, too perfect, and he felt a loneliness like death.

"Liana," Pierre said. He wanted to say: I don't belong here. I will never understand it, I cannot really love it. There is only so much love in any man and I suppose I use mine up on France. But how could Liana understand him since this was her home?

Liana stood very still and she was white against the black trees that lined the beach. Pierre could not see her face but only felt the waitingness and anxiety in her body. The night wind blew her dress tight around her and she looked naked. He found it hard to breathe and his heart pounded.

Pierre stretched out his hand and Liana laid her hand on his lightly. It was a gesture like the beginning of a dance. Pierre tried to see her eyes but they were in shadow. He did not move to bring her closer. Liana took three steps in silence and stopped, almost touching him. Now her face was silver as the sky, and the great dark eyes stared at him. Pierre thought her skin would be cool and glass-smooth. He wanted to warn her that he could not do anything more, that she would have to protect herself if she needed protection, that he could not and would not. Pierre closed his eyes, still hoping to stop himself because he remembered, as if they were part of the same thing, the beach at La Favière and the fact that there was tomorrow as well as tonight.

Then Pierre stopped thinking and put his arms around Liana slowly, gathering her body to him so that he could feel it all, like turning over and stroking a rose in his hand. He did not kiss her at once. He did not understand her entire quietness. Perhaps she too was thinking of tomorrow, but could not save herself. He kissed her and found her lips warm and slowly caressing.

Pierre lifted her in his arms and carried her up to the dry sand. He kneeled beside her. Liana lay with her eyes closed: there were wonderful carven hollows in her cheeks and at the base of her throat.

Later the sand felt cool under his hands and soft against his back. If Pierre reached out his hand he could touch Liana. He did not move. Liana was dark silver and the curves of her body were smooth and hard like stone polished by the sea. Her hair spread out on the white sand. Her face had never been so beautiful. The shape of her face was finished now; it needed nothing more.

"J'ai peur," Liana said.

Liana stretched and the movement of her muscles was delightful. It must be late because the heat had risen to her room and the light was hard. There was a different quietness for every time of day; now it was the waiting resting quiet of noon. I have all the time I want, she thought, and this too was delightful. She crossed her knees and her nightgown slipped up to her waist. She studied her feet and ankles. I could lie here all day, she thought, enjoying myself. She felt wonderfully well and smooth and drowsy. And why not have breakfast in bed, since the house was hers and she was free to do whatever she liked? And why not lie here, bathed in contentment, and spend the time remembering?

Liana wanted to see her face; she wanted to see whether it showed on her face. Her white satin nightgown was rumpled and she stood before the long wall mirror and smoothed the creases. Then she began to stroke the cloth against her skin and admired the richness of her body with the satin clinging to it. She held her face close to the mirror and saw the secret excited look in her eyes and something new about her mouth. Suddenly she kissed her reflection in the mirror. The glass was cool and Liana did not know why she had done this. The dampness of her mouth left a faint mark on the glass. This amused her, and she practiced making wide soft mouth marks on the mirror surface. To her amazement, and like an electric shock, desire ran through her and she looked at herself and slowly blushed.

She flung herself face down on the bed and waited until her heart stopped pounding. Then the sleepy warmth and ease returned and she lay on her back and

114

planned her day. The wonderful thing was that the day belonged to her. There would be three more days, all belonging to her. Liana could not imagine what it would mean to have Marc back; she had forgotten him so easily and so entirely that he seemed dead. There was the question of a dress; which one did Pierre like best? Pierre would come at four o'clock or perhaps sooner, a he did every day. Before that she would have a large comfortable breakfast instead of lunch. She would tell the maid to bring it to her on a tray: sliced mangoes and cold sticks of pineapple, a great cup of pale café-au-lait with the sugar sticky in the bottom of the cup, two eggs baked with cream in a small fluted porcelain dish, and toast and a mound of sweet butter and honey. Liana's hunger grew as she planned her meal and the thought of food was wonderfully exciting too.

At three o'clock Liana waited on the veranda. She wore the white short tennis dress that Pierre preferred and she had pinned her hair up at the last minute, though he liked it falling around her shoulders. But she did not want to be hot and with a damp neck and a crunched sweaty collar when he came. At five o'clock Pierre had not come. Liana tried to read. She walked down to the gate and looked for him on the road. At six o'clock she started to pace up and down the veranda. She felt sick now, with a swimming dizzy sickness like nausea. Why, she asked herself, what does it mean? She could think of no reason for Pierre not to come. Pierre had loved her last night: it was impossible that he would not love her today. But it was not impossible, since he had not come.

She went to her room and lay on the bed. All the happiness was gone from her body. She had no experience to help her and she could not imagine any explanation for Pierre. She could only repeat to herself: he has not come, he is not coming. When the maid knocked to ask what Madame would have for dinner, Liana said that she wanted nothing. She could not cry. There was no release and no escape from this pain. She thought it would always be the same; she would lie here, with the unanswered question like a madness in her brain, and Pierre would not come. The room slowly darkened and grew cool. She did not move. She lay, unsleeping and unthinking, and waited for the morning; but she did not know what she would do when morning came.

It was still dark but Liana did not know whether it was night or the dark early morning. She heard the whistle under her window and rose stiffly, not believing it, and went downstairs in the dark and opened the door. Pierre was standing at the steps of the veranda. Liana walked toward him very slowly. He had hurt her so that she did not see why he came now. There was nothing to say. Pierre did not love her but he did not have to come and tell her: she knew already.

She could see Pierre clearly in the starlight. His face was lined and grave. Liana was surprised to see that he looked as if the long day and the long night had hurt him too.

Pierre had tried all day and most of the night to placate his conscience and his pride. Would they cheat Marc and look for always more secret meeting places on the island, and hunger for each other and be afraid of everyone? Was that how it would go? And would Liana live in this house and be used by Marc? Pierre hated that idea so fiercely that he had to stop thinking of it. It was easy enough to begin; but how would they end? Above all, how would they end? When he could find no answers to anything, and only knew that he needed Liana and at once, Pierre walked very quietly through the town (despising himself for this furtiveness) and out to Marc's house. Seeing Liana's face he believed mistakenly that she too had tormented herself with these questions. His trouble was lighter then because she shared it.

Liana had no idea why Pierre had stayed away; and she did not think she had a right to question him. But she knew that Pierre had come because he wanted her as she wanted him. That was all that mattered and all she needed to understand. She took his hand and walked toward the front door but Pierre shook his head violently. The house revolted him; the house was Marc's; and in this house Liana had always belonged to Marc. Liana followed Pierre down the steps and across the lawn. He led her to a bamboo brake on the hill behind the house. The ground was soft with the leathery dried leaves of the bamboo.

116

Liana said, "We have two more days."

Perhaps that was how it would end, Pierre thought, in two days. That would be the wise way. But he did not believe it. He held Liana and mocked himself for his neat little solution. No man on earth, Pierre thought, would give her up in two days.

The servants knew.

The cook said to Théodore the butler, "Liana better be careful."

"I don't want to hear," Théodore said.

"Très bien, Monsieur Théodore," the cook answered crossly.

The maid said, "That Liana!" and looked frightened and excited.

They heard the room bell in the pantry where they were slowly finishing lunch.

"For her breakfast," the cook said. "The second time. At two o'clock."

"Go and see, Zela," Théodore said to the maid.

"Monsieur will stop this when he gets home. Breakfast in bed at two o'clock. Lucie ought to beat her if she had any sense," the cook said. She put the coffee pot on the stove and poured milk into a saucepan.

"I haven't got a thing to say to Monsieur," Théodore remarked.

"Don't upset yourself," the cook answered sourly, "I know what's good for me the same as you do."

The maid came back. "She looks beautiful," the maid said. The maid was young and ugly. "Love," the maid sighed.

The cook sneered at her. "You talk like you had three mouths."

They would all talk, but not immediately and not openly. They would talk at home and to their friends, making mysterious remarks which would gradually take shape; but none of the things they said would be definite enough to be traced back to them. In a week or two, all the negroes would know about Monsieur Pierre and Liana. They would be fascinated and they would whisper new information around the island, but they would be careful who heard the faint laughing murmur of their talk. None of them, either Marc's servants nor any of the

117

other negroes, would tell the white people. Liana was black, and therefore they would protect her. And Monsieur Pierre had always been kind. Already, in some curious way which none of the servants could explain, this affair was their own revenge. In their eyes, Liana was putting something over on two white men. She was smarter than the whites. They took uneasy pleasure in her cleverness, but her daring alarmed them.

The cook had said, when the maid carried Liana's breakfast tray upstairs, "I promise you, Théodore, this will end bad."

Because Marc was away, and because Liana always lived cut off from the town and the white people, Pierre and Liana ignored the danger of gossip. They had forgotten all the other people on the island. Marc was not there to remind them by his presence that they were not free. They had two days more. They accepted the present as if it would continue indefinitely. Their eyes and their voices were unguarded all the time; they walked down the drive with their arms around each other and kissed each other at the gate. They did not bother to notice whether the road was empty or not.

No news reached the white people. As far as they knew, nothing extraordinary was going on. Pierre Vauclain had been visiting Marc's house for three months now, and everyone knew it. Everyone knew he taught Liana, and after the first surprise that a grown woman should be taking lessons like a child, no one discussed it. It was agreed that Marc would pay well and the salary for a school teacher was barely enough to live on; money was always the soundest possible reason for doing anything.

After Pinelli's denunciation, there had been Pinelli's apology. The apology was believed since Pinelli was recognized as a liar and Pierre had so proved his virtue in a year and a half that no one would easily believe him capable of adultery. When Pinelli left, the scandal he had invented was forgotten. Liana was a sort of invisible freak, a girl Marc had uprooted and sequestered, and was now buying lessons for. (After all, Madame Joffé the wife of the huissier said, Marc probably wanted Liana taught something so she could keep the house accounts.)

And Pierre continued to be the amiable and decent and uninteresting young school teacher, who—as the men pointed out—wasn't quite a man though there was nothing wrong with him, it was just that he kept so much to himself and was cautious as a *jeune fille*.

By accident, Liana and Pierre were safer from talk than any other people on the island.

Liana knew that even if they hoarded every minute they could not make two days last. Marc would come back. She realized that Marc's return was the beginning of danger, but she refused to think of it. If suddenly her heart beat with fear and she thought of Marc, she knew how to stop that. She had only to remember Pierre, or better—if he was with her—she had only to touch him.

What amazed Liana was the light, hard smoothness of Pierre's body. She had not imagined that she could take as much pleasure in a man's beauty as in her own. Her delight in this discovery moved Pierre very much. He was wise enough to understand it. For the first time Liana had chosen what she wanted to love, and so Pierre became truly the first man. She did not hide her wonder and gratitude.

She would run her finger tentatively over the hard ridges of his ribs, and trace the dent of his waist. "Tu es si beau," Liana said with surprise, in tenderness, seeing this miracle, this man she could love.

CHAPTER TWELVE

The calm lasted all day. There were mountains of cumulus clouds on the horizon and shredded cirrus clouds drifted across the sky. The sky was gray white and the sea was blue gray. It looked as if a vast skin had been stretched across the water and the water was swelling under it, smooth still but with an ominous restrained force. A few of the birds that the natives called hurricane birds appeared in the pale sky. They were black and angular and they swooped on sharp wings over the swollen water.

Some fishing boats which had been out all night were

caught in the calm and could be seen rowing for shore with determined haste. The other fishing boats were beached far up on the sand at the end of the sea wall, and two sloops which happened to be anchored in the harbor were moved to the deep water away from the pier and secured as well as possible with double anchors. Everyone watched the weather and complained bitterly about not having radio weather reports because of the war. The barometer dropped but not spectacularly. The people who lived on the harbor front, immediately behind the sea wall, began as usual to feel like heroes or martyrs according to their temperaments. The older fishermen remarked that the island was about due for a hurricane.

The women collected the pathetic-seeming material they used to combat hurricanes: hammers and plenty of long strong nails and thick boards to fasten over all doors and windows. The shopkeepers worried about moving their wares from the ground floor stores; if they were due for a hurricane they could count on an inundation that would ride in from the sea or such torrential rain that the town would be flooded. There was a good chance that everything in the shops would be spoiled by sea or rain water. The town was excited and gloomy and there were many family arguments about moving up to the hills until the weather cleared. The men generally held out against this idea, at least until things got worse, and the women insisted on safety in high indignant nervous voices. They were all unusually anxious and short-tempered because they had no weather reports and had to make their decisions by guesses and the opinions of people who claimed to understand the signs correctly. The sunset was brilliant and lovely and filled everyone with foreboding.

That night the wind started. It began softly and then gathering force blew steadily from the southeast. By morning it was blowing in hard gusts and the sky was a dirty gray. It rained heavily in the early afternoon. The sea whipped up into peaks with foam blowing off the sharp waves. At sunset the wind quieted a little and the optimists began to say that the hurricane was making up somewhere else, probably south near Trinidad or else the storm center was moving toward the Bahama Channel and they were getting only the far western edge of the storm. People did not listen much to what other people said: each one was busy watching the weather for himself.

By night the wind rose again and the stars were covered and it was cold and the trees made a wild noise. The town was dark very early; everyone was in bed where it felt warm and safe. It rained again in the night but the wind was no stronger and slowly, in the soaking blackness, the wind seemed to blow itself out. At daylight the sky had cleared and was a good clean blue with a fresh breeze blowing. At noon people were standing around the streets talking amiably to each other, with the friendliness that comes from relief. The hurricane had missed them; they could not know for sure what had happened, whether there had been a real storm or not and if so where it had reached hurricane force. But their own peril was past and the men bought each other aperitifs at the café and the women talked to each other from the balconies and gossiped outside the shops, recounting their fears and retelling all their memories of other bad winds. The sea was still high and dangerous and no boats went out.

On the morning of the gray calm, Liana and Pierre walked quickly to the deserted Roches Noires beach and studied the sea. Liana said, shining with happiness, "Marc cannot come now."

"But it's calm; he's got a motor boat. He can make it in about eight hours, can't he?"

"Yes, but they won't set out, they won't take a chance. The calm can change very quickly. I am sure he has sent the boat to Statia, Pierre," she said, "he may not be back for days."

Liana sent the servants home early that night and they were glad to go. They would feel safer in their own flimsy homes with their own people. They hurried down the road together, before dark. When the town had shut itself in for the night, Pierre came to Marc's house. He told himself that he was anxious for Liana; she could not be left alone, she would be frightened; a tree might blow down over her room; there were many dangers this wind could bring. This anxiety made it decent to spend the night in Marc's house. They lay in Liana's bed, hugging

121

each other to keep warm, and listened to the beating wind. It was exciting and strange; and Pierre was so thrilled to be cold that he could not stop talking of it. "It's like home," he kept saying, "but one is cold! It is like real autumn weather."

Liana hated the cold but she too was excited by the wind and as the storm mounted she prayed for it to get worse and worse. She told herself that perhaps it would be too bad for the servants to come in the morning and she would be alone with Pierre. If only the wind kept up, they might have the house to themselves for a week since Marc certainly could not leave Saba. They would be alone for a whole week, just as if they were married.

Théodore was the only servant who appeared in the morning and it was easy enough to send him home. He explained that Zela, the maid, and Thérèse were afraid to come out and they were needed in their own houses. Liana said that was all right and he need not come back until the weather was safe again. Théodore was surprised by this generosity: Marc would have said they were fools and ordered them to return at once and get on with their work. During this conversation Pierre stayed upstairs, feeling ashamed and angry with everyone. When Liana went to tell him gladly that they were alone again, she found Pierre with a dark and furious face.

"I'm going home now," he said, "I'm not going to hide in this house like a little gigolo."

"But Pierre."

"I don't want to talk of it."

"But Pierre, we have so little time alone."

"I'm not going to hide from servants. Soon I will be sneaking into closets or under beds. It's grotesque. I'll come back later if the weather gets worse to see how you are."

"You haven't had any breakfast."

"I don't want any."

"What have I done?" Liana said.

"Nothing," Pierre answered impatiently, "nothing."

He had left her alone the first day and now he was going again. He was wasting this time that had been given to them like a rare unhoped-for gift. It was unbelievable. Liana could not understand; what possible use did they

122

have for time except to share it? What reason to go would be strong against the need to be together?

"You don't love me," Liana said, since this was the only way she could explain him.

It's too much, Pierre thought irritably. Women always say the same thing. You would not imagine that they would talk identical stupidities in the Antilles and Europe, but they did.

"Nonsense," he said. His voice was hard.

Liana felt the tears hot in her eyes. What had happened, during the little moment she spoke to Théodore, to change Pierre?

"I can't understand," she said helplessly.

"No, I don't suppose you can." Pierre had not really meant to say it and he had not clearly known what was behind his words. But Liana took it instantly to mean that she could not understand because she was different from him; he was white; and the way he thought and felt would always be mysterious to her.

Her shoulders sagged with discouragement. Pierre might as well go now. She lost hope and found, without surprise, that she had been ready to be hurt and discarded. She had wanted too much; there was no sense in believing in such happiness.

What a great man I am, Pierre thought, what a great and noble man, filled with honorable scruples and a fine pride and a cruelty that is beyond description. He caught Liana by the shoulders and turned her toward him. He was shocked by the desperateness of her face. I must always be careful, he thought, she will never defend herself.

"Liana," Pierre said, "I was ashamed because of the ridiculousness of hiding upstairs so that Théodore wouldn't see me. You must understand that. It made me angry, and I took it out on you and I hope you will forgive me. We'll go and watch the storm."

"Good," she said. But she would need time to soften that pain. Black girl, Liana mocked herself bitterly, do not forget who you are.

It was hard to walk against the wind. They watched the wind hammering at the trees and boiling over the sea. They stood on the rocks above the ocean and had the wonderful fearful sensation that they would be swept out into the water. Liana's hair lifted straight up from her head and blew like a flag and her dress lashed about her. The wind tore their words away and they had to shout against it. Then a streak of lightning ripped through the gray sky and the thunder boomed over the sea. They were drenched by a hard rain that suddenly poured out of the clouds. They ran inland to the shelter of the trees but it was too late. Their clothes hung heavily on them.

"Let's go to the beach," Pierre said.

The walk to the beach was exciting because the whole island had changed; it was dark and fierce with the loud wind. They took off their wet clothes and ran naked on the beach and let themselves be tossed and rolled over by the breakers in the shallow water. They knew it would be crazy to swim out. They shouted and laughed and could not keep their footing against the force of the waves. Then Pierre crawled up on the sand, dragging Liana with him. They were both cold now though the water was warmer than the air. They put on their wet clothes, shivering, and started to run hand in hand up the beach.

"Soup!" Pierre shouted. "Hot soup!"

"Why?"

"To eat, stupid. Warm!"

Liana laughed, panting from the run, and had to stop for a stitch in her side. They climbed through the thorn bushes and found a muddy path and slogged home with the water squelching out of their tennis shoes and their hair flat and dripping down their necks. They went in at the kitchen door, out of respect for Marc's polished living-room, and took off their shoes and dried their feet and legs on dish towels. Then they ran up the stairs trying not to leave a trail of water behind them. When they got to Liana's room they looked at each other.

"You look terrible," Pierre said delightedly.

"Look at yourself."

They stood together before the mirror and saw their muddy clothes and their lank hair and their laughing faces.

"We're happy, aren't we?" Pierre said. It was amazing to feel so foolishly and childishly and mindlessly happy.

"Yes," Liana said. "Nobody can be happier."

Pierre kissed her. She had forgotten again that she was a negro: nothing separated them now. They were the same one.

Pierre carried the pot carefully and the soup slipped around the edges but did not spill. Liana had two cups and a loaf of bread. They climbed into bed and pulled the covers up because now they were quite cold. Pierre filled the two cups. They sat cross-legged, side by side under the covers, and drank the steaming soup slowly.

This is the way marriage really is, Liana thought, being together and loving and having so many happy things to do. She smiled at Pierre over the edge of the cup.

"You're good, Liana," Pierre said suddenly.

"Good?"

"Yes," he said.

That's what Marc does not know, Pierre thought. That's what Marc has never found out. That's why it must not matter about Marc.

CHAPTER THIRTEEN

The sea was bright and a steady east wind kept the waves curling and rolling. For two days the sky had been clean and the sunsets, though red and beautiful as always, did not have the smoking fiery look that alarmed the islanders. There was rain every day and it cooled the land and freshened the trees. Liana knew that Marc might come any time now. He would arrive without warning as he had left his car in town. Any afternoon she might hear the car turning in at the lower gate and then she would hear Marc's step on the veranda and then his voice.

Liana could not warn Pierre because she remembered his furious face when he believed he was hiding from the servants, and she knew how Pierre would resent caution and pretense. But Liana arranged their time so that she and Pierre no longer stayed in the house together and she managed to guide him on farther and remoter walks around the island. If Marc came while she was out he could not be suspicious as she had always gone off with Pierre. If Marc found them together when he returned, Liana was determined that he should not surprise them. But this carefulness changed her and changed the quality of her life with Pierre. She knew this and she felt again that Marc was the enemy and Marc was cheating her as he always had.

On the evening of the third fine day Liana had started to eat dinner when she heard the car turn in at the gate. The taste of the chicken she was eating suddenly made her sick. She pushed her plate away and listened as the car climbed the drive slowly in second gear. She felt a nauseated choking in her throat and her hands were cold. She had not known she would dread Marc's return so violently. Then she folded her napkin, taking great care not to let her hands shake, and went out to the veranda to meet him.

Marc's face was red with sunburn and he looked harder than when he had left, and rested. His breath smelled of cigars and rum but he was not drunk. He had shared a bottle of rum with Gilbert Macon in the boat coming home, and talked about fishing. He had steered half the time and been drenched with spray and then dried out in the sun. The trip had been jolly and everything about his vacation pleased him. He was now a man with a good free life and plenty of friends and a fine house and a pretty wife to come home to. He was tired, jovial and too contented to be observant. Marc did not notice how sharply Liana pulled away from him when he kissed her. The sun and sweat and salt smell that came from Marc disgusted Liana, and she thought she had never seen anything as repellent as his red, shining face with the reddish bristle of a day's beard roughening the skin.

"How is everything here?" Marc said. "Have you been all right? Was the storm bad? Were you worried?"

"Théodore!" Marc shouted. "Get my suitcase. I'll have dinner at once. Tell Zela to unpack. Bring me a whiskey and soda."

The house was suddenly in an uproar. The servants ran to obey him; the cook dropped a plate and then a pot in the kitchen; Zela banged the suitcase against the stairs as she dragged it up to Marc's room; Théodore sloshed whiskey and soda from the glass on to the tray as he hurried to bring Marc his drink. Marc walked ahead of Liana into the house, went to his usual chair, switched on the floor lamp, turned the radio dial, and kicked off his shoes. The room was full of loud rumba music from a Cuban station. "Ah," Marc said, gulping the whiskey, "I was thirsty. Well, how was everything?"

"Fine," Liana said drily, standing before him.

"Did the storm do any damage?"

"Not here. I don't know about the town."

"It was a terrible blow on Saba. Wonderful though. We were actually cold. I should have cabled you but I knew you'd see I couldn't get back. And I couldn't tell exactly when we would leave."

"Yes."

"Were you lonely in the house?"

"It was all right. Did you have a good time?"

"Magnificent vacation. Where's Théodore? Tell Thérèse to hurry; I'm starving. I want to eat and take a bath and go to bed. How about you, Liana?" Marc pushed himself up from the chair, smiling. He patted her cheek, as he passed. "Miss me a little?"

"Of course." Liana felt herself shrinking inside her dress. She thought surely Marc must have noticed that quick shiver of disgust. Marc did not see her; he had already gone into the dining-room. I cannot watch him eat, Liana thought, I cannot bear to. She followed Marc and sat quietly at her place but she did not raise her eyes. She tried not to hear him noisily and hungrily swallowing his soup. Marc did not tell Liana about Saba and Kerstens, as she had never visited Saba nor met Kerstens. He did not think it would interest Liana.

All Marc wanted now was to eat and wash and put on fresh pajamas and go to bed. He had been away for two weeks. It would have been possible to find a girl on Saba, though there were no professionals; but these things could be arranged. He had decided against it because Kerstens was a temperate man and people always mocked the weaknesses they did not share. Besides Marc was not sure that Kerstens would approve if Marc took a negress into the government resthouse. Kerstens might think that would damage the prestige of the local government, or the position of the whites. The Dutch spent a vast amount of time being models of behavior for their colonial subjects. All nonsense, Marc thought, but that was how they were. Two weeks was a long abstinence for a normal healthy man. It must have seemed a long time to Liana too.

"Ready?" Marc said.

Liana did not answer because she could not. Marc waited àt the dining-room door.

"I'll be up in a minute," Liana said. "I have to tell Thérèse something about marketing for tomorrow." It sounded to her as if she were babbling: she was afraid her voice would suddenly leap up so that she could not control it. I must be çareful, careful, careful; he will see it soon.

"All right," Marc said. "But don't keep me waiting."

Liana stayed in the dining-room, looking at the napkin folded beside her plate, the empty wine glass, the chocolate soufflé sunken inside the silver serving bowl. She saw none of this and was only waiting for Marc to call her again, this time imperiously, impatiently. The white ladies in the books could not endure to sleep with husbands they did not love simply because they loved someone else. It was as plain as that. It probably had nothing to do with being a lady and one's color did not matter either. If you loved a man, you could not divide yourself. But what did those ladies in the books do when their husbands returned and demanded their rights? Should I tell him now tonight, Liana thought. And what would happen to Pierre then? What would Marc do to Pierre? Pierre was a stranger and a poor man, and Marc always had his own way. Marc might do anything; he might kill Pierre, he might send Pierre away from the island. Liana did not imagine that Marc loved her but she belonged to Marc. She was his property. Marc would not be kind to anyone who tried to rob him. I cannot go upstairs, Liana thought, I cannot tell him.

"Liana," Marc leaned over the second floor railing. "My God, what are you doing? Are you going to talk to Thérèse all night?"

"Je viens," Liana said. She could scarcely hear her voice saying the commonplace terrible words. "Je viens," she said again. . . .

"Marc will think it strange if he comes home and finds us here. We ought to be on the terrace or else out walking," Liana said miserably. "Oh, Pierre, don't look at me like that."

Pierre tore the fallen bamboo leaves into neat strips and piled the strips into a heap by his side. He was sitting cross-legged and he had looked up from this obstinate silent work to stare at Liana. She lay on her side facing him. The mat of leaves was soft as sand. Sun filtered through the close green leaves and fell in bright slivers on her face and arms. The bamboo boles made a creaking noise like the noises you hear inside a ship.

"What happened last night?" Pierre said.

"Nothing. I promise you, Pierre, nothing." She lied desperately, keeping her voice very reasonable.

"How can I believe that?"

"He was tired," Liana murmured. "Tonight he will go to Le Paradis. What difference does it make if I live in the house? He doesn't really want me, Pierre. It is only a habit."

"Ah," Pierre said furiously, and knocked over the heap of torn leaves.

Liana closed her eyes. She would have to lie to Pierre and lie to Marc; neither of them would help her now. She had fallen asleep at dawn, in her own room. Marc did not wake when she left him. There was only one triumph, and because of it Liana did not feel she was really lying to Pierre. Her body had remained as cold as her mind. She had studied Marc's face, in the pale moon and starlight that entered his room, and taken a slow pleasure in hating him, beginning with his stiff coarse hair and hating separately the veined eyelids, the wide nose and the texture of his skin, his mouth that was half open in sleep and the lips that moved loosely with his breathing. She hated Marc in revenge, taking her time. Then she went quietly to her own room, bathed, told herself that for once Marc had not tricked her, it was she who had tricked Marc, and at last she slept. During the day as she waited for Pierre, Liana imagined that when Pierre came she would forget Marc and be happy.

Pierre refused to stay on the terrace and said it was

129

too hot to walk. He led her again to the bamboo brake behind the house, which was a place Liana considered as intimate as a room of their own. She was afraid to be found here; anyone seeing them here must guess they were lovers. And Pierre, wasting the afternoon, asked questions and looked at her with doubting angry eyes.

"He's paying me," Pierre said suddenly. "We must do some work. After all, he is not paying me to make love to you."

Liana did not answer but simply resigned herself to this brutality. It was another thing she would have to endure in payment for happiness.

The Kings of France, Pierre thought, great authors with their dates and principal works; *Le Bourgeois Gentilhomme, Les Misérables,* the poetry of Lamartine; long division; what is the capital of Turkey; how many *départements* are there in France; name the chief mountain ranges of Europe. What appalling rot it was. From now on, he and Liana would talk of themselves. Pierre could foresee it exactly: they would have jealous arguments or make complicated plans or else—by a miracle —they would be happy and then they would talk of themselves with the easy revealing egotism of lovers.

"I'll be glad when school starts again. Thank God it will only be one more week now," Pierre said. "I'll go mad in this place doing nothing. At least that keeps me busy until afternoon."

"But Pierre, we've had so much to do. We've been so happy. We can go on, Pierre. We don't have to think of Marc."

"I need work," he said furiously. "More work, real work. I'm rotting the way wood rots here, the way everything dead rots at once."

Her silence, her patience, angered him.

"The radio gives only communiqués, or the censored stuff that spews out of every country," he said, as if he had been talking about this all along. "I don't know what's happening. I sit here. Sit and sit and sit. It's enough to drive anyone crazy. It's like being in a beautiful jail, thirty miles long by eighteen miles wide."

Liana rolled over and covered her face with her hands.

"You will leave," she said.

"How can I?" Pierre asked roughly. "Where would I go?"

"It is only that which keeps you?"

"No." He pushed himself across to Liana and pulled her head and shoulders up to his lap and then he bent over and kissed her hard on the mouth. He could taste her tears and her eyelashes were spiky with them. "No."

They listened to the trees creaking in the wind, and falling leaves stuck in her hair.

"How would you feel if I were married?" Pierre asked. "If I was the one?"

"I wouldn't care. I'd do anything. I wouldn't care," she said fiercely.

He kissed Liana again and held her so tightly that it hurt her.

"Darling. *Mon petit.* I'll try to be reasonable. I'll try. It's not easy. We ought to tell him."

"What will we do then?" Liana said.

"I don't know."

She had won now and there was no need to continue this talk. She did not have to tell Pierre that she had won. Liana thought: Marc would hurt us somehow if he knew; he would stop us and he would hurt us. We have no money and there is no place to go. Pierre says there is no place. And Marc would follow even if we ran away. Somehow he would make us pay for cheating him. The only thing Liana knew surely was that they must keep their secret. It would take all her strength and all the lies she could invent to manage Pierre and deceive Marc. There was not too much happiness in this but anything was better than losing Pierre.

Pierre heard the car first.

"Marc is coming home," he said. He did not move. Liana sprang up and brushed the bamboo leaves from her skirt and her hair. Her heart thudded with fear.

"You must leave the back way. Hurry, Pierre."

"No."

"Pierre. Please. In the name of God, Pierre, why do you make it harder?"

"I won't sneak," he said obstinately. "I won't run away. I'm not going to tell him but I will not creep out like a criminal."

"You don't care anything about me. You don't care what Marc will do to me. You only care about how you feel.'

Pierre stared at her in amazement. Liana had never spoken to him in this way, with this bitter and hopeless voice. And what she said, Pierre thought, was true. He had been guarding his own dignity and soothing his conscience with compromises. He had not thought of what might happen to Liana.

"I'll go home the back way," Pierre said.

"Thank you, my dearest."

"Before this is finished, you will not thank me for anything."

"Finished?" Liana said in horror.

"Oh Liana, you must see we cannot go on this way. We can't make any kind of life with Marc around. You must see that."

"I see." Marc, she thought, Marc, Marc: without Marc: it is only Marc.

"Until tomorrow." Pierre kissed her on the forehead lightly. "What hiding place would you suggest for tomorrow?"

"Oh Pierre!"

"I didn't mean that," he said. "Until tomorrow, darling. Here, let me kiss you as you deserve."

For a moment they both forgot Marc. Then they heard the car honking noisily, angrily, commandingly, three times.

Pierre said, "What a way for a man to call his wife."

As usual, Marc made no explanation or apology. He said good night and went out the front door, jingling the car keys in his pocket. Liana waited until she saw the lights of the car flashing down the drive. Then she darkened the living-room and went out to sit on the veranda. The storm had washed away the murkiness of summer and now the cool fall weather had started. This was the finest time of the year, Liana thought.

The stars looked polished and higher in the sky. The weather affected the size of the island: a clean wind or this sort of wide night made the land seem larger. As the land stretched in the wind or grew beyond its boundaries in the bigness of the night, the people had more room to breathe and to live. Liana knew this feeling of lightness and release; in the fall she did not feel locked in by the sea nor conscious of the coast as if visible walls closed in her world.

Liana hoped that Marc would be gone until daylight. He had not seen Marie for two weeks: they would have many things to tell each other. Liana thought about them wryly, wondering what they said to each other. The idea of them making love was comic to her, and unlovely, and Liana did not let herself consider it. Marie, whom she had never envied but always resented, was slowly becoming an ally. Marie kept Marc away; Marie could be thanked for the delicious loneliness of this night.

Where would Pierre be now? He might be walking on the beach near town or sitting at his window where he could hear and smell the sea. He might be reading. If Pierre were reading, he had gone away from this place and from her. Pierre went away too often, suddenly blind to her and to the shining green island. Liana was jealous of where he went. She was jealous of France.

If only I had been there, Liana thought. She had tried to piece together what she read, photographs and maps, and what Pierre and Marc told her, to make an exact picture of France. She imagined that Paris was always soft gray and smelled of violets and the houses shone like dull gold. The people there had voices like Pierre and were graceful and a little sad. Everything was very fragile and fine, the trees and the faces and the music and the furniture and the women's clothes. The Seine was bright as mercury or flowed in a band of flat silver; and the bridges that crossed it were high and curved and hung in the air like cobwebs. It was a rare and beautiful city in her mind and Liana did not wonder that it called to Pierre.

The homesickness of Pierre was understandable but there were other sicknesses that Liana failed to find a name for. They were more dangerous and she feared them beyond her jealousy of Paris and of the unimaginable country that was France. There was the sickness that had to do with war. Pierre had spoken to her a little of the war, gravely and bitterly. Liana had an impression of war as deadly confusion, helpless frightened peo-

133

ple, soldiers who were hungry and lost and fought with the dreadful gestures of men drowning. She thought that war made a wild mad noise, worse than hurricane wind, and that everyone was blown about and despairing in it.

Obviously Pierre hated war, but there was a restlessness in his mind, a feeling of something not finished, not even begun. He kept saying "Ça n'est pas encore fini." He said it with a grinding disgust and anger but also with longing. "Ça ne finira pas comme ça," he would say; and Liana did not know what he meant.

There was the thing of the Germans, and this perhaps was easiest to imagine and understand. Germans were cruel people. Liana had known cruel people. But there were millions of Germans and it was hard for her to imagine millions of men engaged in hurting people who could not protect themselves. It was not as if it were one, like for instance old Monsieur Laborde who beat his servant because he said the servant stole his wine. Monsieur Laborde was crazy, as everyone knew, and he enjoyed being cruel. He had beaten the servant Auguste until he nearly died. But everyone thought that was terrible and afterwards Monsieur Laborde could get no negro to work for him, and for a long time none of the whites would speak to him on the street. The Germans were millions of Monsieur Labordes, Liana supposed, but young and healthy and not known to be crazy.

Naturally Pierre hated the Germans, and he was lucky not to live where there were Germans. Only that was not how he saw it. Once Pierre had said, "J'ai trop de chance. J'en ai honte." He hated the Germans but he wanted to be where they were. He did not hate them and hope never to see them again, which would have been normal. He wanted to kill them, Liana thought, when you considered it plainly. Pierre wanted to kill them himself; it was not enough that anyone else should kill them for him.

And then Pierre had a special homesickness for men. In the beginning Liana thought he spoke of old friends and she could appreciate this though she had no friends any longer. But Antoinette for instance would be miserable if she could not see her brother; Antoinette would die of loneliness if she did not have the two little sisters

134

around her. Liana had asked Pierre whether that man he spoke of, Jean-Louis, was his brother.

"Yes," Pierre answered and smiled.

"I did not know you had brothers. Have you any sisters?"

"I haven't any brothers or sisters. I was an only child."

"But you said Jean-Louis was your brother."

"So he is," Pierre said.

What did it mean? Pierre said later that Jean-Louis worked in a butcher shop in Limoges; Pierre had last seen him on the Somme, they had been in the same company. No, he had never known Jean-Louis before the war. Jean-Louis was a great man, funny and kind and gay, and he played the harmonica.

"There were others," Pierre said. "I do not know where they are either. I never saw them again, afterwards."

"After what?"

"After they signed the papers in the railway carriage." Pierre said that with such bitterness, with such a grimace of hate and disgust that Liana was frightened and tried to make him talk of other things. But that day Pierre had gone away from her entirely, though he lay beside her on the sand. His eyes, which were blue, looked black and were a stranger's eyes.

Pierre lived in his own country and she could not follow. As soon as he left her, he was lost. Liana could not please him then, and she could not call him back. He returned to her when he was ready, but each time his eyes had a blank shine to them as if he saw Liana for the first time or after a long absence. She was the stranger and where Pierre had been was home and whom he had been with were his own people. If she could learn more, or understand better, perhaps Pierre would talk to her and then they would not be separated by the memories but could share them. Liana had asked Pierre once if he got any letters.

"I hear from my mother once in a while."

"Where is she?"

"She is in a village near Tulle. She lives there with some cousins. They have a little land. They are older people."

135

"What does she say?"

"What can she say?"

"And your friends?"

"I don't know where anyone is. They don't know where I am. We are all lost from each other, don't you understand? It is as if everyone was dead. Don't you understand? Please don't talk of it, Liana. It's bad enough to think of it all the time."

The night was not so beautiful any more and Liana did not have that luxurious feeling of space and a cool high world to breathe in. Beyond the black sea was Pierre's world, and in his heart he had never really left it. If Pierre was awake now he would not be thinking of her and of this lovely night: he would be thinking, with pain and some kind of determination, of people and places that she could never know.

Marc hummed to himself and drove slowly. The air grew cooler as the road climbed. The air almost had to have a different color and now on the first hill it should be silver gray to match its coolness. The trees were solidly black along the road and when the headlights picked them up, at a turn, the trunks seemed made of white stone. Then the lights moved and the wall of trees sank into the night. This island is more beautiful than Saba, Marc thought.

Saba has a better climate and it is cleaner and the houses are sounder, I suppose, and in every way it is an island that seems to know what it is doing. Probably because they are Dutch and we are French and we get talkative and worthless in the heat and they get more and more exact. But this is more beautiful. I am glad I live here, Marc thought, and turned the car on the first hill to look at his island in the night.

The sea was divided from the land by a waving soft white line of foam. There were a few lights in the town and they seemed very small and quiet and lonely. The tops of the trees were black fur covering the down slope of the hill and here and there, solitary and superb, palms rose like huge plumes against the night sky. I could not live anywhere else, Marc thought, it is foolish not to be happy here. People are happy in those dreadful hard gray apartments alongside the Gare Saint Lazare, with

136

the trains screaming in and out and the houses and the streets as cold as flint. People are actually happy in Lyons and, more amazing, people were satisfied to live in Lille. Before the Germans came of course, Marc added. We have peace here and the air tonight is like fresh water and three is such a hill to look down: a man is a fool not to be happy.

Marc backed and turned the car and drove slowly on, feeling the slight extra freshness of the air against his face. I'd got myself into a state, Marc thought, with Marie and Liana and Pinelli and a lot of nonsense. All I needed was a change. All I needed was to talk to a man for a while, instead of the digging scratchy talk that women make. But I see it now for nonsense and I won't let myself be an idiot again. Liana looks lovely and is as good a wife as any: what if I were married to a shrew like Madame Merey or a whiner like Madame Bosquet or a slattern like poor Captain Saldriguet's wife? I've done pretty well for myself as wives go, Marc thought with untroubled cynicism, and when I want to talk over old times there is always Marie. She's not exciting the way she used to be but it's good for a man to have a woman to talk to. I'll get out more too, he told himself, I'll go up to the hills and stay a few days and shoot blue pigeons. Next week might be a good time. Perhaps Pierre would like to come along. A man is a fool not to be happy here, Marc thought.

Marie was sitting on her veranda. It was very agreeable of her, Marc felt, always to be there, always ready, always waiting. She had the radio turned on and it poured out a continuous garbled succession of music, advertisements and news. She had it tuned to a Puerto Rican station. As he climbed the steps Marc heard the announcer's voice saying that fourteen survivors of an English ship had been received by the Red Cross in San Juan and sent to a hospital. Marc shook this news off with irritation. He hated the war and everything about it; it was a madness that made the whole world unhappy and no matter how it ended people would be miserable.

Marc greeted Marie and went inside the house to turn off the radio. Almost anything that came from the radio was bad and distracting and it was better not to hear it.

"When did you get back?" Marie said.

"Last night. Kerstens sent you his regards. Madame Kerstens also."

"How is she?"

"Pale. The heat doesn't agree with her. She looks old."

"Kerstens wouldn't be governor of a stupid little island like Saba if he hadn't married her," Marie said with satisfaction. "If he'd had another kind of wife he'd have gone farther in diplomacy."

"Oh, I don't know. They seem very fond of each other. They have nice children."

"What else did Kerstens say?"

"He told me a lot of interesting things about Holland and Java."

"They talk a great deal about the war?" Marie said, with some surprise.

"Yes."

"Well. How was the weather there?"

"Cool. Really fine. Almost like being in the mountains."

"Was the storm bad?"

"Yes."

"It was quite heavy here, but then it blew over."

They sat in silence. This was not what Marc had planned. He had planned to tell Marie slowly all about the Kerstens' and their house and what they talked of, and he wanted to tell her about the island and the comic old colored woman who cleaned the guest house. He had a dozen small amusing memories to share. Marie asked her questions like a lawyer, got her answers, and suddenly there was nothing left to say. Saba was destroyed; Saba did not exist; his trip might never have happened. Marie had taken away his vacation and brought him back to her, to their familiar unchanging life and to the silence of all their evenings. Marc felt cheated and disappointed; he wanted to weep with vexation. He had so looked forward to talking of his journey.

Marc watched a charcoal burner's fire which glowed on the side of the hill. He wondered vaguely whether Marie sold her charcoal or whether she only allowed her laborers to make enough for themselves and for her house. Since there was now nothing interesting to talk

138

about with Marie, Marc took refuge from his disappointment in thinking of new schemes to make money. Marie could sell her pineapple crop in Puerto Rico this year, if she liked: they needed everything there.

This reminded Marc of a letter he had received today from his agent in Florida. He had not thought much about this letter but now he began to consider it. Hawley said that Marc ought to start a shark fishery. There were plenty of sharks in these waters and Hawley said they could sell everything, their skins and livers and meat and fins and nothing was needed to start the business except fishermen, rowboats, line and hooks and salt for preserving. Marc found it hard to believe that people actually ate shark meat but Hawley said it tasted like Norwegian codfish (that must be a lie) and the way things were nowadays people would eat anything. They boiled the livers to get oil and out of that they made Vitamin A, one of these new medicines that allegedly helped pilots to see in the dark. It all sounded like the wildest nonsense but then Americans were constantly taking up wild nonsense and there was usually money in it. The Chinese bought the fins and the skin was used to make jackets or shoes or anything that leather could be used for. Hawley wrote: the Ocean Leather Corporation will take anything you catch and pay you plenty and all you have to do is catch the sharks; skin, butcher and salt them; and deliver them to Puerto Rico. You can use your own schooners, Hawley said.

Marc was lost in speculation about pineapples, charcoal and sharks and had just started to wonder whether he would have to build any more rowboats or whether there were enough on hand. Macon could handle the fishermen. With Puerto Rico so close and so hungry it was a pity not to profit by it. If the Americans really believed they could see better at night by drinking shark oil, a man might as well sell them the shark livers. Marc had heard that since the war the Americans didn't care what they paid for anything.

Marie, who was used to these long separating silences, simply spoke out whatever she happened to be thinking when she felt like speaking.

"I saw young Vauclain in town while you were gone," Marie remarked.

139

"Vauclain?" As if he cared. Marie expected him to be interested in the static gossip of the town after she had spoiled all his stories.

"He looks different."

"How?"

"He looks like a cat that has eaten a plate of cream."

Careful, Marc thought, this is something new she has invented.

"Why?"

"I don't know why, mon cher. I scarcely know the man. Of course you were gone quite a while. I understand Madame Loustelot told some women that Vauclain had stayed out all night a few times."

Madame Loustelot was the baker's wife and Pierre Vauclain's landlady.

"Are you going to continue the fine work of Pinelli, Marie?" Marc asked coldly.

"Moi! Comme si tout ça me regarde! I simply thought you would be interested."

"I'm not interested."

"There is no need for you to be rude to me, my dear Marc. After all, no one invited you here."

"Oh Marie," he said despairingly.

"Well don't start your bullying nasty way of talking with me."

"Oh Marie," he said again, but this time impatiently.

"Ça suffit," she said icily.

They were silent, and Marie rocked as if she were panting. Her chair stirred choppy currents of air in the still night. Marc looked at the high broken tower of the hill and made his mind blank, wiping out her words and her voice. Patiently, he constructed a picture of her as she had been years ago. Patiently and with infinite hope, using the silence to help him, he remade Marie, with a voice that was husky not sharp, and a quiet mysterious face and a smile full of secrets. He was determined not to let his happiness leak away. Slowly Marc built up his illusions again.

"I am tired, Marie."

She did not answer.

"Shall we go inside?"

"If you wish," she said.

The indifference of her voice chilled him. Then Marie

said, "I have a bottle of real Pernod. It seems old André was hoarding a few bottles but he needed money to repair his barn so he asked Drieu to sell two bottles and I heard of it and bought one. I thought you might like a glass of Pernod in the evening."

Marc took this sign of attention as if Marie gave him a priceless and magnificent gift. He felt warm and soft with happiness because Marie had thought of him and of his pleasure, while he was away. He did not know what to say to her. He leaned over and kissed her hand which lay on the arm of the rocking chair, and Marie pulled her hand away nervously, surprised by this sudden gesture.

"Well, come inside and I will fix you a glass," Marie said.

Marc followed her. He was thinking that a man should just take his time and notice the good things that happened to him and that way he would be happy enough.

CHAPTER FOURTEEN

The barometer was high and the trade winds blew steadily from the east. The older fishermen appreciated the coolness and the clean sky as much as anyone, but they reminded people that the hurricane season was not yet over. Wait until October is past, they said. On the other hand the moon was three-quarters full and there had been no break in this healing weather.

From open windows on the Grande Rue, the white women could be heard ordering their servants. Mattresses drooped over balcony rails and pillows were piled on chairs in the sun. A negro servant, wearing a large straw hat and no shoes, shook a rug while his mistress told him shrilly that all the dust was flying back into the house. A negro maid teetered on a stool trying to get the curtains down at the Mayor's house. Painters were working at the Bertholds too. The sewing machine whirred in the hotel salon. All the women in town were busy cleaning their houses and getting their winter clothes ready.

Quarrels which had started in the suffocating summer months lost their value. Madame Joffé the wife of the huissier bowed to Madame Loustelot the baker's wife in Merey's dry goods store, and then asked advice about some flowered crêpe de chine she was buying for a new winter dress. They had not been speaking since July but this was now forgotten. Two sugar planters who had called each other names in the café in August bought each other drinks and did not mention their summer feud.

The white men began to talk easily about after the war when conditions would be different. A rumor started toward the end of October that the war would be over by spring. Spring of 1943, you will see if I am not right, the Judge said in the café. He was taking credit for an original prophecy but he had heard this talk all around the island. The war would not only be over but Saint Boniface would be better off than ever before. There was no explanation for this optimism. Saint Boniface had never been rich or busy; in some mysterious way it would be both after the war. The weather alone accounted for the energy and hope that seemed to sweep the island. Every year in October, if there was no hurricane, the weather played this trick on the people. They thought they had a fine climate and imagined they would always feel as well as they did now.

There were of course realists who pointed out that in November the rains would start (and people would have rheumatism, colds, sinus, and malaria as usual), and that there was no reason to believe the war would end in the spring of 1943, and furthermore what was all this nonsense about Saint Boniface becoming a center of trade after the war. Did they expect Saint Boniface to drift obligingly into the shipping lanes? Did they imagine rubber trees would suddenly sprout from the green hills? Drieu and Captain Saldriguet and the doctor and Marie talked this way, but people preferred not to listen to them.

The barometer stayed high. The palm trees glittered and rattled in the fresh steady breeze.

Pierre said, "We must scrape together a few orchids today. How much have you read in *Le Rouge et le*

Noir? What if Marc asks us? We haven't done a thing this month."

"Oh, haven't we?" Liana said.

"Wicked girl."

Liana laughed at him.

"If we weren't so near the house you know what I'd do."

"Behave," Liana said, suddenly anxious. "Théodore is cleaning the salon. He can see us."

They walked down the drive keeping a careful distance apart.

"I said," Pierre repeated, "we have to bring back some orchids today. Every evening when we get to the house I am afraid Marc will ask what we have been doing. We go off with butterfly nets and we never bring back butterflies. We carry this broken old trout basket and never bring home an orchid in it. We load ourselves down with books and never read. Someday Marc will ask us. Then what?"

"No he won't. He's too busy with his shark business."

"I heard about it in town. The fishermen are delighted. What is it?"

"I don't know. He sells to the Americans. Kiss me," Liana said. They had turned out of the gate on to the road. The road was empty. She stood in the shade of a laurel, close against the fluted trunk. Pierre kissed her.

"Where shall we go today?" he asked.

"To the banyan tree."

"What a bourgeoise you are, Liana. On Mondays and Wednesdays and Fridays, we go to the little beach of the cave. On Tuesdays and Thursdays to the banyan tree. On Saturdays and Sundays to the watercress stream. You're very tidy, aren't you?"

"Yes."

"Not too tidy though."

"No."

"Hurry then."

They turned off the road, going away from the sea, and followed a narrow track that led through a wasteland of thorn bushes and vines and guava trees. The track faded and they picked their way over unmarked ground. They were climbing a low hill and at the top they would come out on a grass bank shaded by a giant

143

banyan tree. This hill belonged to no one and no cattle grazed here. The uncut mat of thorn and creeper guarded the hill.

They were sweating when they reached the top of the hill. They stood, facing the sea, while the trade wind cooled them.

"Such a day," Pierre said. "If only October would last."

He turned to look at Liana.

"Toi," he said. "You know how beautiful you are? You're as beautiful as the island."

"So are you," she said pleasantly.

"No. But I am getting better looking from being with you. I'm a nice color now." He had taken off his shirt as he talked and now stood naked to the waist, feeling the cool air flow over his body. His skin was burned amber-color by the sun. Suddenly Pierre thought: I'm trying to get brown as Liana is. It's true. I've come to think that white is an ugly rather vulgar color. He laughed, thinking this. He was about to tell Liana and stopped himself. She might not think it funny.

"What are you laughing about?"

"Nothing. Just laughing from happiness." He took Liana in his arms. "Do you know how beautiful you are?"

"I'm not."

"Yes you are and you know it. Lie down and spread your hair out on the grass, like that, like a fan. Yes. Oh, my God, you're pretty. You have the loveliest legs in the world."

"Come here. I don't like it when you stand up and look at me."

Pierre lay beside Liana on the grass and leaned on his elbow so that he could see her. The varnished leaves of the banyan swayed high above them. The grass was thick and springy and cool to lie on.

"I'm so happy," he said. "I feel so well. Don't you?"

"Yes."

"I wish it would always be the same weather and we would make love every afternoon."

"Do you?"

"How much I do!" Pierre leaned over and undid the buttons at the neck of her dress. He wanted to see more

144

of her. There was no end to this rushing renewing excitement. /

Liana pulled his head down and kissed him slowly.

"And you, Liana, you?"

"Oh yes."

Pierre's face was close to hers and it looked a little blurred. It was brown and lean with the jaw bone very sharp and the cheek bones showing strongly under the skin. Liana thought she knew Pierre's face perfectly now; but there were still times when his eyes changed and took on a secret look. Or did she imagine that? Pierre had stayed with her all this month, never going silently away from her and from the island in his mind. He did not rage against Marc any more. He no longer said they could not make a decent life, lying and hiding. And Pierre seemed to find her new each day and she made him happy and each time was a wonder to them because it was always a strange wild beautiful country they explored together. Suddenly Liana felt her heart beat painfully. Her eyes, which had been sleepy and inviting, widened with fear.

"Pierre," she said. "You won't ever leave me?"

Pierre put his arms around her so that he could feel her breasts under his hands, and her heart beating. Then he pulled Liana against him and kissed her. Liana thought that she needed no other answer.

There was after all a good side to the war. It did not entirely ruin business, as Marc had thought, it only ruined some businesses but new ones developed. Marc had heard of the fantastic money the Americans were spending on their air bases in the Caribbean but he thought you would have to be in with the politicians or at least be an American to get a share of that prosperity. It seemed however that there was a market for everything and plenty of money was changing hands in these islands. The thing to do, Marc told himself, is to keep your eyes open.

Hawley had been right about the sharks. Marc cabled to the address in Puerto Rico that Hawley gave him, because letters were too slow, and got a long cable in answer. Those Americans did business in a fine large fast way and did not even charge him for their reply cable.

145

He could sell shark meat for fifteen cents a pound and shark livers for twenty-one cents a pound. A big skin would bring a top price of $3.00 but it was better to figure on an average price of $1.00 a skin. Always wiser, Marc thought, not to exaggerate. Fins sold for twenty-four cents a pound for small fins to sixty cents a pound for big ones. Sharks had been a nuisance all these years, eating fish when the fishermen had already hooked them and making the bathing beaches unsafe, and now they turned into a modest gold mine. Due to the war of course, because obviously no one would eat shark meat if they could get anything better and probably these famous vitamins that came from shark liver were in such demand because of the war too.

The fishermen were bewildered and delighted by their sudden wealth. Marc paid them two cents a pound for whole shark and figured that the average weight of sharks was 125 to 150 pounds. Raymond Lesueur earned $9.00 one day which was more than he usually earned in a week. The fishermen's wives were shopping at Merey's and Merey felt pleased about this new industry, naturally. Marc decided to build three more rowboats and that made work for twelve men, not counting the two negroes who hired their carts to drag the lumber down from the hills. Of course, Marc thought, I have to consider that I pay the crews of the two schooners as well. But Marc knew that he need not be too cautious with himself; he was making good money and easy money.

Salt was plentiful and cheap and Berthold was happy to sell it here with no shipping charges. There was no overhead; the fishermen simply built a palm-leaf shack and tables of slats on the beach and butchered and dried the fish there. Fishing had always seemed to Marc a fool's trade but this was a new kind of fishing. If we kill all the sharks in the ocean, Marc thought contentedly, we will be doing a good thing. Though probably there would never be an end to sharks; there would only be an end to the war and people would eat something decent again and stop drinking that vitamin slop for their eyes. All right, Marc told himself, this is only a temporary business but what's the difference. It doesn't hurt a man to make money.

Marc had never been so popular on the island. Ce bon vieux Marc, people said, look what he is doing for Saint Boniface. Even Drieu spoke pleasantly to Marc because the café was doing better business now that every man who could fish had money for drinks. Wait and see, Marc kept telling people, we may build twenty boats before we are through. I figured it out, Marc said to the Judge, we were stagnating here. This is a fine thing for the island, the Judge said. It did not make any difference to the Judge as he was paid a regular salary but he liked to see people in a good humor. I may be able to pay more for the sharks later, Marc said, because he was as happy to be admired as he was to make money. Everyone is very grateful to you, Marc, the Judge said.

Marc stayed in town most days to lunch at the hotel. He said he was too busy to come home but he really stayed because he liked to talk of his new business and he liked to hear people speak well of him. He smiled a great deal and his voice sounded loud and cheerful and confident again. He began to drink in the café in the afternoons before coming home for dinner because men greeted him cordially and asked him to sit with them, and everyone talked about sharks. Even people who did not profit directly were friendly to Marc now. Neatly and without words the new shark business wiped out the rather stale offense of Marc's marriage.

Liana pretended to listen to Marc and flattered him when he bragged of the day's catch as if he had put the sharks in the ocean himself. He brought a big shark steak home and Liana instructed the cook to prepare it with a sauce of tomatoes and onions, and she said it tasted delicious when they ate it. Marc did not ask Liana what she did during the day and often he was tired at night and Liana knew, without his telling her, that she could sleep in her own room. If Marc thought of Liana at all, he thought she was a satisfactory wife as wives go, and certainly a pleasure to look at, and it seemed inconceivable that he could ever have been harassed by women. Marie was satisfactory too. When you did not pay much attention to them they always behaved better.

Toward the end of October Marc decided it was a pity to let the month pass without using the fine weather.

147

Macon was back from Puerto Rico and could keep his eye on the fishermen for a few days. This business anyhow was so simple that it ran itself. Macon would only have to make sure that the livers and meat were well salted before being packed. Marc was pleased to have thought of a vacation: it proved he was again the kind of man he liked to be, a successful well-run sort of person who had plenty of work and plenty of play and no problems. As it was more agreeable to have company, he would invite Pierre and make a week-end trip of it.

In the late afternoon Pierre and Liana returned from their hillside. While Pierre argued politely with Marc on the terrace, the sun set and the sky turned green and water-clear at the horizon. Soon there would be the unbelievable purple blue of dusk which reminded Pierre of the paler softer evening light over the Ile de France. It amazed Pierre that after all this time he could still feel anguished with homesickness every night when the stars came out.

"Stay for dinner anyhow," Marc said, "and we'll talk about it."

"Thank you very much, Monsieur Royer. I don't think I should." Pierre knew he could not plead another engagement. Practically no one had engagements on Saint Boniface.

"No, I insist," Marc said. "We're having guinea hen and I still have some good Bordeaux. It will give us such pleasure."

Marc put his arm around Liana and stood at the front door, looking like a man who is serene and safe in his home. Liana turned her head away from Marc and a dark color rose slowly along her cheeks. Pierre was too embarrassed to invent an excuse for not staying and he wanted to stop Marc from making this fatuous exhibition of himself.

"Well then, thank you very much," Pierre murmured.

Liana went upstairs to dress for dinner. She could not look at Pierre. Marc led Pierre to the comfortable chairs by the radio and offered Pierre whiskey.

"This is very pleasant," Marc said. He was flushed with happiness to have a guest in the house. "You must spend the evening with us more often. We are very quiet here, you know. It's a nice change for Liana too."

Marc tried to conceal his excitement and delight by bringing Pierre an ash tray and a box of cigarettes. Soon he will pat the pillow behind my head, Pierre thought, and was suddenly sorry for Marc.

Pierre drank three whiskeys and soda and began to feel blurred and indifferent. By the time he had eaten guinea hen and emptied his glass of red wine as quickly as the butler filled it, Pierre was drunk enough to listen to Marc without hearing him and to smile easily. Liana did not speak at all. She sat at the head of the table and seemed more the daughter of the house than the mistress, beautiful and child-like. Pierre noticed that Marc gave the orders to the butler and for a moment he resented the obedience and effacement of Liana. He drank more wine to get over his anger.

The cook had made a shortcake with mangoes and curlicues of whipped cream on top and Pierre, comfortable with wine, was telling himself that at least one ate marvellously *chez* Royer. He turned to compliment Marc and met Liana's eyes. A shock of pleasure went through him so that he felt hot and light-headed. Pierre began to enjoy himself. He prevented himself from laughing and from looking at Liana with owning caressing eyes. He considered the beautiful explosive effect of leaning over and kissing Liana, right here at the table. Liana smiled quickly and lowered her head. Pierre watched her eat and thought how elegant sure and unhurried her hands were, and then he forced himself to stop thinking of Liana because he was getting too excited. Marc did not see any of this as he was occupied in putting large creamy pieces of cake in his mouth. There was a smear of whipped cream on his chin.

"Shall we have coffee in the salon?" Marc said and rose without waiting for Liana. Marc walked ahead of her, leading Pierre by the arm, and continued to talk of his shark business. He had only stopped talking of it to eat. Pierre, who had not listened carefully before, began to pay attention to Marc's words. Pierre was quite drunk-and held himself very stiffly and felt that he had never been more sober. Listening to Marc he was suddenly filled with indignation.

"Alors," Pierre interrupted rudely, "Vous voyez la guerre comme une occasion de faire de l'argent?" He fixed Marc with unwinking eyes. Let us see what he has to say for himself, Pierre thought with drunken righteousness. Let him defend himself if he can.

Marc put his coffee cup down on the carved ugly little table and stared at Pierre.

"Comment?"

"Vous allez profiter de la guerre?" Pierre said. Now I have discovered what he really is, Pierre thought to himself. Marc's face wavered slightly before his eyes.

"Mon cher Vauclain," Marc cried, "I provide the Americans with something they need and want. Surely that is not a crime."

"Of course."

"I do not understand you."

"It is not important," Pierre said with great dignity. "Obviously war is not a business which could continue with such success every twenty years or so, unless people gained by it."

"People make money in peacetime too," Marc said.

"You would not sell sharks to the Germans?" Pierre asked coldly. He felt fine. I may have had a little more than I usually take, he thought, but it is not affecting me. What a *salaud* this Royer is, profiteering on soldiers.

"I find that insulting."

"I merely inquired."

"What do you think one should do?" Marc asked angrily.

"I am not a practical man like you, Monsieur Royer. I do not know about business and making money. I only know that millions of people make nothing out of a war, nothing at all you understand. They only suffer. They pay for war with their lives or their deaths." I may be talking too much, Pierre thought, but it is true. Even if I happen to be a little drunk, it is true.

"You aren't suffering too much yourself," Marc said. Then he was distressed to have said anything so brutal since he had not fought in France nor lived in occupied Paris. Hot angry tears smarted in Liana's eyes. She thought, some day I will kill Marc. He does too much harm. He makes everyone unhappy.

Pierre wished he could stay drunk if the drunkenness had given him that certainty of virtue. If he were only drunk enough he would go on insulting Marc but he was

150

not drunk enough and besides what Marc said was true. He felt sobered and dreary and bored with this talk.

"I do not suffer at all," Pierre said quietly. "That is because I have no part in life any more. You are quite right. Who am I to criticize?"

How did this start, Pierre wondered, what a waste of time it is.

"I hate the Boches myself," Marc said, trying to change the conversation. "They tear down the whole world every twenty years. They ruin everything that is built with patience and work."

"I would hate them if they stayed home. I hate what they have in their minds." Leave it, Pierre thought, what is the use in going on?

"How about some brandy?" Marc asked.

"No thank you."

Pierre noticed that Marc did not offer anything to Liana. Marc had obviously forgotten her. Furniture, Pierre told himself, a beautiful piece of furniture except at night. The old anger burned in him again.

"I'll take some if you don't mind?"

Pierre shook his head.

"You must be very unhappy here." Marc had been reflecting on what Pierre said. It followed, from Pierre's words, that Pierre felt guilty to be cut off from the war and the suffering he did not share.

"I am perfectly happy," Pierre said coldly. Marc stopped pouring brandy and looked at Pierre and was baffled by the expression in Pierre's eyes. It was as if Pierre intended that harmless sentence as an insult. But what has happened now, Marc thought in dismay, we were having such a friendly pleasant evening.

I am happy mainly because of your wife, Pierre thought, and because of the climate, the land, the sea, and the funny faces of the children in school. Mainly because of your wife, cher Monsieur Royer. But Pierre could feel the happiness wearing off or else happiness was not what he was really after. He was tired now and the drink, cooling inside him, left him feeling gloomy and a little sick.

Pierre said aloud. "I am not sure being happy is what one needs most."

Liana thought: Marc has done this. Happiness was

all they had, and if happiness was without value then she and Pierre had nothing.

"Nonsense," Marc said comfortably. He held up the brandy glass and swished the brandy around inside the wide bowl and Pierre thought that this had always been a disgusting gesture and never more disgusting than now.

"Nonsense," Marc said again. "Happiness is what life is about. It's what everybody wants. That's all there is."

They sat in silence then, and the echo of Marc's words ate into them. What have I said, Marc thought in despair, as if he had called down a curse on himself. Happiness is what life is about. What have I been doing with my forty-six years then? I cannot fool myself into thinking I have been happy.

Pierre looked at the closed tense face of Liana and the troubled eyes of Marc and he mocked this talk in his mind. Seigneur, Pierre said to himself, here are three perfect specimens thinking about happiness.

It was the end of October and in a few days the weather would change and the gray rains of November would begin. Marc decided he had no time to dawdle around the hills shooting pigeons.

CHAPTER FIFTEEN

There was an ash tray full of cigarette stubs on the table beside Pierre and a glass with the warm sour-looking dregs of whiskey in it. Rain slid thickly over the edge of the terrace roof. At the two corners where the tin waterspouts were the rain seemed to be gushing from a fire hose.

"I think you could get London now," Pierre said, looking at his watch.

Marc turned the dial of the radio and static screamed and jabbered in the room. He turned the dial farther, and in succession they heard the words "This oval soap," "The United Nations firm in their decision to," "You're the tops," then a loud wild wail of saxophones, and the curiously unreal super-homely voice of a woman speaking lines in some radio drama: "Don't worry, Bill, we'll always be able to make out."

"Boston," Marc said, "Boston comes through clearest at this hour."

Liana sat across the room. The lamps were turned on though it was only five o'clock. She held her embroidery in her lap but she had not worked on it. She watched Pierre and Marc with their chairs drawn to the radio, bowed, intent, like men waiting for signs at a strange altar. She turned her head to watch the rain.

"Ah merde!" Marc said. "Nothing. It is the rain."

"We can try later," Pierre said.

Marc switched off the radio.

They both leaned back in their chairs as if they were exhausted from hard exercise. Marc looked worried. Pierre could not keep his eyes away from the radio. He seemed to expect it to speak of itself.

"Too far away," Pierre murmured.

"What will happen next? My God, they must all be mad in Europe."

"It's worse than that," Pierre said. "Why would the government order Frenchmen to fight against Americans? They don't care how they kill the soldiers any more. They don't even bother to think up a good excuse. As if soldiers had no hearts and no minds and no lives they wanted to live. What does the government care?"

"The Maréchal must be gaga," Marc said. "Even if he has to get on with the Germans, he doesn't have to fight for them."

"Why don't the soldiers mutiny? There has been so much lying that no one knows what to believe any more."

"Everyone lies," Marc said.

"If we can believe anybody in this rotten war, you would think we could believe the Americans."

"Why?"

Pierre puzzled over Marc's "why," and did not answer. What had the Americans done in the last ten years that justified his belief in their superior honesty?

"Au fond," Pierre said, "people are good and governments are bad. I don't know why. Look at the French."

153

"They are all dirty sons of bitches," Marc said obscurely. "They can give any orders they please. They aren't going to get killed. You'll stay for dinner?"

"Thank you. Do you think we could try for Boston now?"

When the news finally came through, chopped into by static and fading off and then growing audible again, they learned that the French were still offering resistance in North Africa. Marc turned off the radio.

"I can't listen to it any more," he said. "It is too stupid. It is all too stupid."

Pierre walked up and down the room turning at the base of the staircase and at the front door.

"Now they have a chance to die a second time," Pierre said furiously. "First against the Germans, then against the Americans. I wonder whom the government will think up to fight next; perhaps the Chinese. Let the French have a good big chance to die fighting against everyone. The new motto."

"Shall I tell Théodore to put on another place?" Liana asked.

Marc nodded.

Since the news of the American invasion first came over the radio, Pierre and Marc had not left the living-room. Pierre smoked steadily and the room was hot with the front windows closed against the rain and the smoke choking up the wet warm air. Liana wiped the back of her hand across her forehead. Pierre had not looked at her for hours. He saw only the black ebony box of the radio, the dial he handled with such care, trying to wrench a clear voice from a great distance through the heavy rain-clogged air. There was the radio and unimaginably far away there was Africa where the French were fighting again.

"We can go out," Liana whispered at the front door. "Marc is asleep."

"It will rain."

"We always used to walk in the rain. Don't you remember? It isn't raining now. We haven't been out this week."

"I would miss the afternoon news," Pierre said.

"But you hate the news. Both of you hate the news. Why do you listen all the time if you hate it?"

"And it comes through so badly," Pierre said, "I feel as if I were getting deaf trying to hear it. If only the voices came through clearly."

"But you hate it. Please come out, Pierre, you'll feel better."

"Darling, I have to listen. Really."

"Why?"

"Why?" he said, looking at Liana in amazement. "Why?"

Had she forgotten everything? She had questioned him so eagerly about France and the war. He had tried to tell her the truth as clearly as he knew it, with the carefulness of a responsible person talking to a child. Liana seemed to understand; at least she understood the suffering of others. Pierre had perhaps loved Liana most when he told her of the refugees on the roads of France, and seen tears in her eyes, and known her to be generous enough to imagine a misery and fear and heartbreak she would never experience. Had she forgotten everything?

"As you wish," Liana said. She held the screen door open for him.

"No, no," Pierre said. "Don't move the dial. It was starting to come through there."

"I wonder what that station is," Marc said wearily. "I used to think this was a good radio."

"Wait." Pierre lit another cigarette. He sat with his eyes half shut because of the pain inside his head. Perhaps it came from smoking too much. No, it came from trying to hear, trying to find the right wave lengths, waiting and looking at that damned ebony box. He wanted newspapers as he had never wanted them before; he hungered for them. In any civilized place you could read, you could go over the sentences carefully and make some idea of what was happening. But this way you had to grasp at a voice that spoke suddenly from anywhere. The voices jabbered in Spanish, German, Portuguese, you could not understand what they said. It was easier to understand English spoken by

155

Americans. The voices would whisper or scream, according to the behavior of the air, and suddenly break off in the middle of a sentence. You listened so hard that you did not know what they were saying. It was impossible to imagine Africa or the fighting there; nothing was true, there were a hundred voices babbling out of a box.

A man's voice suddenly spoke from the box. It began very loud and the voice sounded excited and gloating but it trailed off and there was a crackle of static and silence. The voice had said, "Stand by. Stand by. Important news coming to you over."

"That's New Orleans I think," Marc said.

Pierre jammed his hands into his pockets and stood up, took a few steps and sat down. It was like getting ready to abandon a torpedoed ship, it was like waiting outside the operating room while a surgeon worked over someone you loved, it was anything helpless and terrible and suspended in time. I wish I could stop listening, he thought. The noise of the siphon coughing soda into Marc's glass was very loud.

"Horrible weather," Marc said. The rain had not come but the clouds were low, thick and blackish gray. The lawn and the trees looked too green. No wind moved in the trees and the clouds were iron hard and close to the land. In the waiting silence before the storm the radio suddenly chattered and very far away, hard to hear but in a tone of triumph, a voice said, "Admiral Darlan has given the order to cease fire. The French armies in North Africa will join the United Nations. The agreement—" Then the voice disappeared.

"Oh merde, merde, merde," Marc said and began to spin the dial.

"What?" Pierre asked, as if he could not understand the words he had heard.

"Darlan is on the side of the Americans now, I suppose," Marc said. "Anyhow the poor bloody French won't have to fight the Americans any more."

"And how about the ones who died this week?" Pierre shouted. "How about the ones who died before Darlan changed his mind? What about them?" He was standing in the middle of the room shouting at Marc

156

but he was not really speaking to Marc or thinking of him.

"Pierre," Liana said timidly.

"What is this war about?" Pierre cried.

Liana looked at him with love and pity. Marc kept his eyes fixed on the radio.

"Mon vieux," Marc said gently, "the ones who govern us have no interest in human life. Do not break your heart for that. Some day they will be punished."

"What good will that do?" Pierre said. He walked across the room and opened the screen door and let it fall shut behind him. They heard him going down the terrace steps. Marc switched off the radio. Liana put her hands over her eyes. Thunder rumbled like a heavy cart over a rock road. The rain suddenly fell straight down in a gray wall around the house.

It was easy to sleep with the rain soft and cool on the roof and a damp breeze blowing in from the sea. The mosquito net swayed from the rusted iron hook in the ceiling. The mildew-spotted voile curtains were wet with rain and too heavy to flap against the window frames. Clouds covered the thick big stars that gave the nights their particular color. Pierre did not feel that he was lying in a room; the rain on the roof was as close as rain on leaves; the walls of the room did not shut out the smoky night. His bed was narrow and soft. He turned out his light and undressed almost guiltily. Sleep had become his secret pleasure, his vice. His body relaxed and he waited for sleep to stroke him into darkness.

That night Pierre dreamed of Liana. In his dream he was going to the Sorbonne though he was also on leave in Paris because it was the first Christmas of the war. He wore a uniform but the uniform did not mean war and the army and going back to the air-conditioned staleness of the blockhouse in the Maginot Line. There was snow in Paris and this was the most beautiful winter he could remember. Liana and he had a suite at the Crillon, a hotel he had always wanted to stay in so that he could look out of the window while eating breakfast. The Place de la Concorde was lit at night by blue painted lights and snow drifted thick against the rims of the fountains and covered all the street and it looked like a spacious and handsome cemetery. In the daytime it had an air of innocence, as did all Paris cleaned and quieted by the snow, and looked like a village square with war memorials in it. People rode by on bicycles and every one seemed homely and comfortable bundled up against the snow. Liana loved the brioche and café-au-lait of the Crillon and also ate pêche melba for breakfast and was enchanting in the ornate white and gold bed. But she had only sleeveless tennis dresses and espadrilles to wear and she looked cold and strange outdoors and people stared at her. This made her sullen, no, worse than that, hostile and savage, so Pierre knew he would have to take Liana away from Paris. The sadness of leaving Paris hurt him in his throat like tears.

When Pierre woke he never remembered his dreams but only felt that he swam up from deep under water, except that the water was warm and furry and dark. He felt unnatural when he first waked as if sleep was his normal state and the waking was dangerous and the world he waked into was unfamiliar and unfriendly. He was drugged with sleep and had to struggle out of it but he was reluctant to wake. Then from the soft rocking blackness where he had been Pierre was suddenly awake and responsible and knew that he had to dress and go to school, and after that he would go to Marc's house and listen to the radio and then he would come back to town and eat quickly at the hotel. Already he looked forward to the night and to the comfort and emptiness of sleep.

Pierre stood before the small mirror that hung above the wash basin and shaved in cold water. He scraped the lather from his face slowly, feeling his skin getting sore and raw as it did every day. The blade was not sharp enough; there were no more blades on sale in town though a shipment was promised. You will look like a great intellectual with a beard, he told himself. There would not be razor blades or anything else, if he guessed right. The Americans were fantastic nowadays; on the one hand they clasped Darlan to their bosoms which was the same as clasping a quick-witted scorpion, and on the other hand they were starting to blockade the French Caribbean islands. Admiral Robert in Martinique could scarcely be a worse bastard than Admiral Darlan in Algeria, Pierre reflected, so there must be greater mysteries to foreign policy than I will ever understand or else this war is the complete abject confused dung which I have long considered it to be. Why don't you leave it alone, he argued with himself and stared angrily at a small cut on his chin. Haven't you seen enough, do you want any more proof?

It is not so easy, Pierre told himself, standing in the shower. It is not as simple as that. Governments are all alike but there are also the people. The poor bloody people, he thought, now they are fighting with the Americans and against the Germans again. That is anyhow a great improvement. Was there ever a decent war? Was there ever a war where in fact men fought for the ideas they were exhorted to fight for and the leaders did not lie, bargain, conceal mistakes, generously expend others' lives, and survive to be heroic in the next war? Was there ever a war in which a man could die without bitterness or regret or just plain disgust: where he could discount any personal loss, for the cause was as honorable as the speech-makers said?

The water dripped from the rusted tin shower-head and the cement under his feet felt slimy. Pierre stepped out onto the wooden floor of the bathroom and began to dry himself with a sleazy grayish towel. It smelled sour as everything did these days because there was not enough sun to dry the linen properly. His shirt was limp when he put it on and also had the sour smell but it was less unpleasant than the towel.

I'm not going to get into it again, Pierre told himself fiercely, dressing in the middle of the room. I know what I believe in and what I think worth fighting for: la dignité et les droits de l'homme. Pierre said it aloud to see whether the words were as beautiful as he believed: the dignity and the rights of man. What government would make a war or a peace for that? Who believes in that, he asked himself. And then he thought suddenly, millions of men believe in that. Who are the governments anyway; how did they get there; who controls them? What do they matter? Millions of men be-

lieve in that. Why then, Pierre thought, it's like believing
in God but not in the church. You can refuse to believe
in the war but you can believe in the people fighting it.

Pierre was elated to have found this logical solution
for his doubt and disgust. He tied on his espadrilles and
started to comb his hair and all the time he felt happy
because at last there was some order in his mind. The
racking questions that could not be answered were now
answered; he had a system for seeing history and therefore history was no longer heartbreaking and meaningless. The people are decent and fight for something decent; it does not matter if they are tricked or misled or
lied to or wasted. Then he thought, plunging back into
the usual despair: what nonsense that is; what absolute
nonsense. Some of the people are decent and some are
not; they fight because there is a war; they will allow
their governments to make one more corrupt, untenable
peace; and then they will fight again. It is hopeless.

Madame Loustelot's daughter knocked at his door.
Every morning she carried Pierre's breakfast tray up
the outside steps. There was always skin on the milk
and the coffee was lukewarm but the bread had been
fresh. On his breakfast tray there were two soggy soda
biscuits. They will have to make bread of corn or cassawa, Pierre thought, taking the tray; there will be no
more white flour and no more razor blades and they do
not want to believe it. Madeleine Loustelot said bonjour woodenly. She had given up flirting with Pierre two
months after he arrived. Now she did not bother to
brush her hair or wash her face before she came to his
room. She did not even feel angry or disappointed in
him any more. He was the boarder and it was her duty
to carry his breakfast to his room.

Pierre put the tray on his desk and poured the coffee and milk into the thick cup. He could eat his breakfast in five minutes; afterwards he had the habit of smoking a cigarette and reading for fifteen minutes before he
walked to school. He was reading *War and Peace* for
the fourth time and though he had the book open to his
favorite description of war, the battle of Borodino, he
did not read.

I want to go back, Pierre thought, and watched the
smoke of his cigarette waver and fade in the air. The

morning was cloudy but not cool; the coolness came later with the rain. Pierre noticed that there were greenish gray mildew stains on the covers of the books piled on his desk and he got the towel from the bathroom and wiped them off. I want to go back because I am revolted to be safe and I am lonely for other men and homesick enough to die. I want to go back like an unreasoning animal that longs for the herd and home. And then, Pierre thought, you can't tell, maybe it will become a war for the dignity and the rights of man before it is over.

He said good morning to Madame Loustelot, who leaned on the balcony rail resting from having made breakfast or simply standing still as cows do, waiting for the impulse to move. The arch of the pepper trees over the school road was as graceful and perfect as always, and Pierre looked at the trees with gratitude. But he would be glad when this day was finished too and he could sleep again; and escape the grinding argument in his brain.

It rained every afternoon and Pierre had not seen Liana alone for over two weeks. He found that he could scarcely bear to listen to the radio and dreaded the afternoons with Marc: yet he could not keep away from the house and from that groping for news. The French were now dying in places he had never heard of.

They did not notice her as she opened the screen door. She had hoped that Pierre would look at her and say, where are you going, Liana. Just for a walk, she would say. Then he would get up and take his rain coat and tell Marc that he wanted some fresh air. Liana did not care now what Marc might think: she had been afraid of Marc when she had Pierre, but the rain and the radio had taken Pierre from her and being alone with Pierre was all that mattered. Liana did not defy Marc in her mind, she ignored him. Now she had invented this trick to catch Pierre's attention and to be alone with him and the trick failed.

The hateful rain had turned the hillside under the banyan tree into a soggy swamp; the stream was muddy and overflowing and the trees were drowned; the cave by the beach was as cold as a small damp cellar. They had no place to go: the weather had cheated them. They could only be lovers when the climate allowed. Liana had watched the sky and longed for Pierre and said nothing because it shamed her to speak of her need when Pierre apparently was untroubled. Besides, when were they alone to talk? Marc came home every afternoon as if it were his duty to share with Pierre the burden of inaction and listening.

Liana walked down the drive and turned on the road; she would walk to the end of the stone surface. After that there was only red rutted mud. The rain fell in a steady heavy downpour. There was no end to it. But at least outdoors the feel of the fresh water was soft on your face and the air was cool and green. If they could do nothing else, they could walk together on the short strip of paved road.

If Pierre doesn't love me any more that's all right, Liana said to herself. But she knew this was a lie and she was only saying it from vanity and that she could not even say it, if she believed that Pierre had stopped loving her. I have no one else, she thought. Now they were never together and never happy and she could not sleep at night and there were wires pulling inside her body and she wanted to cry ten times a day without reason and she could not sleep and she was growing ugly, with discontented nervous lines around her mouth and eyes, and she felt ugly and unused and unwanted. Liana dug her fingernails into the palms of her hands and walked faster.

I want him, Liana told herself desperately, I want him, I must have him. This was not Marc's fault either; Marc did not bring the rain or make the news. It was Pierre's fault because he would not let himself be happy, he insisted on hurting himself with all those voices that came over the air from America and England. Pierre wanted to be unhappy, it seemed, he liked it, that was what he preferred. He would rather make himself miserable and make her crazy than stop listening to the radio and come walking with her in the rain.

Why would a man act this way? What was wrong with him? What sickness did he have inside himself to behave like this, refusing all the pleasure and delight that was here and now, and tormenting himself for a

162

distant war that did not concern him. It's insane, Liana thought, it's wicked, why should he spoil everything this way?

She opened the front door and let the screen slam behind her. Pierre looked pale and tired and anxious. He raised his head when Liana came in but he did not smile or speak to her. He sat sideways in his chair with his head forward and turned toward the radio as if he were deaf. Marc did not notice Liana and did not appear to be listening to the news broadcast. His face also looked strained and worried and he was apparently thinking of something because he shook his head suddenly, having reached the end of a silent argument, and said, No. Liana walked past them, dripping water on the polished floor, and climbed the stairs. She leaned over the banisters and stared down at them, hating them both, the two white men and their self-inflicted sorrows.

CHAPTER SIXTEEN

Short silver needles of rain slanted before the headlights of Marc's car. The road was black and the mud shone in the light. Reddish water from the potholes splashed over the car and spotted the windows. The electric windshield wipers clicked softly and sleepily. It was hot in the car with the windows closed. Marc drove with care, thinking of something else. There is no use in being bitter, he thought, there is no time for that. But he could not help himself. He raged in his mind against the folly and cruelty of governments. What devious tricks had been played, always secretly, so that no one noticed until it was too late; until at last people were ruled by unknown men who cared nothing for the lives they controlled. We are as helpless as slaves, Marc thought, *they* make the laws, *they* decide, *they* stumble from idiocy to idiocy and we can do nothing. How had this happened? At what moment had men ceased to be free, whatever their label was; at what moment had they all become the servants of the state, which was to say fools bossed by irresponsibles? Politics now was the science of making life impossible. How did they get there, Marc thought, they are above criticism and restraint, like God, and who gave them their power? What miserable patient sheep we have turned out to be, we the governed.

In Martinique, an Admiral (imagine, Marc thought, government is such a joke that they hand it over to admirals) had decided not to collaborate with England and America. It was vastly comic when you considered it. This one bearded, gold-braided man controlled (though God knows why, Marc thought, we are the controlled and we were never asked to consent) the French islands in the Caribbean. From this ludicrous position, this powerless microscopic domain, the Admiral defied the governments of the United States and Great Britain. He said that he did not agree with their invasion of North Africa, he remained loyal to the German-overrun French government in Vichy, and he refused to join forces with the United Nations and with those Frenchmen who were again at war with the Germans. It is too fantastic, Marc thought.

The American government, which had flattered the Admiral into this amazing arrogance by treating him for long years as if he were a powerful friend (and how could you explain that, Marc wondered) now was disgusted with its former protégé the Admiral, and said that since he did not behave and cooperate, French vessels could not take on cargo in any United Nations ports. The Admiral retorted that, this being the case, he would not allow French vessels to leave French Caribbean ports. If you heard it sung, Marc thought, it would be funny as can be.

The orders to remain in port were issued from Martinique; if you disobeyed—which would be possible on Saint Boniface where authority was entirely based on the acquiescence of the governed—your boat might be seized by the Americans when you reached their harbors. That was what Martinique implied and it was too risky to verify. A man couldn't gamble his boat to prove the Admiral was a fool.

It sounded complicated and it was extremely simple. No cargo ships would dock at Martinique and therefore supplies would not be trans-shipped from Martinique to the other French islands in the Caribbean. The belts,

164

Marc thought, which have been tightened these last years will now wind twice around each man's stomach. The Admiral allowed no French boats to carry cargo for sale in American or English or Dutch ports, for fear the crews would remain in those ports of their own free will, or the boats be seized. So Marc could not sell his sharks to the Americans, and this business which had been a sudden hope to the island was destroyed six weeks after it started.

We are put in jail to starve, Marc told himself furiously, because of the accursed bloody goddamn fools who run the world as if people did not live in it.

Marc turned the car and drove slowly up the steep hill to Le Paradis. There was light in the living-room window and the light, streaming out across the veranda, showed the rain falling in a curtain of silver beads. Marc opened the car door and ran up the steps and when he got to the front door he decided he was an idiot, why hurry, the rain would not make him wetter than he already was, soaked in sweat and hot with anger. Marie sat inside by the radio and listened as she always did (or perhaps she did not listen at all) to whatever poured out of it.

At the moment she was listening to a speech by an American politician full of the words that had been corrupted long ago by such speakers. Your children can grow up freely to worship their, free men in free association enjoying the fruits of, sacred rights of the, let fear be banished from . . . Marie understood very little English so that the speech itself did not affect her but the politician's voice thundering and cajoling, seeming to weep, bragging, evidently pleased her. She was embroidering a pillow cover for the living-room sofa. There was a stamped pattern on thick écru-colored cloth: a bird of paradise and a spray of roses. She had a strand of bright purple silk in her mouth and was preparing to thread it in her needle. When Marc unlatched the screen she turned off the radio.

"Bonsoir," Marie said. She was glad to see him.

Marc walked across the room and kissed her forehead.

"Do you know what I had to pay for a can of sardines today?" Marie asked. This had enraged her all day and

165

she could not wait to discuss it. "One dollar! Can you believe it? What do they think they are doing in town? It is robbery. Do you know what else? A litre of cooking oil costs two dollars and five cents. I said I would speak to the Mayor about these prices. You must do something about it. Sit down," she said impatiently. "Can they charge such prices?"

"Probably."

"You must stop them, Marc. It is impossible. We will starve if we have to pay such prices."

That was not exactly true, Marc thought, or at any rate Marie would not starve. He wondered, as he often had before, whether Marie was a miser. Perhaps she loved money; everyone had to love something. He did not know what else she loved.

"Listen," Marc said patiently, "it is not the fault of the shopkeepers. There hasn't been a boat from Martinique for three weeks. The people here don't know when they will get new supplies. If their stocks run out they will have nothing left; they will have to close their shops. They are trying to earn what they can on the supplies that remain."

"There is no more kerosene for sale."

"I know."

"Well, how am I going to run my stove? You know very well it is a kerosene stove."

"You will have to cook with charcoal."

"Like the negroes," Marie said angrily.

"Like the negroes."

"There was a line of women waiting at the bakery today. You never saw such a scene. They pushed and screamed at each other. There is not enough bread so you have to stand in line and try to buy before the bread runs out. Madame Loustelot says she can only bake so much every day, and perhaps in two weeks there will be no flour. She charges six cents more a loaf. I never heard anything like it."

"You will have to eat cassawa bread."

Marie stared at him. Marc's apparent resignation to these outrages only made her angrier.

"It is all the fault of old Berthold," she said slyly. "The women were talking about it."

Marc started to tell her she was a fool, and stopped

himself. Poor Berthold, he thought, they will say it is his fault. And if the women were already quarrelling in a queue before the bakery, what would they do in another month, in two months, when the island's stocks would very likely be gone? The men will get mean if the women do. People will suspect others of having more, somehow, dishonestly, than they have themselves. And if the blacks are hungry and do not understand why, who knows what they will start?

"Berthold has nothing to do with it, Marie," Marc said. "You must believe me. The Americans are blockading us." And also we are blockading ourselves, he thought, but that was too complicated for Marie.

"Why?" she said. "What have we done to the Americans? What are they blockading us for?"

Marc could not explain to her; he was sick of it. Marie would not understand and he was tired of thinking about it and tired of talking about it. He shrugged his shoulders wearily.

"I don't know what I'm going to do," Marie said fretfully.

Marc smiled at her then. Her total unending selfishness was a quality he was so used to that he found it funny.

"I will have to shut down my shark factory," Marc said.

"Oh well, that doesn't really matter to you, Marc. You have plenty of money. You've always got your schooners and the electric light plant and your rents and whatever else you have. I don't suppose that little shark business will hurt you."

"It isn't that." She was too stupid. It seemed to Marc that with the years her face was losing everything except a stubborn rock-like stupid selfishness. She'll have eyes like a pig, he thought indifferently, before she dies.

Marie licked the end of the purple thread and held up the needle and threaded it. She studied her pillow case and sighed with pleasure. It would be beautiful with all the brilliant silk colors. She forgot Marc and her rage against Berthold's mismanagement and all the cheating that was going on in town. For the moment she lost herself in admiring her handiwork.

"I don't know what the fishermen will do."

"What they did before, I suppose," Marie said but she was not interested. She did not want to talk any more. She wanted to concentrate on her embroidery.

Marc took out a cigar and cut the end. Marie frowned at him as she disliked cigar smoke in her parlor. Marc paid no attention to this and said, "I'd like a drink."

"You'll have to get it yourself. The servants are in bed."

When Marc came back from the pantry with the glass, Marie said, "You'd think this rain would make it cool but it doesn't. I can't think when there's been a worse year." The climate, the sardines, the Americans: there was no end to this tiresomeness. "Why can't they leave people alone? We haven't done anything."

"Nothing," Marc said. But that was not the point; it was not a question of guilt and punishment. They would get you wherever you were; misery spread like a stain slowly over the world. No one was safe; no place was small enough and far enough away to escape. I cannot tell the fishermen, Marc thought. This had been a new hope for them all, and not only for the fishermen. Even Mademoiselle Clementine is prosperous because the fishermen's wives have paid her to sew for them. Mademoiselle Clementine was a very bad dressmaker and a pathetic smiling flattering religious old maid, and no one had bothered very much to consider how she lived. She too had money now. She had thanked Marc in the street, only two days ago, as if he organized this entire shark business to enlarge and ease her life. Marc was embarrassed by the pleasure he took in her thanks and in the friendly grateful way people had with him now.

How much would it cost, Marc thought suddenly, to store the livers and meat and skins, and wait until these dirty politics change. The only good thing you could say for politics was that they were not permanent. Perhaps in a few months the Americans would lift the blockade or someone would shoot the Admiral in Martinique and the sharks would sell again. It might cost me three thousand dollars a month, Marc thought with a sinking heart. Impossible, he told himself, figure it out again. But no, if you averaged thirty sharks a day at an average $3.00 per shark to the fishermen, and added the salt, the lumber used in the barrels and packing cases, the four men

168

employed in the factory (which was a palm-leaf shack), the crews of the schooners (My God, I forgot them, he thought), it would easily come to that. Marc had never in his life done anything foolish about money; this was not business, it was charity. He found himself opposed to such charity as if it were a sin. When people started carrying on that way, the whole system would go to pieces.

I can't do it, Marc decided, I can't afford it. Then he thought of the busy evil-smelling palm-leaf shack on the beach with the pier running out from it. He thought of being there early in the morning when fifteen small sturdy white-painted boats sailed in, after a night's fishing. The sails of the boats stuck out sharp and clean and starched by the wind. The little boats seemed to move on wheels, so light and sweet over the dark water. The men dragged the sharks from their boats to the weighing machine. It was very bloody and dirty and there was no time when a shark didn't stink. The men had black sweat-greasy stubble on their chins and their eyes looked tired. They smiled and called to Marc and each one wanted Marc to inspect his catch. Two men came in one day with a five hundred pound mako. It was amazing that two men in a skiff, using a handline, could have fought and killed that monster. They hung the shark's great oval mouth, with the four rows of cutting teeth, over the door of the shack. Marc was proud as they were. He loved to fish too; he knew that beautiful harsh wonder of a man in a small boat alone on the sea. It must be something like what aviators felt, he thought, the freedom and loneliness and the pride of believing you were strong enough to conquer the sea. I won't tell them, Marc thought, I won't shut down the factory. *Merde,* he said to himself, I'll just lose the dirty money.

Marie told him to open the side and back windows as the rain was stopping and they would get more air. Marc did not hear her. She made a little noise of impatience and put down her embroidery and went to open the windows herself.

"Get me another drink please," Marc said.

"I like that."

"Oh come on, Marie, it won't hurt you."

She took his glass and he sat with the wet unrolling

cigar in his hand and stared at it. The light in this room was awful, crashing down from a fancy chandelier in the center of the ceiling. It hurt his eyes. I am probably getting a headache from worry. Perhaps the best thing would be to drink the whiskey quickly and go to bed. Haven't I settled it all, Marc wondered. He would keep the fishermen on, he would salt and pack and store the sharks, he could tell himself that he was taking a reasonable business risk so as not to feel like some sloshy benefactor of mankind. If that was decided, what more did he have to fret about? Marie gave him his drink. Marie, he thought with brief mocking amusement, and her kerosene and her sardines.

What good will the money do them? Marc thought. If there is nothing to buy, what will they do with the money? Say this blockade goes on six months or even a year: Martinique will send us nothing then. I have to think of the island.

When he had thought this, Marc had such a feeling of happiness that it felt like a blush burning all over his body. I am not the Mayor, he warned himself, I have no position here. But this was not a thing of vanity or a desire to dominate other men. Marc thought again, it is my island. He was almost afraid, but still with that hot happiness in his heart. I will not let them suffer. I will not allow those dirty politicians to harm this island. They have ruined the world, they do not care how people live. But this is one place where they can't get away with it. This is one place where the innocent are not going to suffer. I will take care of this island, Marc thought, and the happiness was so fierce that he had to stand up and breathe against the excitement and joy that choked him.

"What's the matter with you?" Marie said sourly.

"We will get together and see what must be done," Marc said. He was talking as if he were drunk, with a strange thick throbbing voice. "We can do it. There's no need to grow cane on the best land. Potatoes instead of rice. Fish instead of meat. We can organize the fishermen. There are enough cows for milk and butter and we will fix the prices. I don't know about shoes but the negroes don't wear them anyhow. Clothes," he was talking to himself now in a low concentrated voice, "don't have to worry. We'll have to make candles; there'll be

170

no gasoline to run the electric plant. Never mind. Marie," Marc turned to her suddenly, "it will be the way it was when our fathers were young. Why not? We can do it. By God, we can do it and no one will suffer and no one will be afraid."

"What are you talking about?"

"About our island," he said.

"The island is Berthold's business. He's the Mayor. He's the one who's supposed to run it. It's his business."

"No," Marc said proudly, "mine."

"Oh nonsense. You must be drunk. You were probably drinking before you came here. I noticed you were a little funny when you came."

We'll show them, Marc thought. By God, we'll show them. We'll show them if they can rub us out without noticing us, when we haven't done anything wrong.

"I'm going home," Marc said suddenly. "Good night." He did not know why he wanted to go home; he had nothing to do; he could not talk to Berthold or any of the other men until morning. He wanted simply to move, to hurry, to begin. The war had started at last and he meant to defend the homeland against the whole hostile crazy world.

"You haven't stayed for a long time," Marie said gruffly. She did not raise her head. She was not going to beg Marc or trouble herself to be tempting.

"I know. Later," Marc said. "Good night, Marie." He kissed her forehead again and she turned her head sharply, in anger, and his lips grazed her dry heavy hair. When the headlights cut out over the grass toward the barn, Marie shut and locked her front door, and took up her embroidery. This is wrong, she thought to herself, there's all that trouble about the shopkeepers and Marc is no good to me and no one cares what happens anyhow. I don't know what I'm going to do, she thought miserably, it rains all the time and everything costs so much and the Americans are blockading us and Marc is no good to me.

The rain had stopped and the wind blowing in from the sea and the wet land was almost cold. Marc stood beside the car on the hill. The stars were covered and the sky was a sooty black; no lights showed in the town. Marc could just see the dark outline of the hill to his

171

right and the rim of white foam along the edge of the distant beach. The town did not interrupt the land; in this blackness the town might not have been there.

My island, Marc thought. The words were enormous, unbelievable. He had lived here and loved the island, but anyone with eyes would love the place. He was rich and people respected him and treated him properly and he needed that. He was no sharper with money than the next man and he had never worried about the island or how people lived here. No one was hungry; there wasn't any reason to worry. He liked many of the men but none of them were his great friends. He had never shared their lives: there was nothing to share really. A man's child might die or his wife and that would be terrible for him but that happened everywhere, to everyone, and it was a suffering that belonged to a man alone and you had no part in it. If people were sick they got taken care of; if they died they were buried. Everyone had some sort of house to live in and even if the negro shacks were wretched and dirty the negroes were used to that and they lived all right. There was nothing to do for the island, it needed nothing. Now the island was threatened.

This fierce exulting happiness bewildered Marc. He had no doubt; he knew they would survive. There would be no hunger and no fear as long as he lived and if they needed money he had money enough. This island was his, and he would protect it from the people who ruled the world as if no one lived in it.

Marc wanted to talk to someone immediately, as a man in love might want to talk. He had never felt this hard defiant pleasure in being alive. He wanted to go through the town reassuring people. He wanted to ring the church bells so all the people would crowd together in the street and take pride and confidence from each other. He wanted them all to know and believe that men lived here, men who would work and be unafraid. They probably never even heard of us, Marc thought, the people who decided to starve us out. Let them go on with their politics, let them spoil the whole world. Here we are going to take care of the land and each other and we are going to live.

Pierre must go home, Marc thought suddenly. I will help him to get home. Every man has the right to take

172

care of his land and his own people, in any way he can. Pierre loved France as he loved this island; it was all clear to Marc now. And afterwards, Marc thought somberly, Pierre must get together with all the others who care for the land and the people on it, and see that the world is ruled so people can live in it. He confused himself readily with Pierre: if I were in Europe and heard they were starving my island . . .

Marc thought he would go that night and see Pierre and tell him. They had been unlucky men, both of them, without a place and without a work. But that was changed now. They have declared a siege, he would tell Pierre, let the *grands emmerdeurs* try it. We will show them. But this is not your place Pierre, and I know it and you can have all the money you want to go back with your own people. I understand how you feel about France. And then he would say; listen, Pierre, when the war is over we must do something. Something. So they treat people properly. So they treat them as if they were alive and decent. So dictators or governments or whatever there is cannot spoil the lives of people they have never seen. Eh, Pierre? Marc said in his mind and felt he was talking to a brother, sure that Pierre would understand and agree. Eh, Pierre? So they remember that it is men they are always pushing around.

The headlights lit up the mud that lay unbroken before the front wheels, a smooth soft curved jelly of mud that would become a dust road again in the December sun. Marc cut off the motor and got out of the car and looked up at the dark windows of Pierre's room. He felt shy then; he could not wake Pierre in the middle of the night and babble these new triumphant truths that had just lately been revealed. He felt shy and ashamed of himself: Pierre would think he was crazy or drunk, and would laugh at him. Anyhow Pierre was asleep. I'm like Joan of Arc and the voices, Marc told himself mockingly. All right, maybe it sounded silly if you talked about it. Then he would not talk about it. But it was not silly when you thought it. He would not ring the church bells and make a speech to the crowd in the Grande Rue. But he would do the work and that was what counted. Maybe he had been a little exalted and that was foolish: but the work remained and the determination. Marc said

173

it to himself in the dark, knowing he would never be so reckless as to speak it aloud: this island is mine and I am going to take care of it.

CHAPTER SEVENTEEN

Liana sat cross-legged in the deep grass of the stream bank. Round white clouds moved as on pulleys across the sky and wind swooped through the tree tops. The solid dark leaves of a breadfruit tree resisted the wind: the leaves seemed to shake themselves free of it. But the eucalyptus floated and swayed with the wind. The high fronds of the palms took the wind most handsomely, streaming out like great flags. Liana's head was bowed and she read with the care and lack of expression of a child. She was reading *Le Rouge et le Noir* aloud. Pierre lay on his back and watched the trees and listened with pleasure to the smooth low innocent voice. He paid no attention to the words. From time to time, at random, he would say: what does that word mean? "Ambition," Liana repeated, dutiful but puzzled, "means wanting to be better than other people." More or less, Pierre thought lazily and told her to go on reading.

He had started the lessons again because he felt obliged to. That was how Pierre explained it to himself. Marc was a pretty decent sort of man, though a man without tact or charm. But he was not bad and it seemed needlessly cynical to cheat him of his money. Marc paid for the lessons: the least Pierre could do was earn his salary. Pierre did not know when nor exactly why he had stopped being jealous of Marc, or shamed and disgusted that Liana lived with Marc. He did not know when he had simply stopped considering that Marc and Liana were married. Perhaps it was because, watching them together, he saw truly that they were strangers to each other. After sharing the radio with Marc during the past month and seeing how sincerely and modestly Marc was now working for the island, Pierre could not believe in Marc as a harsh unloving sensualist. He thought really that Marc was too old for that and too absorbed in his

174

work, and as Liana never spoke of Marc, Pierre readily believed that this marriage, which was a mistake from the beginning, had lapsed and remained only a formality. So that obviously Pierre was not stealing Marc's wife since Marc had no wife: but he would not steal Marc's money.

Without ever putting it into words, because there were flaws in his reasoning which he did not care to examine, Pierre felt that everything would be honorable if only Liana studied again. But more than that, Pierre was happier when they were studying; he could love Liana as a beautiful eager child. The possessiveness of a woman was a trap; but a child could not help being possessive since a child was helpless, and though the woman's claims might fill you with anger or even fear, the child's claims could only be answered with tenderness. If a child did not understand you (not the words but the emotion and experience behind the words) you did not think the child was stupid, or unwilling to accept facts, or narrow, or stiflingly personal. You thought the child was too young, that was all, and would learn later; and you treated the child's incomprehension with patience and kindness. You expected very little from a child except the ability to receive, to take love and care and knowledge. You were decent about children because you knew they were different and themselves and you did not feel cheated or disappointed when they proved to be only children. The selfish way in which a child tried to protect itself by keeping the world small was not only forgivable but natural. You could be friends with a child on its own terms but to be truly friends with a woman she had to be your equal.

And so Pierre thought as he had when first he saw her: Liana is a child. With a child, nothing was final. You could not judge the child and the woman had not yet appeared. It was easier to think of Liana as a child if she were behaving like a child: that is to say, growing. When they had stopped their lessons Liana seemed a woman, not growing any more, static, finished, and though she had been a lovely surprising and hopeful child, as a woman she was simply a child with a closed brain. She is a child, Pierre told himself, with a gift for making love. But that was not extraordinary in the trop-

175

ics, where the child's body ripened and made demands very young; and Pierre thought that Liana's special genius for love was instinctive and she had always had it. It must be that way, Pierre reasoned, women are either natural lovers or they can never learn.

This system of illusion was helped because Liana looked sixteen. If she was sixteen everything became manageable. Pierre could tell himself without anxiety: Liana is so young, she will change when she grows up, this is only her first love. Lianà with a book in her hands, cross-legged on the grass, reading aloud in a soft monotone, proved everything Pierre wished to believe.

And besides, she looked so delicious sitting there with her black hair falling around her face, and the sun making dark bronze lights on her legs. Liana took in her breath (a sort of soft childish gulp) and started off on the next page, and Pierre felt warm with delight. But he stopped himself from leaning over, as he most ardently desired, to stroke those smooth legs, to push away the curtain of hair, to run his finger softly over the soft mouth. None of that, Pierre told himself. "What does the word mean?" Pierre said aloud. "Confusion," Liana recited, "it means when you're caught doing something you don't want anyone to see and they see you."

It is all so simple and personal and tidy, Pierre thought. "Are you tired of reading?"

"No, Pierre."

"Go on then."

What a thing a woman was, Pierre thought. Liana had raised her eyes to answer him; they were clean of any emotion, candid, polite, and a little absorbed (she was trying not to lose her place on the page). But there were times when Liana's eyes were shamelessly wise, dark with knowledge, and they seemed to mock him who would never know what she knew. Sometimes her eyes seemed blind, watching the invisible inward millrace of passion. And her eyes could be welcoming and pleading and (most baffling and exciting of all) shy.

"I'm tired now," Liana said and put a leaf in the book to mark the place. She threw herself back on the grass, and sighed, and watched the moving trees in silence.

If there were many times when Pierre had wished he could talk to Liana as an equal, and that she could understand and answer him as a woman would who had certainly different but equal experience, he also admired Liana's talent for silence. Very few people knew how to be loving and close without talking. Liana handled silence with some special grace: she did not disappear into it, she did not seem to wait and be empty and need words to affirm herself. You could not fail to notice her; she was active in her silence, joined and part of you without saying anything. Pierre thought also how amazing it was that nothing Liana did ever looked ridiculous. No one could have taught her and yet every pose of her body was becoming. So now Pierre raised himself on his elbow, to see her better, and then he wanted more than seeing her.

"Liana."

The wide dark eyes looked at him, welcoming, waiting, secret and somewhere in them (the more disturbing because she yielded in everything and was so entirely humble) there was mockery.

"Liana."

"Yes," she said, agreeing.

Then later, with a gesture that was automatic and funny and shocking, Pierre looked at his watch. He felt himself bathed in comfort and well-being; his mind was washed and orderly; after great pleasure a man could always feel that pleasure was a splendid thing and there were now other matters to attend to.

"It's almost time for the late afternoon news," Pierre said.

"No!"

Liana was not arguing about the hour as he knew; she hated the radio. Pierre felt an instant hostility in him answering her hostility. This was absurd. Liana would no longer listen to any talk of France and the war: she stopped him as if he were speaking of a rival. And she actually schemed to keep him away from the radio. But that was too much: Liana could not expect him to forget the war simply to please her.

"I don't want to miss it," Pierre said coldly. He picked up the book and stood, waiting for her. He stretched out his hand to help Liana and she acted as if she had not seen him. Pierre started to walk away without her.

"Wait," she said, "I'll come."

They walked single-file on the path through the close trees. The trees made a tunnel of dark green light.

"Marc's away," Liana said.

"You didn't tell me."

"I forgot," she said indifferently.

"Where has he gone?"

"He went up-country. He's going to stay a few days with Monsieur Granart. The other sugar planters are going too. It's something about planting potatoes instead of sugar cane."

"Marc is very good about all this."

"He likes it."

"He's very good about it anyhow." Pierre was thinking: I ought to help Marc and I will do whatever he asks me to do. But he could not get excited about it; he could not take this island seriously and it seemed unlikely to Pierre that anything dangerous or tragic would ever happen in this remote insignificant place. However, if Marc or someone did not work to make the island practically self-sufficient, there would be suffering here. But with a secret European disdain, Pierre felt that being distressed for this island was like sorrowing over the tonsilitis of an acquaintance when your own child had double pneumonia. I'll do anything Marc asks me, Pierre thought, I must speak to him about it.

"Pierre," Liana said. "If I send away the servants will you stay for dinner? I'll cook it myself. Will you?"

"Yes, darling."

Liana took his arm on the road and walked beside him, happy and loving, and forgave Pierre the radio and his unnatural need to torment himself. She did not talk any more as she was planning the meal she would cook for Pierre. It would be the first one and it was terribly important that it be fine, so he would see. See what, Liana thought. Well, she answered herself, see what a useful woman I will be. But where and when she would be a useful woman for Pierre she did not know, and she did not want to think about it. The future was always unsafe and no one should go prying and scratching at things that had not happened.

Pierre turned on the radio and Liana went to the kitchen to dismiss the servants. He had difficulty finding the station and then realized he had missed the six o'clock

178

news and would have to wait for the next hour. He had heard a voice remarking briefly that the winter was unusually cold, with great snowstorms somewhere or other. December, Pierre thought, it is already December and they will be hungry and cold in Europe. Cold in the cities and cold in the villages and the hunger hurt more when you were cold. Even in Africa they would be cold, with a slicing wind coming over the desert at night. December, Pierre thought, and looked down at his khaki shorts and his sunburned legs. He felt suddenly more cut-off from the real world since he could not even share its weather.

Liana seemed to float or skip or dance between the pantry and the dining-room. She was setting the table. Then the pantry door closed and she did not come out again; now she would be cooking their dinner. Pierre, not thinking of this, turned the dial with the impatience and anxiety he knew so well. What had happened in the long hours that he had closed his ears to the real world? What were they doing now?

Pierre did not understand the radio nor why voices could be picked out of the air; it was the kind of thing he felt he would never understand. He only knew that this machine was a miracle and a horror and that it obeyed talented people. It obeyed Marc better than him though Marc was no champion technician. So Pierre turned the range-finding dial very slowly, and watched the thin thread move across the ruler-like face of the machine, and marvelled again that one tiny line suddenly became San Francisco and one tiny line quite near it would be Constantinople. He took no pleasure in the loud closeness of the world, all the world babbling and playing music, announcing destruction in ponderous or homely or falsely theatrical tones, all the world so hideously alike, so unavoidably vocal, so sad. He would have liked the world to be again wide and full of privacy and quiet lives.

Pierre found the right place and came in on the foreign language news broadcast from the United States and heard of United Nations air-raids and Russia. He wondered what had happened to North Africa that it merited this silence, until he realized he had found the proper wave length late and the announcer was now summing

179

up the preceding broadcast. It was then Pierre heard for the first time of Mateur, and understood despite the cautious and unrevealing words that there had been a battle against Germans and that Frenchmen too had fought and died in it, and that no matter how the announcer deprecated it the battle had been a defeat. Pierre took this in quickly with his ears and did not think about it, being too intent on hearing to think, until he had switched off the radio.

Then, very suddenly, the meaning of the words rolled over him. He still did not think. The worn flat words simply grew and swelled in shape, towered over his conscious brain, were dark in color and heavy and high as mountains, and had a meaning beyond any other words because they were the words he had been waiting for. He had that curious tricked feeling of having heard them before, as one can suddenly recognize a face or a street one has never seen. He had heard them before and he had known this would happen and yet he had been waiting. In his mind Pierre saw the battle but he did not see North Africa which was unknown to him, he saw Northern France; he saw the faces and the uniforms; the trucks, the tanks, the rifles, the guns, all the old matériel he had used or seen used, despised or admired, and found in any case to be impotent against the enemy. Pierre imagined Mateur as if it were the last failed battle he had been in himself, and he heard of defeat without surprise, but almost with a sense of welcome: because this was what he had been waiting for.

Pierre had known he was going back, but he did not know when. He did not know when the half desire to go back would become a command; nor did he know when he would be able to reject everything he thought, every disgust and doubt, and stop thinking and go. But this was what he had waited for: another defeat. It became essential then to go: it might not have been immediately essential were there news of victory. No other Frenchmen could fight for him, in that specially bitter and hopeless way you fight when you do not win. He could not profiteer on other Frenchmen's lives since the French were again being defeated.

Pierre did not consider whether he believed defeat to be an incurable disease that blighted the French and would destroy them. He only knew that he understood defeat and he hated it with all his heart and that if his people could not escape it, he would not escape it alone, and that he was going home to his army. It surprised Pierre to find how untroubled he felt now that it was settled; and how carefully he had made his plans without calling them plans. He had put together the few books that he could not leave and the three shirts and three changes of underwear, socks, handkerchiefs, one pair of shoes (his only real pair), the gray flannel suit that he would carry was clean, and he had an extra pair of long khaki trousers and two khaki shorts and khaki shirts to wear on the journey. All these things were ready and could be packed into a small suitcase or a big knapsack.

His papers were so tidy that he would have to do no sorting or burning: his table was bare except for his passport, his military papers, his identity card, and an envelope with French money in it. The money which he had saved was obviously always meant for this, for the fare home, though Pierre had not intentionally saved it for such a purpose. He had simply denied himself the smallest luxuries and saved. There was plenty of money, Pierre thought, unless French money had no value anywhere. If that were so, he could not help it; when he gave himself over to the authorities he ceased to be a man who must manage his own life, he became a unit with a numbered identity disc for whom everything is decided and who is provided for less well than if he were machinery or even a horse, but none the less provided for.

He felt quiet in his mind and he had no problems, since he stopped being Pierre Vauclain when he made his decision. He became one of millions who could not have problems because he would have no means to handle them. He would hire a sloop to take him to Anguilla which was the nearest English island; they could sail there overnight. There was probably nothing on Anguilla in the way of government except a colored British Resident, but that man would be Authority, and that man would ship him on to a higher Authority possibly at Tortola. After that, Pierre did not guess or imagine. The voyage home would be long and slow, full of delays and forms to be filled out, probably there would even be suspicion to overcome and there would surely be endless and senseless complications. That was the way things worked. It was no concern of his. Pierre took refuge from thought in reminding himself that he would have to try to buy a waterproof tobacco pouch to keep his money in because he would need the tobacco pouch he now had. As he was returning to the army he would again smoke a pipe.

Pierre felt none of the exaltation that could come from faith or ignorance, and he did not imagine that his living or dying was of importance to any cause or country. It had in fact only importance for him and he stored his own importance away until that future time when a man could be hopefully interested in his own life. He was not sad either because he had not started to think of the reasons for sorrow. He was relieved that the signal had come since he had been waiting for it.

I will go tomorrow night, Pierre thought. Tomorrow he would write a letter to be delivered to the Mayor after he left: the Martinique government did not approve of departing volunteers and though Monsieur Berthold would not be likely to make trouble, it was politer to spare Monsieur Berthold decision in the matter.

They would find a new school teacher in due course: the education of the children would not be damaged by a month's holiday. Pierre thought briefly of the forty-one children who had been in his care. In the twenty-two months he had been on this island, the children learned as much as they would learn in twenty-two months no matter who taught them. They learned by memory and the slowest mind set the pace. I did one thing for them, Pierre thought, I saved them twenty-two months' worth of confusing extraneous nonsense. He had left Martinique hurriedly with a batch of mimeographed paper from the Ministère de l'Instruction Publique in his suitcase. Pierre read this material on the long schooner trip to Saint Boniface and had been, first, outraged, and then contemptuous, and finally amused. With comic speed, the authorities had tried to tailor the curriculum to fit the times. Teachers were supposed to suppress the singing of the Marseillaise and substitute a tinny little song beginning: "Maréchal, Maréchal, we are following, we are following." Teachers were also ordered to play a few tricks with history (refer to pages 18-23 of the mimeographed booklet), which would explain the Fall of France. It all happened because the French did not work, stay home and reproduce, or (if they went out at all) go to church. Pierre had never taken these instructions from his suitcase. It was not heroism, as he knew, to refuse to teach these cheap songs, these vulgar lies: no inspector from Martinique was likely to arrive and note his disobedience. And if, by accident, an inspector reached St. Boniface, Pierre could always act the innocent, the well-meaning but stupid and inexperienced schoolmaster who had not understood his instructions and had been unable to vary the traditional teachings.

Maréchal, Maréchal, we are following, we are following, Pierre thought. He was not going to admit, even to forty-one ungifted children on a microscopic island, that France had reached such depths of absurdity. It was well to have spared the children this. As every European knew too bitterly, the absurd, the grotesque had a way of changing itself into poison. By the time the new schoolmaster arrived, the imbecile songs and the tricked history would have been abandoned as inoperative. Well, Pierre thought, dismissing it from his mind, a month's holiday is not going to hurt those children, nor a two months' holiday as far as that goes.

He continued with his time-table of departure. He would leave his rent in an envelope on the table and in another envelope he would leave the money he owed the hotel for meals this month. There were no other debts. It gave Pierre an almost uncomfortable feeling of lightness to realize how easily he could disappear. But then he had always been waiting.

Finally, since there was nothing else to plan and no further way to escape it, he thought: I will have to tell Liana.

He had not always been waiting, after all. Pierre told himself that having known the signal would come, he should have waited even in this. It was useless to regret the three months that they had been lovers and ungrateful and absurd and hackneyed, and he could not regret them. He regretted the manner of their ending: if only he could have left Liana safer somehow, somehow less alone, somehow better able to live. But before Pierre could sink into the guilt and sorrow that leaving Liana meant for him, before he could take time even to imagine what it would mean to be alone for him as well as for her, he told himself the reassuring lying phrase: Liana is a child. Nothing is final for her, anything may happen to her, she is a child with her first love and first loves never last but their ending is not ruin. There is so much time for her, Pierre thought, hoping it was true, insisting it was true, and refusing to see that time would not change Liana's color and that she would stay here because she could not do anything else and time would only mean the years passing. I will tell her that I'll come back afterwards, Pierre thought, and hoped that was true too and did not let himself wonder what difference it would make, what lastingness would he have to offer then?

Pierre did not have to think of himself without Liana because he did not have to think of himself at all; he had decided to go home to an army and so he forfeited his own life as all the millions of other soldiers had. It was too soon to feel the loneliness and the ache of desire for a loved irretrievable woman's body. It was too soon, and when the pain of this foreseen loss suddenly darkened his mind and made his heart sick, Pierre closed it away from him and forced himself to think again of Liana.

I will tell her tonight, Pierre thought, I will find a way to do it and she will forget me or at least get over the hurt later because she is so young, no hurt can stay with her forever.

Liana had sneaked up the back stairs, when the dinner was almost ready, to make herself pretty for Pierre. She came down the front stairs now and Pierre did not hear her and suddenly he felt her lips soft on his forehead. She smelled faintly of gardenias. She wore white and her eyes shone so that Pierre had to turn his head away. There was the other thing about children which he had forgotten: there was the trust.

Liana had lit candles on the dining-room table; the room was less square and hard in that wavering light and she had read somewhere about candles on a table. They had never used them before in this house, as Marc liked the glaring light of the chandelier so he could see

184

his food properly. The candles made the meal and the room a special thing of their own. Liana held Pierre's chair and he felt embarrassed and then mocked his embarrassment. She wished to be his servant, she wished to do everything for him. Pierre turned and kissed her hand that rested on the chair back and Liana flushed with pleasure. If only, Liana thought, I really knew how to cook. She brought the meal in on a tray and lifted each plate from the sideboard and a small frown of doubt and anxiety wrinkled her forehead. Would the potatoes be hard? The lima beans were not as green as when Thérèse cooked them. The red snapper, covered with tomato sauce, looked a little disorderly. There should have been more to eat and it should have been handsomer. She wanted to serve Pierre food as beautiful as hibiscus flowers and diamonds. He would not like this dinner; he could not. When she had finished placing the serving dishes, Liana looked unhappily at the table.

"Liana," Pierre said. "You didn't tell me you were a fine cook. What a marvellous fish. When did you learn to do anything so elegant? Come, sit down. I can't wait to start."

So then Liana felt perfectly happy and reassured and took her place at the head of the table and served Pierre with great dignity. He was her husband and he had just come home from work as he did every night and she had cooked the dinner for him as she always did and now she would give him the best of everything and scarcely eat herself in order to make sure he lacked nothing and to be ready to get him anything he wanted, before he knew that he wanted it. We always eat by candlelight, she thought, it's cooler and it rests my husband's eyes. Pierre poured the wine. My husband takes care of the wine, Liana thought proudly. She could not speak for happiness and because the occasion was too important and serious for words.

Pierre, who believed that Liana was worried about her cooking, began to tell her stories. He told her how he had set out on the *metro* when he was seven years old, with a cardboard doll's suitcase packed with handkerchiefs, to find Père Noël; and how he had been brought home in tears from the Parc Montsouris station, believing he had taken the wrong train and so missed

Santa Claus. He told her of a fight he had with another little boy in the lycée who spoke disparagingly of Maréchal Ney. Pierre remembered, though he had forgotten for more than twenty years, his first love, a little girl with dark curly bangs; and he told Liana how they had made up and repeated words for a marriage ceremony under a lilac bush in his grandmother's garden at Ville D'Avray. He spoke of the children at school in town and the latest joking gossip of the island. By the time they were eating dessert (the remains of a cake Thérèse had baked, and sliced bananas: it all looks so poor, Liana thought, in passing despair), Liana had forgotten her rôle as the dignified young matron.

She now sat in the way she was most comfortable, with her legs crossed and her elbows on the table, leaning forward to see Pierre and leaning forward to listen. Suddenly both of them thought: this is her first party. This was a party, this was what she had always imagined, only it was far better, it was unlike every other meal or anything else they had done together. But that was the wonder of Pierre; he made everything into a surprise, each day was new, he could invent happiness. No matter what they did it was always a first time, and though Liana could not believe anything would be happier than their picnics, now they had a party and it was the gayest and happiest of all. And Pierre was sad. He looked at Liana gilded with her joy, and knew that being a child made it no easier. The heart, he thought, breaks irrespective of age: one can only believe that it heals better in the young.

Pierre stretched out his hand and felt her arm smooth and fresh under his fingers. Then he leaned over and blew out the candles and heard Liana take in her breath with amazement. The white night came in through the windows and he saw Liana sitting cross-legged on the chair, still and silvery and with the great waiting eyes. He went to her and picked her up silently and Liana lay in his arms as he would always remember her, cat-soft and light and with a perfect yielding ease because she knew she belonged there. Pierre carried her quietly up the stairs: there should be no noise to disturb this. He could not speak and he could feel the blood hammering

186

in his head, but he walked steadily and the color of the night lay in lighter and darker strips over the stairs.

Liana did not understand how she could breathe as she always did; how she could lie so quietly in Pierre's arms. The story had changed and this was the bridal night that had never happened and she was being carried to the bridal bed: this too became a first time. She closed her eyes and there were streaks of flaming light in the darkness and she felt her body to be flame too but still waiting for Pierre, always needing Pierre, she had no body really until it became his. Liana turned her head and pressed her lips against the coarse khaki of Pierre's shirt and felt the hard flat bones of his chest under her mouth.

Pierre looked down at her face, seeing only the smooth cheek and the heavy shadow of the eyelashes and the hair that hung straight down over his arm.

He knew he could not tell Liana good-bye tonight.

CHAPTER EIGHTEEN

Liana sat on the terrace steps where she could watch the drive. She had waited in the salon and tried to read because Pierre wanted her to read. Then she went to her room and used a long half-hour varnishing her nails which did not need varnish. But now she could not bear the house any longer and yet she did not want to stand at the lower gate and perhaps be seen, anxiously staring toward the town. Five o'clock, Liana thought, Pierre won't come before dark. It always seemed to happen this way: it was impossible to understand but by now she should be hardened to it. After special joy, when Liana felt that nothing separated them, Pierre failed to come for her or came as a different man who had forgotten the night. Deep in her mind where Liana would not allow it to take shape in words, there was the deadly thought: if I were white, I would understand why Pierre behaves this way.

She put her head down on her knees and amused herself by listening to each separate small sound in the green world around her. She heard a mocking bird and the rumble of two pigeons on the roof, and a cricket, and some bees, and the rattle of the palms, and she was now trying to decide whether that brittle yet slurring noise was a lizard racing across the dead leaves in the flower beds. Then she heard Pierre's step on the gravel of the drive and raised her head to see his face, fearing some look she would not understand but that would hurt her. Pierre seemed only preoccupied and a little tired.

"I'm sorry to be late, darling." He sat beside Liana on the steps and put his arm around her shoulders, careless of Théodore who might be watching from the salon. "I had some extra work to do at school."

That, Liana knew, was all Pierre intended to say.

"Let's go swimming," Pierre said. Now in December the water would be almost as cold as in a proper ocean; and he wanted hard exercise to tire his body and rest his mind.

During the afternoon Pierre had worked to put his old school desk in order for his successor. It was more than a question of leaving the grade book fully marked, and the supplies tabulated and in their place, and the children's notebooks ranged in alphabetical groups. Pierre wanted to tell the next man what he, Pierre, had learned about these children so that it would be easier for the children as well as for the new teacher. It was difficult in a few words to a stranger to explain the backgrounds and the talents and failings of forty-one unexceptional children. The new man would have to grow fond of the children before Pierre's notes would mean anything to him. Yet Pierre did not want to leave the children unidentified and therefore unexplained. It had taken him months to attach the children's names and faces to the houses they lived in and the parents they lived with.

"Want to swim?"

"Yes, Pierre."

They walked to their own cave on the small beach that was shut in by black boulders. The boulders curved in a wall to make a pool here that was ice-clear and shallow. No one bothered to push through the uncut thickets on the shore and no one could see into their private beach from the sea. They always swam naked, swimming out through a narrow opening in the porous black rock into suddenly deep blue water and swimming back to lie half covered with white water on the white sand of the inside pool.

Pierre thought of nothing except the color of the water and the sky, and the sting of the water on his body, and the good hard pull in the muscles of his legs and arms. Liana swam fast and very smoothly. Her skin glistened under water as if it had been oiled and she moved with the gliding silent motion of a water animal. She was completely at home in the sea and the way she swam without effort was a marvel to Pierre who was himself a fine swimmer. Suddenly Liana swam against him so that Pierre felt the cold flashing brush of her skin as if a fish had struck him, and then she swam under him and rose before him laughing, and saying, "You swim so hard, Pierre. Where are you going?"

Pierre raced after her but could not catch her, and followed through the opening into the rock to where she lay on her stomach drifting with the tide in the shallow water. He anchored himself with his elbows in the sand and looked down at her breasts. The water partly covered them and underwater the skin seemed lighter. They were round and full with the skin very tight and cold over them. Pierre thought he would never again see a body as beautiful as this one. Liana's hair lay wet and black and flat as cloth down her back, and suddenly she tossed her head and her hair fell like a screen between him and her naked breast.

"What are you thinking?" she said.

"That you are beautiful."

Liana kissed him and Pierre tasted the salt water on her lips. But he did not want to build up happiness again; it was unfair now that he was leaving. Every moment that he saw Liana, and saw her better because he knew how little time remained, Pierre found it harder to think of leaving and impossible to speak of leaving. If only Liana were not so happy and if only she did not look at him with this lavish confidence and love. Since Pierre did not have the courage to talk to her, he decided that in all cases he could not leave until Marc returned. He would need Marc's permission to hire one of his boats and he had to say good-bye to Marc anyhow. It was all right then to postpone those unimaginable words. What would he say when finally he had to say something? "I am going away. Thank you for a kind of happiness I never had before?" Oh my God, Pierre thought, who ever talked like that?

But if he could not tell Liana the truth, he could at least avoid building up happiness as if he built her a tower to fall from. You could do that with a wife because you were partners and you could make happiness to hold in reserve, each one equally, against the day of return. But you could not let a woman love you and let yourself love a woman until you both felt safe in your happiness and then walk off muttering something about loved I not honor more.

"I'm cold," Liana said and showed Pierre her brown arm prickling with goose flesh.

Pierre did not want to move. Every action brought the time nearer, the time of telling and the time of leaving. He had to go back to his army and he wanted to go and he meant to go: but this moment in between, when he had tidily attended to everything except to the breaking of Liana's heart, was unbearable. If he did not move nothing happened, and nothing need be said. The perfect solution would be to fall asleep for two weeks (the old vice, Pierre thought) and wake two weeks farther away from this island, with the comfortable male conviction that Liana was beginning to understand, Liana was getting over it.

"Please," Liana said.

"Oh, darling!" Pierre was distressed that he had ignored her. Because of course, he thought bitterly, I wouldn't let Liana catch cold if I could possibly prevent it.

The sunset burned along the sky in the magnificent fierce colors that Pierre sometimes loved and sometimes hated, depending on whether he was homesick for another sky. They were tired after the swim and walked in silence, hand in hand where the path was wide enough and arm in arm on the road leading to the house. Pierre saw the curving drive and the low white house with new and grieving eyes: he had thought of his departure so rigidly in his mind that he had not guessed how painful it would be for the unreasoning, always lonely, safety-seeking heart.

"Will you stay tonight?" Liana asked at the open front door. "I'll make dinner again. It's going to rain too. We'll be cool in my room, listening to the rain. Will you, Pierre? Marc may come home any time; it might be our last night together for a long while."

For a long while, Pierre thought. He wanted to stay but he thought that to be a coward was enough, at present; he need not also be a hoarder. Each night made the necessary words of farewell less decent. I will not stay tonight, and tell her perhaps tomorrow afternoon when we won't have such close memories to make it cruel.

"I can't my darling. Not tonight."

There was nothing in Liana's training which permitted her to protest. She turned her face up for his kiss, like an obedient disappointed child. Pierre caught Liana to him and kissed her with the desperate longing remembering of a man standing in a railroad station on a long platform, where hundreds of other uniformed men are waiting with their women, and the train is just starting to move very slowly out of the dark steel cavern of the station, and some women are already stepping back to see the train go, their faces flat and meaningless with grief.

"Je t'aime, ma petite," Pierre said. It sounded as if he were crying. He had never said this before. Never, Liana thought, no, he never said that to me before. Pierre had said he adored her but that was a different and lesser thing, and he said it in another voice and at night. His voice was heavy with sorrow and the words that were so beautiful did not make her happy. Liana reached out her hand to touch his face, believing that through her fingers she would understand what she could not understand with her brain. But Pierre turned from her as if he wanted to hide, and hesitated, and then walked quickly down the steps and down the drive and did not look back.

They could not have seen Marc's car in the garage. The garage door opened at right angles to the drive behind the house and the car was parked well inside. No light came from Marc's window over the terrace because

191

he had been undressing in the fading cool light of the sunset, wearily taking off his sweaty clothes and thinking with pleasure of a cold shower and a drink beside the radio before dinner. They could not know that Marc, hearing their voices, came out of his room on bare feet planning to go down and greet Pierre and invite him to stay for dinner. They did not see Marc in the dusk at the head of the stairs.

Marc heard without wanting to hear and saw their bodies outlined against the red and gold sky, and he turned and went silently back to his room and shut the door.

Marc sat on his bed without moving and his face was like that of a man returning to consciousness after a bad accident with his memory blurred and fumbling and only the pain and the shock clear to him. He sat straight with his feet firmly on the floor and stared at the foolish dressing table beside the bathroom door. The shock wore off and Marc wished that he could freeze again into the stiff emptiness that had spared him thought.

It was true, Marc thought. The sentence said itself over and over again in his mind: it had no meaning, simply the sound of the words. It was true, it was true. But he himself had changed, or else he had worn out one set of emotions and could never use them again. Marc remembered, but not with any feeling, his passion of shame and anger when Pinelli had first accused Liana and Pierre of being lovers. He remembered the fury of being robbed and the anguish of being mocked: and he felt none of that now. At the time he had believed that there was no worse misery but he had been wrong. He was always wrong. If you waited you would find that your mind was capable of stretching itself limitlessly to hold new and different suffering. What Marc felt now was despair for himself.

He had liked Pierre always and admired him and trusted him: and when Marc knew he loved his island as Pierre loved France, Marc believed that he and Pierre were the same man. They shared a special kind of knowledge and love, like brothers. He understood Pierre and in this understanding he thought he had escaped loneliness. If you could know the heart of one man, then other men need not be secret and enemies. His understanding of Pierre guided him now and made it possible for him to treat with the island men as friends and allies. Marc believed that they were all as united in their hearts as he was with Pierre, through love of a land, though none of these men had the time or words to speak of that love or of their comradeship.

But if everyone fails a man, Marc thought, and the roots of his life are always rotten, he would have to be insane to blame others. If they show you often enough, Marc thought, then finally you must know that the failure is your own and so is the rottenness. They don't go out of their way to show you because they don't care enough and it isn't worth while. But they show you.

Marc did not consider Liana then. She was only a woman, not even a woman, a beautiful mindless animal. She had no obligation to him that Marc considered real; he owned her but ownership was nothing. He had given Liana nothing that counted and expected nothing that counted in return. Liana did not matter in this.

But Pierre mattered. For either Marc had been a fool, and chosen to trust a liar and a cheat, or else he Marc was diseased in some way and infected others. Something cheap and evil in him was catching and could taint decent men. It wasn't true when Pierre spoke to me about it, Marc thought confusedly, I know he did not lie to me then. They must have started afterwards. Pierre didn't lie to me that day. It was desperately important to believe that Pierre had not lied. It was more important to believe that, and so save his faith in Pierre, than it was to help himself. He could not stay locked inside himself, wronged and virtuous and with nothing left for others except suspicion. It was better to find excuses for Pierre. Anything was better than the absolute loneliness of shutting yourself away from everyone in hate or disgust or fear.

Liana knocked on Marc's door. Marc had forgotten to lock the door and he was so horrified at the thought of seeing Liana and of having her see him that he could not move.

"Théodore just told me you were home." Marc did not notice how choked her voice sounded. Liana had run up the stairs and she could not get enough air into her lungs. She was choked with terror. "Shall I come in?"

193

Oh, God, Liana prayed, help me now. Her face felt stretched with fear and the muscles around her mouth were so hard that she could not smile. She stared at the door and held both her hands hurtingly down on her breast, to try to quiet this wild short breathing. If Marc had not seen them or heard them on the terrace, he would surely know by looking at her now.

Liana did not realize how long it took Marc to answer. I can't see her, Marc thought in panic, I don't know what to do yet. He had to hide and heal before he could start again the exhausting business of managing life so that at least life looked all right even if it was rotting.

"Don't come in," Marc said, "I'm not dressed." This sounded ridiculous to him but Liana was too frightened to notice. "I think I have a touch of malaria. I'm going to sleep right away. I don't want any dinner and don't disturb me. I'll see you in the morning."

"I'm sorry," Liana murmured and stayed by the door.

"Please go away at once; I don't feel well," Marc said, and his strained nerves made his voice convincing, angry and rasping and unreasonable.

"Good night," Liana said and tiptoed across the hall to her room and locked the door behind her.

"I'm not going to keep the supper warm all night," Thérèse said, at nine o'clock. "You, Théodore, go up and see what's the matter with them."

"Not me," Théodore said.

"You, Zela," Thérèse ordered.

"Not me either."

"What is it, Théodore?" Thérèse asked, suddenly anxious.

"I don't know," he said. "I just got a feeling. Feels bad around here. I just got a feeling this is it."

"Sainte Vierge," Thérèse said. "I'm going home."

"I guess so," Théodore said. "There's no sound from up there. I guess we better go home."

"Will he kill Liana?" Zela asked. "Look, I'm shaking like with a chill."

"Shake your way home," Thérèse said coldly. "Monsieur Marc is a gentleman. Don't you talk that godless law-breaking talk in your street when you get home either."

After a long time, Marc felt his back cold and stiff

194

with strain. I'll take a shower and go to bed, he thought. If I sleep I may be able to think better. He did not turn on the light. There was a milky cloud-covered sky and he could see his way around the room. The light would wake him up, or wake his mind: in the light, seeing himself, he would have to do something brutal and traditional. He would have to behave like a man, instead of handling his thoughts carefully as glass. If he saw himself he would be ashamed of his inaction. In the light, everything would become stupid and simple: beat Liana and shoot Pierre or vice versa. Marc walked silently to the bathroom and turned on the shower. The noise was too loud; it would wake him, too. He let the water trickle from the shower head and stood under it absentmindedly, taking comfort in the freshness on his body. When he found himself sitting on the edge of his bed again, in the same stiff unnatural position, Marc roused himself and lay down and tried to keep his eyes closed. If sleep settled nothing it cured pain for a time. But he could not sleep. He watched the pale shadow of leaves on the ceiling and listened to a nightbird that screamed suddenly from the bamboo brake behind the house.. There's no way to get out of it, Marc thought, I must know what I mean to do by morning.

Marc was bewildered by fatigue too, having been up since six that morning and on horseback until afternoon and then driving home with the sun in his eyes along the torn backroad. It was almost impossible to think and his feelings alarmed him because they were unexpected. It was the absence of anger that alarmed Marc. Was he getting old then, and dried-up and near to that mysterious hateful borderline where a man stopped being entirely a man? It was certain that for a long time now Marie had not meant to him what she once did. He had thought this was Marie's fault, the fault of her ugliness and meanness. He had imagined that when his hope slowly turned into habit, it was natural he could not truly desire her. The desire, Marc reasoned, was desire not only for a woman's body but for a kind of woman, and Marie would never be anything but herself and Marc knew what she was now beyond any chance of self-deception. So desire itself became a habit, and not an urgent one. Marc had not worried about this and his

195

sadness in Marie was spread over so many years that he did not feel any special sadness now. Though he had freed himself of Marie now that he considered it. Or had he freed himself: had time freed him, the same time that now made him tired and quiet and despairing and gentle, when he should feel plainly murderous?

And though he had never loved Liana, he had surely lusted for her with all the power in him. If he had seen Pierre and Liana sometime ago (when? Marc wondered, at what moment exactly?) standing with their bodies and their mouths melted together, he would not have gone silently back to his room. He would have tried to kill Pierre; he would not have let any man take from him what he so violently wanted himself. That feeling too had faded or else the excitement had gone from it, and Liana had become another habit. Was this time again, time weakening him and he, so naïve and so arrogant, believing that he was the one who decided, not time working at his body? For whatever reason, there was the fact: he could do without Liana. Since Marc had seen her with Pierre it was more than doing without her. He would not have her. He never wanted to have Liana again.

But surely this was all wrong. He should hate Liana because she had tricked him and he felt nothing except weariness and the sure gray feeling of something that has come to an end. Perhaps it was because he knew Liana loved Pierre, and loving Pierre she must be revolted by Marc's older coarse unwanted body.

Marc saw himself as clearly as if he stood before a mirror and suddenly he felt an emotion he recognized, remembering how coldly Liana had allowed herself to be taken, how cold and separate she remained when he was lost in pleasure. But, then, Marc had not thought of her and it was only now that he realized Liana's loathing. This at least he understood, this furious shame. He could hate Liana for his own blindness.

I am too tired, Marc thought. No hate was strong enough, no hate was worth the effort.

His life had been deformed by women and the women could not touch him any more. It was incredible to remember how he had tormented himself through the bitter wasted persevering years with Marie, and the prison

196

years with Liana when he tried to substitute lust and revenge for love. If I had known it would matter so little
in the end, Marc thought, I could have saved myself. I
could have done something with the time, if I had known
that in the end all those years would be meaningless.

It was terrifying to lie there in the pale dark and see
his life as a long imbecility for women who really did not
matter to him at all. I made money, Marc thought, I did
that. And that was all; just the money. He did not know
how to spend the money. The money would not buy
Marie nor pay for Liana. The money bought, respect;
he needed respect. But the men of the island respected
Gilbert Macon who worked for Marc Royer and earned
800 francs a month; they respected Captain Saldriguet
despite the fact that he was drunk half the time. They
did not respect Berthold because he was a pompous in-
decisive old politician; they did not respect Drieu because
he was a crook. They respect my money, Marc thought,
correcting himself carefully: so the respect is without
value.

I'm getting mixed up, Marc thought, perhaps I can go
to sleep now. This is just the jumble and confusion that
comes before sleep. He closed his eyes and saw Pierre
with swift appalling clearness, Pierre on the day he
shouted, "What is this war about?" and turned with a
drawn, sick face and left the house. Better to keep my
eyes open, Marc thought, I haven't settled anything. It's
about Pierre and Liana, he reminded himself, and what
I must do.

I should never have come back to this island, Marc
thought. I should have stayed in Europe and never come
back. That was when I made the choice that wasted all
these years; when I came back. But no, Marc said to
himself, that is the worst folly of all. I love this island.
This is my island.

Marc found the rock he had to stand on, quite suddenly, so that all this night before seemed like a dream
of falling, a slow speechless stricken falling from nothing
into nothing. He had come safely to this rock: his island that he loved.

Marc knew who he was when he thought of his island.
There was no denying the waste of the past, but until
you were dead you had time and you could learn and

197

you could change. Nothing very great and surely nothing spectacular would happen to him. If a man has misjudged and mismanaged for forty-six years, he cannot expect suddenly to build a superb life from such foundations. But as long as he is not dead he has time, Marc thought, and he can try to make something not useless and not lamentable out of that time. If he knows what he has to do, anyhow, and stops thinking of all he failed to do. And an island was different from a woman, an island was a safe investment for love.

There was however very little time. It was not that he was forty-six, because he was not going to plunge into old age as a quick excuse for irresponsibility; even though now, lying here, forty-six seemed as old as a man could get and as tired. There was very little time for the island and there was no time at all for Marc to spend on himself. Besides, Marc thought grimly, I have taken a great deal of care of myself all these years and I might have spared myself the trouble. If I don't take any care at all, it will work out as well and anyhow it could not work out worse.

Marie doesn't matter and Liana doesn't matter and I don't matter, Marc thought with amazement and relief. I only have to arrange about Pierre and Liana but I don't have to suffer. Not if I don't want to, Marc added, and Christ I am tired of the mess of my life. Then he thought: it isn't such a mess, little man: courage! it isn't such a mess. You did a good job with Granart and the others. They started out wanting to defend their cane fields with shotguns and now they are sensible citizens. They are even rather pleased with themselves, and feel good, and are respectably excited. They feel proud in not a bad way. Old Vaneau, who isn't given to such drama, suggested that we were the last reasonable men on earth and they were all delighted (though they kept saying voyons, voyons, modestly) because the French love to be reasonable, that's what the French always feel conceited about.

Marc found himself smiling in the dark as he remembered the ten rich men (rich for here, he thought, only rich for here) sitting in Granart's salon which was as ugly but not as elaborate as Marc's own. At first no one wanted to talk because everyone thought if he talked he would say something careless and be cheated; then they interrupted each other in explosions of bad passionate French. Each one felt the neighbor could easily make some sacrifice though his own situation scarcely permitted it. Each one said, with obstinate wishfulness, that the war was going to be over by the spring of 1943, at the latest in six months, and then where would they be if they had cut down on cane to plant vegetables. Marc neglected to say they would be exactly where they were before which was nowhere in particular, tiny men producing tiny quantities of sugar. They wore out their mistrust and their illusions in words and slowly they began to talk like comrades. It was very slow but it caught them and in the end they were talking as loudly about what they would do as they had talked about what they could not do. Marc was still smiling to think of it and there was pride in him too because it had been his own eloquence and his example (he was the richest, you might expect many things of Royer but not that he would be foolish about money) which forced these ten unread unthinking men to accept facts.

Suddenly Marc thought, here I am forgetting what I have to think about. And he thought, with reviving healthy optimism (because he was somebody after all, he wasn't simply a man whose life leaked away in miserable little failures): *crotte,* I have more important things to handle than love affairs.

Still it had to be handled and now he could face the problem with detachment as if he were not involved. Marc had confidence in his judgment as long as he was not judging for himself. The thing to do is hang on and use your head, Marc told himself complacently, and was filled with admiration for his own calm. The problem is really Pierre since Liana does not count. Now Pierre is noble and he probably thinks he loves Liana. If Pierre had been any ordinary island man, he would have no emotional complication: he would have slept with Liana, as who wouldn't if the chance offered, and that would be that. I will assume, Marc told himself, that Pierre loves her. Then Marc thought: I am going pretty fast now and seem to know a lot. It is at once too easy and too hard, the way I see it. Pierre is an educated European and he is clever; he is not color blind; he also probably knows

199

Liana better than anyone does and he must know that she couldn't be his equal ever. So perhaps Pierre just thinks he loves Liana or perhaps he is grateful to her or sorry for her. In any case, no matter how Pierre feels, he is apt to do something chivalrous because he believes he ought to.

This was the dangerous place and Marc could see it with painful precision. Pierre must not ruin his life as Marc had ruined his: Pierre must not now start on the long slow years of waste and futility because of a woman who would not fit and because of an idea that would not fit the woman. That was vital. It was an impossible liaison, it would never work, but Pierre was the kind who would break his heart and his life trying to make it work if once he started. And Pierre, Marc said to himself, is worth saving. Pierre has work to do. Pierre has a place and a land. Pierre must go home where he belongs and get on with the work the men have to do. What Pierre really loves is France, Marc thought, as I love my island: I've got to get Pierre out of here. And I've got to get him out of here quickly.

It wasn't so difficult after all, if you stopped thinking of yourself. And I have nothing to do with it, Marc thought, I never really had a wife. I will tell Pierre that I understand how it happened and do not blame him; and I will make him see what he already knows, which is that he must go home; and then I will send him in the motor boat to Anguilla. They can arrange to land at daybreak and they can run the boat close to shore but not beach her, so those silly Anguillans won't think they have to do anything heroic and seize the boat, and he can wade ashore and from then on it's his lookout. I'm not going to carry him all the way to Europe in a steamer rug, Marc thought irritably.

As for Liana, Marc said to himself, that's the easiest of all. She will go back to her mother's house tomorrow and stay there. There's no problem about her. She'll cry her eyes out for two weeks and get over it; that race doesn't go in for tragedy and besides she's too young to be sad the rest of her life. Marc was not going to keep Liana in his house any more. It was all finished with Liana. Marc told himself coldly that Liana was a hindrance in the work he now had to do: he needed all his time,

200

he needed personal tranquillity, and furthermore he needed his house. Liana was an embarrassment by her very presence, and as she obviously cared nothing for him and was not even happy here, there was no reason for her to stay. The island had either forgiven him his marriage or decided to ignore it, but Liana was a *gêne*. Marc thought: we can use this house for offices and for meetings and when Granart and the others have to come in town on island business they can stay here.

It was all practical and serene and Marc denied to himself that he did not want Liana to stay in his house one day more because he would never forgive her the months of his blindness when he had believed (like the most fatuous *cocu*) that her body still responded passionately to his. He could not forgive Liana the knowledge she must have of him, while she had lain unfeeling and watched his solitary and therefore shameful satisfaction. But that Marc buried in his mind and would never look at again: he would have no part in this affair, not even the part of poisoned vanity.

I will tell Liana tomorrow morning, Marc decided, that she must leave in the early afternoon. I'll talk to Pierre in the evening and get him off the next night at dark. There's nothing more to think about. It was as orderly as the account books in his office in town.

The sky had whitened and the birds woke and made a dawn racket in the trees and a breeze suddenly slapped in from the sea and beat at the leaves and blew over Marc's bed. Marc found he was cold and his eyes burned after the sleepless night and his mouth tasted sour and dry. I'll go downstairs and fix myself a drink and then get a few hours sleep, Marc decided. He knew he would sleep now.

Marc walked quietly on the stairs, not wanting to wake Liana. In the salon he found the whiskey decanter and a siphon and was too tired to go for ice to the pantry. The drink did not taste specially good, being lukewarm and too strong, but it rinsed out his mouth and gave him a comfortable warm feeling in the stomach. Ten hours ago, Marc thought, I was in despair and I feel fine now. I feel as cheerful as if I had made fifty thousand dollars.

This was extraordinary; he had not slept, he could

feel the sleeplessness cold around his shoulders and hot in his eyes, and you would not normally consider it a privilege to see your wife and the one man you wanted as a friend kissing each other like lovers at your own front door. I'm free, Marc thought, that's what makes me feel so fine. I'm cleaned up; I haven't any kind of a life to stumble over any more. There's the work and that's all I want. Marc raised his glass and drank, smiling as he remembered them, to his pals: *aux copains,* he said softly, thinking of the ten men who had somersaulted into citizenship at his urging. And to our island, he added.

Marc could see the low first streaks of red over the sea. He thought he would stand on the terrace and watch the sunrise and then he thought, hell, just because I feel like a new man is no reason to get sentimental about sunrises. I've seen hundreds of them, and went quietly to bed.

CHAPTER NINETEEN

Madeleine Loustelot had told Pierre when she brought his breakfast tray that Marc was back. She had seen Marc's car passing through town yesterday afternoon or she had seen somebody who had seen it. It was never clear how news spread on the island but no incident was too small for observation and there was always plenty of time to talk and very little to talk about. Pierre decided he would call on Marc in his office after school that day and then go to the house and tell Liana. Marc, who was so efficient and fast, might help him to leave the island this night. As the leaving became a fact, and not an unfixed date and a series of neat but uncertain plans, it began to seem like diving into darkness from a great height. Pierre wanted to hold his breath and close his eyes and dive. It was unbearable to think about it; it simply had to be done.

The children had straggled home at noon and Pierre sat at his school desk with his lunch spread on a not too clean napkin. The lunch was meagerer every day and

what with hard bread, miserly butter and an almost un-
varying ration of sardines and a boiled egg, Pierre usually found it a difficult meal to swallow. Today he could
not eat at all, and sat smoking with unsteady hands and
nervousness like a gag in his mouth. He was trying not
to think of anything and was telling himself, as if these
were complicated directions for crossing dangerous country: I will walk to Marc's office and get there at quarter
past three. It should not take more than an hour to explain to Marc. Then I will walk down the back street
behind the garage and along the main road and I should
be at Marc's house at quarter before five. Then I will
see Liana and I will say . . . But what would he say?
There were no suitable words because Liana would understand none of them.

Pierre did not blame Liana, he sorrowed for her and
he recoiled in advance from her pain and his guilt as
the one who brings pain.

The screen door of the schoolhouse opened and Liana stood on the steps, but she was looking behind her
not into the long whitewashed room. Before she turned
Pierre was stunned to see her here and frightened by the
odd jerky way she moved her head. When Liana turned,
Pierre saw that her hair was uncombed and sticking to
her forehead with sweat, the bones under the skin of her
face showed so plainly that they almost seemed to shine
white, and her eyes looked crazy.

"Liana," Pierre got up from the desk and went to her.
"What's the matter? Why have you come here? Why
do you look this way?"

"Marc knows," Liana said. Now she was staring out
the windows as if she expected to be trapped and killed:
it was appalling to see her. She could not hold her body
quiet.

"Knows what?" Pierre said stupidly. He tried to take
Liana's elbows to steady her but she wrenched away
from him.

"About us," Liana said. She was whispering. "He
didn't say so but I know. He came to my room this
morning and he stood in the door and then his face
looked very strange and he said he could not talk there;
I was to come to his room. He shut his door so Zela
wouldn't hear because she was sweeping in the hall."

Liana shuddered suddenly and Pierre put his arm around her and led her to one of the low wooden benches in the front row. He made Liana sit down and sat beside her. She would have to stop peering around her this way. He could not understand what she was saying as he watched her eyes crazily and suspiciously flicking at the room.

"Then?" Pierre said.

"He said, 'You will pack and leave for your mother's house early this afternoon.' I said, 'Why, Marc, why?' He looked at me with stone eyes and did not say anything. Then I said, 'For how long, Marc?' and he said 'For always.' Pierre! I started to cry and I said no, and he stood up, always with the stone eyes and the stone voice, and said, 'I will not discuss it. Be sure you leave early this afternoon.' Then he walked out of the room and took his car and drove in town. I could not come to you then because I knew the children would be here, so I came now."

Liana took a deep shivering breath and seemed to shrink or collapse. She was hunched up on the bench and her body looked shapeless. But the bones still pushed through the skin of her face. She had closed her eyes for a moment and Pierre was glad of that, as if a sharp intolerable noise had stopped.

He heard everything Liana had said, in the same words and in her voice, a second time like a record repeating. The second time Pierre understood her. Now, Pierre said to himself, now, now? Now on the day of leaving? There is no time. It cannot be now. It can't have happened now because I have no time as I am leaving.

"Pierre," Liana whispered, "you won't let him?"

"No," Pierre said automatically.

"We'll have to go away," she said. "Otherwise he can make me. I'm his wife; I have to obey him. We'll have to go away or he could do it. And I'd never see you. He could do it here where I am his wife. We'll go away."

Pierre said nothing. He did not look at Liana. He was the one who was going away; it was settled, all the plans were made. In a few hours he would have told Liana. But then everything had been settled; Liana had been settled in her house and he had been settled in his journey.

And now Liana said they must go away and she had no house. Go away where? Where he was going he had to go alone. Where else was there?

"Théodore said the boat from Martinique was coming this week. I heard him talking to Thérèse. Because there is no meat and almost no flour. He said it was coming; someone heard the radio operator say so. We could go back on that boat to Martinique."

Martinique? Pierre thought. I am going to Europe. It is all arranged. Martinique, he thought again, what would we do there? How would we live? How long would we have to stay?

"What would we do in Martinique?" Pierre said. His voice sounded to him like the voice of a half-wit, slow and thick and unused to speech.

"Pierre!" He was staring in front of him. Liana could not see his eyes. "You won't let Marc send me away from you?"

Pierre did not answer because he did not hear. He was thinking: Martinique. Then what? Stay in Martinique doing nothing, for always? Pierre was so shocked at this unimagined ruin of his plans that he could not think beyond the word Martinique. The name itself was a horror. It had an ugly and final sound; it meant the waste of all the rest of his life. His plans had grown in the dark of his mind and his heart for long months and he did not really know they were growing. But when finally Pierre made the decision that had already been made, he knew he was doing what he had to do, and there was no choice, and it was right this way. Suddenly from nowhere and without warning, there was Martinique and an eternity of sun and fiercely green land and a too-blue sea, and all of this meant nothingness. Pierre felt panic drowning him. Martinique, he thought, *no:* and the awful bursting panic of a man who hears himself condemned to prison for life pounded in him so that the schoolroom blurred before his eyes and he had to force himself to sit quiet and wait until he could control his fear.

The panic was catching, it spread like a smell in the room. It crept out from Pierre's skin, from the line of sweat around his mouth and from his eyes. Liana caught it. Pierre's silence meant that he would do nothing; he would abandon her. Her loneliness and her helplessness now became unbearable, and more unbearable because she had never doubted that Pierre would help her and Pierre would stay with her. Liana had her own image of prison: the filthy shack in the hills, the life of her family, the days that never ended and were always the same. And she would be caught in it, buried in it, knowing that Pierre had never lifted his hand for her, Pierre had not cared enough to save her life. The panic exploded in her brain. Liana climbed up on the school-bench and stepped on the narrow unsteady wood table before it and jumped to the floor. She turned to run toward the door. She had come for safety and found only this silence that said, No. She must run somewhere else to hide before they trapped her and took her away. Her face was twisted with fear and she sobbed with her mouth open.

"You won't help me," Liana cried, "you won't help me." She was running to the door as if she were wounded, awkwardly and with pain.

"Liana!"

She did not stop but she moved very slowly. She was crying so that she could scarcely see the free space between the wall and the benches.

It was Liana's fear against his. Pierre saw this clearly and Liana was the weaker and he was the responsible one. He could not let her go away alone with her fear.

"Liana!" he said again.

Liana stopped near the door. She no longer expected Pierre to help her or understand her. She was lost and there was no one now to trust. She did not speak to Pierre, since he was deaf, but to herself. She spoke out of despair. Her voice was bitter with loneliness and her eyes were black and dead in her face.

"To be a negro," Liana said. They had taught her to be a white lady. Marc had taught her with money and Pierre had taught her through love. And now both of them thought she could change after the long schooling and go home when she had no home and no people.

Very suddenly, Pierre saw what he and Marc had done. We really did it too, Pierre thought. If we had let her alone she would have whatever kind of life they have, not very good, but at least there would be people

206

in it, she would have a place in a world of people. Now she belongs nowhere. The whites will never forget the color of her skin and the blacks are strangers. We made the blacks into her enemies because she had to learn to fear them so she could escape from them. We should have done a complete job while we were about it, and changed her skin, since we took it upon ourselves to change her life.

Pierre put his arm around Liana's shoulders and pulled her to him. Her body was hard as wood to his touch and unyielding. Liana had stopped crying and her face looked bony and hollowed out. She did not try to use her body or her suffering to win Pierre. She waited for Pierre to speak but it did not matter what he said. He would say something clever and comforting and untrue, as a white man would, and then she would go away alone.

Pierre said, "Don't be afraid. I'm going to take care of you, Liana." Liana stared at him, unbelieving.

He said it again. "I promise you," Pierre said, "don't be afraid."

Then Liana softened in his arms and hid her face against him and wept with relief and with gratitude. She could trust Pierre after all. She had misunderstood his silence and she was ashamed to have doubted him. Pierre would help her, she was not alone.

Over her head, Pierre saw the children trooping down the road under the pepper trees. It must be nearly one o'clock.

"Liana," Pierre said gently, and shook her away from him. He gave Liana his handkerchief and she buried her face in it, remembering how she looked now that her looks again had value. "You must go home, darling. The children are coming back; you won't want them to see you like this. I will talk to Marc tonight. Wait for me. Don't be afraid."

Liana nodded and wiped hard at her face, trying to scrub away the marks of misery. She wanted to smile but it was too soon; her face would not obey her. She could not recover so quickly, though it was all right now. Pierre would take care of everything. Trust in Pierre. Love Pierre who would not fail her.

The children were puzzled and excited to see Liana

(it had to be Liana; what other colored girl dressed that way?) stumbling across the school yard with a handkerchief held up to shield her face. They were also interested by the way Monsieur Vauclain behaved, forgetting to correct the recitations and allowing big pieces of silence to fall in the class when he called on no one. The best of all was when Monsieur Vauclain dismissed school a whole hour early. None of them had watches but they knew the time when school should be out as if unseen bells rang with beautiful clarity in each small head. The children left the building quietly but when they were outside the door this wonder of unexpected free time was too much for them, and they started to shout and swat at each other and chase their way across the yard through the trees. Pierre listened to them go.

He sat at his desk with his head in his hands and gave himself up to weariness. He did not let himself think of the sloop setting out at night for Anguilla and he in it dreaming of a war that would someday be won, that had to be won; dreaming of his own people fighting and winning. He did not let himself think of France. I tried to get something for nothing, Pierre thought, and no one can. The bill may be presented late, that is all. No force stopped him from hiring a fishing boat and leaving tonight without ever going to Marc's house. The fishing boats were small for that trip and Marc owned the only sloops and motor boats but it was not too dangerous to chance the crossing. He could still go, telling himself that it was more important to go. Whatever he owed Liana was less than what he owed other Frenchmen and his country. Only it wouldn't work. Pierre knew what he would become with that treachery in his mind; he did not think a dirty heart was proper baggage for such a journey.

Parents were supposed to be responsible for their children on the simple grounds that the children did not ask to be born. But surely no one ever asked to be *déraciné*. The whole world was struggling against that; all the uprooted people were struggling to have a home and live in it, to be part of a human world, to have identity and place and safety. He and Marc had overlooked a good deal when they assumed black could be white, and now they were responsible for one human being they had

208

made homeless. Marc was responsible too, even if he threatened and shouted adultery at them and tried to reduce this to a conventional scandal. Pierre would try to explain it to Marc and if Marc did not hide behind outraged vanity, they could discuss how to care for Liana together. Pierre knew Marc did not love Liana: there was no question of the heartsick husband who finds himself betrayed by a beloved wife.

Dismally and without much conviction, Pierre began to make a chart for himself. I do nothing but plan, he thought, but I am beginning to lose confidence in all my fine schemes. He and Liana would go to Martinique. Marc must let Liana stay in the house until then. They would try to leave quietly to avoid embarrassment for Marc. In Martinique they would find a place to live. (Here Pierre's heart turned cold inside him: the walls of that unknown house were gray concrete, the windows barred with steel.) Pierre's saved money would help now. Perhaps, later, if Pierre could find a companion or a friend for Liana so that she would not be as homeless and abandoned in Martinique as here, he could leave her there. No, Pierre told himself, stop trying to bore a hole in the wall; stop planning your escape so cheerfully in advance. Still it might work out like that. Martinique was closely governed and patrolled; to leave it would not be as easy as to leave Saint Boniface. The nearest English island was a sizable sea voyage away in whatever small inconspicuous boat he would be able to hire. There wouldn't be so much money to throw around either. But just possibly, he could get to St. Lucia. He'd send his pay to Liana. That made Pierre smile. His soldier's pay would perhaps buy her an egg a day. Liana could find work. What work was she trained for? Nothing, really. Liana was trained to be the wife of a rich man. She could only be a servant. All right, Liana can't work. Marc will have to help.

I'm still in Martinique, Pierre thought grimly, it's too soon to arrange for Marc to support Liana while I'm in the army. Better figure out how you will do the supporting in Martinique. Pierre could not imagine this: it exhausted and bored him to consider it. He would have a negro mistress, which wasn't exactly recommended for young schoolmasters, but still it happened in the islands and would probably pass. In the islands, Pierre thought, and remembered with a mixture of dismay and amusement the quiet professorial bourgeois world that he belonged in, in France. It would be hard to know who would suffer most there, Liana or the wives of the men he knew in his profession. That's impossible, Pierre thought, not France. But he was not in France, nor did he know if he ever would be, and he certainly did not know what would happen to his little world after this war. My mind jumps like a burned frog, Pierre told himself, try to think about Martinique. He might get away though, having provided for Liana in his absence, and come back to Martinique after the war was over.

Suddenly Pierre hit the desk with his fist, in rage. "Fool!" he shouted, "fool! fool!" The noise of his voice surprised and quieted him. Stop fiddling with your hopeful silly little plans, Pierre told himself. Only one thing is sure: you will take Liana to Martinique on the next boat. Think about the rest of it as it happens. Some of it might be great fun, as Liana was young and beautiful and loving and he cared for her very much. And on the other hand, it might be hell. But none of that mattered. He could not let Marc condemn Liana to the negro shack and the negro life. He could not let Liana be destroyed. He would go with Liana to Martinique, as there was no other place, because if he did not go a piece of rottenness would fester and spread inside him and he would not want to live with the smell of it.

If you just stopped saying the word "Martinique" to yourself, Pierre thought, you'd be better off.

Marc had said, "I thought you understood you were to leave this afternoon?"

Liana cowered away from him, keeping the bed between them, as if she expected Marc to beat her. Marc did not like this picture of himself as the man with the knout. He was uneasy before the animal fear in Liana's face.

"I couldn't," Liana whispered. "I didn't have time. I couldn't pack. There wasn't time."

This all embarrassed Marc a great deal; he became a monster simply by looking at Liana's eyes and hearing her voice. Marc had not meant to be cruel. It was just that he wanted to clean up this disorder as soon as possible and get on with his work in peace.

"All right," Marc said. "You can go tomorrow. I'll have Zela bring your dinner on a tray."

Liana locked the door, turning the key very slowly and holding her breath for fear Marc would hear her. Pierre had said tonight. Pierre would not be afraid of Marc; he would speak to Marc with his beautiful proud voice and tell Marc they were going away and then she would be free. She would not have to fear always that Marc would catch them and punish them. She would not have to live in terror of what Marc could do to Pierre and of the life Marc could always send her back to, the hated unlivable buried life. Liana remembered with horror the smell inside the shack, the hot greasy bodies of the children, the shallow latrine. She could see her family's life in its miserable unvaried detail: the cracked plates, the smoking kerosene lamps, the mud floor, the mosquitoes, the work in the fields, the valued filthy pigs, the ugliness of it, the living only to exist.

Pierre would come and she would be free. They would take their love to a new country and she would belong to Pierre and she would care for him day and night with all her heart and all her body. There was nothing to fear now and only a few hours to wait. Whatever Pierre said would be right because he was wise and faithful and she had no other thing to do now in life except love Pierre and serve him. Liana could not however stop her heart from pounding in her chest; she could not sit quietly and wait as she should. To be in the same house with Marc frightened her and if for a moment she stopped thinking of Pierre's strength she was frightened for Pierre because Marc was wily and violent and perhaps he would hurt Pierre. She should have warned Pierre this afternoon.

Liana sat on the floor close to the crack of her door to listen. As soon as Pierre came she would go downstairs to be with him when he talked to Marc so that she could warn Pierre if she saw that Marc was dangerous. Pierre did not know Marc; he would not be able to see the signs for himself.

When was tonight exactly? The time would not pass; the sunset stayed in the sky and the sun would not drop into the sea. Pierre perhaps meant that he would come after dinner, yes of course that was it. Pierre did not want to eat with Marc; he could not very well accept Marc's food now; and since they would have to talk a long while Pierre would not want to come before dinner. Perhaps Pierre thought it better to wait until the servants went to their own quarters so they would not be listening at the pantry door as they always did. Liana began to wait for darkness. She had never seen such a slow sun.

When Zela knocked on her door Liana said she wanted nothing. Soon now, Liana thought, now Marc will be eating in the dining-room with the light pouring down from the chandelier. In that lovely unknown house in Martinique, where Pierre and she would live, they would always eat by candlelight. Martinique, Liana thought, caressing the word. She had never been away from this island. What could be luckier than to take their love to a beautiful new country?

Liana heard Pierre coming before he reached the terrace. Marc heard too as he was expecting Pierre. Liana unlocked her door and walked quietly out to the stairs. Marc called, without turning around, "Go back to your room and stay there, Liana." She had to obey. This was terrible. Pierre would be alone with Marc, with no one to warn him. She had a right to share in their talk; it was her life too and Pierre was hers and she must take care of him. Liana undid her slippers and turned off the light in her room and opened her door a few inches so that she could hear Marc. When she heard him cross the lower room to unlatch the screen for Pierre, Liana ran silently down the hall and down the back stairs and out the back door.

The moon was bright and Liana could see easily but she tested the ground before she let her weight down on her feet. She was breathlessly afraid Marc would hear and order her back to her room again and she had to be near Pierre; she could judge from Marc's voice alone what Marc would do. Liana turned the corner of the house, moving slowly and without sound, and pressing to the sidewall she crept toward the window by the radio. She could hear the men's voices there and she guessed they would sit in the chairs they were used to, on either side of the radio, with the heavy fringed lamp standing beside them and making a hard circle of uncomfortable yellow light over their faces and the chairs and the tea wagon that Marc used as a movable drink tray. Slowly, Liana warned herself. She flattened herself against the wall, and fearing that if she had to stand a long time she would move and make noise, she squatted very cautiously on the damp earth of the flower bed. Liana was directly beneath the window and she could hear as well as if she had been in the room. Now Marc could do nothing sudden and murderous against Pierre. She would be able to stand and shout at Pierre if she thought Pierre was in danger.

Liana had missed the beginning.

"Bonsoir," Marc said. Pierre did not expect this easy cordial voice. He had not foreseen Marc would be so ready for him, so calm and with a sly kind of amusement behind his eyes. Pierre wondered suddenly how he looked. He was afraid his face was too stern, too determined, or fierce or strained. He regretted his nervousness on the long walk from town. It seemed ridiculous now to have steeled himself for this meeting, with Marc's voice and face so pleasant in greeting. It was like steeling yourself for manœuvres in which the ammunition is not loaded.

"Will you have a drink?" Marc said.

"Yes, please."

"I think we need it, eh?" This was incredible. Pierre stared at Marc. Marc is acting as if we were two boys who have been caught out in some minor scandal by their families: conspirators, pals.

Pierre drank too much of his drink, recognizing his own nerves by the way he emptied half the glass without stopping. When he looked at Marc again there was in Marc's eyes that same speculative amusement. Suddenly Marc realized that he was upsetting Pierre and he changed his manner and grew serious but still perfectly amiable.

"Well," Marc said, "this is all very awkward. (What a word, Pierre thought.) But I am sure we can work it out."

"I hope so."

"What are your plans?" Marc enquired. It sounded so

213

odd that Pierre almost laughed. What are your plans? Are you going to Mont-Dore or to Hyères this summer; are you leasing that flat on the Rue Monsieur or have you decided to stay there in the old one on the Rue de Varenne? I must pull myself together, Pierre thought.

"Marc," Pierre began, and the old training of the lycée reasserted itself. Given and to prove: one, two, three, with subheadings. "We won't talk about what has happened unless you want to. I take it that you know."

Marc nodded. In his eyes now there was a sudden darkening of pain as if something in his body ached briefly. This was the part Marc would be glad to forget: this was the part that he could not work out in his mind entirely. He would ignore it, believe what he wanted to believe, and blame no one. Pierre had not valued him enough to tell him the truth, and Pierre was capable of trickery. It was best to forget it. Probably Liana made Pierre keep quiet, Marc thought.

"I will only say," Pierre put in stiffly, "that I am sorry not to have told you myself. But," Pierre wondered at his recklessness. There was no use provoking Marc. What vanity forced him always to clarify his own moral position? "I did not believe you would care too deeply in any case. I assume, Marc, that you do not love Liana. Forgive me for speaking of it but it is necessary to know, as I wish to take Liana away with me."

So, Marc thought. Pierre behaves exactly as I imagined. Now it begins. It will take me all night to make Pierre see how silly this is, without offending him. I'll have to be cautious about it or he'll get angry and rush off with Liana just to show me what a fine man he is. Marc thought that Pierre was being a fool and it irritated him very much. I don't know why I bother, Marc thought, let them do any idiot damn thing they wish. But then Marc calmed his irritation and remembered who Pierre was and what he thought of Pierre and how he knew Pierre was worth saving. He remembered that Pierre and this island and France were all somehow part of the same thing.

"I hoped to be able to discuss it with you," Pierre said uncertainly.

"But of course, Pierre. We'll discuss it. You want to go away with Liana. You are a young man, thirty or so

aren't you? Military age anyhow. I imagined you would
be wanting to go away but I thought you would want to
go back to Europe. There's an army again; they'll form
some sort of reasonable government outside of France.
There's everything except the country. I imagined you
would want to help get the country back. Since it is your
country and I know that you love it."

"Naturally I want to go back. You don't have to talk
to me about military age and tell me my duty."

"You said however that you were going away with
Liana."

"The situation changed," Pierre said coldly.

He means I found out, Marc thought, but how exactly
does that change the situation? What has Liana got to do
with his going back to Europe now, since he didn't
think of her before?

"Have another drink," Marc said. Let's get tight, he
thought, and pour out our woes on each other and have
a fine time. This has got to be settled tonight. If I know
us, we'd never be able to talk about it again. We'd get
embarrassed or bad tempered or we'd start being roost-
ers. You can't expect men to forget forever that they
used the same woman even if the woman doesn't matter
to one of them.

"As a matter of fact," Pierre remarked, "I was coming to see you in your office this afternoon about it. Not
about this. I mean, I was coming to talk about leaving
here. I decided definitely a few days ago that I wanted
to get back in the army."

The ball-up at Mateur, Marc thought briefly, that
decided Pierre. We're a slow moving pair, we are; I need
a blockade and he needs another defeat, but we do move
at last.

"Why didn't you come?"

Pierre ignored this. It had become absurdly difficult
to speak of Liana and himself. Marc seemed so uninter-
ested; it was almost rude to bring it up, like annoying a
stranger with intimate family problems.

"You see," Pierre went on, "I thought you'd help me
with a boat. I planned to go to Anguilla but it's a pretty
long run for one of those fishing skiffs. I thought maybe
you'd let me hire your sloop, that thirty footer *Louise*.
If I can get to Anguilla, the English will have to send me

on. It's a long haul of course from Anguilla to England or wherever they train now, but once you start you take it however it comes."

"I'll lend you the motor boat," Marc said. "It's much easier. That way you know exactly how long the run takes. The wind is uncertain now and weak at night; you might be flapping around within sight of Anguilla all day. I haven't any idea what the regulations are but everything's such a stinking mess in these waters that the best is to get to Anguilla in the dark and simply show up at the Resident's office in the morning."

"You would?" Pierre said eagerly.

"Certainly. Won't cost you a sou either. You can make it in five hours easily in the motor boat. They can pole her out of the harbor here at night so the gendarmes won't get excited hearing the motor. Not that I think those men would get out of bed for murder. But you can do that, and run in the dark. Macon knows the channel perfectly. He'll drop you close to the beach so he can turn her and get out in a hurry if those patriotic English negroes think they ought to seize the boat for their King. You can wade in. From then on it's up to the English."

"That's perfect," Pierre said. "That's even better than I'd thought."

They drank in silence. That was easy, Marc thought, too easy.

"Thank you very much, Marc," Pierre said warmly, "I appreciate the offer. I can't tell you how gratefully I'd have accepted it yesterday. But things have changed now. I won't be able to go as I'd planned. We'll be leaving for Martinique on the next boat and that's what I've got to talk to you about."

Here we go again, Marc told himself, now be patient. Anyone can see the man is crazy to get back to his army. This other stuff is just muck and can be arranged. It oughtn't to interfere with the work a man has to do in his life, nor a man's need to take care of his country.

"Let's talk about it," Marc agreed. "You want to take Liana to Martinique. What are you going to do there?"

"The first thing is about Liana now. I don't know exactly when the schooner arrives from Martinique. I will promise not to see Liana if that suits you; but I want

216

you to let Liana stay here in the house until the boat comes. I'll arrange the passage without mentioning names and Liana can come on board at the last minute. There won't be any talk; we'll be careful. But between now and when the boat sails Liana has to have a place to stay. She can't go up country to her mother."

Marc said nothing and Pierre took his silence for obstinacy and refusal. Pierre leaned forward and said, "Listen Marc, as far as I'm concerned you have a right to shoot me if you feel that way. You can be as angry as you like and we can do anything you damn please about honor. But it's different for Liana. She's your responsibility too. You took her out of that shack in the first place. You took her away from her own people; you did that six years ago. For six years you've accustomed her to the life of a white woman. It's even better than the lives most white women have here. You've trained her to live your sort of a life, on a comfortable basis of being clean. You cannot ship her back to one of those rotten negro shacks and expect her to be a negro again. You can't play God and then disown what you made."

"I wonder," Marc said. But he was remembering Lucie's shack and he was thinking how he hated all those shacks and always tried to avoid going inside them. Marc remembered Liana's face when she came back the last time from that filth and how he had known Liana would always obey him because she feared to return to that life as much as he would have feared it. And it was true: he had picked Liana out, she hadn't asked for it. She hadn't asked to be his mistress or his wife; now that he remembered, Liana had never asked for anything. She took what he gave and she had learned how to use it. Marc remembered too, with sudden and surprised pity, how Liana practiced when they were first married to be a white lady.

I'm not mean, Marc thought defensively, there's a lot wrong with me but I'm not mean. I'll have to find something else to do with Liana so she can live decently anyhow.

"You wonder?" Pierre said, angered by Marc's silence. "How can you? You've used Liana exactly as it suited you all along. Now it doesn't suit you and you kick her out. You never loved her but that's your own

217

business. Only you have some kind of obligation to her, or don't you accept that idea?"

"Do you love her?" Marc asked suddenly.

The light shone blindingly in Pierre's eyes. His shirt was sticking to his back though the night was cool. It must be the whiskey or nerves or all this welter of feeling that had made the day hideous. If Marc won't let Liana stay here I will take her in town with me, Pierre thought, and it will be a jolly little scandal and make a noise that will bore us to death.

"I care for Liana very much," Pierre said. "She's good. She has been generous and good to me. And I know what she fears. It can't be too easy to be one of a kind, anywhere in the world, but specially not on a little island like this. And I understand how she feels about going back to that squalid negro life. I helped take her out of it too. It doesn't make any difference whether I love her or not," Pierre said warily. "I only know I can't leave her in this mess and live with myself, in case you can understand that."

"Mon vieux, I understand you," Marc said gently. Marc was wishing that he had ever been Pierre's age, with Pierre's conceited and touching and fervent judgments on right and wrong, and that he had found a woman to spend all that feeling on. Pierre was young and he would find one of his own people, a woman who came from the same country (the same passionate Calvinist country of the heart). Pierre would put on a little weight when his conscience did not have to turn like a dynamo twenty-four hours a day. The woman Pierre would find would take some of the burden of that conscience from him. Marc was very sorry for Pierre. It did not seem so bad to be forty-six and unencumbered, with the illusions stored away like old fashioned, worn out clothes.

"What will you do in Martinique?" Marc asked.

"I don't know. I've saved a little money. I thought later, after we get settled, I might try to go home to the army from there and then I'd come back to Liana after the war."

"You'd come back to Martinique?"

"Well, yes."

"You won't do that, Pierre."

"That's my affair. All I want is to know you will keep Liana here until the boat sails."

"What will Liana live on while you're in the army, providing you could get there?"

"Name of God, I don't know," Pierre said impatiently. "I don't know. I haven't planned. I'd never thought of this; I don't know how it will work out. I was just as *crapuleux* as you."

Unexpectedly and to their mutual and almost shocked surprise, they smiled at each other.

"I was," Pierre insisted. "I never thought beyond the day. I was happy and Liana was happy and I didn't think. And now I don't know, but we'll manage somehow. I had no right to live from day to day. It was fine for me but there's Liana too."

"You know you can't take Liana to France?"

"Leave it, Marc. I don't see that we have to go into that."

"You do know?"

"Yes," Pierre said fiercely.

"It won't work, Pierre."

Pierre leaned back in his chair. He wiped his arm across his forehead. Sweat was running off him like rain. He was exhausted now: perhaps there really was no argument with Marc and he had been arguing all evening with himself. Marc certainly had none of the feelings you might expect. Marc seemed to forget that Liana and Pierre were lovers and he was the abused husband. Marc was very far away from this; Pierre was the one spinning and whirling in it, flailing with his mind, spinning round and round and getting dizzy and confused and despairing.

"Please give me another drink," Pierre said.

Marc poured the whiskey. "It won't work, Pierre," he said, handing Pierre his glass. "You know that. It won't work for either of you."

"All right," Pierre said. "It won't work." He was too tired. I never thought it would work, Pierre reminded himself, nothing has changed. "I still can't go off and leave Liana in a mess."

"But we can fix that. There doesn't have to be a mess."

Pierre thought: I hope this isn't something new. I

219

hope we don't have to start a whole new argument that will move slowly in a circle toward an ever-diminishing point. I'm too tired. No one wants this much personal life.

"It's like this," Marc said. How cool he looks, Pierre thought, and I am soggy with sweat. "You want to get back to the army and you should; that's where you belong. You can't live in these islands and Liana can't live with you in France. You care very much for Liana and you wouldn't want to do anything dirty to her; so you decide to go away with her. It will be a hardship because you won't be able to provide for her properly, at least not for some time. If you give up France for Liana, you will gradually take that out on her. Don't argue," Marc said. "For Christ's sake, be a realist for once. But you are not willing to see Liana miserable. You mean, really, that you don't want her to live like a negro again. And I say: she won't. That's all. I guarantee it. Liana will stay here until I can build a house for her, a good house that you would be contented to live in yourself; with servants and all the other things I have accustomed her to, as you say. I'll give her money every month; plenty of money. She won't have to do anything for that money. It will be as marvellous as that American system of alimony which always seemed to me the easiest way to earn a living I ever heard of. She will be free, well-off and her own mistress. She can do anything she likes, not that there is much to do here. But that was true even before you came. And you go back to Europe and get on with your work. What a pair of splendid sensible men we are. Eh, Pierre? How about it?"

"The way you tell it, it sounds so wonderful I wish I were Liana. I don't know, Marc. I'll have to ask Liana. I'll talk to her tomorrow."

"Bon," Marc said. But he knew it was all right. It was arranged. I'm not mean, that's one thing, Marc thought. I don't have to be and I wouldn't be. That's a thing I can't stand, meanness.

Pierre's eyes were circled with black and he felt a chill through his shoulders as the sweaty shirt dried in the cool night air. He was almost ill with tiredness and the strain of the day, in which he had twice decided to

220

leave the island but in different directions and for different purposes.

"I'm a little drunk I think," Pierre said. "Anyhow I've got to sleep. Good night, Marc."

"Good night, Pierre. Women always make things into tragedies, but it isn't true. And we've got our work to think of."

Marc latched the screen behind Pierre and stood watching him disappear down the drive. I hope he doesn't get fever so he can't leave, Marc thought, he looks pretty bad tonight. Marc was tired too but he felt certain of himself and relieved that this evening was well over. Everybody's life was snarled in stupid knots and he undid the knots, the ones he had made and theirs. Soon they could forget this disorder and busy themselves doing something that showed results.

CHAPTER TWENTY

The lamp had been turned off and the first floor was dark. Moths stuck to the screen, purposeless now that the calling light was gone, or fluttered off into the moonlight. In the ground beneath her the hurrying life of the warm earth went on. She could feel ants cross her bare leg; it felt like a blade of fine grass stroked over the skin. The night bird who lived somewhere in the bamboo brake screamed with that furious unexpected voice. The moon rode clean in the sky, with no clouds around it. The grass seemed covered by frost in its whiteness and the trees were solid, soft and black and cast a black shadow.

Marc moved in his room and then in his bathroom and suddenly his light went out. The house was in darkness. There was no noise anywhere. The wind had fallen so that the trees stood still.

Liana sat with her back pressed to the wall of the house. She could feel the ridges of the board, hard against bone. There had been no need to warn Pierre. There was no need to shout a warning and run to help

221

him; if she could have moved, she would have run with all her strength to escape their voices and their words. Pierre was in no danger. They were two white men and they understood each other. They agreed on everything; their voices never sharpened in anger. Marc was not the enemy, he was the friend. He was Pierre's friend. They had nothing to quarrel about, only Liana. They were two white men: why should they quarrel over a negro girl?

It doesn't make any difference whether I love her or not. It doesn't make any difference whether I love her or not. The words had no voice in Liana's mind: they ground themselves out slowly, each word separate from the next, and made a flat whirring sound that a machine could make, turning and turning.

Pierre has taken care of me, Liana thought. He promised. Do not be afraid, I'll take care of you. She would not be sent up the hill track to live in poverty with her family; she would not be sent away where her heart would sicken for Pierre and her eyes would see only the path through the forest that led back to him. Marc would build her a fine house and she could live there, comfortable and safe, and her heart would sicken for nothing since her heart was empty and her eyes would watch no.path, no road, no sea, since no one was coming for her from any direction. Pierre had not promised to love her but only to take care of her. It was so easy: a few words between friends and instead of a filthy evil-smelling shack you had a new made-to-order house. It would be a fine cold house to live in all alone.

Pierre had never loved her. The two white men did not find this strange; they did not stop to mention it. It seemed natural to the two white men that neither of them loved a negro girl. They did not ask whether she loved Pierre. Pierre would not leave her in a mess, he said. He meant he would not leave her in a one-room shack where she had to sleep in the same bed with her mother and Antoinette, who had never taken a proper hot bath in their lives. That was a mess. Pierre could leave her in a house that had a tiled bathroom. That was not a mess. Pierre had been planning to leave for days though he had not spoken of it. The night he carried her upstairs in his arms, Pierre was planning to leave her. How Pierre must have hated her when she came to the school house and spoiled his plans; she imagining that Pierre loved her, she believing he would not want a life without her any more than she wanted a life without him. Pierre had not suffered long; only from noon to night. He talked with his friend, the two white men together, and there was no reason for Pierre to torment himself now. His plans held. Pierre could go. He was not leaving Liana in a mess. She had a cold house now and the promise of another cold house. What could a woman want more than two houses?

Then suddenly Liana imagined the other house, the one in Martinique where they would take their love and eat by candlelight and where she would have no other thing to do but serve Pierre and love him. Liana bowed her head on her knees and wept for the shining warm lovely house that she would not have, and for the beautiful new country, and for Pierre who never wanted to go to that country and live with her in that house.

Liana rose with her back hurting and held herself very straight, making no concession to this little pain. She walked quietly from pride. Marc must not know she had heard their talk and Marc must not see her. She had now only her pride to strengthen her and she did not name it nor recognize it. Liana thought: Marc will not see the light by my bed. I can write there. She had things to do at once, tonight, quickly. When she had done what she must do she would have time to cry and perhaps that would help the dry pain in her eyes, and her dry throat and this sickness that ached in her body.

Liana had never written a letter. She had no letterpaper and realizing this she felt suddenly terrified and defenseless. She had to write a letter. This letter was the last thing she could do to help herself. She would send the letter with Théodore and then Pierre would not come to her. And there was no paper to write it on. Because of this, she must suffer more than she knew how to suffer. She could not see Pierre and hear him, the false gentle unloving words, his eyes that would pity her and deep inside them the gladness of leaving.

There were the notebooks. Liana found the one in which she had drawn laborious sketches of the fish they saw in the reef. She did not look at the pictures. Liana took the paper-covered book to her bed and started to cut out a clean page with her nail scissors. She did this neatly, trying not to let the scissors curve down and scallop the edge of the paper. She moved her bedside table so that it made a desk and brought a pen and ink and placed these things in order on the narrow glass top of the table. It was serious enough to write a letter when you had never written one before and would never write one again; she must write it perfectly, with every word properly spelled and every accent in place, and she must find the right words.

Now that the table was ready, Liana could not think what to write. She could not say: don't come to see me tomorrow, I know you are going, go then, but do not hurt me with your face and your voice. Leave me alone since you have left me entirely. She did not want Pierre's pity: she did not want him to read her letter and come to comfort her, as if he could ever comfort her again.

Liana drew rather than wrote the words. She spoke each phrase softly aloud before she wrote it, and in her mind she checked the spelling. The ruled cheap paper did not look well but if she wrote a fine hand and fine exact words it would look well enough.

"Dear Pierre;
I have reflected on our problem. (*Bien réflechi?* she thought, would that be better?) *Marc has made me a good offer. I will be independent. It would be difficult for us both to live on your salary and I have no profession.* (A stenographer, Liana thought, explaining it to herself, or working in a store.) *Naturally Marc would not make me this offer if we continued.* (Continued? Liana thought. What did Pierre have to continue?) *I think then that it would be wiser if you left the island alone. I am sure you will always succeed but it would be hard for me to live anywhere else and I will be well taken care of here. Please do not come to see me, for any reason.* (Liana underlined this, with a straight firm line of dark blue ink.) *I do not wish Marc to have an excuse to change his offer. Thank you very much for everything.* (Thank you for the months when I believed you loved

me, Liana thought, thank you for the house you arranged to leave me.) *Good luck on your travels.*

Your friend,
Liana.

Liana read it over. As far as she could see there were no mistakes. There was nothing Pierre could pity. She was as cold as he was. I lived from day to day, Pierre said. Let him think she lived from day to day too; and the days had changed. Let Pierre think she too had her plans.

There was no envelope either but there was the glue she had used to fix her butterfly collection. Liana folded the page and glued down the loose end, lightly, so that the paste would not soak through and tear the paper when Pierre came to open her only letter. She addressed it neatly, in discreet small letters, and put it on her dressing table. There was nothing more to do now except tidy the room and undress and lie on the bed and wait for morning when Théodore could carry the letter to town.

Liana undressed and put away her clothes. She washed as carefully as she did every night and brushed her hair fifty strokes. She began to rub a lotion on her hands, and stopped and looked at the pretty glass bottle with its frivolous painted paper band and said to herself: what am I doing this for? What's the use of this?

She lay on her bed with her eyes open and the room glowed in the moonlight. If Liana looked at the room she would have to remember Pierre in it, Pierre and she in it together. She could not keep her eyes closed so she stared at the ceiling which was like staring at a flat windowless wall. The night went on, shining and quiet, with no wind.

In all her memory now there was nothing Liana could think of without pain. Even long ago, before she had known Marc or Pierre, was hurting to remember; the careless and uncertain, not unhappy, poor life of a negro child stayed like a sin in the past; she could never escape it. Because she had been such a child, she was now this woman who belonged nowhere. Belonged nowhere and had no place to go, except to a cold fine house that would be built for her like an asylum or a prison or a tomb. If her mind moved backwards a week or ten years it found no safe place to rest. I won't think, Liana decided. But if you could not sleep, how could you make your mind black and still?

Slowly, in trying to escape from everything she knew, Liana began to think ahead to what she did not know. But she could not think of the house Marc would build and herself frozen inside it. Without wanting to, and with a kind of tired softness, Liana started to imagine the house in Martinique. It would be on a street that climbed a hill and from the hill they would see other houses, roofs and the sea. There would be a terrace all round the first floor to keep the rooms shady and cool, and the terrace would rest on slender white pillars which rose to hold the balcony. Everything would be so clean that it shone like silver because she would have cleaned it. Perhaps the house would be painted pink. Wisteria and white bell flower would hang like fringe around the pillars and from the railings of the terrace and balcony. The house would look very small and bright when you came up the hill toward it; it would always look as if there had just been a light spring rain to wash it. She would be inside waiting at sunset, never tired or cross or wearing a hot soiled dress the way some wives did. She would be as fresh as the house and she would wait behind the wisteria perhaps, until Pierre came up the hill, and when he opened the gate she would stand on the front steps to welcome him. His eyes would be eager and loving and he would say, "Bonsoir, ma petite," in that quiet voice, his voice, his voice that was more beautiful than anyone's.

But Pierre would never come and never say, Bonsoir, ma petite and there was no house. She would not wash the windows and sing in the kitchen because there was no house. There would never be a sunset when Pierre climbed the hill to that home. The time will pass, Liana thought. Do not think at all and the time will pass. But it would not pass; each hour would be the same in every day, in every month: each year would be the same. She was twenty-two and there were innumerable years still to come, but the time would not pass. There was nothing to mark the time or drive it on, there was nothing to wait for, there was no use for the years. The time would never pass.

"Oh, Pierre!" Liana said and pressed her mouth against the pillow to hush the sound. "Oh, Pierre, Pierre." But she could not cry. She held the pillow against her, sinking her hands into it, crushing it against her face and her breast. In this aching screaming loneliness it was better to hold a thing than to lie empty-armed.

Marc sent his colored clerk to buy beer. Marc knew there was no beer on the island, and he presumed the clerk knew, but the clerk would walk obediently to Drieu's café and the other little café that was only a closet open on the street and to the two grocery stores. The clerk might even try the hotel since the weather was cool and walking was no effort. When the clerk left, he and Pierre had the office to themselves and could talk.

In the winter the office was a little too cave-like and chill for comfort. The thick stone walls, which supported the wooden house above it, closed out all light; only the wide doors let in air and the pleasant December sun. Marc's desk was a scarred ugly roller-top, badly varnished and not too neat. A mass of papers on a man's desk showed that the man had many irons in the fire and was struggling contentedly against a weight of pressing business. Only failures had ordered, empty desks. Pierre had pushed through the swinging door that opened in the waist-high railing which separated Marc's so-called private office from the rest of the dark stony room. Pierre sat on a straight chair, whose wicker bottom was torn, and waited until the clerk disappeared into the outer sun.

The two men smiled at each other with false embarrassed smiles and shook hands quickly as convention demanded when doing business. Marc had known they would both be shy today and not too friendly. But their business was brief; Marc had already seen Macon and need only give Pierre instructions. This was the end of whatever had been between them. There had really been nothing between them except an idea and a hope of Marc's and Pierre's grudging, reluctant, slow-growing sympathy. It was a pity, Marc thought, that in all this

227

time they had never really met each other. There were no other men on the island for either of them, but they had never found the way to be friends.

"I've seen Macon," Marc said. "He is filling the tank now. The crew will come to the harbor tonight a little before eleven. You won't have much luggage?"

"No."

"You should bring it down yourself quietly at eleven. Macon wants to get off then. He thinks it may take six hours to reach Anguilla, which would get you there around five. That's a good time. All right?"

"Fine."

"Macon says you better take some provisions; some rum maybe for the trip and a few cans of things. He hears they are badly off on Anguilla and if you have to wait around a couple of days while those negroes make up their minds or find a way to send you on to Tortola, you'll be glad of your own food."

"I'll see to that."

"A blanket too, perhaps."

"Yes."

"I won't come down to see you off; no sense in having anyone hear my car. The less fuss the better."

"Parfaitement."

Marc had decided to talk as if Pierre was certain to leave the island. He did not know, when he began, what Pierre's choice was. Marc thought Pierre might interrupt him and argue and he was ready to bring out all the reasons Pierre had for going home to his army. If Pierre insisted on wasting his life for a woman, which was the emptiest waste of all, Marc would have accepted that, feeling that he had done what he could and was not going to use any more of his own time meddling with another man's fate. Though Marc hoped very much that Pierre would decide to go home because he believed anything else would be cowardly and indecent.

A man had a right to waste his life in the fat years, if he wanted to be such a fool, but not in the lean years. A man had to work now: it was not honorable to squander your brain and your arms when all were needed. Each man in his own country had to do the work. It was important work too, because they had to settle something. They had to see that these idiot dis-

228

asters would not be shoved off on innocent law-abiding people again. If men like Pierre and himself did not do the work now, the crooks would take hold again and mismanage the world as they had before. Marc believed that he and Pierre were average men; it was the average men who would have to run the world if it was to be sane, not these strange remote creatures who spoke on the radio, got their pictures in the papers, rushed about the globe bossing and babbling and had no real life anywhere, nothing to do with real people, and no roots. It was the men with honest roots in every country, the men who knew how all the other average men had to live, who must work now to save the present and make the future.

Marc was pleased to believe that Pierre reasoned as he did and was too intelligent to waste words discussing it. But he wished that Pierre looked a little tougher and more cheerful. Pierre's eyes were still circled with black, his face looked very thin, and he kept locking his teeth together silently so that a muscle jumped in his cheek. Pierre was awfully grim about doing something that was a good thing to do, and Marc hoped that by a miracle the clerk would find beer and they could drink some kind of jolly toast to the journey and to the work ahead. The work, as Marc saw it, was a fine challenge and release for all a man's energies and the work could not fail. Marc thought he would have been a great deal happier than Pierre looked, if he were starting home.

Then Marc remembered Liana. He had not entirely forgotten her or at least he had not forgotten his promise to Pierre nor his own dislike of being mean. That morning Marc had studied the rough land map of his properties and fixed on a place some way down the road from his house where he owned a little hill and a patch of ten acres around it. The land was too hilly to cultivate and thorn covered it so it was useless for grazing. There was a fine view from the hill, as Marc remembered, and ten acres was plenty of land for a small farm if Liana wanted to amuse herself that way. Marie ran a farm and it evidently kept her busy. That morning Marc instructed his clerk to hire eight men to start clearing the land. It was not going to be easy to get building materials these days but the black market always worked and Marc would send Macon to Guadeloupe later on, in the forty-ton schooner, and Macon could probably locate whatever was needed. They would build the main frame of the house with local woods. With luck they might make a house for Liana in three months.

Marc had spoken to Liana before coming in town. He told her that she was to stay in his house until a new one was built for her, and seeing Liana's face, he had added pleasantly that she remained the mistress of the house as before and could eat her meals alone or with him as she saw fit. He wasn't going to be mean about this. Marc could afford to be kind since he found he really did not care at all, it was like having a visitor whom you did not know well and did not intend to know but to whom you would be perfectly cordial while the visit lasted.

Pierre sat on the straight chair in silence, not as if he still had something to say and was waiting for a chance to say it, but as if he could not remember what had been said and that everything was settled and he should go. The muscle jumped in his cheek and his eyes were not only circled in black, they were bitter and sad.

"Perhaps that negro will find us some beer," Marc said amiably. "He's been gone long enough."

Pierre said nothing.

"Have you seen Liana?" Marc asked. His voice was casual. He wanted to make sure there would be no late change in their plans and he also wanted to know what to expect at home.

"No."

Oh, *crotte,* Marc thought, now there is all that to go through.

"She sent me a note," Pierre said. His eyes really looked very strange. "She does not want to see me."

"Oh?"

"It appears Liana was delighted by your offer of a new house," Pierre said. "She doesn't want to see me for fear you'll change your mind. She doesn't want any trouble, apparently. It is clear," Pierre said stiffly, not looking at Marc, with the sad bitter eyes staring at a rather dirty calendar on the wall behind Marc, "that I somewhat exaggerated things in my mind."

What disgusting cheap grasping bitches women are, Marc thought furiously, and was hurt for Pierre. Not that I didn't always know it, Marc told himself untruthfully, they have nothing in their hearts, there's no use expecting it of them. But what a way to treat Pierre now when he's leaving. Just send a note and say I'm getting a new house and that's what matters to me so I don't want any complications with you. Marc was appalled by the mercenary cruelty of this. No wonder Pierre looks so awful, Marc thought. Pierre was willing to ruin his whole life for her, go to Martinique and spend the rest of his poor bloody life taking care of her: and Liana doesn't give a damn about anything except getting herself comfortably fixed.

Marc could not speak for indignation at this further proof that you wasted your life on women and got nothing except shoddy heartlessness in return. And he was sad for Pierre and wanted to say something to help Pierre. Then suddenly Marc thought, I am absolutely ridiculous. The next thing I'll be crying over Pierre because my wife mistreats her lover. No really, Marc thought, let's get finished with all this god-damned nonsense.

Marc spoke more gruffly than he intended. "There's nothing more to arrange, Pierre. I have some work to do now. You'll be at the harbor at eleven then? Bon voyage. I hope you get back to Europe quickly."

He stood up and Pierre rose awkwardly, having just remembered that he should not go on sitting here all afternoon with his hurt and his disillusionment numbing him.

"I can't thank you Marc."

"Don't talk about it."

"Good-bye, Marc. Good luck with the island."

They shook hands well this time and for one moment they looked at each other like friends.

Pierre walked down the street simply to get out of Marc's sight but he did not know where to go. There was nothing to do except wait for night. Well, he could buy some tins of food. That would take up a little time. And then he could read. He had always told himself Liana was a child. What did you expect of children: they were not supposed to be other than themselves.

231

They naturally wanted safety and the known thing; no wonder Liana was happy to see her life provided for and sure. No wonder. It was better this way. Did he prefer to have her suffer; was he so selfish that he would rather leave Liana broken-hearted and miserable and lonely?

Pierre walked down the sunny street and sat on the sea wall at the harbor. A steady wind blew from the east and the waves bounced in neat white-capped rows over the deep blue-black of the water. The breakers foaming in against the sea wall made a regular comforting sound. It would be pleasant to stretch out here in the sun and let that steady slow beat lull him to sleep.

I didn't want Liana to suffer, Pierre thought. Why are you so unhappy then? What did you want? You can't have it both ways. I wanted her to miss me, Pierre decided; I didn't want it to hurt her, but I wanted her to think of me and remember and love me without having it hurt her. You wanted a lot for yourself, didn't you, he jeered. Yes, Pierre thought soberly, I wanted a lot; I wanted insurance, I wanted someone who cared what happened to me. I didn't want to go away really alone. Stop feeling sorry for yourself, Pierre told himself, you were expecting to hurt Liana and you find you are the one who is hurt and it's much better that way. You know she's all right and you won't have to worry and you travel very light now.

For the promise of a house, Pierre thought, she forgot at once everything, everything. It hurt badly; there was no use denying it. It hurt too badly.

I'll go to see her, Pierre thought. I can't leave it like this; it's such a miserable way to end. It makes everything that went before pointless and untrue. But it wasn't untrue; it wasn't for me. And surely Liana couldn't make her eyes lie, her voice, the shape of her face, the very way she walked. God knows I don't blame her, Pierre thought, I wasn't offering her anything; but not to end like this. Liana has to feel this way now; she's afraid. She has to grasp at Marc's offer because it's the only safety. But why such a cold, hostile grasping?

Then Pierre thought, I wasn't too marvellous to her when she came for help to the school house. I wasn't marvellous at all. I thought I made it all right but obviously I didn't. That would hurt Liana enough to make her write such a letter. Or perhaps the letter was protection for her pride: perhaps when she truly considered their going to Martinique Liana was forced to accept the fact of her color, and she had known how little chance they had of making a happy life together. How little chance there is now, Pierre amended. He mistrusted the word *now*. When would *now* stop, when would *now* be any different? *Now* was the tricky word, the slippery word, the word he could not quite manage.

I was offering Liana nothing, Pierre thought again, if I saw her I could only say: good-bye; take Marc's fine new house. Oh Christ, Pierre said to himself furiously, despairingly, what do I want? What shall I do? Liana could only have written that letter when she was hurt, and I am well hurt too, but perhaps that is the easiest way for us. I can't think at all, Pierre told himself, I don't know what to do. I don't want to do anything. I don't want to think.

Pierre took off his shirt and wadded it into a pillow, put it under his head, stretched out on the gray stone wall and closed his eyes against the glare. He had not slept last night, trying all night long to imagine some way to tell Liana that he was leaving alone. Pierre was not even sure, at dawn, that he could tell Liana, though he knew it was the only thing to do. If ever they could make a life together, they could certainly not do it now. Pierre had compromised finally by deciding to tell Liana he would come back next year, in two years, whenever the war was over and they could then choose freely what they wanted to do. It was a waste of sleep since it had not been necessary to tell Liana anything. Théodore brought Liana's note while Pierre was eating breakfast.

The sun was warm on his chest and his face; it loosened the muscles in his body and softened the hard weariness and the hurt in his mind. Pierre knew he could not think his way out of this sadness; it would have to wear off with time. He must neither fight it nor feed on it; he must leave it alone and let it wear away as the wood of the pier wore away in the sea. And he was very tired and the sun was good and sleep was the loveliest, the best, the alluring escape.

CHAPTER TWENTY-ONE

Liana looked at the pretty bottles and jars on her dressing table and thought: I don't need them any more. She had started to brush her hair but it tired her and besides what was the use. What difference whether her hair shone or not? Liana stood uncertainly in her room and did not know where to go in it: one chair was as good as another if you had nothing to do but sit and wait. Wait for the time to pass. Know that the time will not pass. Know that every day will be like this one. There was no need to care for an unloved body and nothing would fill the emptiness of her mind. I might as well sit down, Liana thought. That was something to do anyhow. First you stand and then you sit and that way you wait for the time to pass.

The morning lasts four hours, Liana thought, from eight until noon. Then there is lunch. Afterwards there is the afternoon which lasts five hours. Then there is dinner. The night lasts longest of all, the night takes ten whole hours to pass. She had almost waited out the morning. In the afternoon she would sit in another chair and feel the time like rock burying her. In the night Pierre would leave the island. There must be some way to escape those ten hours.

Then Liana thought, I have something to do. She did not begin at once because she could not move quickly and it was good to save action; if you did not hurry it would take longer and use up the hours. She started slowly, giving herself orders as she went: open the bureau drawer, Liana told herself, take out the frames of the butterfly collection. Liana piled these carefully on the floor. Open the second drawer, she told herself, and take out the coral and the pressed flowers. These drawers were crowded and disorderly and looked as if they belonged to a little boy. The paint box was in her dressing table; the notebooks were in the closet on a high shelf where they would not easily be seen. Liana took her books from the hanging shelf she had ordered specially for them, but she put them back again. The books did not really belong to her; books belonged to everyone. She found the mask she had used for goggle-fishing and the cheap knapsack. When everything was stacked in heaps on the floor it did not look like much but it was all she had of her own. Have I forgotten anything, Liana thought. She opened all the drawers and the closet again and the medicine chest in the bathroom but nothing remained that was hers. Everything else was Marc's.

Liana dressed quickly and without care. She did not put on shoes, having forgotten them, and she had not washed. She lifted the frames that held the pinned butterflies and carried them down the back stairs. She did not carry more than she could hold safely and without strain and she walked slowly. A stubborn bemused will drove her on: once she stopped, halfway to the cane brake, and could not remember what she was doing with an armful of notebooks and a sun-faded knapsack, walking barefoot across the yard.

When all her possessions were collected under the bamboo trees, Liana looked for dry wood. This was pleasant to do because you only had to watch the ground and think of picking up fallen twigs from the mango trees or broken brown bamboo stalk. It could not be done quickly either; it needed many loads of wood to build the fire. But finally there was enough wood, and Liana scooped a clear place and used some of the dried bamboo leaves as kindling. Now she had to go to the kitchen for matches. That was another trip. This is a long and time-taking work, Liana thought. Perhaps it would take all afternoon to finish. Thérèse gave Liana the matches and stared at her face. Thérèse whispered to Théodore, when Liana had walked back to her fire, "Liana looks a little crazy to me, like she don't know where she's at or what she's doing."

"She forgot her lunch."

"Don't bother her," Thérèse said. "Looks like she has to be by herself. That Lucie ought to feel proud of how she fixed her own child."

"What you talking about?" Théodore said. "Liana's got more than any colored girl on this island. Look at where she sleeps; look at the clothes in her closet. She don't work; she don't have to do nothing. I wish my daughter would be fixed like that."

"I don't," Thérèse said gloomily.

"What you talking about? You talk like a fool."

"I don't talk like a fool, Monsieur Théodore," Thérèse said angrily. "I got a daughter myself. I got a daughter that don't have crazy eyes. I can work for my daughter myself. I'm not like that worthless Lucie who wants to own a farm and be a rich woman."

"You make me tired," Théodore said. "And I got silver to polish."

"I wouldn't want to tire you, Monsieur Théodore," Thérèse said acidly. "Go on and polish your silver."

Thérèse peered out the kitchen window to see Liana but the close green leaves of the bamboo trees hid her. This is going to end bad, Thérèse thought, it's not natural, that's why.

Liana lit the dry leaves and they caught fire and burned and the light twigs above them burned too. Slowly, stick by stick, she placed more wood on her fire. Now it was burning high and the heat scorched her face. Sparks leapt from the fire and caught the near mat of leaves and Liana hurriedly beat out the sparks and scooped the leaves away, leaving the black earth safe around the blaze. Methodically she built the fire until its flames roared up in front of her and its heart glowed thick and red. Then she dropped her possessions into the flame. The rubber of the diving mask made a sickening smell and the coral only blackened, but the notebooks burned brightly and the frames of the butterfly collection snapped in the fire.

Liana stood back to watch. Fire was slow too; slow as time. She stood with an empty face and watched these things she had loved burning or turning ugly and useless in the fire. She did not want them; she would have no use for them again. They were part of her happiness and of her long, ignorant hope. She had thought she could learn to be as fine as any white lady; if she studied hard enough she would learn. She had studied to please Pierre too, and all the time she believed she was making herself ready. There was nothing to be ready for. It had been her mistake. The lessons were a trick since they led nowhere. The lessons were a cheat since

236

no matter how much she learned no one would admit she had changed.

What would burn had burned and now she was as poor as when she started. I must put out the fire, Liana thought, it is dangerous to leave a fire in the dry season. She raked the ashes with a stick and went to the garage for a bucket of water. When Liana had poured water on the mound nothing remained except the melting rubber and the cracked glass of the diving mask, and the blackened coral. Liana heaped dead leaves over these; if they would not burn she wanted to think of them as buried.

Liana's dress was scorched and she had black smudges on her arms and face. Now there was something else to do: she would bathe and put on fresh clothes and that too would eat away the hours of the afternoon. But when it was time to dress Liana found she had no energy for that. She took from her closet the only ugly kimono she had, unconsciously selecting something that did her damage and made her body shapeless and her skin muddy. Liana sat on another chair, looking at the wall, and thought: the night lasts ten whole hours.

But it was too much; it could not be endured. Time gnawed in her brain with sharp poisoned teeth; the emptiness around her turned black and threatening. She had to talk to someone, she had to be near people who moved and breathed and were alive. Liana went downstairs and opened the pantry door. She felt shy to be coming here, where she had only come to give orders. Liana was looking for friendship now but she did not know whether these three colored people whom she had held away from her with pride and the power of Marc's money would treat her as a friend.

The servants were eating their supper. They stood up when Liana entered the room, as they had been trained to do. Théodore, who was quite proud of his manners, swallowed furtively so that Liana would not see him but Zela went on calmly chewing with her mouth open.

"You wish something, Madame?" Théodore said.

They were all surprised to see Liana dressed this way. No one moved. "Sit down. Go on with your supper. I'll just pull up a chair," Liana said uncertainly.

The servants looked at each other with puzzled eyes

237

and made room for Liana. They ate in silence, uncom-
fortably, trying to finish their meal. They did not like
having Liana watch them eat any more than they would
have liked Marc to sit with them.

Liana stared at their food and without knowing it she
wrinkled her face in disgust. Zela had poured plantain
juice over her rice and mashed it together with the black
beans and fried meat and the food looked as chewed-
over and dirty as swill that was ready to be thrown to
the pigs. The servants were beginning to resent Liana
now that the surprise had worn off. Why did she come,
here to spoil their supper that was always a pleasant
chatty meal? What did she want sitting there staring at
their food as if it were bad? Thérèse bit off a piece of
dry bread and chewed it angrily.

"Coffee, Théodore?" she said.

"No thank you."

"Why not?"

"All right then."

Thérèse made a loud angry rattling sound in the
kitchen, shaking up the coffee pot that she kept on the
stove all day long in case any of them wanted a cup.
What's Liana doing here, Thérèse thought, with her
crazy eyes and wearing a kimono like any common nigger? We got a right to be like we want, Thérèse thought,
we're good enough for ourselves. No need for her to
come in here sniffing at us.

Théodore cleared off the plates though usually Zela
did this. He was glad of something to do. They could
not very well tell Liana to go away. He started to wash
the dishes too, and Zela stared at him in amazement.
Théodore was not a man to do work he didn't have to
do; the servants' dishes were Zela's job.

"Get a bottle of rum, Théodore," Liana said suddenly.

"Madame?"

"A bottle of rum. Let's have a drink together. It will
be nice. Marc won't be home for another hour." Liana
blushed when she had said this. It sounded so vulgar
and sneaking. It sounded as if she were a servant too,
trying to cheat the master.

"Hurry," Liana said sharply. "And bring four glasses
and ice."

The servants were now standing around the table looking at the rum bottle as if they were afraid of it.

"Oh, sit down," Liana said. "It won't hurt you."

"I don't believe I want a drink, Madame," Thérèse said with dignity. Look what things were coming to now. The next thing Théodore would be stealing Monsieur's liquor, after Liana set them off this way, and she'd have drunks in her kitchen and nothing but trouble.

"I want you to," Liana said. "We must all have a drink."

They sat down reluctantly and drank in silence. Why did I come? Liana thought. This is worse than being alone. I'm alone now with them to see me; they hate me, they don't want me here; they wish I would go. Liana had nothing to say to the servants; whatever they talked about was unknown to her and nothing of hers was suitable for them. She could not very well talk about the house-cleaning or tell Zela to stop forgetting to take the spots out of her green dress. She could not talk like that when they were supposed to be drinking together as friends.

"Have another, Théodore."

"Thank you," he said. None of my business, Théodore thought, this is a sweet old rum though and I'd never get any like it if it wasn't for this. He rolled the liquor around on his tongue and smiled with pleasure. Théodore's smile freed Zela from her shyness and she held out her glass too.

"That's a nice drink," she said.

Thérèse sniffed.

"Come on, Thérèse," Liana said. "We'll have another too."

Seeing that Théodore's glass was empty, Liana filled it.

"Man," Théodore said happily, putting away his third glass, "that is certainly a fine class of rum."

Zela giggled.

"I wish my Réné was here," she said.

"Who's Réné?" Liana asked.

"He's my young man," Zela said. "He works in Monsieur Laurent's garage."

So Zela, scrawny and ugly, flashing smiles, had a young man and was happy.

239

"My son don't drink," Thérèse said coldly.

"Oh, I don't know," Théodore remarked cozily, "I don't see nothing bad in it. Me and my wife go out sometimes and have a little drink with the neighbors."

They all had someone; they had homes they went to and people waiting for them. They had things to do. They were not afraid of time.

"Have another," Liana said. "Let's all have another."

But Liana had nothing to say to them; there were no confidences she could share with them. There was no one she could talk to. And they would not talk to her; they were saying little things because they were getting drunk but they would never talk freely about what mattered to them. Their secrets were their own, their happy secrets and their bad ones. Liana had no place with them and she knew it and she did not want a place. She had come for friendship but she did not really want it. They were too different; she feared their kind of lives. Now Liana only hoped to escape the time that was waiting for her in her room. She would stay and drink with them and some of the time would go away. The servants would be happier to drink without her and Liana knew it. They did not hate her now, but she was a stranger.

"My son says a man who starts drinking don't notice when it gets ahold of him," Thérèse said. "But one day he finds he can't stop himself no more and there he is, bending his whole life to getting liquor. My son wants to get himself a farm and leave something for his family."

"Your son," Théodore said firmly, taking Thérèse's remarks as a personal insult, "is the most serious boy I ever see. He don't have no fun worth staying alive for. I think a man ought to have a little fun whilst he's alive."

"That's the way Réné is," Zela said happily.

Thérèse drank sternly.

"You and Réné," Théodore nudged Zela. "When you going to get enough money for the wedding certificate?"

Zela threw back her head and laughed as if she had never heard anything so funny. She laughed until tears ran down her face and Théodore laughed too, in the easy glad-to-laugh way they had. Thérèse looked at them and shrugged. She appreciated good liquor as much as anyone but she didn't have to get drunk right off, the way these young fools did. Liana watched the two laugh-

240

ing. They talked about a wedding certificate and laughed with joy as if it were the funniest and the most natural thing in the world. Liana wished she could get drunk and laugh too but the rum would not warm her. The laughter had nothing to do with her, nor the negro faces with their bright eyes and shining teeth, nor the negro voices, nor this room, nor this house. Nothing had anything to do with her. She stayed here because she had no place else to go.

Suddenly the laughter stopped. Théodore sprang up from the table upsetting the bottle at his elbow. Zela ran into a corner of the pantry and held her hand over her mouth and stared with unblinking eyes at the pantry door. Marc had opened the door behind Liana. They were making too much noise to hear Marc's car or hear him in the salon. Thérèse stood up slowly and waited for the punishment that was coming and that was deserved. She would be punished with the others but it was better that way. Monsieur would see to it that these goings-on stopped and the house became again the kind of place it ought to be, and not a wild place where the mistress sat in a kimono getting drunk with the servants.

"Go to your room, Liana," Marc said.

Liana found it difficult to walk; her legs felt heavy and soft. There was a blur in front of her eyes though the pantry was very bright. She clutched at her kimono, holding it close to her throat, and it opened as she walked showing her legs bare to her thighs. Liana passed Marc, swerving, and walked very slowly because of the soft way her legs bent under her.

Marc stepped into the pantry and shut the door behind him.

"Clean this up at once," he said. The servants were so quiet that they did not seem to be breathing. "Do not speak of this and see that it never happens again. Do you understand me? If it ever happens again you know what I will do."

The unspoken threat was worse than if Marc had promised to beat them. His voice was terrible too, so low and so hard. Thérèse went to the kitchen to finish preparing dinner. Zela and Théodore worked in silent haste to tidy the pantry. I've got my headache already, Théodore thought, from being scared into it ahead of

241

time. Why did Liana have to come down here and make us all bad trouble? If Liana ever comes again I'm going to say I can't stay in the pantry with her and I'm going to wait in my room. Even if she does bring rum, Théodore thought. No sir, I'm not going to have Monsieur Marc after me.

Marc thought he ought to speak to Liana at once but probably. it was useless; she was too drunk to understand.. He had looked at Liana with horror. The drink widened and thickened her mouth; it made her skin darker. There she sat in a dirty kimono, showing her legs to the servants, her hair matted and her face greasy with sweat and loose with drink: acting like a blowzy nigger tart. Marc stood in the middle of the room thinking, Good God if she's going to take that up. If I'm going to have a drunk slattern on my hands in this house. Liana can do what she likes when she leaves here, Marc thought, she can drink herself to death if that pleases her and slouch around in a dirty half-open kimono for all I care. But not here, by God, Marc said to himself. If the servants showed any signs of remembering this evening, he would beat them and the hell with the law. This was a white man's house, he wasn't going to let those niggers turn it into some kind of disgusting black gin shop.

Marc went to his chair by the radio and poured out whiskey with a shaking hand. This was something he had not foreseen when he made his promise to Pierre. Just when he thought their lives were at last sensible and settled, Pierre leaving for Europe, Liana tranquil and soon to live her own life, Marie no longer buzzing in his brain, Liana started this ghastly repulsive business of getting drunk and going about dirty and half-naked. Pierre said Marc had no right to send Liana back to the negro life. It seemed that was what Liana wanted. What had she looked like except a negro; who except a negro would go about undressed and get drunk with servants? I ought to beat her now, Marc thought, so she'll know it's serious and I mean what I say.

Marc drank the whiskey, not tasting it, and thought: goddamn women. They will never leave a man alone. You can't trust them to behave decently for a minute. Thinking about women calmed him: Marc could see

242

Liana as a woman now and not as a negro, not as that sly always-spreading menace that threatened to overwhelm the whites and drag them down into fatal, careless squalor. Liana probably felt she had to do something dramatic, Marc thought, women are such fools. They like theatre. She was making a big tragic gesture to show her heart is broken. Liana probably liked the idea of herself drinking to forget. Marc felt no sympathy for Liana: had she not written to Pierre telling him that she was getting a new house so she did not wish to see Pierre any more? They want everything, Marc thought, they want to be queens of tragedy and at the same time they are hard as flint, figuring out what is the best bargain. She'll sleep it off, Marc told himself, her theatrical drunk and her false heartbreak, and tomorrow she'll want to know how many rooms there are going to be in her new house. I know them, Marc thought with disgust, but I'll make it clear to Liana that she had her little comedy tonight and it is the last time.

Liana sat on the bed staring at the small clock on the night-table. This was fascinating, like watching ants at work. Sometimes, because she stared so fixedly, the gold and white clock face smeared in front of her eyes and then the fine gold hand would click forward another line and she would not have seen it. It was very interesting to watch and it was good to see time exactly measured, made small, concentrated in one swift-tapping little clock. Her body still felt heavy and soft, as if the flesh weighed too much for the bones and the bones would not hold her straight. Liana could feel the clock ticking as well as see it. It was comfortable to sit here in this dull slumped way, breathing with the clock.

The liquor, which had never touched her brain, slowly seemed to melt away from her body. The invisible warm wet towels that had been wrapped around her turned cold; and then there was nothing except herself, the one she knew, narrowly watching the clock. For all this care she had taken to help the minutes go, the gold hand had only moved half round the dial.

I know, Liana told herself, I know. Pierre is leaving; Pierre did not want you. Pierre is leaving for his own country where he would not take you. He always meant to go home to his own country. The night is ten hours long and all the other nights. You are twenty-two, Liana told herself, think how many nights that is and how many days. But you don't have to, if you don't want to. No one can make you. No one can make you wait all those nights and all those days. You don't belong to any one. No one can make you.

I don't have to wait, Liana thought very carefully, there is no reason to wait. It was foolish of me not to see this before. I need not have waited so long.

Without believing it, and without really hoping it, Liana had hoped all day that something would happen; something as impossible as snow falling through this hot sky. Pierre would come to her and say he could not go without her; he loved her; he had not understood. Liana had not believed in this because she remembered the words of the two white men and their voices; the wary doggedness of Pierre, his half-shamed reluctant relief when he went home, and Marc's voice that was reasonable and final, speaking truths that no white man would deny. But there was always the hope that was behind consciousness, the longing for miracles. Now it was night and there would be no miracles. There was at last nothing to wait for at all. Liana imagined Pierre would leave as soon as it was night; she had only heard Marc speak of crossing the channel in the dark. The night was beautiful and dusty with stars outside her window, and Pierre had gone.

Liana turned out the ceiling light and lit the small lamp by her bed. She opened her door and walked quietly across to Marc's bathroom. Marc was in the dining-room and would not see or hear her. She found a new package of razor blades and opened the blue paper cover and took out one blade in its stiff envelope. It was the last package Marc had. Marc will be angry with me for using this, Liana thought.

Liana closed her door behind her and now she was safe. She would not have to hurry. She opened the envelope that held the razor blade. There was a thin greasy coating on the blade, to protect it from rust, and Liana disliked the feel of this on her fingers. She washed the blade in her bathroom and threw the blue paper covering into the waste basket. It was necessary to do every-

244

thing with care and in order. Liana hung the ugly kimono in her closet and found her finest nightgown that was made of white satin and trimmed with lace and smelled of gardenia sachet. She washed her face and put on lipstick and combed her hair. Liana moved without noise but steadily, knowing exactly what she wanted to do. She must be clean and fresh, her room must look pretty and spotless, there must be nothing nasty or soiled to leave behind.

Liana was finished with thinking. What she did now was natural and obviously what she must do and she did not have to think any more. It was not even very important; it was just that she was not going to wait.

She sat on the edge of her bed and examined the room. The razor blade lay on the glass table top and caught the light and for a moment that flashing light seemed big and blinding and wrong. Then Liana picked up the blade, holding it daintily, and laid her left wrist flat on the table. She did not want to hurt herself; the idea of pain was shocking in this neat, silent room. I must do it quickly, Liana thought, and as it should be done.

She had been almost proud of herself because, without any help, she had seen what she ought to do and she had known how to do it and she had gone ahead in a calm, sensible way with her plans. But now Liana felt her breath coming faster and she was alarmed by this. Be quiet, Liana told herself, be quiet. It is just the way it was before. See, everything is ready. Now, don't be afraid. You have only to look at your hand to find the place. Then just once, deeply, along the line of the vein: it will not hurt; it will only take a second; even if it hurts, it will only be for a second. And you scarcely have to look, and afterwards you will close your eyes and lie on the bed, and it is nice and quiet in here and there is no hurry, and you will lie on the bed afterwards and then. And then there would be whatever came, but she did not have to think about that; that happened, and she would not see it or feel it. The waiting would be over without her knowing it. Liana thought, with a sudden last pleasure, that she had managed everything well and need not be ashamed of how she would look.

It is all right now, isn't it? she asked herself encouragingly. Her right hand held the blade firmly. She looked at her wrist and looked away, and then she thought: but it can't hurt, there is so little to cut. She saw the vein, almost purple under the skin, and she forced herself to see it clearly so that for an instant it was all she saw. She did not really see her right hand or the washed blade, and she commanded herself: *once deep quickly*.

Liana dropped the razor blade and stared at her wrist. A narrow jet of blood pumped from the single deep cut the razor had made. With every heartbeat it spurted up, fresh and light and strong and almost gay, curved and showed red in the light, and fell. First it fell and stained the satin cloth over her knees. Then, as Liana moved her hand away from her body, it spattered on the bedspread. Stupidly, Liana stretched her arm over the side of the bed and then she could not see where it fell; but when she leaned forward she saw it dark on the white rug. She could not understand this, and she stared unbelievingly at the floor until she saw it widening and creeping over the white fleece of the rug. It could not be her blood; she had not done this.

She closed her right hand around her wrist, still not understanding but only knowing that she must stop this at once. She had made some terrible mistake through not knowing enough; but she could stop it. She would have to stop it. Obstinately, she thought only of that: I can fix it, she told herself, but she was afraid; I can fix it so it will be right.

Now her hand was wet and warm; she could feel the blood pressing against her fingers, trying to spurt out again. But that must not be, because if it leaped out, moving without her doing anything and against her will, then her room would be ruined and she could not lie on the bed and close her eyes. She was crying now. I didn't do this, she thought, I never did this.

Suddenly Liana knew she must hurry. She got up from the bed, holding both hands in front of her, and felt it trickling through her fingers on to the floor. She wanted to be careful not to step in it, with her bare feet, but she could not watch her hand and the floor too. The bathroom was very far away and she had to walk carefully and watch her hand to see that nothing new happened. Then Liana realized, because everything took so long, that she would never get back to her room again. She would have no time to make her room clean and peaceful so that she could lie on the bed, the way she had planned. Now she did not know where she would be, nor how it would be; it was rushing towards her and she was not ready.

If she could only wash and be clean and clean her room, then she would have time to make herself ready as she had been before. Oh hurry, Liana thought, and now she was in the bathroom and had found the light switch. When she took her right hand away, to press the wall button, the stream was loosed again. She could not defend herself against it; she did not know what to do with her hands. But the washbowl was so near and if she could turn on the water, she would be safe. She held her wrist under the tap and turned on the water.

For a moment Liana believed that it was all right now. This had been a fearful and horrible mistake, but it was all right now and she would have time. The water washed her right hand clean and, in its force, washed her wrist free of blood. She splashed water on the tap to clean away the stains her right hand had made, and she thought confusedly that she would take a wet towel back in her room and clean there too. For a moment she rested in this safety, holding herself up against the washbowl.

But now the water was not clear any more; it swirled inside the bowl and slowly darkened. It seemed to Liana that the water itself was very loud. She closed her eyes, because she was not sure she had really seen this changed water, and because also the walls of the bathroom were too white. The water was very loud. She opened her eyes and the water was coming closer. It climbed in a circle and all the time it grew darker, so that now it looked red. Liana forced herself to hold her body steady so her wrist would stay under the tap, but the water did not help her, it did not stop the blood. The bathroom was getting smaller and there was not much air to breathe and all the time the water came closer. It would spill out of the bowl and splash on the floor and then this room too would be ruined and there was no other place to go. Liana thought she was calling; she could feel her voice beat in her throat. She would have to turn off the water. No one would hear her because of the water.

Pierre she called in silence, *Pierre, Pierre.* If she did not turn off the water it would spill out of the bowl. Her hand was slipping but if she could close the tap she would have time. She got her fingers around the porcelain knob, but she could not move it. I can't stop it, Liana thought, I can't stop it. *Pierre,* she screamed silently above the roar of the water.

The water ran, quiet and clear, inside the washbowl. Liana lay curled on the floor, now, small and still and with a childish careless ease. Her hair was soft around her face and her cheek rested on her arm. The satin nightgown had twisted about her and slipped above her knees and this way the stains were hidden, so she looked almost as neat as she had wished to be. Her face was tired and gray against the white tile of the bathroom floor.

The noise of the water running in Liana's bathroom irritated Marc. It was so wasteful. Could she have gone to sleep with the water on? At least Liana was saving electricity and that was something; Marc did not see the oblong of light that fell from her window on to the front lawn if her room lights were burning. It isn't the water, Marc thought, it's the gasoline for the well pump. You would think Liana could understand that. I'll have the water turned off during certain hours of the day and every night at nine or ten, Marc thought. The only way you can keep them from wasting is not to give them a chance. He ought to go up now and tell Liana for God's sake to shut off the tap; but perhaps she was still in her bathroom getting ready to go to bed. *Oh foutre,* Marc thought, I don't want to see her. I'm sick of having to discipline everybody around here. I'll be glad when Liana has her own house.

Marc sat at a small table by the side windows, with only one lamp lit, making a list of people who owned dairy cows. It had been decided that day, at a meeting in the Mayor's office, that Marc should handle this matter. There was almost no cooking oil left in the stores; raising the price to a spectacular three dollars a litre had not prevented the supply from disappearing. Marc said, if there's no oil the women will have to use butter to cook. This seemed extravagant and reckless; butter was

248

a luxury, you didn't fry fish and plantains in butter. But if there is no oil, Marc said, we can make butter; there's no reason why we can't make plenty of it. We reverse everything here, Marc thought with amusement, butter instead of guns.

Marc had already listed the white owners of dairy herds, and he was trying to remember what negroes kept cows. His clerk would have to take a careful census over the island; now Marc wanted to make an approximate calculation of what they could count on in gallons of milk per week. It was comforting to see how many cattle there were on the island; we're pretty well-off here, Marc thought contentedly, we're richer than we knew. The negroes, and most of the whites, put their cows out to graze; Marie had good grazing ground and some of the other whites did, but mostly the cows were scrawny from living off poor country. It would be necessary to arrange better feed for all, and if they were going to pool the milk supply they would have to work out some required rudimentary system for pasteurizing the milk and for controlling the health of the animals.

There was also the problem of storing butter since the island had no ice-house. Perhaps the women would have ideas on that; it was the kind of detail they were good at. We'll have to choose different stations around the island where the butter can be called for, and then we'll need a transport system. Well, that part was easy: they could use his car. Saldriguet's boy was seventeen and if he didn't know how to drive he could learn. Young Jacques was reliable and he could be the butter chauffeur. We could probably build some kind of cellars, Marc thought, that would stay cool so the butter won't spoil and Jacques can distribute it two or three times a week. That wouldn't use up too much gasoline. A couple of the farmers ought to supervise the cattle end; and if there were any sensible women in town, two of them might organize the farm women for the actual butter-making.

Marc wrote names thoughtfully on the long page of yellow paper. He wrote in a small careful hand; he was not even wasting paper. Everything had to be saved; the island needed everything; everything belonged to the island.

Marc looked at his watch. Pierre would be leaving in another hour. It was a clear windless night; they would have an easy crossing. Marc thought he would drink to Pierre's trip and then get on with his work. He would miss Pierre in a way; as long as Pierre had been here, Marc could always imagine the day they would be friends and the life they could make for themselves with that friendship. But it was right for Pierre to go, and Marc thought there was no sense in feeling sad now at the hour of his going.

Marc mixed a whiskey and soda and stood near the front windows where he faced the sea, though the sea was ony a distant blackness under the black sky. Do your work, Pierre, Marc thought, and good luck.

He carried his glass back to the table and bent again over the paper. Marie would raise hell about sharing her grazing land or selling her milk at a fixed price. She had already gone into a fury when Marc told her they were sending laborers to make charcoal in her woods. Charcoal was the only fuel the island could count on now. There were others like Marie but not too many, and if they could not be persuaded, they could live by themselves and see how they liked it; no contributions, no benefits. Ces foutus imbéciles, Marc thought impatiently.

It was rather wonderful to feel this island tightening itself, drawing in, with all the decent people thinking and working as if they no longer had to scheme and wangle for themselves because they belonged together, they were the same one. It was wonderful; the island had never felt better. The island had never been a better place to live.

Marc yawned and finished his drink. He might as well go to bed. There was nothing more he could do now alone. He felt well tired and there was tomorrow, another good hard day to work through. Marc had forgotten Liana and he no longer noticed the sound of the running water.

Pierre turned to look at the dark shore. There behind the high thin landmark of the palms was Liana's house. No light showed. She had not waited for him; she had not marked his going. It hurt badly. It hurt all the time.

250

Pierre had not imagined he would be leaving so completely. He had counted on someone to miss him and to remember, since the journey was long and he did not know what the end of it would be. But there was no light.

That's the way it is, Pierre told himself harshly, and better for everyone. Why did you think you could have it specially easy? By what right? He could not help himself; it hurt him, it was a black and lonely leaving with no light to watch.

Pierre turned from the shore where there was nothing to see and nothing to wait for. He made his way forward, holding to the sides of the boat. The little boat dived into the trough of the waves and knifed its way up again. Straining and stubborn, it moved slowly ahead through the huge black sea. Spray rose over the bow of the boat, fanning out in a triangle. Pierre's wet clothes hung against him, and at each rising obstinate thrust of the boat the spray lashed his face. Pierre stood in the narrow bow and held to the side of the boat to keep his balance and waited for the whip of the spray.

He looked ahead in the night to all the unknown countries that lay like stepping stones over the sea. Suddenly his mind was washed of the past and there was no lightless shore behind him. He said it aloud to himself, with his voice for company in the dark, "Kill the bastards and go home to France." And there was France, wide and green, touchable, grown simple and majestic in his mind. France the wise, the old, the tower of beauty. France that was worth any man's life. France made pure and perfect in his love. Pierre lifted his face to the blow of the spray, and thought: pour la dignité et les droits de l'homme.

The little boat moved slowly, smelling of gasoline, and creaking in the sea. It dived and rose through the dark vast strength of the water, and the colored crew bailed out the spray with rusty tin cans.

THE END

AFTERWORD

My distinguished publishers believe that a novel of a certain age, like this one, requires a preface or an afterword by way of explanation. I disagree profoundly but it is a house custom and though any self-respecting writer will argue a publisher to the death before changing a word or a sentence, this is a matter of formality and since no one else is available for the job, it falls to me. I have done it once before for the same reason and chose then as now to write an afterword which is easier to ignore.

I do not think that this novel or any work of fiction needs explanation. Fiction is story-telling; the story explains itself. Perhaps the original date of publication is useful to readers but that is printed on the first page of a book along with all the other small type business. Fiction, story-telling, is a direct transaction between writer and reader. Readers have the right, without the intrusion of anybody's opinion, to judge the story for themselves, to understand in their own way, to enter into the story, into the piece of a world the writer has invented; or to reject it.

In my opinion there is only one iron rule for fiction: it must not bore. Fortunately there are innumerable readers with every possible variety of taste, so all writers have a fighting chance of an audience, of whatever size, who will not be bored by their particular brand of story-telling.

Writers do not know that invisible audience, apart from generous enthusiasts who send a thank-you letter. Even those are strangers. Writers wish to be read, they hope for the invisible and mysterious audience; but, in the end, as they cannot know who is out there, the story-tellers are telling their story because it fascinates them.

If readers are interested in the theories or techniques of writing fiction, there are books on the subject. If readers are interested in the lives of writers, biographies and autobiographies abound. I find such information irrelevant to the end product: fiction. The writer of fiction has worked out his/her way of story-telling so that readers keep turning the page to learn what is happening next to these people who have come alive through black marks on white paper. I am a fiction addict and I am almost certain, from a lifetime of talking with others, that no readers react in the same way to the same book. Readers put into and take out of story-telling something personal to themselves which may be quite different from the writer's intention if, in fact, the writer had any intention beyond a private wilful wish to tell that story.

It may be of interest, though hardly important, to mention that *Liana* is the only one of my books which fetched up on the *New York Times* Best Seller List. Not at the top, of course, but in the respectable middle. The Theater Guild of New York, a grand institution then, like a small private version of the National Theatre in London, wanted to make it into a play, changing Liana to a "creole". "Creole" is an elastic word and means anything except black. Apparently love scenes between a white man and a black girl would be too tough for their public. Full of artistic principles and besides deeply absorbed in more urgent affairs (reporting the war), I refused.

The book went into paperback, a piece of information that somehow escaped me until—passing through New York—I saw a copy in a drugstore. The cover was a picture of a beautiful light black girl, scantily clad: luscious. I wondered who on earth would buy this book in drugstores; then thought, sadly, maybe all the girls of Harlem, hoping to meet themselves. It sold 150,000 paperback copies, as I remember. Not memory but fact, because I discovered the contract during a recent clean-out of files: my royalty was one penny, one U.S. cent, per copy, half of which reverted as usual to the hardback publisher. How to become rich and famous.

Liana grew from a wonderful lunatic journey through the

Caribbean in 1942, about which I have written elsewhere.* My transport was a potato boat, a thirty-foot sloop with one sail and a hold for hauling potatoes between the islands. We were becalmed on a very small island for four days. I lived in a swoon of joy, hoping the wind would stay dead. I thought that chance had brought me to the last best place in a crazed suffering world. These little islands were always isolated, but at that time—the hurricane season and German submarines—totally isolated. I realised that Eden is a subjective state, and even here people could manage to make themselves unhappy.

Many weeks later, returned from the journey, I began to write this novel. I wanted to be reporting in the Western Desert but for domestic reasons I could not depart then, so instead I settled in imagination on the perfect island. About ten years ago I went back there again by chance, while searching the Caribbean to see if any of it was left as once I knew it. A runway for Jumbo jets had been built on my Eden, and the island was covered by hotels, boarding houses, boutiques, eateries, villas and hordes of tourists. The taxis, owned by islanders, were Mercedes. Progress: absolute ruin. You might say this novel records a world that is lost and gone forever. But that is not the point; it is story-telling and succeeds or fails according to the iron rule: it must not bore.

Martha Gellhorn, London, 1986

Travels with Myself and Another